BELVIDERE.

IV

X
Sans Nom

ISBN: 978-1-950804-27-6

Title: **Belvidere.**

Summary: *A mysterious man is sent to a dead-end town; to do what, and to whom, he simply doesn't know. It's all part of a game he neither understands, nor controls. He befriends those he will likely betray; there will certainly be trouble if he does not. A fantastical, mysterious journey; an ephemeral olla podrida of raw erotica, graphic violence, racism, heathenism, bigotry and vulgarity, all buoyed by the providence of friendship, love and kindred souls.*

1.   Fiction-General.   2.   Fiction-Fantasy.
17 18 19 20 21   j i h g f e d c b a
First Edition - American

A Special Note To The Reader Who Is A Self-Appointed Observant Orthographer:

To this special group, the spelling and grammar police, please put your pencil down; I will save you the suspense.

This novel may be a grammar and sentence structure nightmare to people who obsess about such things. The pages that follow are vaguely, or not so, reminiscent of Beat literature, which can be described, by some, as a rejection of standard narrative and linguistic values, including, but not necessarily limited to, syntax, punctuation, sentence structure and morphology. The writing style is idiosyncratic; it is how the author thinks, and how the author believes this fictional account should be told. And just as important, it's how real people speak and communicate in the real world, which is rarely textbook or *correct*. It is real, or at least how this author perceives reality, which is all that matters between these end-papers.

In any event, there **will** be mistakes. And all the mistakes in this book were purposeful, and will be defended as such, even if they weren't. After two long years of editing, this writer simply got tired of re-reading and proofing. So what you see is what you get, whether it's *right* or not.

My suggestion is to take the broader view: simply enjoy the characters and enjoy the ride they take you on. Along the way, if you feel the need to get enraged, do so at the abject violence, the graphic sex, the racism, the bigotry, the coarse language, the heathenism....but for God's sake, don't get enraged at punctuation....leave the poor periods alone.

WARNING:

This novel installment contains adult-directed narrative and dialogue not suitable for children, including, but not necessarily limited to:

racism, bigotry, heathenism, vulgarity, graphic violence and raw erotica.

Proceed at your own peril....

CHAPTER 114 – OH MY GOD!

The following afternoon, Wednesday, July 5th, day number seventy-seven, and still no word.

Cord was stuck in Aisle Two; he had nuts on his mind. Whole, shelled and salted, chili-dusted; he was contemplating a new product line, talking to customers about favorites, sampling the wares, envisioning placement. But despite the immersion, he was distracted.

He couldn't wait for dinner and the pre-show he planned. After the goof, surely he and Earl were dead men; Earl was fast, but she could run faster than the both of them. Since Cord was the slowest, he would simply be dead meat, the sacrificial lamb. But it was still worth it, he thought, as a wry grin creased his face; tonight was going to be fun.

He called Lilly from Mae's last evening, much to Mae's delight, asking if he could postpone her big July Fourth dinner surprise till the following night….tonight; he had run into a *slight conflict* he couldn't shake.

Mae, as the *slight conflict*, listened with glee, gloating as Cord rescheduled Lilly around a sleepover with her. Little did Mae know she would have been dropped, but quick, if Lilly gave any pushback, but, surprisingly, she didn't. Earl figured C was on a sex-bender, and didn't bother to whine about his absence.

Lilly's big surprise would have to wait a day.

C's disappointment lay with the certainty that Lilly must know the conflict was a sex session with Mae, and she didn't seem to care. That was an ego blow, just another sting to complement Earl's comments about Button at the *Big Crack.* Would Lilly have cared if it was Button on a bender, even with a senior citizen?

Most certainly.

But he took the sex; it was important to Mae, and getting another taste of her was never much of an arm twist, especially when there was no other bar to belly up to.

He closed the shop solo, in quick order, and was home by six o'clock; he knew he had plenty of time to prepare. Of course, Earl was at his side, deliciously giddy and over-the-top nervous at the same time. Although Cord couldn't hear him through the mumble, it was clear Earl was rehearsing.

Lilly was in a rare good mood.

She had to teach a beginner kick-box class at the old Mill, beside the Town clock, across from the Belvidere Hotel; Wednesday night was the late night, but no matter, she was already set for dinner and the extra day provided sweet time to relish the scam she had been running against Ay for the past three months.

It didn't sound like a big deal, barely moving stuff around in his apartment to see if he'd notice; saying it aloud actually sounded kind of dumb – not some big gotcha moment. But getting the better of that obsessive bastard was always satisfying to her, no matter how insignificant the increment. Spilling the game, from moving the soup can that first time, to the foil wrap amoeba-dots, which he *still* hadn't found, was going to be sweet. Maybe *Mr. Anal* wasn't so anal after all; someone else as obsessive as he claimed to be surely would have found those foil dots gone awry.

She laughed aloud at the thought of how bad she was going to get him.

Of course, the real prize was the segue into what was *in* the foil packets; it couldn't be anything but money. And what was in the mystery box? She was tired of wondering; she wanted some answers from the worm-man of *Seattle*. If it was money in the foil, she wanted to know why; where did it come from and why the elaborate wrap? And more importantly, she wanted to know what was in that taped-up box, with the writing, the words, those fateful words; why were they there? What did they really mean? She was convinced it had some tie to her mother; or was it just silly hope?

The clock took forever to catch nine pm; less than five minutes after the bell, she shuffled out the last of the fat-asses and took a quick jog home….all of two blocks.

Lilly took her sneakers off at the base of the stairs and hustled up the flight, past her landing, and placed her ear gently against C's door – no noise. She knew it wasn't locked, it never was, so she cracked the knob and stuck her head into the kitchen, whispering softly.

"C, I'm home; you coming down to dinner?"

No response.

The lights were all off, which was a bit odd. A few scattered candles quietly licked in the kitchen, shifting shades of gray and black across the cabinets. From her vantage, a scarlet glow from his bedroom, and from the front room down the long hallway, suggested more candles, hidden from view. The effect barely illuminated the apartment; a dim, amber glow washed the ceiling and walls, the flicker of flames casting long, dancing shadows.

It was eerily quiet; too quiet.

Cord frequently left a few white candles burning, even when he ducked out of the apartment; that always unsettled her, frightened her – it seemed dangerous. But there were never as many candles as there were now, and the lights were never all out.

Strange.

And stranger still, gone were the white candles; these, at least the candles she could see, were blood red.

Being in his place right here, right now - alone, dimly candle-lit and empty, simply creeped her out. She couldn't place it, but it didn't *feel* completely empty; it was as if something else shared her space in his apartment, something she couldn't describe. From nowhere, the hair on her neck and arms rose and the flesh-creep settled in; a deep feeling of spook.

With no more warning that that, she turned tail, shut the door haphazard and hustled down the steps, before something emerged from the shadows to grab her. No way was she waiting around to find out what it was. A last shiver shot her spine as she descended the staircase to the second floor.

She looked back up the flight from the safety of her second-floor landing, half-expecting the door to open and something unspeakable to stick it's head into the hallway. She waited a few seconds, staring at the blackness in the window pane at the top of the stairs; but nothing happened.

She smiled, exhaled in relief, and felt a bit foolish, like one does when they feel safe, after they just felt unsafe. She grabbed the knob, gave it a half-turn and entered the sanctity of her apartment.

Three words dripped from her lips....*Oh my God!*

CHAPTER 115 – IT MUST RUN IN THE FAMILY

Her apartment was dark, except for a dim glow painting the ceiling and walls from the flicker of blood-red candles, scattered about the kitchen counter and set along the floor of the long hallway.

She didn't own any red candles.

More candles burned out of sight in her bedroom and the front room. She was sure they too, were crimson.

It was as if Cord's apartment seeped through the ceiling and followed her down the stairs; the long, dancing shadows beckoning her entry.

And it was eerily quiet; too quiet.

She flipped the switch beside the door; no lights. The hair on her arms and neck again stood upright and a dull tingle raced her spine; her feet were leaden, glued to the wooden floor.

There was *definitely* something hiding in her apartment; she could *feel* it. The spook resettled, quick and hard.

But what she didn't do, what they never do in times of trouble, what she always yelled at the idiots on the movie screen to do, was *run*. Here she was, front and center, and she didn't hear what her mind should have been yelling....***run!*** Instead, she did what all the idiots do; she froze.

"Lilly?"

Came a low, empty voice from down the hall, toward the kitchen, just beyond sight. It was barely above a whisper. It kind of sounded like Earl, but the throaty call was muffled and distant; a portend of trouble.

"Earl?! ***EARL?!***"

Her voice trembled as it rose.

Then she heard music, faint music. It was a deep baritone, from down the hall, hidden in the kitchen; chamber music.

"In the pantry; help me; come get me out….*please!*"

The words trailed to silence; only the sound of the orchestra remained….haunting music.

She didn't remember her sprint from the doorway to the kitchen; never once did she think of her safety, or the foolishness of the act.

She stood in the dim kitchen, heart pounding, and saw the pantry door wide open, the soles of Earl's shoes and a part of his pant legs were partly visible from beneath a blanket thrown atop him in the pantry which was illuminated by more blood candles, set on the shelves.

Lilly's eyes quickly darted across the pantry; it had been transformed.

Everything, **everything**, was neatly stacked on the shelves, all the labels pointing forward, all the cans stacked in uniform rows, not a item askew, just like that movie that scared the shit out of her, *Sleeping With The Enemy*.

The music suddenly jumped in volume, as if it leaped at her. It was *inside* the pantry, under the blanket; her legs became wobbly and the blood drained from her face.

It was then, that the tall thin figure, in a black trench coat, with a black mustache, stuck its head from behind the pantry door and bellowed baritone.

"Relax, Princess, nothing to worry about."

She barely heard the last word; she certainly didn't hear
the laughter that followed. Down she went like a sack of
potatoes, fainting on the spot.

It must run in the family.

CHAPTER 116 – BELLY LAUGHS AND RAISED GLASSES TO THE WITCHES SABBATH

Lilly blinked her eyes and tried to focus; it took a moment to realize she was looking at the kitchen counter. Her body still tingled. She looked around, blankly, out-of-body, taking in the scene, and realized she was sitting up, firmly held in place by a set of big arms.

"Are you *sure* all the knives and forks are hidden?"

C asked earnest, a second time.

"*Yes!*"

Earl responded, nervous; his heart racing.

All the lights were on, the candles blown out, and the blanket gone, revealing a pair of Earl's pants and shoes, stuffed with newspapers like a scarecrow, standing on the pantry floor, exposed for Lilly to see the fraud.

Both were afraid to talk to her at first, so the three of them shared the silence.

Earl broke the fragile ice.

"Are you okay Lilly?"

Earl said sheepishly, quickly followed by:

"It was all C's idea."

"You mother-fucker! I can't believe you threw me under the bus!"

C shouted, still wearing the mustache.

"Well it *was.*"

Lilly let out a sigh.

"It's okay, I'm okay. That was a good one C….good one. I'm okay, Earl; good joke….hah hah, but let go, so I can get up."

"Nice try. Sorry Lilly, we're not falling for that one."

Cord said, as he peeled off the hair on his lip; the wig was sitting on the floor, next to the box he stood on, behind the pantry door.

Earl tightened his grip, as if girding for an explosion.

"Listen, I knew you've been moving stuff around my apartment from day one, starting with the *soup can*. You really think I didn't know? Moving the *Sweet-n-Low*, messing with my underwear, touching the foil, erasing the dot; come on Lilly, do you think I'm *that* dumb?"

"Yes."

Was all she could muster.

"So, when you had to spill the big fat *secret*, I figured I would beat you to the punch, and play a little preemptive trick on you; I didn't mean to have you faint; I wanted to call the whole thing off, but Earl insisted."

"*Did Not!*"

Earl screamed hysterical.

Cord just smiled; Lilly didn't.

"Hey, you've been fucking with me for three months; if the shoe was on the other foot, you would be rolling on the floor, laughing your ass off at what a wimp I was for fainting….come on now?"

As if Cord had to justify the stunt.

Then he stuck out his hand in a signal for a truce.

Lilly tried to reach up to grab it, but Earl had her cinched tight.

"Earl, let go."

She said, sans emotion.

So he did, just like that.

She shook C's hand, and mustered a half-smile to boot. That was as good as it was going to get. She stood up, brushed herself off and asked the question she felt she more than deserved the answer to, given the ordeal she just endured.

"What's in the foil?"

C didn't hesitate; he knew he couldn't fuck around anymore, not now.

"It's what you think it is."

"How much, and where did you get it?"

"I don't know."

"You don't know what?"

"I don't know how much."

"Guess."

She said sarcastically.

"Couple thousand, maybe more."

"Are they ones, tens or hundreds?"

"The latter."

"Then it's a *lot more*."

She snapped. Cord didn't answer.

"Where'd it come from?"

"Savings."

"Well, you didn't open any of those packs, so where did the money come from, for the *girl*?"

Lilly didn't have to specify black girl….*girl* sufficed.

"Underwear drawer."

"No it didn't, I went through your underwear drawer, remember, moving shit around; there was no money in there….you're a God-damn liar!"

"I'm not a liar; there's still a bunch in there."

"Prove it! If you're lying, I get to keep it….***all of it!***"

Lilly barked.

"Fine, and what do I get if I'm telling the truth?"

"The right to not worry about when I'm going to stab you in the fucking chest for scaring me like that, making me think Earl was hurt; that wasn't funny, not at all....that was wrong. You don't do shit like that, you just don't."

Cord just looked at her, with an air of resignation, and embarrassment.

"Hey, you're right, that was wrong. Fun is fun; Earl told me that movie freaked you out, but making you think Earl was hurt was over the line. That was my idea, and for that, I apologize, I really do; I'm sorry."

Lilly didn't quite know how to respond, so she didn't; she simply half-snorted an acknowledgment. Then she marched down the hallway, opened the door and started up the steps to C's apartment. C didn't follow.

"Come on! Let's see if you're a lying sack of shit."

"You're going the wrong way."

Came Ay's voice, monotone, from inside her apartment.

She walked back down and entered the apartment, hands on hips, looking at him with disdain.

"What the fuck is that supposed to mean?"

And with that, C walked down the hall to the left and hooked a right into the rear bedroom....Lilly's bedroom. She just stood there, mouth open.

"You had *better* be fucking kidding me!"

She followed him in, and watched as he slowly slid open her upper dresser drawer, chock full of underwear - every candy-color under the sun; then the second drawer, also overflowing with frilly pieces of fabric, most of them so small they would be sucked into the crack of Cord's ass, like dental floss. Although she only wore them half the time, at best, Lilly simply loved to buy underwear, and never got rid of a pair. Half she never wore once.

"You have over one hundred pair of underwear in these two drawers; did you know that? That's got to be some kind of record, by the way; half still have the tags on them. In fact, to be exact, there are *one hundred thirteen* pair; I counted *every* one, *including* the crotchless ones, rubbing them all, of course."

This was clearly much worse than the fainting episode; Lilly turned crimson.

"I cannot believe I have been wearing underwear that you were fingering with those grubby, sweaty hands of yours!"

"Wait a minute; first of all, my hands aren't sweaty. And besides, you don't wear *half* these underwear, because there are still tags on them! I've been hiding money in here for the past two *months*, and you haven't come close to finding it; here, look!"

And with that, Cord started to dig through the satin, cotton and lace, flipping out bricks of bills, wrapped in rubber bands.

Lilly screamed.

"Get out of my underwear!"

As she ran over to shove him away.

Lillian tried to push him aside, but he just laughed at her. Earl kept his distance from the whole scene, embarrassed, as his sisters panties flew around the room.

When Cord took a slinky, scarlet pair of thongs and strapped it around his head, it was time for Earl to leave.

*"All this money is mine; **all** of it!"*

Lilly screamed.

Cord laughed and walked out of the room, thong snug around his head, the crotch stretched around his jaw, like a chinstrap.

"Fine, keep it, but I get the thong."

"Give me that back!"

"You never wear this thong; I know that for a fact - it was right in the middle of the bills. Probably rides your crack anyway; that can't be comfortable.

"I'm warning you!"

"Okay, the thong or the money? What'ya got there? I'd say at least a couple thousand bucks, probably more; you want the dough or this piece of red nylon that would barely cover my palm, and I have small hands."

"I want *both* asshole."

"Sorry, make a choice; I'm getting attached to this thong."

C said defiant.

"Earl!"

Lilly yelled, but to no avail; he was long gone, staying *far* away from this one.

"Make a choice, Lillian; money or dignity?"

"What's in the box?"

She spilled, out of the blue, as she sat down on the side of the bed, in a resigned posture, not sure if she really wanted to hear the answer.

Cord took the thong off his head and placed it gingerly on the bed; then he sat quietly beside her.

"Why do you care what's in the box, Lilly? It's just a stupid box."

"Because it matters to me; you don't have to know why."

But Cord *did* know why, and he couldn't tell her how....that Sam had spilled those beans that first night in the *Palace*. He let out a long sigh.

"Lilly, what's in that box has to do with when I have to make a decision, an important decision in this particular case; part of some grand scheme I don't control, and that I don't really understand myself....that's all I can tell you. Just like I don't have to know why you care, you don't have to know what the decision is. I'm not trying to be a jerk, it's just something I don't want to talk about....I know you get that. But I *can* tell you this; that decision, *my* decision, has, and will, become much harder, in the three months since I landed here, then it was that first day I stepped off the bus, if that makes any sense."

"Are you here because of Earl and me? *Are you?* Are you here for some reason to see us? To tell us something?"

Lilly's voice was trembling, which in turn got C a bit upset; he knew Lilly was referring to her mom....*Open When Ready*....angels....something.

And then Cord did something he never did before, without even thinking. He put his hand gently on the inside of Lillian's thigh, in comfort, and slowly ran his finger in small circles as he spoke to her. And to his surprise, and hers, she let him.

"Lilly, I promise you, when I came to Belvidere, it had *nothing* to do with you and Earl; I didn't know anything about you or your brother till we met that first day....honest. But if I told you that I'm not really sure why I'm here, I wouldn't be lying to you either; stuff has happened in this Town, with you and Earl, that doesn't make sense to me, stuff outside of the rules, and I don't know if I even believe half of it. But I can tell you this, and this is the truth, I've never met anyone like Earl, *never;* and as for you, well...."

Cord didn't finish his sentence. He lifted his finger off her leg as gently as he placed it, got up and walked out of the room, to look for his best friend.

And the three of them enjoyed a quiet dinner of Earl's absolute favorite – chicken and ravioli (with a whole pile of pasta, sans meat, that Lilly labored over especially for Cord, about which she complained incessantly, fishing for the martyr vote).

After, with their stomachs full and in good spirits, wine in hand, they all took turns messing up the pantry, to the haunting sounds of the *Symphonie Fantastique,* Fifth Movement, with belly laughs and raised glasses to *The Witches Sabbath.*

CHAPTER 117 – RIGHT THEN, RIGHT THERE, SHE FELL IN LOVE

Sunday, July 9th; eighty-one days since he stepped off the Greyhound, planting himself in this strange place. Still no signal to act, no suggestions of trouble to come. Maybe this was to be a long stint; he hoped as much.

"What time is it now?"

Earl chimed, for the sixth time.

"Jesus, Earl, I'm gonna havta pop ya!"

Cord replied, in mock anger.

"Leave him alone; it's 11:18."

Carol flashed a sweet smile at Earl as she spoke; he returned a weak half-smile, embarrassed.

It was a bit overcast, but the day had the feeling of blue skies on their way. A lone navy and green tent was set in front of the Courthouse, partly visible through the trees, from the vantage point of Carol's rambling porch.

The low, steady rumble of an idling diesel engine from a vintage troop transport cut the air, till someone turned the key and it fell silent; calm again blanketed the Park. A false calm, or so they all hoped.

A group of parishioners did a slow sachet down the sidewalk past Carol's porch, fresh from a weekly chat with God, distracted amongst themselves in idle chatter. A group of talkative starlings gathered in the sycamore in the Park, closest to the Episcopal Church; others trampled the clover in the green Square, making a general raucous, looking for eats. Earl gazed toward the Courthouse and counted silently to himself, right to left.

"There's six so far, including a jeep and a medical one."

He whispered, as if spilling a secret.

"How many come?"

Carol asked, always trying to engage Earl.

"Lots!"

That's usually what she got back….one word. But it was still worth it, to her, and Carol smiled just the same.

Hardwick, Mansfield and Third Streets were lined with church cars, which had to make way for the spectacle en-route. A nondescript gentleman in a loud yellow shirt, with a little-shit lap dog, the kind old ladies carry, walked by, waving wild at Earl from across the street. A tiny see-through bag containing mini pellets of dog shit swung in time with his gait, slapping him in the thigh.

"Hey Earl!"

The man yelled.

Earl ignored him, not out of rudeness; it was just what Earl did when most people talked to him. The man paid no attention and took no offense, disappearing down the Park-side sidewalk.

Earl heard a rumble.

"What time is it?!"

Inquiry number seven.

"11:25."

Carol answered politely. She didn't care if Earl asked her the time every minute; she would never tire of Earl asking.

Just as she spoke, a large camouflaged troop transport, with a flashing yellow beacon on the cab roof, coughed petrol, passing off to their left, up Third Street. A large banner was stenciled across the transport door:

Rolling Thunder – Chapter III

The belch of diesel wafted across the porch; it hastened the mood.

A blue jay screeched intermittently in the distance; that sound always reminded Cord of childhood. Blue jays begot instant memories, good memories, of being a kid – the two always paired. It made him smile; a rare smile of a happy past, before twelve, before things turned south.

The anticipation was building; Cord could see Earl trying to quietly, discretely, rub his hands together, hidden on his lap. The rubbing was getting quicker and more animated. When he caught himself doing it, Earl tried to stop; but would invariably start again a few minutes later. He couldn't help himself, the excitement was simply too great.

Cord's jay-smile stayed, looking at his best friend. This pending show was for him.

Another family, in their late-thirties, with three young boys and two younger girls in tow, ambled by the porch, preoccupied in disjointed chatter, only bits of which the three of them could hear.

"….take about an hour to get there."

"….take care of that."

"….are you gonna do it?"

The wife caught sight of Earl, a once-cute wiry blonde, now middle-thick and road-worn from pumping out a team of kids over the past ten years.

"Hi Earl!"

She tossed, followed by a heartfelt smile, which Earl, again, ignored.

It didn't seem to bother her a bit.

But the salutation caught the attention of the youngest one of the kids, an adorable little blonde of no more than four, straggling behind her parents and siblings, shuffling her feet along the slate sidewalk. She didn't say a word, but it was clear she knew Earl; her face glowed at the sight of him. Shy, she half-waved at him, hesitantly; it was a secret little wave, meant just for him.

Earl's face awakened, and a pirate smile took hold. He didn't say a word, he just raised his hand ever so slightly and returned a little, secret wave, just like hers, meant just for her. The little girl beamed and let out the tiniest squeak of joy, like only a little girl can.

Cord missed it, the whole thing; it was over in an instant. But Carol didn't.

Looking back, years later, Carol came to realize the gift that little girl gave, because it was right then, right there, she fell in love.

CHAPTER 118 – ROLLING THUNDER IS COMING AGAIN

A last, large wave of Methodists walked past the porch on their way to their cars, followed by a couple of elderly stragglers, then no one.

It was 11:34 am and the sidewalk before *L'antre du Lion* was empty once again. A large, portable grill fired up in the distance, the smoke puffed and curled into the trees at the far corner of the Park. Otherwise, all was quiet. Another two minutes passed.

By 11:36 am, the anticipation was too great for Earl; he stood up, without warning, huffed, and made a beeline for the Park.

"I wanna go look at the trucks!"

With that, without answering, Cord and Carol followed….myrmidons. Earl was the veteran; Carol and C were simply along for the ride – *Rolling Thunder* virgins.

The trio made their way along the loose grit path to the center of the Park, which was empty. Earl sat on the bench across from his mom's bench, his bench, to get a better look at the vehicles parked in front of the Courthouse, fully expecting C to sit beside him. Carol had other plans and planted herself next to Earl, her thigh purposely grazing his as she landed on the seat; she kept it in light contact. C stood on the other side of her, missing the subtle flirt.

Once Earl realized what happened, he shot to attention. Carol tried to put her hand on his thigh to stop him, but he was quick when he needed to be.

Wow, that was close Earl thought, letting out a sigh of relief.   Carol was disappointed, but smiled at the spectacle; she would eventually win him over, just like the little girl.

The aroma of grilled burgers wafted over the center of the Green. The sun they expected had arrived, breaking through the clouds; a patchy blue sky snuck up on them, appearing from nowhere.

One of the vendors, setting up, loaded a disk of 60's staples; a step back. Martha And The Vandella's 1965 pop *Nowhere To Run* was the first song of the day; the anticipation grew. It was 11:53 am, and Earl looked up at the sky.

"Hey! The sun's coming out; I knew it would!"

Which got him antsy all over again.

"Let's go look at the stuff!"

And, with Earl sprinting ahead of Carol and C, off the three went, over to Second Street, in the shadow of the Courthouse columns.

They were greeted by a rag-tag convoy of vintage World War II hardware parked along the curb, including five canvas-topped troop transports, a medical van, a heavy wrecker, three trailer rigs, three jeeps, an amphibious track-mounted vehicle, camouflaged farm tractors, a trailer-mounted artillery gun and a lone tank, the barrel ominously pointing down Second Street. Eighteen relics in all, most painted in shades of drab green, sporting white stars and strings of non-descript serial tags. Some were pristine, but most were underlain by rust, decades of slow corrosion, waiting to resurface through the most recent coat of fresh paint. Earl was in awe, walking around each one, running his hands lightly along the armor and diamond plate, looking at the oversized, black tires and sticking his fingers in the zagged tread….really big *Tonka* toys.

The next two '60's spins drifted down Second Street; *One* by Three Dog Night, followed by The Beach Boys *Good Vibrations*. It was shaping up to be a great day, shared by three good friends.

The walk down Second Street scanning the vintage hardware was quick, and by straight-up noon, they were back on Carol's porch, asses planted, waiting for the party to start. Leaves rustled in the Park; the sun dimpled the ground where the rays found their way through the weave of overstory green.

Hunter lounged on the ottoman, nestled against Carol's feet; Zeke was prone on the wooden deck, striped, gray and the definition of cool. Both, along with Big Banana, were shelter rescues by Ji-Sue just two weeks prior, and they quickly acclimated to a privileged life at the Lion House.

Hunter was already fattening up; Carol smiled as she ran her bare foot gently across the chubby girl's belly. She knew Ji-Sue probably played her; more cats meant a bump in the babysitting fees, but the cause was good, and in her heart, she knew the Korean really loved the cats, especially Big Banana. He was older, no one knew how old, but he lost just about all his back teeth over time and earned the dubious distinction as the longest resident cat at the shelter, a full two years. Big B scaled in at twenty-four pounds, a bulbous belly set atop too-skinny legs; he looked like Mrs. Ackerman from Brookfield. But he was sweet as pie. He had the added insult of a perpetual crusty ass; he couldn't quite clean himself that well on the far end….too fat.

An old fat cat, with a crusty butt, destined to die at the shelter, living on borrowed time.

Until he met Ji-Sue.

He waddled over to her in his second story wire cage, one of seventy-five cats in the west ward. Rarely did he get to venture from his cage, which wasn't much bigger than Banana himself. He gently placed his paws on her shoulders and rested his head on her chest, closed his eyes and began to lightly purr. He had been saving that trick for anyone who would open his cage and give him a chance, it was the only one he had. Ji-Sue did, and she fell in love.

So out the door Big B went, along with Hunter and Zeke.

The shelter even cleaned Big B's rear end for the car ride home; he was royalty for the day.

And, of course, Earl and Big B became the best of friends; he immediately ranked above Louie the Lobster, who dropped yet another notch, down to sixth-best friend. But lobsters don't mind, so Earl didn't feel bad.

On the news, Carol put the kibosh on future Ji-Sue shelter runs; even with Earl now helping, eight cats was the absolute limit for *L'antre du Lion*. She had enough strikes against her in Town; she was sure the *Crazy Cat Lady of Belvidere* was the next inherited moniker, and Carol was sure Lilly already started the whisper campaign to seal it.

The real after-party parishioners hobbled down the Hardwick Street sidewalk; the last of the last. The older they were, the longer they lingered in the church lobby, hobnobbing with the minister himself, organizing pig roasts, scheduling bingo, more face time with the big man – extra credit; important stuff when you're trying to cement that ultimate train ticket home.

It was 12:03 pm when the first bikes finally arrived.

Earl always remembered the first one; this time it was a teal and white Suzuki, atop same was a hefty blonde, with a long, thick braided rope of hair running half-way down her back. A second black bike tailed her....the boyfriend. A third bike, straddled by a butch-dyke, rumbled by. The trio rode up Third and hooked a right onto Hardwick, swinging past the porch front.

"This is exciting!"

Carol said aloud, to no one in particular. It was exciting to her, but more so because it was exciting to Earl; he could barely contain himself.

"That's nothing! Wait till they all come in; the whole Park rumbles! Lilly and I watch it all the time together!"

Neither C nor Carol responded to that comment, but it was clear Carol was disappointed this was an Earl/Lilly affair. Just her luck she would show up too, and put a damper on the makings of a good day with her two favorite boys.

Another bike rumbled past, husband and wife in tandem; they rolled to a stop and idled in front of the Methodist Church.

"Hey, there's two more, across the Park, with headlights on!"

Earl yelled, like a birder spotting species on the wing.

California Dreamin by The Mamas & The Papas played in the distance; the song ended and there was more waiting, and more quiet, more anticipation building after the tease of the first half-dozen bikes.

By 12:16 pm, a whiny bluesy song, with a solo harmonica, played across the Park; the three of them racked their brains and laughed, trying to figure the name to a song they all knew. No luck.

They finished a second round of coffee and *V8*, still waiting through the tease.

The music ended, and the Park fell silent yet again. Carol slowly leaned back in her chair, content. Big B jumped onto the ottoman by her feet and laid hard against her ankle; she could feel the vibration of his purr against her leg.

In the fourteen years since she stumbled upon this Town, never once was she here for the annual *Rolling Thunder* run; in fact, she had never even heard of it. Too many important parties, attended by important people, to venture out to Podunkville. Man, she thought, those parties didn't mean shit. She couldn't remember a one, and none ever had a military convoy, *Rolling Thunder* motorcycle brigades, screeching blue jays, and, most importantly, friends she cared about. None ever came close to touching this, sharing coffee and *V8* with the two men she honestly felt she could spend the rest of her life with, and never grow tired.

Well, with Cord, maybe she could tire of him; he was a royal pain at times. But in the end, it was always better with him, than without; he always seemed to redeem himself, somehow. With Earl, well there was no question about that one; she would never tire of Earl.

Her thoughts were broken by the piercing of silence across the Park; a lone musician, sans warning, had begun to play a haunting tune on the bagpipes, which seemed to bring the goings-on in the Park to a standstill, stopping all in their tracks.

Earl slowly stood up, and turned to Carol, whispering for the eighth, and final, time.

"What time is it?"

"It's 12:23 pm."

Carol whispered back.

A slow smile creased the big man's face, as he looked at the two of them.

"12:23 is my new favorite time, C; you know why?"

He didn't wait for Cord to answer.

"'Cause they're almost here; *Rolling Thunder* is coming again."

CHAPTER 119 – THE THREESOME SMILED QUIET

A low, rumble at the far corner of the Park began to drown the lilt of the bagpipes, spilling along Mansfield Street, like the rolling in of the fog. The percussion grew louder; the skin on the back of Carol's neck began to tingle as she slowly leaned forward in her chair.

And then they appeared; *what* a sight!

A gnarling, throbbing mass of motorcycles raced up Mansfield, turned the corner onto Third, gunned down the length of the Park, and crossed onto Hardwick, a tangled, indistinguishable thread of leather, rubber, petrol and noise; endless drum-shaking combustion, belching and barking naked power….raw emotion.

More and more came, an unbroken chain, with no end. You couldn't help but stand in awe at the spectacle; two hundred hogs circling the Park; a pack of wild, barking dogs. Cord and Carol stood and soaked it in; it gave them goosebumps.

Yet, as quick as they arrived and circled the Square, causing a heart-thumping raucous, the bikes fell silent, parked in sentry around the perimeter of the Green, including dozens in front of *L'antre du Lion*, just twenty feet from where the three of them sat on the porch.

The bagpipes fell silent along with the bikes, and the sixties rejoined the party. Marvin Gaye and *I Heard it Through the Grapevine*, followed by The 5th Dimension and *The Age Of Aquarius* lit the Park.

The music played while hundreds of bikers milled in the Green, canvassing a half-dozen vendor tents affront the Courthouse, buying tee-shirts, wallet chains and bandannas, while chowing on burgers and dogs.

Carol was standing on the curb, talking to Frank and Fob Berry, two old-timers, both well in their eighties, gossiping about the new Methodist minister. Carol had been waving to the two of them on Sundays and making small talk, on and off for the past ten years, never once knowing their names. It's odd how that happens; you get to a point where it is much too awkward to ask, so the charade of polite, nameless conversations drag on, for years.

Except that two months ago, Earl told Carol their names; of course Earl knew them since he was a kid. And ever since, Carol called out to Frank and Fob by name, like she knew the given names from day one.

They were the only parishioners that ever talked to, or even acknowledged, Carol sitting on her porch on all those past Sundays, for years.   They were a sweet couple, the kind that get into heaven regardless of organizing pig roasts or scheduling bingo tournaments.

It was 12:51 pm and *Johnny Comes Marching Home* lilted through the Square. Only twenty-eight minutes after the *Rolling Thunder* first stormed the Park, the first biker parked in front of Carol's house mounted to leave; a minute later, two more saddled and left.

Such was the case every year; just as they came….in a trickle, then a blast, the bikers left.

Earl always got sad when the first motorcycle skirted away; it felt like losing a friend.

But despite the few who departed fast, the bulk of the bikers were congregating at the far end of the Park, by the War Memorial. The true rally hadn't even started.

"Come on, we gotta get closer, or were never gonna hear!"

Earl urged impatient; so the trio made their way back to the same bench, and settled in to listen to the tap of the microphone, and the opening remarks by the Chapter President. After hats were removed, the invocation performed and perfunctory introductions of distinguished bikers in the crowd finished, the 2006 bike run was devoted to the former *Rolling Thunder* Chaplain, who recently died of cancer. A moment of silence was followed by a solemn tribute to prisoners of war and soldiers missing in action – POWs and MIAs; comrades to which *Rolling Thunder* was dedicated to bringing home, to locate and assist them….give them help, hope, encouragement and the strength and patience to endure.

Earl didn't understand most of it, but he hung his head respectfully and listened with all his might; he knew what they said must be very important.

Earl knew some people in Belvidere were a bit frightened of the bikers, because of their tattoos, long hair and leather jackets, full of scary patches. But when Earl raised his head and looked around, he didn't see anything scary; he saw a big family, most of them hanging their heads, standing together, because they all missed their family and friends….a lot of them had red eyes, and some were quietly crying. Big scary-looking people, missing family they cared about; Earl knew all about that.

Carol saw the troubled look on Earl's downward face; she stood next to him and gently grabbed his pinky finger with hers, squeezed it for a bit, and let it go. He didn't acknowledge the act, but he also didn't flinch or pull away when she did it, and that alone made Carol happy.

The Star-Spangled Banner played, followed by the *Pledge of Allegiance*; over two hundred men and women sang proud, in unison, getting louder with each stanza. Both songs were followed by thunderous applause.

A tear creased Carol's right cheek.

Why did she miss this? *How* did she miss this? All those years of *Rolling Thunder,* right in front of her house, and she never even knew it existed, that it came and went year in and year out in her absence, a special neighbor she never met. Looking across the mass of bikers, she couldn't believe how such simple gestures and time-worn songs could engender such feelings of pride and emotion in her, standing in the Park.

But they did; it opened her soul. She was sad for all the bike runs she missed over the years, knowing Earl was out in front of the house for all of them, without her, not even really knowing her. And she was wasting time somewhere else, far away, on something that wasn't nearly as important as this....not even close.

Earl's eyes had gotten red; he whispered to the two of them.

"I know they all look kinda scary, and I'm afraid to talk to them, but you know what? I *like* them; they care about people left behind, people who are scared and lonely…..people like Fred, before Fred got hurt."

Carol knew the Fred story; she gently rested her head on the lower part of Earl's chest and kept it there for a few seconds.

"You're a good egg, Earl."

She whispered quiet.

And Earl smiled at the both of them.

It was 1:06 pm, and the President laid a wreath at the base of the small War Memorial, to the left of the Courthouse steps.

"To our friends, our comrades in the Army, the Navy, the Marines, the Coast Guard and the Merchant Marines, brother and sister veterans....God Bless America."

The crowd barked loud in unison: **Semper Fi!**, followed by a single **Hooah!**

"What's that mean C? They say it every year."

Earl asked.

"It kinda means always faithful, loyal, brothers in arms; something like that."

Earl thought about it a second, and then turning to face his two friends, said gently:

"Semper Fi."

And the two of them replied.

"Hooah."

And the threesome smiled quiet.

CHAPTER 120 – NOT ANOTHER WORD WAS SPOKEN

The clock swept to 1:07 pm; that's when it started.

It only took two notes to realize what he was hearing, and even then, Cord couldn't believe it. Adrenaline raised the hair on his forearms and calves; he quietly stepped backward and eased down onto the bench and shut his eyes, immediately thinking of *her*.

He didn't think he would ever hear that song again and *not* think of her. Carol knew what was going on, hearing the stories from Cord.

As usual, the event did not cause Earl to cry. To the contrary, he was happy, like always. The bagpiper played the entire song amidst silence in the Park; no one even moved.

C's lip quivered, and he looked down, so Carol wouldn't see him get upset, see his eyes wet. He didn't know why he got so worked up, for a woman he never knew, and would never meet.

The three of them, along with the throng of bikers, two hundred strong, stood together as one and listened to a haunting rendition of that beautiful song.

Amazing Grace

The song ended, and there was no acknowledgment, nor applause, the crowd simply, quietly came back to life. Earl turned to the two of them.

"They play that every year; I usually sing out loud, if Lilly isn't near enough to hear me, but this time I decided I...."

Earl stopped mid-sentence, something at the perimeter of the Square caught his eye, and caused him to fall silent. Neither one had to venture more than one guess, and they were both right.

Sitting alone, atop a picnic bench as far from the War Memorial as you could get, sat Lilly, head staring straight ahead. You could see the scowl from fifty yards. She wasn't looking at the three of them, but they all knew for damn sure she knew they were there. That scowl was for them....guaranteed. Earl didn't say a word, he just shuffled off toward the table.

"Well, that's the end of that."

Carol said, with disgust.

"Hey, come on, Earl's in a tough spot; if he didn't love you as much as he does, he would never risk her craziness....never."

"Really? Do you really think so?"

Now the question Carol was asking had to with the first statement; and of course she knew it was true....Earl loved her. But she wanted to hear C say it again. But he wouldn't indulge her ego, and let her question lie unanswered.

Lilly set her jaw hard; Earl wasn't going to get off easy.

"Hi Bibby."

She didn't answer.

He saddled up next to her, sitting atop the picnic bench, as close as he could possibly get to her without touching legs, the space between no more than the width of a sheet of paper. Usually when he did that, she would move her leg toward his, ever so little, just to initiate contact, a kind of unspoken handshake between the two.

But this time, she didn't. And Earl noticed; he was meant to notice.

"Sorry, Lilly."

"How 'bout stop saying *Sorry Lilly* and stop doing things that you have to say sorry about to begin with, how 'bout that?"

No answer.

"Having fun with your girlfriend?"

"She's not my girlfriend!"

"I meant Cord."

"You like him too, I know it."

"Do *not*."

That answer didn't convince either one of them.

"You better not have sung that song, Earl."

"I didn't sing; I was just smiling, is all....I didn't sing."

"Especially with *them*. That was *our song*, her song, our song; it's not for **anybody** else, you hear me?"

Lilly glared at Earl with wild eyes, the ones that really scared him.

"Yes, Lilly."

"You know, we're supposed to come and see the bikes together Earl, like always; that is what *we* do. Well, I guess *we* don't anymore. You want me to go away? Cause I will; I'll just leave one day, no note, no warning, nothing! And you can stay with your new friends; is that what you want?"

Earl put his head down.

"Well? **Is it**?"

"No; sorry Lilly."

Was all Earl could think to say.

"We should go over there! She's yelling at him, like always, treating him like a little kid!"

"Stay out of it; Earl knows way better than you or me how to handle Lilly, trust me. And when she gets like this, she's unpredictable."

"I'm not afraid of her!"

"I know, I know, your tough, she's tough, your both tough; just stay out of it."

Carol huffed at him, disgusted.

"I'm going back to the house."

And with that, she left Cord sitting alone on the bench.

Two peas in a fucking pod Cord muttered under his breath, watching Carol storm away. Then he sat down on the bench in a casual manner and watched brother and sister sitting on the picnic table, in the distance, waiting for the drama to play out, like it always did.

They sat beside each other in silence; Earl too afraid to talk, and Lilly too hurt to talk anymore. And so they sat; minutes past, simply silence. Both looked straight ahead, at nothing in particular, waiting for something to happen.

It was 1:16 pm, and the closing prayer was read by the new Chaplain. Two minutes later, the final song of the rally was sung by the crowd, *America the Beautiful*.

O' beautiful for spacious skies,
For amber waves of grain;

"I'm sorry Bibby."

Earl said again, barely above a whisper, to no response.
They sat is silence, listening to the bikers sing.

And crown thy good, with brotherhood,
From sea to shining sea!

And just as the last words were sung, before the echo left
the air, Lilly, ever so lightly, moved her right leg
outward, and gently touched hers against Earl's; she
never moved her head or made any other gesture to
acknowledge the truce.

But that's all he had to feel.

"I don't *ever* want you to leave; I love you Lilly."

He said tenderly, still looking forward.

"I'm not going anywhere; I would never do that to you
Earl....*ever.* I love you too."

She answered in an equal tone, never turning her head.

And then they were silent once again; not another word
was spoken.

CHAPTER 121 – DADDY WASN'T HAPPY

America the Beautiful had ended, it was 1:20 pm, and less than an hour after their arrival, the bulk of *Rolling Thunder* began to disburse from the War Memorial area, heading toward their bikes along Mansfield, Third and Hardwick.

Every year it was the same; over the next fifteen minutes, three-quarters of the bikers would mount and ride out of Town. An hour and a half later, the last stragglers would leave, the military vehicles would be driven back to storage, the vendors packed up – before 3:00 pm rolled in, there would be nary a trace a single motorcycle had entered Belvidere.

Earl always hated when they left, dreading when the stragglers would finally stroll over to their bikes, strap on their helmets, and ride away. He would watch them sad, one by one, until the very last one mounted and disappeared, and he would have to wait a whole year till they came back again.

He sat by Lilly, eyes darting around the Park perimeter, trying to guess which bike would be last. He played that game with himself every year, and never once picked right. But he had a feeling this year was gonna be different; he was going to finally pick a winner.

"Here; do I want to know why?"

She said, more than slightly annoyed.

Earl shook his head no; he didn't need to get into another pickle with her.

"I figured as much."

Lilly had retrieved and handed Earl a small piece of yellowed paper from her back pocket. It was lined, with big spaces – the kind you write on in grade school. The date, *December 16, 1976*, was written in trying-to-be-neat block numbers, separated by slashes, in the upper right corner of the paper.

Earl rubbed it between his fingers; he hadn't looked at it in over twenty years.

"Earl, you know that was one of her favorite things of yours….you *know* that, right? Don't go giving it away or doing something stupid!"

"I know, I'm not dumb! I just wanna show it, is all."

Lilly frowned; every little piece of him, every special part, every sacred memory, shared with others, especially that bitch *other*, was like a little piece of their past, their family, whittled away from her….and she didn't like it. Not one bit.

"Make sure you give it back to me when you're done, so I can put it back, keep it safe….okay?"

He nodded just a bit, but she didn't see it.

"Okay?"

She said more forcefully, with a nasty twang.

"I said okay!"

"No you didn't; you didn't say anything."

"I nodded."

"We'll I didn't see it; speak up next time."

"OKAY!"

He yelled at her.

And she flashed him a wicked look that could kill.

"Don't you raise your voice at me, not now, not after what you did to me today! You hear me?"

She wagged an angry finger in his face.

He put his head down, and didn't say a word.

He put the creased paper carefully in his front pocket, for later.

He wondered what C and Carol were up to; he looked around discretely, not to attract Lilly's attention, and saw Cord sitting on the bench where he left him, in the middle of the Park, but there was no Carol. He sighed in disappointment.

Now, how could he get back over to C without getting Lilly upset? He wracked his brain, but there was no way out. He looked around, frantically trying to find an answer.

And that's when he saw it. He couldn't believe it at first, and blinked to be sure his eyes weren't playing tricks.

But they weren't.

Less than twenty yards behind them, perched quietly in front of the Episcopal Church, lay the lady of his dreams.

"Lilly...."

He whispered, grabbing her lightly on the arm.

"*Look.*"

Lilly turned, and followed his finger, but she didn't have to look very hard. Earl had shown her pictures a hundred times; she figured it must finally be one, in the flesh. He grabbed her by the arm and led her over to the curbline, approaching in reverence, like one kneels before the altar.

"It's a police *Knucklehead* Lilly, a real *police one*! All black! Look at the red seat, Lilly; see the valve cover? That's what that's called, you know, a valve cover; it covers valves. It's a *real Knucklehead*! The cover kinda looks like a fist, with two knuckles sticking out, doesn't it? I can't believe it's really here! I don't know why, but I just like it, a real lot; don't you?"

Earl ran his hand gently over the leather seat, which looked more appropriate for a bicycle, not a motorcycle. His hand tingled in excitement.

"Come on Earl, you know why you like them; you think they're cool because mom thought they were cool, and she told you she used to ride on one a long time ago; it was her favorite."

Actually, Lilly knew it was more than that, much more. Although she never knew why, Earl somehow convinced himself years ago the man who rode their mom around on one of those bikes was the father he never knew; it was more than just a *Knucklehead* Harley to Earl, it always was.

"So, I can still like them!"

Earl was defiant.

"And I never saw one, for real, till now. I never saw a police one at *Rolling Thunder* till now, never! Isn't that kinda weird?"

"You didn't look at *all* the bikes; there were *hundreds*, just like you don't look at every bike every year. There could have been police *Knuckleheads* here before and you never saw 'em, is all."

Earl didn't answer; he just shook his head no, still defiant.

"Don't shake your head at me."

She scolded.

So he stopped; but he still thought *no;* Lilly couldn't stop him from thinking about shaking his head no, no matter how much she yelled at him.

Earl was mad at her for yelling at him; she was always yelling at him. And, although he didn't realize it, he started rubbing the bike seat harder, thinking about Lilly scolding him all the time.

Cord saw the two of them standing at the bike, talking, and he was debating as to whether it was safe to join them.

It was right then that he heard the terrible crash, and he saw a big man clad in black leather go from stop to a full sprint, straight toward the Episcopal Church.

Daddy wasn't happy.

CHAPTER 122 – STEP BACK ASSHOLE, OR YOU'RE GOING DOWN!

Cord and two bikers, all in full sprint, reached the fallen *Knucklehead* at the same time; Lilly and Earl were standing by, ready to right the machine.

The one biker, clearly the owner, was a strapping, forty-something bouncer, six-foot-three and three hundred pounds plus. He was used to intimidating people with his size and grizzly menace, always the biggest guy on the block.

Except for today.

Like the car you flip the finger to, before seeing how big the driver really is, the biker started yelling from afar, focusing on the downed bike, and not the size of the man who put it there; that was usually never a concern for him.

Except for today.

He found himself looking up at a *very* big mulatto, with a ripped physique, muscle atop muscle. And he immediately regretted the obscenity-laced rampage run. His mind was racing, trying to formulate a partial retreat, damage control before the black behemoth pounded him senseless.

Then he heard Earl speak.

"I'm sorry, I'm sorry, I'm sorry! I was just rubbing the seat and it fell!"

Earl was flush in the face and looked ready to cry; his head down in submission.

The biker's fear quickly morphed to relief, which turned to anger once again. The grizzly got his dander back, and was ready to unleash, when Lilly lit in.

"You mother-fucker! You say one more word to my brother and I'll kick your fucking teeth in, and the fucking police are already on their way, cock-sucker, so try something....*go ahead!*"

Lilly shoved her cell phone at his face.

The two bikers were taken aback; they didn't know how to react to the visceral response from the twig blonde, or the lack of one from the guy the size of a fucking tree. So they just stood for a moment, silent....regrouping.

And that's when Cord spoke.

"Listen to her pal, trust me, she's not kidding, about any of it."

The two turned to look at C, who up to that point had gone largely unnoticed.

"Now, Earl, that's the big guy standing there *[Cord pointed at Earl]*, knocked the bike over by mistake."

"It's a *Knucklehead*, C! The *police* one!"

Earl whispered.

"Really? Well, that explains it. See, my friend here, he has something for *Knuckleheads*, and until today, had never seen the black police one, so he got a bit excited. Sorry."

The biker sighed, and in a low, sarcastically polite tone, offered his rebuff.

"Well, I appreciate the interest, I really do, but you just don't go touching a man's bike without permission. And sorry doesn't pay for all the damage that touching costs, man."

"Understood. Well, I assume you have insurance; make a claim, and we'll pay the deductible."

"I'm not making no claim and getting dropped, man! You'll pay the full repair cost, using *my* repair guy, and you're lucky I'll end it there, let you off; that's the way this is gonna roll."

"Fuck you shithead! Marty will handle this; he'll put your fat ass in jail for harassing me! How 'bout that *roll*, asshole!"

The biker slowly turned toward Lilly, and spoke in a condescending tone, wagging his finger at her face.

"Now, I haven't said a word to you little lady, *not a single word.* I suggest you let the men here handle this and you can just keep that pretty little mouth shut and you'll stay out of a world of hurt; we're all trying to be civil here, on such a fine day."

He biker's buddy shook his head in silent agreement.

Lilly was lit up, the fire in her eyes vermilion. She was already in a wicked bad mood, and this just added a whole load of fuel. This guy had no idea of the hornet's nest he was poking.

Instinctively, both C and Earl stepped back from her, waiting for the viper to strike. They knew it was coming with that comment, it was just a matter of how and when this poor sap was going to get fucked.

She inched a bit closer to him as she spoke.

"I'm sorry, I don't think I heard what you just said; can you repeat it for me?"

"I said you have a bit of a temper; I see you don't get that from your *brother.*"

The fat man pointed his thumb toward Earl, and the two bikers laughed.

Now this guy was *already* done; but that was just about the worst comment he could have heaped on top. Implying, because Earl was black, that he couldn't be Lilly's real brother, with the subtle racist inflection, head tilt, thumb-jab and sarcastic chuckle to boot, turned Lilly's ears crimson. She stepped just a bit closer to the big-bellied man, her sights, and foot placement, were set clearly on his easy-access nut-sack.

Why is it fat guys always take that wide stance?

The man turned to his buddy to finish his chuckle….fatal mistake.

It happened so quick, Cord almost missed it, and both he and Earl knew it was coming. Earl had enough time to look away; Cord wouldn't have missed it for the world.

A small yelp from Lilly preceded the swift viper-strike and the dull thud of her foot on his groin, and just like that, a ripple ran across the loose skin of the fat man's belly, like a stone tossed in a pond. He stiffened, let out a gasped groan, like a hungry sea lion looking for a fish, and fell toward *L'antre du Lion,* axed timber, both hands never leaving the too-late cradle they made around his swollen nuts.

Fat guys always hit the ground hard.

The other biker, before thinking, instinctively took an aggressive step toward Lilly, but Cord stepped in the path. He was noticeably smaller than his companion, but a thick man nonetheless. He and Cord stood about eye to eye.

"Another step, and I'll snap your neck."

C said with dead eyes.

The police cruiser, lights on, screeched to a halt curbside, kicking gravel, with the tire rubber dangerously close to the *Knucklehead*, which still laid on its side.

And an uneasy truce set in, while Marty slowly opened the cruiser door, night stick in hand. He was always psyched for a Lilly rescue, his adrenaline dialed to high.

Marty focused on the upright biker, pointing his club ominous at the man's head.

"Step back asshole, or you're going down!"

CHAPTER 123 – TAKING UP THE ASS END

In less than five minutes, tempers cooled and Marty had the situation well in hand.

"Listen, you guys do a great thing; I love *Rolling Thunder*, but you just have to cut Earl a little slack is all, he meant no harm, trust me."

Marty summed up, after getting his arms around the details, which went something like this: accident happens, someone talks, Lilly gets mad, Lilly attacks; Marty cleans up the mess.

Pretty much the same story every time.

The downed biker had regained some semblance of composure, and had been helped onto a Rotary Club bench, along the sidewalk. Of course it was Earl who helped him up. He wasn't afraid of him anymore.

"My name's Earl; I'm sorry about your bike….it's my most favorite bike, *ever!*"

"It's okay man, really, just keep your crazy sister away from me, okay. She's got a wicked quick foot….*damn!*"

"I know!"

Earl said, as the fat man gingerly rubbed his nuts, trying to lessen the dull throb.

"My name's McLeod; Mac is fine. Thanks for helping me up; I'm not too easy to get off the floor, need to lose some weight."

As he grabbed a generous handful of fat from his bulbous stomach, folded in rolls on the Park bench.

"Why don't you join my sister's kick-boxing class!"

Mac just looked at Earl, and gave him a half-cocked smile.

"Classic. You're okay, Earl; I gotta tell ya, I don't like many people, but I really like you. Sorry I did all that yelling, bad temper, bad habit; gotta get better about that….take a deep breath, or something."

Mac exhaled long and slow.

"I don't care, my sister *always* yells at me. Hey, maybe someday can I take a ride on your bike? Maybe? Someday?"

"Sure, you got it, done."

Cord walked over to the two of them.

"Hey, whatever it takes to fix it, whatever, I'll cover it, no problem. And use whoever you want, do whatever you have to do; doesn't matter."

Mac looked over at the downed *Knucklehead*.

"I'll take a look; I'm sure its nothing that can't be buffed out. If not, I'll cover it; Earl's okay. But thanks for the offer, appreciate it."

"Mac said maybe some day I can take a ride on the *Knucklehead*!"

"Very cool."

Cord whispered at Earl.

Lilly saw the three of them talking and, reluctantly, after a small push from Marty, walked over to the bench. Instinctively, Mac took a defensive position, and clamped his legs shut. You don't need to beat this dog more than once; he was trained.

She walked up and faced Mac head-on, with her head slightly down.

"Sorry."

Was all she said, in a barely-whisper; it was as much as she could muster.

"Whoa!"

Both C and Earl said at the same time.

"You don't know just how rare that statement is, my friend….frame it."

C said to Mac.

Mac stuck out his hand in peace; Lilly grabbed it lightly, and let it drop.

"Marty made me do it."

She said under her breath, to no one in particular.

Earl let out a little snort from his nose, trying to hold in his laugh.

"Nobody makes you do anything, Lilly, who are you kidding?"

C said, smiling.

Mac rescued her.

"Thanks. Hey, Lilly *[Mac kind of ducked his head down, then looked up at her downcast eyes]*, I'm sorry too; what I said to you and your brother, about your brother, that wasn't cool. You're all good people, I can tell, especially you, Earl, you're the real deal…what you see is what you get. Anytime you want a ride, just let me know, you got it, no question."

Earl smiled.

And to everyone's surprise, Lilly spoke, nicely, to Mac.

"Hey, let me ask you a question; how long have you had this bike?"

"Long time, bought it in 1981; big year for me, never forget it."

"81? *1981?* Are you serious? Who'd you buy it from?"

Lilly's voice quickened.

"Why?"

Mac asked, surprised at the tone.

"Was he black?"

Lilly asked.

"No way!"

Mac chuckled.

"This guy was as white as they come, some rich dude, from Far Hills, had a whole garage full of collector bikes – a whole garage built just for his wheels! Must have had thirty or more bikes – all super high-end collector shit, and a separate one for vintage collector cars, with a vineyard in between the two....pretty fucking crazy. Anyway, this guy puts his bike for sale through my dealer, sent my guy a photo, and I see it pinned to the wall behind his desk, call the dude, and bought it on the spot, right out of his garage.   This is one expensive, valuable bike, and he was selling it for next to nothing; I could *never* afford to pay what it was worth, so I figure something royal must have been wrong with it, but there wasn't – it was perfect; he just didn't want it anymore, didn't say why. Don't know why he sold that particular one, it was the only one for sale; but I never asked, didn't care. Why?"

"No reason, just curious."

As she looked at Earl, who was looking at her, with eyes full of disappointment. He thought for sure that was the bike his Mom rode, he could just feel it. Maybe she would tell him, but he would have to wait; she hardly ever came around when he and Lilly were together…almost never.

Lilly didn't let it go.

"But you don't know when, or who, he bought it from, right? He could have bought it from anyone?"

"Sure, I guess. Why not?"

And with that, Lilly walked over and whispered something in Earl's ear, and kissed him on the neck.

"Thanks."

Was all she said to Mac, then she walked away.

"Do you remember the address?"

C asked.

"No; long time ago dude."

"But it was from where? What was the Town you said?"

C pressed.

"Far Hills, from what I remember. I probably have the Bill of Sale somewhere; I don't get it….why do you guys care?"

Cord didn't answer.

"Hey, seriously, thanks for being stand-up about the whole thing. Give me your number, okay, that or your email….something, so we can keep in touch. Earl will definitely take you up that offer for a ride; we'll have to set a date."

Cord said, as he bent down beside Mac.

"Sure….**Jones!** That's it! The guys name was Jones. Man, I can't believe I remembered that; that's fucking weird, just popped in my head. I remember he looked like Barnaby Jones, that TV show guy, you know, the Beverly Hillbilly, white haired dude, Buddy Ebsen….that's it! Better looking than him, rich does that, but reminded me of him. Fuck, thought it was funny his name was Jones and he looked like him. Man, that's weird, remembering that; fuck, I never remember anything."

Mac's voice trailed off, lost in a distant thought, from long ago.

And with that, Mac and his buddy righted the *Knucklehead,* checked out the damage, which was just a nick or two in the black paint, started her up, and slowly headed out of Town. They were the very last two bikes to leave on that gorgeous Sunday, on the 9th of July, with Mac following his buddy, taking up the ass end.

CHAPTER 124 – PETTING BUMBLEBEES AND A BIG FAT NO

"Earl be careful, you're going to get stung!"

Earl snickered.

"No I won't, they like it; besides, they're too busy working."

Earl took his big pointer and gently with the lightest of touch, stroked the furry gold bristles just behind the bumblebee's head, then ran it slowly down the length of its folded wings along its back. The bumblebee paid Earl no attention, furiously working the pollen onto its rear legs and buzzing its wings now and again, to Earl's delight.

Earl smiled.

"I've been petting bumblebees since I was a kid and never been stung, never once! My mom was the best at it; she taught me. Here, try it."

And with that, without really thinking, Earl carefully grabbed Carol's tiny wrist and slowly brought it close to the working bee. Even though she was afraid of the bee, she let herself be led by Earl, surprised at the contact; his hand was warm, and felt good on her arm.

She extended her pointer tentatively and barely touched the bee, first on the wing, then behind the head. Cord could see how thrilled she was.

"Petting bumblebees in Belvidere; it doesn't get much better than that."

C said as he leaned against the black top-rail, watching the two of them crouched in front of the tea roses, by the topiary set against the front porch. They were both lost in the act.

Out of nowhere, Carol kissed Earl on the right cheek; she did it quick, without warning, so he didn't have a chance to pull away, or run.

Earl was taken aback, both flustered and ecstatic.

"Thank you?"

Was all he could come up with.

Carol gave him a warm smile.

"You're welcome. Now every time I see a bumblebee, I'll think of you."

"Great, thanks a lot!"

Cord jawed sarcastically, interrupting the moment.

"What?"

"What? I'll tell you what! I'm going to have to hear, and re-hear a thousand fucking times, about that little sneaky kiss - explain it, discuss it, dissect it. Earl is like the tide, he keeps on coming, never stopping, with the questions and commentary....relentless. And this one's huge! A full week's worth, for sure; and now every time he sees a bumblebee? All over again....Christ!"

"Well it's good for you! Ask as many questions as you want Earl."

Carol shot back.

Earl blushed, he was in a perpetual blush whenever stuff like that happened with Carol.

Now was as good a time as any, he thought. Earl bounded up on the porch and whispered in C's ear as he slid his hand into his front pocket, handing the yellowed

paper to C, who carefully unfolded it, concentrating as
he read.

"Really? This is great Earl. Hey you, stop petting the
bees and come up here!"

"Why? They like me; this is really fun!"

"Uh huh, well, this is more important; come on, sit your
butt down."

C said, as he patted the seat cushion of her favorite chair.

Carol reluctantly came on the porch and faced C, with an
annoyed face, refusing to follow the instructions of his
cushion pat.

"I was busy!"

"Yeah, sit down."

C barked, as he playfully pushed her into the seat.

"Okay, ready? This is a poem Earl wrote, when he was
in fifth grade, just ten years old. And he got an A+ on it,
his only A+ *ever*. And the teacher liked it so much, she
had him read it to his whole school, over the loudspeaker
in the morning, during homeroom, and….what?"

Earl tugged at C's arm and whispered frantically into his
ear.

"Oh, right. Earl didn't actually read it, big surprise, he
made Lilly come to his school and read it. Anyway, it
was Earl's mom's favorite too."

Earl had his head down, too embarrassed to look at
Carol or Cord.

"Anyway, Earl wants me to read it to you, to show you
he can be smart and get good grades sometimes, as a

kind of gift for being so nice to him all the time, and letting him watch the cats with Ji-Sue, and making breakfast, and all the other stuff too, and never yelling at him."

And with that, Earl had about as much as he could bear. He got up to run, but Cord grabbed hold of his shirt before he slipped away.

"Whoa, whoa, you run, and I don't read. Now just sit there. This is really good Earl, I know you're proud of it, and so is your mom. So just listen while I read it."

Earl sat down, scared to death. He answered C in three soft words.

"Okay, go 'head."

Earl squeezed his eyes shut, covered his ears with his big mitts and scrunched his shoulders, like he was waiting for a firecracker to explode.

Both C and Carol smirked, and Cord began, as he gazed lovingly at Carol, instead for Earl.

The Night Before Christmas

The feel of Christmas floats through the halls,
All are happy putting up the balls;

The tree is up and we go to sleep,
Trying not to make a peep;

We can't resist and look and see,
And there is Santa under the tree;

I looked again and he was tired and sad,
My gosh he looked just like my dad!

C put the paper down and Carol's eyes were red, like she was about to cry. Earl was still clamped shut, eyes squeezed as hard as he could.

Carol got up and gave him a second kiss, a long one, on the forehead, as she grabbed his hands and pulled them away from his ears. He unscrunched his shoulders and warily cracked open his eyelids, to see her nose entirely too close to his.

"Earl, that was beautiful; thank you."

"I don't know what my dad really looks like, so I remember thinking, maybe he looked like Santa Claus, maybe. I would give you the poem, but Lilly said I can't, that my mom wouldn't like it. But she's wrong, I know she wouldn't care; my mom likes you....*a lot!*"

"Earl, you *did* give it to me, you just did. I don't need the paper; I've got it right here....and here."

Carol pointed to her head and then to her heart, which made Earl unknowingly focus right on her breasts, which he stared at long enough for Carol to notice. She smiled mischievously at the unexpected attention, and Earl realized his little lapse was noticed....busted.

"Should I leave you two lovebirds alone?"

C said, getting up in a mock exit.

"NO!"

Earl screamed, a little too loud, and in a girlish high pitch, which made them all laugh.

What a way to end a *Rolling Thunder* day; petting bumblebees and a big fat no.

CHAPTER 125 – WHO EVER SAID I WAS THE JAGGED GLASS?

Earl turned back and waved six times as he crossed the street and disappeared into the Park; you couldn't wipe the grin off his face. *Rolling Thunder,* police *Knuckleheads,* bumblebees, Christmas poems and Carol kisses, lots of kisses. Earl had a good day, a real good day.

"He's got some major damage control at home; better him than me."

C said, waving back until Earl was out of sight.

"Why does he put up with all her nonsense?"

"Why? Because he loves her, more than just about anything."

"Then why didn't he go home before, *with* her?"

"Because he loves you, more than just about anything. But you already know that, and just like to hear it, over and again."

C said, as he took a long toke from his *DeMuth,* sitting on the porch loveseat.

"You know, I'm tired of this seat; I want your seat."

"Really? No problem."

Carol said, as she made not even the slightest hint of an effort to vacate her chair.

"You are such a bitch, you know that?"

"Only to certain people."

Silence.

"You know, if you just asked politely, instead of demanding, you might just get what you want; ever think of that?"

Cord resettled in the loveseat, shifting his ass around as he cleared his throat.

"Excuse me, Ms. Crowe, may I sit in your favorite chair? For just a bit mind you; it would be an honor."

Cord sat upright and proper during the delivery, with the air of an Englishman.

She studied him with deep conviction, took a long drag from her *Davidoff* cigarillo, and sighed.

"No."

Was all she said.

"Bitch!"

She laughed.

"Yeah, but I at least gave it a pretend thought."

C looked out over the Park; muffled thunder barked in the distance.

"I didn't know it was supposed to rain."

He said, but she didn't answer, instead taking an extended drag, gazing out at nothingness in the empty Green.

"I gotta do some work; coming out here is a great escape, but it's just that. I'm coming out here too much, getting buried at the office. And the worse part is, part of me doesn't really care; that's never happened before."

This time C didn't answer, instead taking a long toke on the big *DeMuth.* Awhile later, he broke the silence.

"What are you working on, that new Fund?"

"Yeah, trying to find property whose environmental risk I can understand and quantify; I don't understand all the science, and haven't found anyone I can really trust to explain it to me - lot of acronyms, guesses and bullshit it seems, with no straight answers on what things cost to fix, and how long it will take to do it. Plus I'm thinking of transferring the Brownfield Fund *in toto* from Cayman to Bermuda; Cayman's been good to me, but Bermuda has been making it much more attractive for funds to establish on the island.

C smiled, reliving memories of both locales, but he said nothing aloud. She saw the smirk.

"So you've been?"

C looked at her with a puzzled face.

"C'mon, I can see it; which one? Both?"

"Yeah."

Was all he said, taking another drag; he loved the *DeMuths* Woody fed him.

"Well, I prefer Bermuda; it's closer and I have a house there which I rarely use, a *pied-a-terre,* you know, a summer place *[she defined the term, since Cord didn't speak French].* It's a Greek Revival, 1913 I'm told, outside Hamilton, North Shore. Don't get there nearly enough; it's too big, really....too big."

A bit of a brag, which she rarely did. In fact, after the words left her lips, and the slip of French to boot, she felt awkward and pompous, and wished she could take it back.

1142

He answered with silence.

"Tell me this; why is it a grocery boy has been all over the world? Everywhere I mention, no matter where it is, you've been there; isn't that a bit odd?"

"Why, are you the only one allowed to travel? Traveling makes one a more interesting person, don't you agree? Can I have your seat?"

"No, and I agree. But that doesn't explain how you find the resources for this little hobby….wanderlust."

Cord sat quietly, thinking.

"One hundred people; if the world could be categorized, represented, by a group of only one hundred people, how many of them would have a college education? How many wouldn't even be able to read?"

She just looked at him, annoyed at the lesson she knew was coming.

He took another drag; the low rumble of thunder was getting closer, preceded by the sky-wide glow of sheet lightning. The wind had picked up a bit, sporting an unusual chilly bite for a summer evening in July.

"Two and seventeen."

He answered himself, then he said it again aloud, still amazed at the numbers.

"Two and seventeen; unbelievable."

"So what? Most people are stupid; is that supposed to be a surprise?"

She said, more annoyed.

"Are you stupid?"

C asked, deadpan.

"I don't think so; are you?"

"I don't think so."

Cord said, in a drawn-out response.

The first drops of rain hit the bluestone walkway.

"Twenty of those people hold ninety percent of all the wealth in the world....*all of it*. The other eighty slobs fight over the scraps....ten percent."

Now she was starting to get mad.

"Again, so what? Should I apologize for being successful?"

"I never said you should; can I have your seat?"

"NO YOU CAN'T! And you never answer my fucking questions; you obfuscate and hope that I forget; I'm not a dummy!"

"I never said you were; can I have your seat?"

"Oh for Christ's sake, take the fucking seat already!"

"No thanks; but thank you for the offer."

"Jesus Christ! I can't believe you! You are so fucking annoying! How can Earl, how can *anyone*, like you?"

"Earl loves me."

C whispered through an exhale of smoke.

"I *know* he does, and for the life of me, I don't know why; you don't deserve it."

"I treat Earl better than I've ever treated anyone."

"Really? Do I have to remind you?"

And C turned ugly, in an instant.

"**Nothing happened** *[Cord wagged an angry cigar at her]*! And we said that was a mistake by *both* of us, and we would *drop it!* So fucking drop it!"

Carol was taken aback, and retreated.

"Agreed, sorry."

She said meekly, knowing she was in the wrong. But she was still irked at his commentary, and stewed.

They both sat in silence, each looking out at the Park, watching the rain grow steady and waiting for the next thunder clap, which was getting much closer. The storm was gaining on them….fast. The wind started to whip now and again, but not enough to drive them from the porch. Yet.

Enough time had passed, and the air between them had calmed, so she spoke.

"Well?"

"Well what?"

He said.

"You're unbelievable! Answer my fucking question!"

"What question? I forgot."

She shot him a dagger, which said, quite clearly, that she was done playing his games.

"How 'bout I tell you a story?"

"It better be good, and it better answer the damn question, for once!"

"I was in Hamilton awhile back; it was a beautiful day. I took a run in the morning, just a couple miles out I stumbled upon this little park, right on the water, called *Spanish Point*. It seemed like no one but the locals went there; the inlet, right off the parking lot, was rocky, shallow, kind of unattractive. I remember this big hulk of iron, half-sunk out at the end of the inlet, about a hundred yards off shore. It was a rusted dry-dock some plaque said it was from 1902. Kind of eerie, sitting out in the water, the waves weaving in and out of the corrosion holes. The whole scene was pretty ugly, which is kinda hard to find in Bermuda. Anyway...."

"How do you remember this stuff? By the way, my place can't be too far from there. Never been there, to that park; where did you say it...."

Carol interrupted, then stopped when she saw C was waiting, annoyed, for the interruption to end.

"Sorry."

She said sarcastic, waving dismissive at him to continue.

"It's not *your* kind of park; a lot of locals pitch tents and sleep there, drinking themselves to sleep, and waking up to drink some more. Been there, done that.

Anyway, I walked over a small knoll, just off this ugly inlet, beyond a row of tents full of drunks and dozens of broken beer bottles smashed in the grass, and made my way down to the water, and it felt like another world....it was beautiful. Looking out at the bay, light breeze at my back, utterly peaceful. It couldn't have been a prettier place on the island, as long as you didn't turn around and look at the broken bottles and rubbish, or the proles in the tent-city behind you.

Anyway, the surf here snuck in and around a bunch of rocks on the shoreline, creating these little beaches, you know, side by side, some no more than ten to fifteen feet wide….outwashes really. And when I looked in the water to the left, some of the broken shards of a beer bottle had found their way into the water, where they must have been rolling back and forth with the surf, endlessly, till they were worn smooth, the sharp edges rounded to little green gems - the kind people stick in their pocket to take home. Sea glass….mementos.

And to the right, no more than ten feet away, was a little eddy, and stuck in the rocks, just above the high tide line, were more broken pieces of the same green glass, wedged between the rocks. But these shards were sharp, dangerous….ugly. The kind that slice your foot open. And no matter how long they sat there, they'd stay that way, dangerous….nobody's memento. Same green glass bottle, from the same drunk that threw it in the surf, long ago.

I'll never forget that. I turned and walked back over the knoll. And you know what? The old dry-dock, and the inlet, they really weren't so ugly; it's one of my favorite spots on the island."

And the story ended, as C took another long drag on the cigar, staring out over the Park, in reflection.

She just looked at him, incredulous, her ears turning red.

"I ask a simple question: How do you travel everywhere on a grocery-boy salary, and I get *Aesop's Fables,* to make me feel bad about being successful, the luck of the drunken bottle toss. I'm smooth glass and your jagged, but we're really all the same, you're just as smart, and could be just as successful, it's just where we happen to land. Well, I'm from bum-fuck Missouri, asshole, and I earned everything I have – no one gave it to me - I *took* it! I suggest you get off your ass and move to the inlet on the left."

She was steaming, and angrily stuffed the remnant of her *Davidoff* in the ashtray for effect.

Cord just looked at her and chuckled under his breath, then took another long, leisurely drag on his *DeMuth*. The rain was coming down hard, the wind blowing mist onto his shoulders and bare legs; tiny water droplets clinging to the hair on his shins.

He stared out at the Park; the sky lit bright with lightning, then went pale purple again, with the thunder right on its heels.

It was a beautiful early evening in July; he loved staring down the face of a storm.

"What's so God-damn funny?"

She barked at him, as the darkness rolled in.

He slowly exhaled a trail of smoke, and answered in a low monotone:

"Who ever said I was the jagged glass?"

CHAPTER 126 – BIT OF A BRAIN DUMP

"Wait a minute, what's that suppose to…."

"I'm getting wet, can we go in?"

Cord cut her off.

"No, not until…."

"I can't go in? I have to stay outside? Are you my mother?"

"No, but yes, yes you do; now be quiet for a minute while…."

Carol had yet to finish a sentence.

"Did I tell you I've been having dreams about my mom? And not good ones."

Cord said, in a hollow voice. Carol stopped, and listened.

"You know, I haven't dreamed about anything, for years, decades; no dreams, at least not any that I can remember when I wake up, anyway. Maybe I dream and just don't know it. Anyway, I certainly haven't had any in the….*[Cord looked out at the Park in thought]* what, eight years, Jesus, eight years already, since she's been dead. And I come here, to this place in the middle of nowhere, and meet Earl, and they suddenly start again….very strange. And they're almost always about my mom, in some peripheral way. I don't ever really see her, I don't think I've *ever* seen her; she's just nearby, out of sight. But I can definitely *feel* her. I smell her smells, her perfume, soap, cocoa butter - I even feel her warmth, and I know it's hers, it's not anybody else – I remember how her radiance felt. Sometimes I hear her voice, but it's always in the next room, just beyond the corner, so to speak. Last night, we were in the same room; I just missed her - she must have *just* gotten up from the table – all I saw was her favorite pen was still lying there, next to a letter she hadn't finished. The pen was laid down and she was in the middle of writing a sentence, that she didn't finish; it was if she abruptly got up and walked away, right before I got to the table, but I could feel that she was nearby, just out of sight, and I hoped, in the dream, that she would come back in the room, and finish the letter, but she never did. Strange."

Cord closed his eyes and sighed.

"I miss her sometimes; I can't say I've really had that kind of feeling in years. That doesn't mean I didn't love my mom, I did....but *miss* isn't one of those feelings I've really had; can't say why.   You either have it, or you don't; you can't make it up – can't fake it. And I haven't had it, until recent, anyway, and it only comes in my dreams. Strange."

Carol didn't say anything, she just stared at him with slate blue eyes, looking at a man, a friend, that she barely knew. In fact, she didn't really know him at all.

Carol's eyes pierced him; they were hypnotic. C slowly turned his head to look at her, and focused on her eyelashes, at how long they were, and the slight cleft in her chin. She didn't wear a stitch of makeup, clear nails, no rings, no jewelry of any sort....nothing. Her skin was a perfect, even tan, on the light side. She smiled at him, a faint smile shared amongst friends, which cracked her lips just enough to reveal the small, designer gap between her two front teeth, just a sliver....her trademark.

The wind died down and the rain, still heavy, fell vertical outside the safety of the porch. The storm had passed; the thunder had quickly left them, a lonely traveler, heading east.

"Hey, I think I have a Brownfield property for you."

C announced, out of the blue.

"Really? Where?"

"Right here, in Town, over on the river; an old plastics plant that Earl showed me."

"Here? Get out! I've been here fourteen years and I never heard of any plastics plant on the river."

"Well now, you don't venture down by the river much, do you?"

She shook her head in a regrettable *no,* understanding what he meant. River area meant away from the safety of the Park, into Lilly territory, which until recently she avoided like the plague.

"How does Earl know about it?"

Cord just looked at her, incredulous.

"Come on, Earl knows everything in Town, between his sister, Marty, W and Sam, all major spokes on the information, cum gossip, wheel. Plus, Marty watches the place for Georgia-Pacific; once a month he does a quick walk-around."

"Georgia-Pacific? Are you kidding me? I think I know some people on their Board; I can't believe this!"

And with that, Cord told her all he knew about the plant from Earl, which wasn't all that much. But what she heard intrigued her.

"Right on the Delaware River? Ten acres? But what can I sell; what can I do here? It's too small, really, but it would be a cool plus for no other reason than it's

here! But I can't do that, can I? How could I make this work?"

She said aloud in questions to herself, the whole string barely a whisper. Her wheels were spinning wild.

C broke in.

"I have some redevelopment ideas - phased development approach, options to test the waters, so to speak, shit like that. The contamination is likely an easy work around, but will undoubtedly have some riparian, flood hazard and wetland impacts to jockey along the river, which might be a more limiting factor – too early to tell. All my first-cut ideas are a bit off-the-wall, non-conventional, but possibly some attractive cap rates in the end. Plus, it might be the right, first draw to Town, to springboard other development, other destination-location ideas. They're talking points nonetheless, a bit of a brain dump."

Carol looked at him with head cocked, interrupted mid-thought. Where the fuck did *that* come from? She was taken aback by the interest, and the versed vocabulary, from a grocery clerk. So she asked.

"Okay, where the fuck did that come from?"

"What, you're the only one that reads the *Wall Street Journal*? I read a lot about real estate and finance – it's interesting to me, and for some reason I retain it; no big mystery. Figured maybe I could put it to use helping you."

He left it at that; and for now, so did she.

"Well, okay, let's hear it; the phased development, destination-location, the attractive cap rates, the *bit of a brain dump*."

CHAPTER 127 – SPILL ABOUT THE NAUGHTY DISK

The two spoke excitedly about the dilapidated plastics plant for a good hour or so, and it was clear they both shared a fascination with transforming the hulking brick industrial artifact, half-hidden amongst the trees and understory on the east bank of the Delaware; they were lapidaries working an unpolished gem, found by circumstance.

The conversation weaved in and amongst potential end-users, areal population counts and day-trip radii, conservation set-asides and remedial strategies, architectural preservation, pro forma layout and distribution lists, financing and unique recreational components to focus on water features along the lazy stretch of Delaware, just upstream of both the bridge and the Foul Rift.

Although unsaid, it was eminently clear that C, grocery-boy, knew the language, the concepts and the business model, even as he tried to half-hide it, purposely stumbling on words and ideas, clumsy attempts at ignorance. How did he really know about such things? This was pretty complicated stuff when you got into the weeds, but he seemed too in-tune, too comfortable with the whole process. She guessed, much to her surprise, that he might even know as much about the subject as she did; maybe not that much, but close, anyway. She tried to make inroads on the subject, call him out, but he deftly shut her down with the same tired reading-the-*Journal* excuses, till he got tired of the constant prodding and denials, and changed the subject to Earl's surprise fortieth birthday party.

That chewed up another half hour; their excitement shifted to the prospect of seeing Earl's face on the big day, D-Day….he was going to be in hog heaven. They both laughed at the thought, and couldn't wait to see his reaction when the vinyl disk for *Song No. 40* dropped onto the jukebox turntable. You couldn't wipe the smile off Carol's face for that one; she wished it was tomorrow.

Carol had her own surprise plans for Earl that day, plans she didn't, *wouldn't*, share with Cord. It was her own special birthday present for Earl; a fortieth present he would remember for the rest of his life.

She hoped anyway.

Water ran steady along the curb line, marching into the storm drain on the corner of Hardwick and Third, a faucet barely on quarter bore. The muffled sound of the gathered rain dropping through the cast iron rain chains out in the evening darkness was a pleasant backdrop.

The two of them never left the porch; Carol fetched a narrow bottle of golden Chilean *Semillon*, a chilled glass of nectar, and they slowly polished the contents and smoked more cigars as the rain kept on, lessening to a light drizzle by the last swig of grapes.

They sat in darkness on the porch, save for two aspen candles set on the side table, which danced between them, sending off just enough of a golden glow to trace their silhouettes, and glaze their faces.

They both spent time throughout their jag, now and again, just looking at the other in silence, reveling in the enjoyment of the company they shared, quiet smiles acknowledged the thought. This was the Cord Carol liked; why couldn't he always be like this? *This* guy was a guy she could call a true, lifelong friend. But he wasn't the one who always showed up; Cord had proven that time and again.

Finally, Carol sighed. That unhappy feeling of knowing the weekend was ending had crept onto the porch and saddled beside her. Nowadays, time always seemed to fly too quick when she was in Town.

She felt that little pang in her stomach; the Sunday night stomach churn before school the next day. She loved her job, and once she walked into the office, she immersed herself headlong into the goings-on of a typical non-stop day. But that didn't negate the empty feeling sitting on the porch, knowing she wouldn't see Earl and C for another whole week.

She was just about to speak, but C beat her.

"Hey, you know, you still never told me the naughty story about that dagger you threw at Lilly in the market, something about a disk."

She smiled; the query diverted her attention, and gave her a good enough reason to not-just-yet blow the candles and gather her belongings for the long, lonely ride back to the City. Cord had served up a welcome reprieve.

"Yeah, and you never told me about Brockton Point, Little Apple Creek or Amsterdam."

"You go first."

Cord said, knowing that would never fly.

"Yeah right, sure; how about *no* to that. Tell me two of yours first."

"I'll shoot you for it, fair and square."

"Shoot for what?   For who goes first?"

"Yeah."

"How many stories do I get?"

C thought for a bit, and said.

"One; I'll give you Little Apple Creek."

She took the bait before the worm hit the water. No way was he telling her about Little Apple Creek, so if he served it up, she'd likely toss it like trash. It worked like a charm.

"No way! That story must suck if you're giving it up; I want the other two."

"Nope, pick one."

Carol studied Cord's poker face, trying to figure the better story, not realizing he already had the nuts.

"Brockton Point."

"Fair enough, odds or evens?"

"You pick."

Carol said, sitting upright in her chair, excited at the gamble.

"I'll take odds."

"Forget it; I want odds!"

Carol yelled, figuring him taking odds somehow gave him an advantage; she didn't know how, but it must.

C sighed.

"Fine, I'll take evens."

She was disappointed he took evens back so quick; maybe she should take them instead.

Cord mouthed the game instructions.

"Shoot on three, okay? One, two three!"

They both shot out ones; C with a pointer, Carol with her middle finger, aimed at his face.

"Fuck! Best of three!"

She yelled.

Cord just smiled, savoring the win.

"I never lose a shoot; did I fail to mention that?"

C said, through a shit-eating smirk.

"Void; cheater!"

"How did I cheat?"

Cord said, incredulous.

"I don't know, but you did somehow; you *always* do."

"Suck it up, loser."

Carol sighed; she always seemed to be giving in to Cord, and it drove her crazy. But a bet was a bet, no matter how bitter the pill. C smiled, as the rain still lightly fell, unseen in the black pitch beyond the porch.

"Is this gonna require another bottle? Two? Let me smoke one of your *Davidoffs;* I need to settle in for this one."

And with that, C dashed into the house like a little kid prepping for a camp-out, and came back out with a handful of cigarillos, two more bottles of wine, and a wide grin. She sat and watched the spectacle, happy for the stay on her City-bound trip. She used to think of it as a trip home, but she wasn't sure where home really was anymore.

C hastily poured them both refills, lit their fresh cigars, straight from the humidor, and squirmed on the loveseat, getting his ass in a comfy spot, ready for story-time. Sufficiently content, and ready to gossip like a little girl, he gave her the send-off.

"Okay, dish it out; spill about the naughty disk."

CHAPTER 128 – MIDNIGHT….DOUBLE-DOWN, DIRTY GAMES AND ALL

Carol lazily raised her head from the newspaper and gazed across the Park.

It was quiet and sunny, a typical late summer day; the Green was empty, save for a bike quietly peddling toward her along the gravel path, and a sole dog-walker. She laid the paper on her lap, stretched her legs and wiggled her toes, took a long swig of her favorite, a diet *Stewart's Orange Cream*, and drank in the scenery. The slightest summer breeze tickled her cheek; this was why she came out here, she reminded herself. Where could you find this so close to the City, so close to home?

For eleven summers she had sat on this porch, once a month or so, and she never tired of the scene, the smell, the feel, of this little backwater. At least her little island on the Square, anyway.

A lone figure, walking along the sidewalk, Park-side, caught her eye. It was a thin man, and even from a distance, she could tell he was muscular, in shape. An obvious confidence accompanied his gait, relaxed….in control.

She shifted in her seat and craned to get a better vantage as he approached. She lifted her paper as camouflage and peered sneakily around the edge, waiting for him to enter her ken; a spider in waiting. It seemed forever until he passed in front of the house, across Hardwick. But it was worth the wait.

He was a *stunner,* someone she had never laid her eyes on before. He looked to be about her age, and was just under six feet, she guessed, with a back straight as a board, a shaved head, and sporting a several day shadow of dark brown stubble on his chiseled face. She moved the paper slowly to the left in step with his gait, leering at him just beyond the left margin. She felt like a little kid, spying; it was kind of fun. He continued to the corner of Hardwick and Third, crossed Third, walking toward the funeral home, a block further down Hardwick, away from the Park, and soon was out of sight, hidden behind the low greenery of the street trees.

She placed the paper back on her lap and sighed; that was a nice, unexpected distraction, she thought. She smiled and took a sip of the orange cream, bent over and played with her toenails a bit, lost in thought, wondering who the handsome, exotic stranger was, where he was off to, and why was a looker like that hoofing around in Belvidere?

"Name's Button."

She jumped in her seat, startled to see the same man standing on the walkway halfway between the sidewalk and her porch, no more than fifteen feet from where she sat. How the hell did he turn around and get back so quick, without her even noticing?

But more important, *my God,* he was even better looking up close, if that was even possible.

"Uh.."

Was all she came up with at first.

"I saw you watching me from across the Park; you should really sneak a look over the *top* of the paper, then you don't move it so much. It's kind of a give-away."

She blushed.

And she obviously knew the name, even if she rarely left the porch; she knew that name almost as soon as she knew Lillian's, right after she landed in Town. And in the ensuing eleven years, she couldn't help but hear that name countless time, tied to her nemesis. But in all those years, she had never laid eyes on the man who

Lilly called her own, her prize possession, the crown jewel. And as much as she hated to admit it, he was gorgeous; if *she* had him, she sure as hell would parade him as the eye candy he was.

Button never waited for the invite.

He simply strolled onto the porch and extended his hand, which she met with her soft, delicate own in an inadvertent fish-shake, which she immediately regretted; she hated the thought of being seen as weak....as a *girl*. He sensed it, and his firm handshake turned to mush mid-shake, to follow her lead. The whole exchange enraged her, mad at herself for letting him get the upper hand.

He, on the other hand, settled into the typical *player* stance, a mode in which he was quite comfortable. He leaned back on the railing in exaggerated comfort and just smiled at her; my God, she thought, this guy could easily get into any girl's pants that he wanted, and he knew it. And she didn't even care; he was that good to look at....a player's player.

She had to be careful, to remind herself who was the spider, and who was the fly. And to focus on the question at hand; namely: *after eleven years, why was this guy standing on her porch?* She sat up, shaking the doe eyes and assuming a defensive stance, figuring this was some sort of Lilly-trap being laid.

He sensed the change and worked to put out the smolder. He was still sizing up his prey, although he pretty much figured she was in the bag. Button never had to give it much of an effort.

"Lilly doesn't know I'm here; I assume you know who *I* am."

What a cocky bastard, she thought.

"Not really."

She shot over the bow; he shot right back.

"*Not really?* Does that mean *no*? Or does that mean *yes*, but I don't want to act like I know?"

Oh my God! This self-important jerk-off was tailor made for Lillian, Carol thought; never mind that he was dead-on right, and she got snagged. Instead, she got annoyed.

"What do you want?"

"Direct; I like direct. Okay, here it is; my girlfriend just found out, today in fact, that the year lease she signed three months ago with the owners of the *Palace*, is now a lease with a *new owner,* one she has a *bit* of a problem with. This is where you come into the picture, as you can imagine."

Carol was basking; what a coup! And she was mad at herself for not figuring it immediately; of course that was why this guy was here.

The storyline circulating about Town goes that Carol ran into the original *Palace of Sweets* family heirs, walking around the Park, who, after a bit of a talk, and with a dash of serendipity, offer to have the Estate sell her the building on the spot, full asking price, with a quick all-cash closing, to pay off the out-of-town relatives, who had no ties to Belvidere. Sound a bit far fetched? Well, it was….actually.

The *real* story had Woody calling Carol, saying the building was going up for sale real soon, but hadn't hit the market yet, knowing Carol would buy it in a minute with Lillian living on the second floor. But W could never admit that to Lilly – she would stab him in the chest with a pair of scissors for sure. So the made-up *Park story* saved his hide, made him a sweet, easy commission, and allowed him to commiserate with Lilly about the whole dastardly deed, and the bastard *Palace* family members who sold out. If he had only known, he could have tried to stop it. Classic Woody.

"What's the problem? If she wants out, just pay me the balance of the year, and all the utilities too, of course, and she can go, *maybe*. I'll have to look at the terms of the lease."

That *maybe* was just to be a dick.

"Yeah, well, Lilly doesn't have that kind of money, readily available."

"Gee, that's a shame; nice to meet you. Goodbye."

Carol picked up her newspaper, ready to resume her reading.

"I said *she* doesn't have the money, *but I do*."

Carol looked at him with the slightest of interest; the idea was to keep Lilly in the lease, to see her suffer, to laugh at her predicament as she wrote a check every month to Carol! The irony that Carol was her landlord was simply too sweet to ever give up; she bought the building for that reason, and that reason only. Why was she even listening to this release nonsense?

Actually, she knew why; because she was angling as to how she could turn this little impromptu visit by the Prince of Belvidere to her advantage, and she didn't mind the eye candy, even though he clearly was a pompous ass. She invariably found that her eyes would end up staring at the bulge in his crotch, no matter how much she tried to train them anywhere but. She wondered how big his cock was, and when he last had sex with Lillian, and how he liked to fuck her, and how Carol would fuck him, knowing she would give him a better ride than that bitch downtown ever could. And that's when the bulb went off, and the ever-widening smile creased her face.

"Okay, so what, are *you* going to pay me for the rest of the year? Maybe I don't want the money; maybe I could give two shits about that."

"I would be willing to pay you *double* the nine months rent, on a couple simple conditions."

Now Button clearly didn't have any appreciation for the league he was trying to join. *Ten times* the balance of the years rent was a daily interest rounding error for one of Carol's tertiary accounts; the money meant absolutely nothing. Nothing at all. But she realized he was clueless, and it worked to her advantage; so she let him play….the spider had set the trap.

She assumed a serious demeanor, contemplating his stakes.

"Really, double down? Now you're talking some *serious* money. What kind of conditions; give me a *such as.*"

This time, Carol made it obvious she was talking to his cock; she never even made eye contact – she burned a hole in his fly with her stare. Of course Button noticed; even a dolt would have noticed. And being entirely too impressed with himself, he ignored her ham-handed gesture and smirked; as expected, his looks got him anything he wanted. He quickly assumed the relaxed stance of a winner; this was cake. He might even get out of paying altogether, he thought to himself, and tag a bit of new snatch to boot; an all-around win. Now it was his turn to check out her crotch, which he did unabashed, to let her know he was looking. Carol left her legs slightly ajar, and ever-so-slightly opened them wider, for him to graze as much as he wanted. She got a quick throb in her pussy, thinking of the risky game she had just cracked open.

"I want her to move in with me, to my place, but I can't get her to shake that retarded nigger pretend brother of hers. This should do the trick."

Now Carol didn't know Earl, she never met him, although, like the name Button, she had heard Earl's name around Town over the years. And, unlike Button, everyone seemed to like Earl; no one *ever* had a bad thing to say….this was a first.

Carol never forgot the first time she met Earl, which was the month *following* this little Button-story she was telling. He hand-delivered the first rent payment to her door; she doesn't know why he decided to do that, but he did. She never did ask him that question.

After she opened the door and saw Earl, all six-foot eight-inches of him, looming at the doorway, she was taken aback, and scared. But that quickly melted, when she saw the puppy behind the façade. He just stood there, in his light-blue button down Oxford, staring at her like a deer in headlights, smiling, holding a bag of barbecue chips and a bottle of *Vernors*.

Every time since, he wore the exact same outfit as that first day, always with a bag of barbecue chips and a bottle of *Vernors*. Always. Except, of course, for the time he showed up on her porch with a stranger, by the name of Cord.

She remembered him smiling, long after he let go of the envelope that first time. Even after she shut the door, he stood there smiling at the door. He eventually made his way off the porch, looking back every couple steps, all the way across Hardwick. She watched him, through the dining room curtain, cross into the Park, walk to the center and sit on a park bench, it turned out to be *the* bench, *his* bench, and just stared at her house. She remembered being a bit scared at the time; why was he staring? She chuckled thinking back at it now.

She remembered getting instantly mad at Button for what he said about Earl, even though, at that point, she had never even met him. But she quickly regained control of her anger; this was too important an opportunity to squander.

"What's wrong with Earl, I've heard he seems nice enough, and...."

Button rudely cut her off, annoyed she even questioned his motives.

"That's between him and me. Listen, I just want to tell her I made a deal with you to get her out of the lease, and get her to move in with me, and unload her brother on his Uncle, or wherever else she dumps him, I could give a shit, and not have you tell anyone what I paid you to make it happen. How I present it to her is my business, my end; no concern of yours."

Then she dropped the bait.

"I don't know, I'll have to think about it; maybe you can sweeten the pot?"

Now she looked even more deliberately at his crotch, for a long period of time, opened her legs just a bit wider, an almost imperceptible move, and raised her eyes a tick to meet his, while she seductively licked her upper lip, done in the most subtle way, but meant to be noticed.

She continued.

"No one has to know; just between you and me. Maybe *that* will make it worth my while, for my own reasons. Plus the double rent, of course, because, you know, business *is* business."

Who said this woman was so smart, so cunning? She was just another girl after his cock; they were all the same. Button reveled in him gamesmanship; he was good, he kept telling himself….he was so good, it was scary.

And a little taste of the cutie on the porch was a just dessert, and certainly something Lilly didn't need to know….spoils of war. At forty-three, he could still get any girl he wanted to spread her legs, with minimal effort; he cracked a grin of self-congratulation.

He eagerly stuck out his hand.

"I think I can provide a little sweetener, well, not so little. Deal?"

Carol smiled as she pointed her spinnerets at Button, the spider's silk slowly entrapping the fly.

"Deal. Tonight, come over around midnight; can you get out to play?"

Button nodded his head slowly, in a most-definite yes.

"And I like to be dirty, to play games, to be in control; are you up for that *Button*? To be controlled by a girl?"

He just smirked.

"I control, always; but I'll make an exception, this one time, for the greater good."

"Good boy."

Carol said, smugly.

He lazily pushed himself off the railing, looking into her piercing green eyes.

"I hope you're in for a long ride; I'm a long-distance man."

She didn't answer, she just smiled mischievous.

Button looked back at her with that model face as he made his way down the porch steps, extending his pointer at her pussy as he spoke smug.

"Midnight....double-down, dirty games and all."

CHAPTER 129 – ALL THAT REMAINED WERE SHADOWS

Carol waited on the porch, expecting him to be late; guys like that were always late.

Button was true to form, showing up close to quarter to one, hands in his front pockets, in no particular hurry, with no pretense of apology. She flipped her cell phone shut and waited for his leisurely approach across Hardwick, from the Park.

"That girl is outta control; couldn't get her off my cock!"

Was all Button said as he saddled up to Carol, leaning on the porch rail by her chair and squeezing his crotch for effect, looking for a Lilly-related reaction. He got none from Carol; she was in full game mode.

"I hope you've recovered; it's gonna be a long night."

She delivered the line with a slight cock of the head, in an even voice. He smiled and leaned in close, whispering.

"Never a problem on this end, *darling*. Had to rinse off; didn't figure you'd want to lick her pussy off my dick, unless you're into that sort of thing. Are you? Maybe I shouldn't have showered."

Carol ignored his taunt and offered one word.

"Drink?"

As she handed him a stout. She figured him a beer drinker, and was right, as she smelled the heavy aroma of stale suds on his breath and saw the glaze of a lingering beer buzz in his beautiful blue eyes.

Like most nights, he had downed a couple at the apartment, chased by a couple more at *George's Place*, a hound-dog dive downtown, half a block from the *Palace*. It was Button's home away from home since he was a teenager; he started drinking there when he was twelve, stealing booze while he swept the floors for George.

But tonight, he drank more than most nights; he was off-his-ass drunk.

"Surely."

He slurred.

"It's a milk stout. Nursing mothers drank it one hundred fifty years ago; good for the baby, so they said."

"Whatever."

Button said dismissive, as he took a hearty swig of the warm swill, which he immediately blew in an exaggerated spray across the front shrubs.

"What the fuck! That's disgusting!"

"Mother's milk; don't you like it?"

Button threw the bottle in her shrubs, disgusted; it disappeared, sinking in a sea of English ivy.

"We'll get that later; maybe I'll try the real thing."

With that, he leaned into her and went to cup Carol's chest, seeing the faint outline of her stiff nipples through a thin white cotton top. Carol was stoked, and her nipples proved it, but it wasn't for the reason Button suspected.

"Hold on cowboy, we need to do this right, and we need to set some ground rules. I'm in control, remember? Number one, you listen to what I say, and do what I say, without question. You don't, just once, and the game ends; the lease stays as-is and you go home, without a taste, and without your new roommate. Understand?"

Her palm was planted firmly on his chest.

"Yeah, whatever."

As he leaned into her stiff arm, to try again for his own taste of mother's milk.

"No, not *whatever;* if I squeeze this button *[Carol held up a small remote],* the police will be here in less than a minute; you understand?"

"What? Marty to the rescue *[Button chuckled]*? Please, the man is a moron, and probably asleep somewhere, running radar. So you see, *little darling,* it's just you and me, and we have to have a little thing between us called trust....right?"

"No, I don't think so. You see, these are what you call *private police,* and they're not very happy men, coming all the way out here to the boonies in Belvidere, on such short notice, and especially being made to wait till one in the morning, for a meeting I said was supposed to start at midnight."

Carol touched Button lovingly on the nose, a love tap.

"Brick."

Carol called in an even voice, matter-of-fact, into the darkness enveloping her porch.

And with that, a black man no less than six foot four, and well over three hundred pounds, not fat, appeared from nowhere, emerging from the shadows swallowing the front yard. Without being asked, and without being told where to look, he bent over and removed the stout bottle from the ivy bed, dumped the rest of the contents gently into the ivy, and quietly tucked it under his immense, black, tailored double-breasted jacket.

He didn't say a word, staring straight ahead, wearing black shades in the dark.

"Thank you dear; tell the boys to sit tight, we should be fine. Button, *darling*, do we have an understanding?"

Button didn't say a word; he just stared blankly at the immense black figure planted at the edge of the ivy bed.

"How can he see?"

Was all Button came up with; a comment she ignored.

"By the way, did you say you had a problem with black people earlier today? You know, like Earl? I believe you referred to him as a *retarded nigger*, is this right?"

Button rarely retreated; he was a no-nonsense bad guy, the kind who never shied from a fight. But this was the exception to the never. There was tough, and there was stupid, and in this instance, Button wasn't stupid.

"No problem, we have no problems here. Look, maybe I should go."

"Go? Hell no, I've been waiting for this wild ride all day! The boys are harmless, as long as we go inside and play nice, by the rules, *my rules*. Just forget they're out here."

She said, with a dismissive wave of her hand.

"That's a little hard to forget."

He said, pointing at the large mass of man standing rigid in the front lawn, arms folded across his massive chest.

"Trust me, I think I can distract you; you're gonna have the ride of your life! And look at the prize, Lillian for life, under the same roof! Then you can finally *shake that retarded nigger;* isn't that what you said? Anyway, looks golden for you, all around."

With that, she gently grabbed him by the hand and led him like a little boy across the porch. Just before they crossed through the double doors, Button looked back.

The Brick had vanished; all that remained were shadows.

CHAPTER 130 – THAT ASS HAD A NAME.....BUTTON

C stared intently at Carol, eagerly listening to her recount, as he lit his second cigarillo.

He liked the story so far, because he liked that Carol put the cock-sucker in his place. God, he hoped she didn't fuck him; please have the story end with no fucking. He didn't want that guy to have gotten into her pants, especially since he wasn't getting in anytime soon, if ever. Because of Earl, likely never.

Sitting on the porch, in the dark, that was the only angle that mattered to Cord, as Carol continued the tale.

As they walked into the rear parlor, Carol discretely held the remote by her leg, and softly pushed the upper right button. A red diode silently pulsed to life across the room.

"You like to ass-fuck? I think this should be an ass-fuck, a dirty ass-fuck."

Carol said, as plainly as asking if he wanted a drink.

Holy shit, the mood certainly changed in a hurry. The beer buzz had already blurred the recent messiness outside; Button smiled at her raunchy talk, flashing those gorgeous too-long eyelashes at her in a wink. His blue eyes were piercing. He joined her in the mud.

"Ass is my specialty darling. Lilly's was an ass-virgin till I took her; no one goes in but me. It's mine; I own it. I own it all, actually, every bit of her, but especially her tight little ass."

"Really? Does she know that? That you own all of her; that you *own* her ass?"

"Fuckin–A right she does; even some day, when I move on, that door is closed to *anyone*, for good! We've had that discussion; I'm the one-off in that hole; anybody else tries...*big* problem."

"That's a little hard to enforce, isn't it; I mean, you know, when you *move on*?"

"Lilly knows better; she knows the consequences."

Button said, in a serious tone.

"Is that because you're a tough-guy? I asked around; word is, you don't mess with Button."

"Fuckin–A."

He said, as he walked over to her, and lightly squeezed her left nipple, still stiff, and slowly rolled it between his fingers.

"Remember that darling, don't ever mess with Button."

He whispered to her, smiling, gently touching her trademark, the ever-slight cleft in her chin. He had already forgotten the big black man in the front lawn.

She let him indulge a bit, then stepped back, and reached behind a pillow on the sofa to pull out a rubber vibrator, jet-black. It wasn't an overly thick or long cock; rather, it was a right, manageable size. Perhaps, if categorized, it would be called a solid *medium*. Not too hot, nor cold, but *just right*.

"You don't need that thing, trust me, I think I can take care of you just fine."

"Really? So what do you think Lilly would say if she knew you were going to have sex with *me*, of all people."

"Knowing her, she'd probably cut my balls off while I was sleeping."

Button chuckled nervously at the thought, knowing, even drunk, that wasn't so far-fetched.

"And you'd risk that, risk hurting the girl you love, losing your nut-sack, to have sex with me? How sweet."

Carol dripped sarcastic, which cleared his head by a foot.

"Who said I loved her? Well, when my cock's in her mouth I sure do; she sucks *good*, no doubt; but most other times she's a leech, Christ, she has no life, so she's always sucking the God-damn life out of me *[Button shook his head in disgust]*. Listen, there's lot of shit Lilly doesn't know, and this will be just another. No big deal; she knows not to question me, ever; my business is not her fucking business. And she'll still perform if and when I tell her to, end of story. She's a bit addicted to my cock; I have to dole it out or she'll go crazy. And what guy, real guy, would tag just one pussy anyway? *Boring.* What's the fun in that?"

Carol smiled devious; she couldn't have possibly scripted this better if she tried.

"Sounds like you two have a *real* special relationship. But what if we like it? Are we fucking again? And again? Are you gonna keep coming up here for pussy and ass when I call, like a dog on a bone? A dirty-ass dog? I like dogs."

"Darling, there's no doubt you're gonna like it, you're gonna fucking *love it*, and you'll be back for more, trust me. Let's just see if you can keep up, and if I'm willing to keep doling it out; who knows, you might not be that good."

He smiled cocky, as he put his hands on her ass, cupped her cheeks and pulled her in, grinding his hard cock on her pubic bone. He wasn't being gentle.

"Whoa, step back! Remember the rules."

He hesitated for a bit, and gave one last thrust and grind, just to be defiant. Button released and took a half step away, willing to play along, for now, but he was getting antsy, and tiring of the charade; it was time to fuck her, and fuck her hard. How quickly the drunk forgot the Brick.

"Okay, take 'em off; let me see this cock of yours you keep bragging about, the one you're gonna share with both Lillian and me, *our* cock. We'll, since I know about it, and she doesn't, I guess that makes it more *my* cock. I guess I own it, your cock that is, right?"

"Take it easy honey, more like a rent-to-own plan for now."

But as he said it, surprisingly, he obeyed, unceremoniously unbuttoning his jeans and pushing them down, along with his boxers, stepping out and showing her a stiff bone, not nearly as big and impressive as she expected, given the hype. But rock-hard it was, sporting a dark brown arrowhead birthmark, perfectly shaped, on the underside of his shaft, conspicuous due to the stiff attention at which it stood, announcing its presence to all in the room.

"Interesting; tattoo? *That* must have hurt."

"*Au natural,* right from the womb; pretty isn't it? In case I forget, it points in the direction it should be going....*in*."

Button said, grabbing his cock and admiring it, like a proud father, and giving an air-thrust for effect.

"Lovely."

Carol said nonchalantly.

"Now, get on your knees, my dirty little dog."

Carol barked.

"What?"

Button said, caught off guard.

"No *what*, just do what I say. This isn't Lilly, your little leech bitch; you control Lilly, and *I* control you, right? You own Lilly and I own you, right? Which means I *own* Lilly, right?"

Button didn't answer; he just stood there, wary, not sure what to make of this sudden forceful turn in Carol's demeanor. The one who needed to be on their knees, ready to receive, was *her*. He started to reach for his boxers, to pull them back on until this strange situation played itself out.

Damn she thought, her mind racing. She jumped in too fast and strong; she was afraid she was going to lose him. So Carol quickly softened the delivery, and revealed a seductive smile, sporting the sexy little gap between her two front teeth, which were pearl white and perfect in every other sense.

The chin cleft and the tooth gap – the boys always loved them, and Carol never shied from bringing them to attention, when the situation called. And this situation certainly called.

"Come on, I'm just playing around - it's just a game, remember, and you said you like it dirty….remember?"

"No, *you* said that, *not me*."

Button was still wary, not buying the back-down just yet. So she stepped forward and kissed him on the mouth, a sensual lingering kiss, slowly running her tongue along his lower lip. She whispered in a seductive purr, as she gently pushed down on his shoulders.

"That's right, I did. Now on your knees; this is part of the deal, and you'll like it, trust me. Don't be afraid; I'm not gonna hurt you."

She licked and gently kissed his neck between her sultry words, laying it on thick. He let out a fake laugh, more of a bark, and, surprisingly, succumbed to her push, dropping quietly to his knees, still upright. She knelt down beside him, facing him, and cupped his shaft with her delicate right hand, and slowly started to jerk him off, while she spoke, louder than necessary.

"Do you want to fuck me?"

He looked down at her hand working his cock, and didn't answer right away.

"Well?"

As she stroked him a bit faster.

"Yeah."

"How bad?"

He didn't answer, so she stopped, and let go of his cock.

"Real."

He said, so she grabbed it again. His cock was hard, rock hard; she had soft, warm hands; they felt good running his shaft.

"You get this hard for her?"

He didn't answer.

"I can't hear you."

"It's so hard, it fucking hurts."

He said, in a little whine.

She smiled, turned toward the wall, and smiled wider.

"Good boy."

Carol grabbed the vibrator, quarter-turned the end knob, and slowly raised it to her mouth; the humming head barely touching the lips of her slightly parted mouth. Then she extended her tongue, and licked around the top of the molded black cock. Her other hand jerked him off, faster. Lilly never did anything like that, like this; what a fucking *turn-on;* this girl must be some sort of nympho, he thought.

"Who owns your cock?"

She purred.

He didn't answer.

"*Say it;* tell me who owns it."

She was jerking him off double-speed; no one ever did that to him before, and it felt God-damn great.

"Fuck! You do, okay? You do. Jesus! Just don't stop."

"Good boy."

Carol said, as she slid her hand up and down his shaft, now slowing to a deliberate, relaxed rhythm. She could feel his cock throb in her hand; it was hot and red from the friction. Without talking, she put her hand on his shoulder, and guided him down onto all fours, doggie-style. To her surprise, he conformed, without question. That was half the battle, she thought, and he did it without any struggle at all….*sweet.*

But the real test remained.

His eyes were closed, focusing on her slow, steady pump of his shaft.

Now came the tricky part.

She took the black cock out of her mouth, and slowly lowered it, till the vibrating head was between his legs. She inched it closer to him, till she was barely touching his balls with the pulsing tip.

Most straight guys would immediately, instinctively, react to that ploy, and pull away; another cock by their balls, even a fake one, was a definite no-fly zone. But Button didn't flinch, not a bit.   To this day, that still surprised her.

She let go of his prick, and slowly ran the head of the vibrator up his shaft, to the tip of his cock, and held it there, while she barely kissed and licked his ear, breathing warm air into him.

"Feels nice doesn't it? Good boy, good boy, enjoy, good boy….good boy."

She repeated seductively, as she gently ran the vibrator back down his shaft, over his balls, and planted the head in the sweet spot, halfway between his sack and his asshole, and just rubbed it gently, back and forth. *No one* had ever done that to him before; it felt incredibly good, and he felt vulnerable, which he didn't like, but the feeling was unbelievable. Regardless, more reflex than anything, he tensed, and she knew she was at a critical point.

"Shh; remember, I'm a bad girl, a dirty, dirty bad girl."

She said, preemptive, while she placed her other hand on his ass, running her fingers through the fine hair, down between his cheeks, till her middle finger found his butthole. She traced light circles around the outlet.

"Whoa, whoa, what the fuck?"

He quasi-protested. But surprisingly, it wasn't a *stand-up and stop-the-play* statement; it was more of a hesitation, the kind that says stop, but doesn't put an exclamation point on it.

And that was good enough for her, and there was no stop. She just kept the status quo, and that's how it stayed, in silence, save the steady drone of the vibrator.

After a bit, Carol lifted her hand from his ass and placed her middle finger in her mouth, seductively, and sucked it, tonguing it good, lubing it up with saliva, making sure he was watching.

Then she slid it inside her shorts, and worked down to her pussy. He couldn't see what she was doing, but it was clear, from her face, that she had slid it into her cunt, moving it in circles.

"*Very* wet."

Was all she whispered, her eyes closed, licking her lips.

Out it came, and she held it up for him to see, glistening with her pussy. Then she was back at his ass, rubbing her lubed finger on the outside of his butt in a tight circle, putting more pressure on his hole this time.

That prompted an instinctive flinch.

"Hey, no way! Get that...."

He didn't finish his sentence.

She quickly shoved her middle finger deep in his ass, all the way past the second knuckle, and just held it there, without moving it, and let him adjust.

He didn't shoot to his feet, or even move; just a deer in headlights. Unbelievable, she thought….golden. Then she twitched her finger, ever so slightly, the vibrator still working the skin just south of his balls.

"Now you know why Lilly likes it in her ass so much? Feels good, doesn't it?"

Carol whispered, as she stuck her tongue in his ear.

"Oh fuck."

Was all he said. He still didn't move; he just let her be, while his rock-hard cock got harder.

And by that point, when Button hadn't sprung vertical in protest, when he didn't scream – violated as he was – and try to choke her for what she had done, for going into that special place that few straight men stray, that most sacred one-way street, she knew she had him….she truly owned him.

She smiled sly; there *was* going to be some dirty ass-fucking after all.

And that ass had a name….Button.

CHAPTER 131 – TAKING AN ALPHA DEEP, LIKE A DIRTY LITTLE DOG

She kept her finger in his ass, and slowly ran it in and out; her other hand jerked him off, increasing the speed. The vibrator lay on the floor, humming away.

"You like that? You like my little finger in your ass? Just like your gonna pump me in my ass?"

"Oh yeah, pay back is a bitch, I'm gonna pump you *good* after this."

"But you like it?"

"I'd never admit it to anyone, but that feels fucking good; holy shit....*real good.*"

"I know something that feels even better, trust me. Here, take over."

And with that she let go of his cock, and he choked himself, picking up the jerk-off where she left off. Carol snuck behind him, pulled her finger out and kissed his ass-cheeks repeatedly, in a loving, yet obviously sarcastic, way, which was all but lost on him, but not to anyone else who might be watching. Carol's show was clearly for others.

She grabbed the vibrator, shoved it in her mouth, and lubed it with her saliva, till it ran thick down the shaft.

"Now stay still *darling.*"

She commanded, and before he could answer, she shoved the black cock in his ass, till the humming head was out of sight.

"Fuck! Mother fucker!"

Was all he said, as she slid it further into his ass, easing it in. She simply couldn't believe it; other than the initial jolt, more from the surprise than anything else, he didn't fight it at all. She buried it half-way, let it stay in on its own, and slid under him.

"Good boy; now you get a little treat. Time for me to take a little taste of my own."

And with that, she buried his shaft in her mouth. She had decided early on *not* to blow him, not to give him the satisfaction, to be yet another coming of Lillian and all the other weak women he had taken. But she couldn't help it; contrary to the plan, she had no idea she would be, could be, so incredibly juiced, more so because he surrendered, succumbed, so completely to her. Carol's pussy was throbbing, and she had to have a taste of that beautiful hard cock; she wanted it, bad, and she wanted it now.

So into her mouth it went.

She worked his cock furious, sliding her tongue up and down his shaft, then sucking on his head, while she jerked him fast. She could taste his come, a small tease here and there, as it leaked from his head. She swore he got harder with that cock in his ass, his prick stiff as glass.

He wasn't going to last much longer; she could sense he was close, his cock pulsing in her mouth, him grunting and moaning, quicker, louder. So she worked him even faster, sucking hard on his head, waiting for him to unload.

"Shit, shit, shit!

She could feel his cock start to contract as he tensed up. And as much as she wanted to take it, all of it, no way was she going to swallow his load. So, at the very last instant, she quickly slid his cock out of her mouth and kept jerking him off. Seconds later, he unloaded, but good, painting the green floral carpet in spots and stripes of cream, the black vibrator still at attention, lodged deep in his ass.

"Ahh."

He moaned as he finished the last shots onto the rug. Hunter and Big Banana were laying under the coffee table, mere feet away, watching the whole episode with an utter lack of interest.

She smiled in disbelief, *never* figuring she would have gotten half this far. This was golden; a coup of epic proportions.

"Does your girlfriend swallow?"

Carol playfully asked, but when she looked at Button's face, it was clear the mood in the room changed, like the flip of a switch, and not in a good way. The atmosphere was ice.

How quickly that carnal charge, the juice in sex that makes one do things unwise, turns to shame, anger and self-doubt once you come, and return to ground; all the above were clearly written across Button's face. The beer buzz had receded, which made his immediate regret that much worse.

But there were no take-backs on what happened, on what he did tonight; she made sure of that, looking at the steady red dot hiding across the room.

Button quickly yanked the vibrator out of his ass in sheer disgust, squeezing it in crazed anger, his eyes wild. His cock was still rock-hard; he had a second come in him, easy. No way he was going soft, not until he got *major* payback from the bitch before him. He barked in an ominous tone, eyes with the look he had before a hunting kill.

"She does whatever I *tell* her to, and keeps her fucking mouth *shut*, unless she's sucking my dick, which is how the rest of this night is gonna go for you. Games over; you're gonna shut that fucking trap like the bitch you are, until I tell you to open it, and how wide I want it."

He was beyond rabid, his mind squirming; unhinged at what just happened, and crazed for letting it happen. This game was *so over,* and this cunt was going to pay for that little stunt, and it was going to hurt, badly. Of that, he was sure.

Carol cautiously backed away, her blank eyes locked on his, which were wild, unpredictable....on fire. She saddled up to the near wall and reached back to flip the chandelier switch, casting the room in an amber glow. It was her SOS. *Please, for Christ's sake, please be watching* she screamed in her brain.

Button mirrored Carol across the room, cutting the distance carefully, like the deliberate stalk of prey. The playful banter and innuendo was long gone. He spoke to her plainly.

"First, your gonna get on your knees and clean my ass off this thing, and clean it good. Then it's my turn to describe how *you* get fucked, and for starters, that sorry ass of yours is getting reamed, but good, dry, with a real cock, and you're gonna bleed, bleed bad. And you're gonna scream to please make it stop, and I won't....trust me, I won't. And if *anyone* finds out what happened tonight...."

She half-smiled, involuntarily, even though she was scared shitless. They had better come *real* soon.

He was just about to pounce, to shove his ass-vibrator down her throat, hard; but the violent crash of the front door stopped him dead in his tracks.

Before he could turn his head, Brick, flanked by two even bigger *Bozaks*, pumped full of adrenaline, were towering less than three feet from his side, snarling like animals, sporting contorted faces full of rage, waiting for Carol's smack-down signal to break the little bastard in two. The anticipation of inflicting violence had danced in their heads all night; nine hundred and eighty-five pounds of black meat were a hair-trigger away from beating Button to a bloody pulp. The three immense men dwarfed him, rabid dogs, pulling hard on the chain. If Carol had simply nodded, they would have killed him, right then and there, in her back parlor. It would have been over, simple as that.

But she didn't; so he lived.

Button's dick, at full attention, quickly deflated, an ignominious end. It was only then he realized he was still holding, in a death grip, the vibrating black cock. He threw it hard to the floor, against the parlor pocket door, in disgust and humiliation.

She breathed a deep sigh of relief.

"Thanks guys. Just wait in the foyer for a bit, I have a couple things to finish up with our friend here, before you escort him out."

The three reluctantly stepped out of the room, sorry for the missed opportunity to hurt something. Brick eyed Button with venom, slowly sliding the large pocket doors three-quarter shut, leaving Carol and Button alone. The trio never uttered a word.

Having the upper hand once again, Carol finished him off.

"That wasn't very nice; it looked like you were going to try and hurt me."

He just stared at her with those wild eyes, somewhat sober and seething.

"It's not my fault you liked it; honestly, I'm surprised you like cock, didn't think you had it in you. But you never can tell with some people; homosexuality takes on many forms."

"Fuck you, I'm no fag."

Button spit, as he buttoned his pants, the end of a quick and indignant redress.

"Could've fooled me. Most guys who don't like cock wouldn't have a big *black* one shoved up their ass when they shoot their load halfway across the room, especially nigger-haters. Maybe you really *like* niggers?"

Button just shook his head; what the fuck did he get himself into? How did he get here? What the fuck just happened? He was getting angrier, his mind racing on what to do, a cornered dog, looking for an out. For a second, he thought of beating her senseless, snapping her skinny neck, wondering how much pain he could inflict before the baboons returned and ripped him apart.

She could see it in his eyes, and beat him to it.

"I see that temper of yours can be a *big* problem. So let's cut to the chase and discuss how the rest of this story is gonna play. Here's the script; you're going to leave, and you're gonna cool off. Someday maybe you'll realize, on some level, you had a pretty good time, for a bit. You have to live with whatever that means. As for you and me, you'll never step foot on this property again, or my friends, next time, won't be so kind. Oh, and your girlfriend, not me, that is, but the other one, the dumb blonde leech that you're cheating on, the one that's got no fucking life....yeah, that one; she's gonna stay in her lease. Maybe *you* can bunk with Earl; I'm sure his cock is a bit bigger than the tiny sausage you packed tonight. Who knows, maybe you'll fall in love."

Button just smirked, an evil smile which said he wasn't listening to a single word Carol spewed; his wheels were spinning elsewhere, in all directions.

She saw the dis, and spoke sternly.

"Let me be crystal, asshole; Brick and his friends, I told them you're a nigger-hating Cracker, and they *hate* Crackers, and they think you're the fucking poster-boy. So even though I am paying them a lot of money to keep an eye on you, beyond tonight that is, for now and forever, they would just assume break you apart for free, just for the fucking thrill, and I mean break, darling, bust up…broken for good, for life. There are different levels of bad, and trust me, you're not in their league."

Button never wiped the smirk; he never stopped staring at her face, and never stopped smirking, a maniacal smile.

"We'll see."

Was all he said in the end, as he slid open the pocket doors, walked quietly by the three *Balubas* standing just inside the door, never making eye contact. In seconds, Button shuffled off the porch and dissolved into the darkness.

Carol let out a long sigh, and asked the boys to stay in Town for the night, putting them up at the Belvidere Hotel, half a block away. Brick stayed at the house, in the third floor guest room, just in case. And for the first time in eleven years, she locked the doors.

As the boys dispersed, Carol casually walked into the rear parlor with a smugness of victory savored, still in awe of how the night played. She leaned gently on the edge of the armoire and stared directly at the red diode silently glowing in the dark, sporting a shit- grin while she whispered at the vermilion speck.

*"Shrimp dick, likes black cock up the ass, and a cheating bastard who doesn't think much of you, you leech – his words, not mine; sounds like you picked a real winner….certainly the kind of shit-bag you deserve. Oh, be sure to have the rent in to the landlord, that would be me, by the fifteenth; hate to see those nasty late charges accrue. My-oh-my, payback's a bitch, isn't it….**Bibby?**"*

Her smile widened, she grabbed the remote and pushed the upper button; the red eye faded into darkness, and she walked out of the room. Victory.

And that is where her recount to Cord ended. The next chapter, later that night, Carol declined to share with her friend on the porch, but it swam in her head just the same.

An hour after Button had disappeared, Carol was still wired, juiced from all that had happened, reliving the episode in her head over and again. My God, he was a dangerous, disgusting guy, with an absolutely beautiful body. And his cock wasn't as small as she alluded to Lilly on the recording, or to him as he left. In fact, truth be told, attached to that body, his cock was just the right size....perfect. And Button knew it. She couldn't stop thinking about it, jerking it off, sucking it. Her pussy was still wet, and it started to throb as she pushed hard on her pubic bone while she brushed her teeth, getting ready for bed. Brick was already tucked away in his room, and a scatter of cats surrounded her on both the floor and atop the vanity, beside the stone sinks.

It was then she decided to take a long, hot bath. Carol had a large clawfoot tub, reclaimed from a lakefront hotel she once owned, set on an elevated platform in the master bath. It took three big steps, fashioned from progressively taller petrified logs, set upright, to get upon the tub landing, which was a good four feet above the regular bathroom floor. She called it her *tub tower*.

She stripped naked and slipped into the warm water; it felt good. Almost immediately, she did what she had been wanting to do since she blew him; she spread her legs as far as the tub would allow and rubbed her clit, eyes closed, mouth barely open. She came almost immediately, thinking of Button's cock pulsing in her mouth; but this time, she swallowed every last drop, feeling it run warm down her throat. Christ, she hadn't come that hard in years. As soon as she finished she went at it again, pushing her spread legs hard against the sides of the tub, letting one finger rub a light ring around her ass, probing a bit inside her hole, just a bit....a tease. The other finger rubbed her clit, till she let it slide in her pussy for a bit, then quickly out again, and back to her clit.

She lost track, but it must have been four or more orgasms, one running into the next, as Button tore off her clothes in the rear parlor, ripping them from her body in a rape, revealing more of her flesh with each peel of fabric. In seconds, he stripped her naked, her top gone and her shorts and panties pushed to her ankles. He mounted her alpha, controlling her, manhandling her, while she screamed and struggled to break free. But he was simply too strong for her; there was no Brick to save her. Exhausted, like prey run down, she submitted to him, and her surrender was complete, letting him do whatever he wanted to her, for as long as he wanted. She gasped and said nothing, her screams had turned to muffled grunts and moans with each thrust of his cock. He pumped her fast and hard, bent over the couch, pinning her down, choking her, as he pounded her pussy, deep.

She couldn't stop coming to the thought of Button fucking her multiple ways, her powerless to stop him. Carol was always in control, in business, in life, in every aspect of her being. But here, in her head, she could finally give herself up, succumb, surrender. And the fantasy fueled her orgasms. And that she was taking what was Lilly's prize possession was simply a cherry on top.

Carol saved the best fantasy for last, teasing the scene for as long as she could, to have the orgasm that lasted the longest, and felt the best, by far. Now she was on all fours, legs spread limit, ass in the air, compliant and completely submissive, as Button mounted her doggie and entered her ass. One thrust, and he buried his whole cock in her, till his balls were pushed against her ass. Then he pumped her fast and deep, while she moaned, begging him to come inside her.

With legs spread wide in the tub, with fingers buried in both her butt and her pussy, Carol came hard to Button's cock pumping her ass. She moaned low and long through her orgasm, fantasizing about Lillian's prize, taking an alpha deep, like a dirty little dog.

CHAPTER 132 – WHY DID SHE HAVE TO BLOW HIM?

Cord stared, mouth ajar; he was ecstatic she didn't fuck Button, but not happy she blew him. Those were the two most important things he took away from her story.

"That is some fucking story; never quite expected that. So then what?"

C asked.

"Well, I watched the video, just to be sure it all worked, and captured what I hoped it would. Christ, it was better, or worse, depending on one's viewpoint, than I even remembered, as it was happening. What a bombshell. Then I fucked around with the disk, made some minor edits, made some copies, then held onto it for a bit, about a week or so, just to see, you know, what the fallout would be. You'll never guess what happened."

Cord smirked; it was hard to imagine the fireworks that ensued.

"I can only imagine."

Carol leaned forward and whispered.

"Absolutely nothing, nothing at all."

"What? Get out!"

"No, seriously, it was like the night never happened. I never saw Button's face again; haven't seen him to this day. I asked the boys to stick around for the week; I was sure there was going to be some sort of retribution – vandalism, threats, him showing up with a bunch of skinheads, something….*anything*. But nothing happened. The boys were disappointed and bored as hell, mainly playing cards and listening to music on the second floor wraparound porch at the Hotel. I kept them on retainer for a couple weeks after that, and then told Brick that if *anything* ever happened to me, anything strange, anything at all, he knew who to call, and what to do. That was three years ago, and he's still waiting. Brick wants to break that boy so bad he can taste it….still does."

Carol smirked.

"So what about the disk; how did Lilly get the disk?"

Carol shook her head in disgust.

"You know, I felt guilty about the whole thing, right after it happened; I guess that makes me a *little* better than her, doesn't it? Because you know sure-as-shit she would have hand-delivered that disk to me personally the next day, right?"

Cord didn't answer.

"Anyway, so I sat on it, figuring it would be an ace I could pull out some day, if I ever needed it. Believe it or not, even though I bought the building to fuck with her, for the most part, she had let up on me after eleven long years. A sort of *détente* had set in; two nations in a Cold War. I had the Vatican; she had Rome. And don't bother, I'm sure you've been to both."

C smiled silent.

"Anyway, if she had left well enough alone, I would've sat on the disk forever. I kept it and the copies in a safe in my office; the copies are still there. It was cathartic for me, strangely enough, a weird sex act like that. I didn't realize it until it was over, but it had a healing affect. I think I would have been okay never giving it to her. It kind of served its purpose, for me anyway, and no one knew it existed, not even Brick and the boys; my own little secret. No one was the wiser."

Carol shook her head in disbelief.

"But Lilly can never just leave it be, she just can't; I don't think she's capable."

Carol frowned shaking her head at the thought. It was clear she was conflicted, still conflicted, three years later. And C knew she *was* the better person; Lilly would never doubt her own actions. For better or worse, Lillian makes a decision and sticks with it, consequences be damned.

"I don't know what transpired between the two of them during that next week, God knows it couldn't have been good. Anyway, my only peripheral contact was Woody, who generally doles out information sparingly, unless he's got some angle. There's no gossip for free from him, and, as you know, no one else in Town really talks to me. So I was operating in a vacuum.

Anyway, my guess is that Lillian must have been really stewing, going fucking crazy, about me buying the building, and when she ragged about me, to him, I figure Button sure as hell didn't want to talk about *that* topic. Honestly, I really don't think he gave a rat's ass if she ever found out what happened, probably *wanted* her to know, in his demented mind, considering how little he really cares about her.   But what he didn't know was what my intentions were, and I think he was amazed that a week went by without *me* spilling the beans. So my guess is he didn't want to do anything to tweak me, provoke me, so that I would do something that, for some reason, I hadn't done yet. Namely, blab the story. And he sure as shit didn't want *that* story hitting the streets, him with a big black cock up his ass, and enjoying it to boot. Not to good for the rep, so to speak; and a story like that, about *him*, in Belvidere? That would take about *fifteen minutes* to spread from one end of Town to the other, easy! So, because of that risk, and that alone, I can't imagine he was too interested in the subject of the landlord. So he probably blew it off to her, which just made it worse. Again, this is all just a guess. And remember, he didn't even know I had a disk! My guess is he figured it was my word against his, and he would survive, and discredit my story as some sort of unbelievable tall tale, because of my trashed reputation in Town. But with the disk? Christ, there was no denying that disk. He didn't even know I had that nuclear option.

Anyway, after a week of simmering, however it happened, whatever the set-up was, there clearly must have been a blow-up. Not too hard to imagine with Lilly as one of the parties in question. Frankly, I'm surprised it took as long as it did. Anyway, all I heard were the repercussions a couple days later, from Woody of course, when he wanted something, about how Lilly went on a bender, dissing me and spreading a whole set of mostly recycled rumors, all lies, and, of course, everyone in Belvidere downed them whole, without chewing. Of course I never heard any of them directly, but according to Woody, they were bouncing off the walls from one end of Town to the other, worse than usual. He figured I'd want to know; kind of a heads-up."

"Like what?"

"Oh, a whole range of shit; standard fare, rich spoiled City girl, it's somebody else's money she got by being a sleep-around whore, she's put together with plastic surgery....blah, blah, blah. Same old crap I'd heard for years. And if had been limited to that, even though she stirred a shit-storm, I probably *still* would have held onto the disk, since it was nothing new. But the last one, the last fucking lie was the straw, and she had no idea of the irony *[Carol smiled at the thought]*. She said I was a rich girl who liked to hang with boys from the hood, that I liked to be gang-banged by crackhead rappers, that I craved black cock – her words, and that I was going to be bringing all sorts of unsavory blacks into Town, criminals, you know, drug-dealers, devaluing the neighborhood. And she pointed to the boys, *my boys,* who stayed at the Hotel, as proof of the bad *element* I was already bringing around."

C chuckled.

"Oh man, she *so* fucked herself with that one."

"Ya think? Anyway, when I heard that, I figured *enough;* she couldn't keep her little trap shut, so it was time to send the disk. I called my florist in the City; this guy is great. I bought a bouquet of a dozen, huge, beautiful white lilies; of course they had to be lilies, the biggest and best bunch you've ever seen. And I had them place a hand-written note in the bouquet, a little delivery card. The envelope simply said:

Darling

on the outside; on the inside, it read:

To the one and only girl I have ever loved;
Just you and me, faithful forever.
The disk is my special present, to show my true feelings
for you;
I hope you enjoy watching it,
As much as I enjoyed making it.

Love, Me

And I put the disk in a sleeve and had them slide it in amongst the flowers.

Cord leaned back.

"Holy shit, that was fucking cruel!"

"Yeah, kind of; well, more than kind of, but she brought it on herself. Anyway, the next day, I heard from W that Button had simply left, gone, no one seemed to know where, just vanished, and he hasn't been back, in three long years. I don't know what happened; all I know is the florist said a blonde woman signed for the delivery, and I made sure they mentioned the disk, on the off-chance she didn't see it, and to be sure to tell them to read the note first; it was important to read that note first. Anyway, the delivery guy said she yelled to some guy in the background, but I don't know if it was him, or Earl, or someone else. Jesus, to be a fly on the wall *that* day!"

"That's it? You don't know anything else?"

C asked, incredulous.

"Nothing.   Three years and no radar; he left and everyone settled back into their routines, I guess. I don't think the disk story ever got out though; I can't imagine Woody wouldn't have sprinted to my doorstep with *that* one, for free. For all I know, Lilly never told a soul, except him, I presume, since he went AWOL."

"We *gotta* ask Earl; he *has* to know something!"

C said, in earnest.

"Aren't you the little girl? Well, if you want to ask Earl, go ahead, but not with me around. If it's good, tell me solo; I don't want to be that way in front of Earl. If I knew him then like I know him know, I never would have done it, no matter how nasty she got to me. Earl doesn't need me to be like that; I'm forty-five, and I don't want to be like *that*, not anymore."

"I understand, but I'm still getting the scoop! And hey, how about letting me see that dirty disk? I never saw this jerk-off; sorry, poor choice of words. In fact, never mind; I don't want to see you and him like that."

She stared stern.

"First of all, there is no *me and him.* And you, nor anyone else, will *ever* see that disk; it's embarrassing on all fronts. I'm ashamed of it, frankly. I don't know why I even keep the copies; kinda feels like an insurance policy I don't want to lapse, I guess. I haven't even watched it since I sent it to her, three years ago; no reason to revisit that nonsense."

Now that was one big fat lie; there was *plenty* reason.

Truth be told, Carol, three years on, still masturbated to that encounter; it was her go-to ditty, a sure quick thing. And although she would admit it to no one, she had downloaded the video to a thumb drive, and had come countless times to it, both at home, and behind her desk at the office, working late. She would watch over and again her stiff nipples pushed against the thin of her white cotton top, her ogling his thoroughbred body, with washboard abs, watching as she sucked that beautiful hard cock, with him spraying his load across the carpet. She must have replayed the video a hundred times, even more, always finishing to the vision of Button's swollen cock. Oh the irony; she probably mind-fucked Button more than Lilly, and had an orgasm *every* time. She regretted not reworking that night better, not getting to feel, really feel, Button's hard cock inside her. On that one front, she had a tinge of Lilly-envy; Lillian got to mount the real deal. Carol missed her only opportunity; what a shame, she thought, because Button surely did have a *go-to* cock, and it was right there, so close, and ripe for a long, hard ride.

Cord was looking at her, but Carol was staring off into nothingness, seemingly lost in thought. She sighed, letting out a long exhale. Cord figured she was thinking what a mistake that night with Button really was; C was happy she came to that conclusion.

"Okay then, I guess it's my turn."

"Yeah, but hold onto your hat, I'll give you a reprieve; I'm taking a rain check. I really gotta get back to the City and get some work done tonight, procrastinated long enough. Can't see that happening if I continue to sit here gabbing with you, as much as I love the company."

She smirked at him.

"Cool. Promise you'll get Brockton Point when you come back; a deal is a deal."

"Yeah, whatever; it will give you some time to find an excuse not to tell me."

"Probably."

And with that, she scooted inside to grab her overnight bag and briefcase.

"C, would you mind just cleaning up the glasses and stuff? I really gotta run."

"Sure, I'll be your domestic, but just for tonight; that story was worth it."

She gave him a peck on the cheek and squeezed his bicep as she did it; although it was perfunctory, he liked it just the same.

Five minutes later, he watched the red glow of the Ferrari taillights disappear down Hardwick Street, and he was alone on the porch. It was quiet, save the steady patter of a drizzle bouncing off unseen leaves, and the distant sound of curbside rainwater running into the street corner storm drain. He shook his head and sighed.

Why did she have to blow him?

CHAPTER 133 – HE FOUND A GRAY-HAIRED ROOMIE

"No umbrella; never a fucking umbrella."

He muttered as he cracked his knuckles, looking at the rain, which had ramped to a steady, hard pelt in just the last minute.

He thought about staying on the porch awhile, sitting and hoping for a let-up, but he didn't want to stay at Carol's any longer. With her gone, he was antsy to get home. He resigned himself to a thorough soak; even a sprint home wouldn't save him. He knew he would be drenched before he reached the other side of the street. He took the first step into the gauntlet.

And that's when he heard it. A tiny, almost imperceptible cry barely heard above the beat of rain.

He stopped, stepped back under the cover of the porch, and strained his ear, trying to isolate the rain, the rustle of the leaves in the night wind, the stream of water along the curb, to compartmentalize them. He waited half a minute, frozen-in-place, afraid to make any noise for fear of missing it.

Then he heard it again; it came from behind Carol's house.

He leaped off the porch and sprinted toward the driveway to get closer before it sounded again, and he hop-scotched across the back yard, honing in on the beacon, dead-stopped between calls, which sounded every fifteen seconds or so.

It was a weak cry, and he was drenched.

He found his way to the front porch of the small house behind Carol's, which she also owned. It was empty, dark; Carol didn't want anyone living behind her, so it sat vacant, ostensibly for guests she never invited to Town.

And again; a small, helpless cry.

C fell to his stomach, lying in the wet ground cover peering through the lattice work surrounding the front porch skirt. His eyes took a bit to adjust, but there, along the foundation wall, about four feet away, was a wet, tiny ball of fur, a kitten, alone, barely the size of his palm.

It cried again.

He tried to force his hand in between the lattice, but it was too small, and he immediately grew angry and ripped the lattice from its framework, tossing it across the front walk.

Soaked, his front full of dead leaves and mud, he slithered partly under the porch, grabbing blindly, straining to reach the scared kitten; but it sensed his hand and curled into an even tighter ball, away from him, meowing louder.

"Fuck!"

C screamed.

He stood up and searched for a tool, anything, in the dark, and found a broken rake beside the garage. He slid it under the porch, and in one swift motion, scooped up the bounty and dragged it to him. It shivered in his hand, both eyes glued shut with crusted secretions; rock-hard eye goop, covered in mud and wet, dead leaves.

Into Carol's house he went; she never locked it, and found a cotton towel, the ones he never used to help dry the dishes, and cradled the kitten, which cried loudly in his arms.

"Shh, take it easy."

He used a wet cloth to clean its fur, a beautiful light gray, a *Russian Blue*, and dapple water on its eyes, which were crusted shut. He gently pulled on the lids and ran his finger across its eyelids, trying to coax them open. No luck, just more frantic cries from the tiny bundle in the towel.

"Okay, okay, take it easy."

One last crack at the left eyelid, which looked pretty clean of gunk. A quick pry and he saw the faint glimpse of an orb. A second later, it worked itself open, revealing a large yellow/green doe eye, a half-size too big for its tiny head.

It was beautiful, and it looked right at him. C smiled, and right then, right there, it owned him….and they both knew it.

No luck with the other eye, it was sealed shut; it must have only one eye, he thought.

He slowly ran his hand down its back, now dry, more to take a break and give it a rest from his poking and prodding. The shivering had ceased, but not the constant, sometimes frantic, mew.

"Shh."

He said again, and surprisingly, it did.

The newly found quiet was soon interrupted by an almost imperceptible sound; C put his ear down to the kitten's little belly, and there it was….a low, intermittent purr. He took his pointer and gently stroked its head, as he thought.

"*Columbo,* that's your name; Peter Falk had one eye….just seems right."

He cradled the soft gray ball of fur in the towel, there was not a flaw in its fur, except for an irregular dab of white on its breast, and made his way onto the front porch.

The downpour had ended; the crisp smell of after-rain ozone filled the summer night sky; errant drops of precipitation fell off tree leaves, late to the party.

Cord kissed the kitten gently on the head and made his way into the night, heading home.

He found a gray-haired roomie.

CHAPTER 134 – A BLEEDING FIST POUNDING SPLINTERED SLATS

Early Monday morning, July 10, 2006; day eighty-two. As he first came to wake, in that opaque period, he thought this might be the day; it had the beginnings of that feel.

But it turned out to be nothing but a bit of a brush, the makings of a tease. It clearly wasn't *the* morning, for it lacked the fateful words, the feeling of impending doom, followed by the resignation that the ride never ends.

And for that, he was thankful.

It was the first time he remembered being thankful the players weren't saddled beside him, dancing in his head. As much as he despised them, he usually welcomed their arrival, marking the end of yet another sorry chapter.

Rather, he thought of Earl, of Lilly, and of little Columbo, who was asleep, curled up snugly, sapping the warmth from his belly. He pulled over the little white blanket from the base of the bed, the one he slept with in his crib, and tucked it carefully around the tiny ball of fur. The blanket reminded him of his mom, of her warmth. His mind wandered to her; he tried to think good thoughts, relive some good memories, but his mind would have none of it....not this morning. And his thoughts turned dark.

It wasn't a good night; his sleep was fitful, but he couldn't remember why. And like the flip of a switch, his mood turned anxious and volatile, and his mind began to race in a vicious loop. It frequently happened that way, without warning. He shook his head to reset; the shake somehow fixing the malevolence swimming in his head, like a reboot. Sometimes that worked.

Not this time.

He remained agitated through his morning exercises; push-ups, leg-lifts and sit-ups - eighty each. His belly was flatter; he had dropped twenty-plus pounds in the last three months, and people noticed. Without fanfare, the Lilly and Carol fat-belly jokes had quietly faded away. He should have been happy, but he wasn't; he was angry.

He looked over at the dresser beside his bed, at the herring gull feather lying there, the *memento mori;* it reminded him why he was here, how he was here, in this place, any place….every place. It answered questions, and it didn't. It was both, and neither. It made no sense, which made all the sense in the world, at least in his world.

He stared at it with emotionless eyes, breathing heavy and lost in a trance, sitting on the floor, his legs pulled up and wrapped by his forearms, the end of an eighty sit-up set. He looked about the room and found his eyes wandering the apartment, for no particular reason. Everything was in order, neat, not an item askew. He was looking for *disorder*, for something to get angry about, that was not in its place, so he could fix it, reset *it*, reset *anything*….but he could find nothing to move. And *that* stirred his ire, that he could find nothing tangible to anger over.

He eventually sighed, showered, got ready, dressed and made his way outside, to find supplies for Columbo, including a Sherpa bag and some toys at the tiny pet shop a few doors down from *Nonpareil*. He didn't stop at Earl's like he usually did in the mornings; in times like this, it was best for him to be alone. A curt talk with Sam gave him the morning off, the whole day if he wanted. Sam let C do pretty much as he pleased, and he could see Cord was *off;* Sam had seen that look before, and it made him wary.

C grabbed a cup of black coffee and a *DeMuth* from behind the counter, the morning paper and the new

Sherpa – Columbo safely tucked inside, and made his way across Town to the Park. Monday morning should be quiet, a chance to let his mind ease, to let the fret fester and pass without incident, without trouble. Anyway, that was the plan.

The sun shone brightly and the Park was awash in soothing shades of green. He set upon Earl's bench and immersed himself in the news, his hand subconsciously pounding the wooden bench slat, till it hurt, till it bled, till he noticed.

He stopped, looked at the meat of his palm, flush red, the skin split fresh, and closed his eyes; a single tear ran down his right cheek – he let it go. He wasn't sure exactly why it fell; it could be from one of a dozen reels squirming in his head. The trail soon dried; he could feel the remnant line lightly pinch the skin of his cheek.

He opened his eyes to the lazy summer sunshine, and caught a familiar scene. His fist started up again, and he failed to notice.

"No, not today; *please,* not today."

He said through clenched teeth, a bleeding fist pounding splintered slats.

CHAPTER 135 – AT SOME POINT, THERE HAS TO BE A SCARIEST

Buck and Vinny were arguing at the corner of the Park, the same corner from which they emerged on Day Two, three months prior. Cord hadn't seen either one since, not once.

C leered at them; Buck was on foot, Vinny rocked restless back and forth on an undersized bike.

After a half-minute of rising voices, Vinny flayed his arms in disgust and rode off, kicking up gravel in the process. He slowly circled the Park sidewalk, sitting high on his bike, keeping a confrontational eye on Cord. A good hundred foot buffer and a set of wheels provided the means to make the teenager play tough with the man who choked him to fetal in their first encounter.

Cord followed him with a hard gaze, deciding whether he should attack.

Buck lowered his head, sighed, and headed straight for the center of the Park, toward the man who made him piss his pants.

C stood up in an aggressive, offensive pose, to face the lanky, muscular eighteen-year old, with knee-length jean-shorts hanging below his boxers and a muscle tee showing off his pet dragon, wrapping his neck and resting on his deltoid. The two silver eyebrow rings were absent. Buck saw the preemptory move and fired the first volley.

"I don't want trouble, I just want to talk."

Bucks hands were raised in an act of conciliation.

C didn't answer, he just pounded his bloody fist lightly against his right thigh, eying the two interlopers, back and forth. Ay spun his head; Vinny straddling his bike like a horse, stopped directly behind C, less than a hundred feet away, in front of the Presbyterian Church. His right hand slid into his pocket, where it appeared he was grabbing something; but his hand stayed in his pocket, out of view.

"Tell him to keep moving, or we have a problem."

C said to Buck, never taking his eyes off the little-shit on the bike.

Buck yelled to Vinny.

"Get lost man! I'll talk to you later."

Vinny sat still, ignoring the order, staring Cord down, hand still buried dangerous in his pocket, as if daring C to call his bluff.

Without warning, from a dead-stop, Cord launched into a full sprint toward the Presbyterian Church, an enraged bull.

Vinny saw the sudden charge and a cannonball ran his spine – a spike of fear. He pulled his pocket hand, empty, and fumbled his foot on the peddle; it slipped and he nearly fell over. C was less than fifty feet away, coming hard; the delinquent wasn't going to be as lucky this time, evil distorted Cord's face.

The bike somehow righted itself; Vinny pushed off, recovering in the nick of time to skid away from C's outstretched, diving hand. Ay snatched his shirt, but Vinny skinned out safely, a frayed fragment of fabric ripped from his back, buried in Cord's white knuckles as he tumbled across the sidewalk, ending face-up on the curb.

Vinny quickly sped away to safety, his heart pounding in his chest. Looking back, he saw C slowly righting himself in the road; with his brio back, Vinny screamed over his shoulder.

"Yours is coming, mother-fucker! Dead man!"

Vinny laughed and whooped, loud and forced, as he air-pumped his fist in victory over his head, looking back several times as he sped away, to ensure he wasn't being chased. C was enraged; he looked back to the center of the Park, expecting Buck to have cut and run too. But he didn't; he was simply standing there, shaking his head and frowning.

C walked calmly, slowly, back to his bench, rotating and rubbing his right shoulder to try and ease the ache. He stood beside the bench, not making eye contact with Buck, nor approaching him in any manner.

"You need to leave, now, *right now*; trust me."

C said ominous; it wasn't a suggestion.

"I'm not leaving. I'm scared, but I have to talk to you. Please, I'm not with that jerk-off."

C looked and saw Buck's hands trembling; he sighed as he slowly sat back on the bench.

And with the sigh, like a light breeze, the morning fret seemed to pass, an invisible weight lifted.

"What?"

Cord said, annoyed, tiring of the interruptions.

Buck gingerly sat on the far side of the same bench as C, facing Carol's house.

"I already saw Earl this morning and apologized; I don't know why it took me three months….because I'm an asshole, I guess. I woke up this morning and decided not to be one, not anymore. Earl didn't even know why I was apologizing, and he ended up apologizing to me for not being around to play, if I wanted to *[Buck shook his head and laughed in disgust at himself]*.

C didn't say anything.

"He calls me Billy, the only person who does. I like that name….Billy. That's what my dad used to call me, or at least my mom says he did; I was like, two, when he left….asshole."

"Was Lilly there?"

"Where?"

C sighed, annoyed that Buck wasn't following the conversation, annoyed he was even talking to this jerk-off.

"With Earl, when you apologized."

C said, in an annoyed tone.

"No way! I made sure she left before I went up; I don't like being anywhere near her."

"Smart man."

C said, staring into the distance, at nothing.

"Did you know she used to babysit me? I was a little kid, like six years old, in first grade."

"Yeah, I heard; I would have broke your fucking jaw."

Buck looked at him, puzzled.

"She said you used to chew with your mouth open to fuck with her, like a little shit."

"*That's* what she told you?! Did she tell you *why* I did that? It was my only defense; she used to terrorize me, man, tie me up to the porch railing with fucking big-ass, industrial-size rope that weighed more than I did; I couldn't even move, or stand up….like a fucking chained dog. She'd laugh at me, laying on the porch, exhausted, fighting the rope. I was only six! And she would cook spaghetti, my favorite, and eat it in front of me, while she made me eat stinky fish cat food with maybe three or four strings of spaghetti mixed in with the fish gook; she'd boil it in little plastic baggies, and then dump it in a cat bowl and make me eat it – I would almost puke just from the smell! Or she'd fill my mouth up with so much whipped cream, you know, from the spray can, that I would choke and gag, while she fucking laughed her ass off. And the worst, she used to lock me in the fucking attic! The more I'd cry, the more she would laugh and leave me up there, in the pitch dark, telling me the fucking monsters were going to get me if I closed my eyes! I slept with the lights on for years, *still do;* man, she fucking damaged me! *Guess she didn't tell you all that, did she?!*"

Cord laughed loud.

"Yeah, she kinda forgot to mention all that."

"Yeah, thought so. So chewing with my mouth open to annoy her when my mom came home was my only way to get back at her; I was six fucking years old, man! And I knew it would just make it that much worse the next time she watched me; Lilly doesn't forget *anything*! But I did it anyway, I had to. I used to beg my mom, cry, to leave me with Earl, but although she trusted him, she was afraid in an emergency, Earl wouldn't know what to do. In an *emergency, can you believe that?* She left me with Lilly in case of an emergency; Lilly **was** the fucking emergency!"

C laughed again; maybe this jerk-off wasn't such a jerk-off after all.

"She babysat me for a year; it felt like a fucking lifetime….at six, a year *is* almost a lifetime. She lived two doors down from us, on Fourth Street; I would walk a block out of my way, and cut down the back alley, just so I didn't have to walk by her house. This tattoo? *[Buck pointed to the dragon]* it's because of her, partly anyway. She always made me feel weak, like a loser. Had to do something. I'm still afraid of her, to this day; I would *never* speak to her, still don't. If you say the wrong thing, or even look at her wrong, she can get pretty fucking crazy, scary-crazy, you know?"

"Yeah, seen that, first-hand."

C said, matter-of-fact.

"Anyway, I just wanted to apologize to you; I know you're friends with Earl, and what I did, used to do, was really bad, and I don't even know why I did it, I really don't. After what happened, what you did, it was kinda a wake-up call; I didn't like who I was – not even sure how I got to be that way, and I don't know what I want to be, but I know I don't want to be like that, not that, not anymore *[Billy just shrugged, then continued]*. Earl was always like a big brother to me, and he always bailed me out, the only one who ever did, the only one who ever really believed in me, cared about me. And look what I did in return, to look cool to a bunch of fucking losers *[Buck shook his head]*. Even when I was mean to him, he never turned on me; I don't get it."

"Earl's different. You, or me, we'll never be like him. You can only try to do your best, but there's only one Earl. I appreciate you apologizing, it's not easy to do, trust me…..we're square."

And C nodded at Buck, and that was that.

"Well, I'm changing; I've changed, and I have you to thank for that….kind of a kick-start *[Buck laughed nervously]*. Anyway, it's time to return the favor."

That caught C's attention.

"How's that?"

"I assume you know about Button?"

"Heard the name."

C said, flat.

"Yeah, we'll he's heard yours too, and the word is….it ain't good."

"What's that supposed to mean?"

"The kid on the bike, Vinny, he's been feeding a friend of a friend of Button all sorts of bullshit about you and Lilly and Earl, most of it crap – stories floating about Town, puffed – made worse, some just made-up-shit to get Button to take you down. Button is very possessive of what's his, of what he owns.....and he owns Lilly, he always has. And everyone around here knows that and pretty much stays away from her, for their own good. Well, Vin's been saying a load of shit about you and her, to get him riled, and apparently, it's been working. Vinny wants you taken down in the worst way; he's fucking obsessed with it."

"So that's the *dead man* shit I just heard?"

"Yeah."

"So where's this cock-sucker? I thought he skipped Town about three years ago."

Buck shrugged.

"He did. I don't know where he is; no one does – at least no one I know."

"It's always the little fucking shits, you know that? The little guys, with little dicks, they're always the ones to stir the pot *[Cord shook his head....then he just shrugged]*. Well, whatever."

Cord said, stretching his legs.

"Not whatever; do you know anything about Button?"

"A bit."

"Yeah, well he's a crazy dude; he's fucking psychotic....scary mean."

"What makes you think I'm not?"

C said, still staring ahead.

"I'm not saying you aren't, especially when you handed me the bat. But you're friends with Earl, and more importantly, Earl's friends with you; you're his *best* friend – that's what he says, if he says anything. And if someone like Earl thinks you're a good person, that makes you very different than Button, *very* different. I'll tell you an interesting story."

Ay sat silent and listened.

"All this happened way before I was ever born; but shit like this, in this Town, the stories live forever; *especially* Button stories. I've heard this one a fucking hundred times, half from Button himself. Over and over and over.

Button's in high school, seventeen, just got his license, even though he had been driving all sorts of shit since he was probably thirteen, on the farm. Anyway, he used to carry around an old newspaper article, probably still does, kept it in this black, leather mini-notebook he had; it was a national newspaper, can't remember which one it was, but a big one, and the shit made TV too, the whole bit. He was very proud of it.

Button had driven down to A.C., you know, Atlantic City, with this guy, CJ Hammer, he used to like to call him *The Hammer,* his best friend – who's dead, by the way, died before I was even born. Anyway, they steal a car, some half-assed *Datsun;* a souped-up, black shit-box, you know, with bolt-on fins and shit, the kind wetbacks drive, and go to a burned-out section of A.C. - most of A.C. was burned out back then - and bought a whole load of fast food greasy fries. They pile them up in the middle of the street, right in the middle of the fucking ghetto dude, and they wait.

Before long, the first seagull comes along and lands in the road, you know, to eat the fries. There isn't any real traffic on these streets in the City; too dangerous. People avoid them, drive the long way around. And the delinquents that do live here don't own fucking cars, that's for sure. So it's pretty desolate, on the street, anyway.

So Button barrels down the center of the road, sixty miles per hour, past these burned out row homes, and flattens the bird, I mean he *smears* it, all along the pavement. The two of them are fucking laughing, spin around, and the next set of gulls comes down, and they mow them down too. And the next, and the next, and the next; birds caught in the grill, in the tires, a fucking bloody mess. Twenty passes and thirty-five dead gulls, feathers everywhere, bodies piled in the road like a red, oozing speed bump; blood smears thirty yards in both directions. But not all of them died right away; they laid there, squawking, with broken wings, broken backs, suffering, wailing….real bad. The police never saw anything like it; they had to kill the last of them, the ones that didn't die, just to put them out of their misery. And the fuckers never got caught; pictures of a pile of dead birds all over the national news. I never saw Button laugh so hard as when he told that story.

He told me when they were done, CJ wanted to bolt. Hell, he wanted to bolt after the first bird, but Button couldn't get enough, and they weren't leaving until *Button* had enough; that's how it always played with those two.

So before they go, Button gets out of the car, jumps on the hood and screams at the top of his lungs, in this burned out all-black neighborhood, not a white person for a fucking mile, with dying white gulls laying on the road around him…crying as they died. He ignored them like they didn't even exist.

'Take a good look, mother-fuckers! If anyone wants to come out and remember this face, you'll see me again, and I won't be killing white birds! I'll be killing fucking porch monkeys! Takers? Anyone?!'

He said as he spun around on that car hood, laughing, knowing all eyes were on him. He told me he knew they were watching, but not a door opened, and not a call was made. That part never made the news, and that's the part Button lived for; he had no remorse, no regret, none at all….the suffering of those poor birds was the part he lived for. And he knew the black neighborhood wouldn't do shit to a white boy; he fucking *hates* blacks. He thought the whole thing was one big fucking joke.

"Weak people hurt animals….weak."

C said low, with pursed lips.

"Maybe, but he hurts people too. Like Earl, like Lilly….especially Lilly."

C sat up and turned toward Buck.

"What do you mean?"

"I mean he hits her, hurts her; everyone *knows* he does, but she'd never admit it, nor would he, so it's this big secret, that's no secret, that no one talks about. No one dares to; too afraid of what Button would do to *them*. And he wants to kill Earl; he's always wanted him gone, for good, even back when Lilly's mom was alive. At least that's what I hear, anyway; that was way before me. If it wasn't for Lilly, Earl would be dead, for sure. Button hates blacks, and he hates Earl most of all."

"He hurts Lilly?"

C said, in a stronger tone.

"Okay, I'm gonna tell you a story, another one. But this one, no one knows about but me, *no one*. Just me."

Cord nodded once, waiting for Buck to continue.

"I was nine years old, and I was at Earl's old house, out on Fourth Street *[Buck pointed across the Park, south]*. Earl and I used to play together all the time; his, and my, favorite game was hide-and-seek. He liked when I hid and he had to find me. I could always hide where Earl couldn't find me; I was real good at hiding, not making a noise.

But this particular time, I wasn't trying very hard, so I just ran and slid under his bed. Earl always looked there pretty quickly, so I knew I was gonna get caught.

So I hear him calling *'Billy....Billy'* and he's getting closer, real close, just outside his room. I know I'm gonna get found real soon, and my heart is beating like crazy, even though I know he's gonna find me; it's the anticipation, you know, before you get caught. But anyway, just then, the front door busts open, like a fucking bomb, and slams into the wall when it swings, you know, *really* loud; scares the shit out of me. I think I yelped, but no one heard me.

And all of a sudden, out of nowhere, I hear screaming, and I know it's Button. Earl's scared, and getting upset;

I can hear it in his voice. They are standing right outside of Earl's room, five feet away from me, hiding under the bed. And I can hear Button hitting Earl, slapping him hard across the face; he always does that, and Earl just lets him. Then Earl usually starts crying. He was always afraid of Button, even though he could break him in half, easy. But he never knew that, never realized it; it just wasn't how Earl thinks, you know?

Somehow, this bullshit yelling spills into Earl's room; now they are inches from me hiding under the bed. I'm scared to death; and all I can see are their feet and ankles, and all I hear is Button yelling and Earl crying, telling him to please stop hitting him. I think Earl was trying to get away from Button, but he followed Earl into his room, screaming at the top of his fucking lungs. Earl would never put his arms up, you know, to protect himself; I don't know why, but he never did.

Lilly apparently had bruises all up and down her arms, from Button grabbing and throwing her around, and Earl saw them. They were worse than usual, *way* worse; usually Button tried to hurt her in places that no one could see, under her clothes and shit, but this was right out in the open. So Earl saw the bruises, got scared and told Sam, who confronted both Lilly and Button.

Lilly denied it, of course, and Button told Sam if he ever accused him of hurting Lilly again, *ever*, he would regret it; Sam knew exactly what that meant, and he shut-the-fuck-up. But Button wasn't done, not by a long shot. So he came looking for Earl.

I froze under that bed, trying not to cry, not to move, not to even breath loud, as Button slapped Earl over and over across the face, *real* hard, like he was winding up or something. Button told him to sit-the-fuck down, which he did, right on the bed, inches from me, and berated him, telling him he was bad to his sister and, deep down, she really hated him, and that he was a stupid retarded nigger with no real daddy, and that

Button could kill him anytime he wanted and no one, *no one*, would care….just another dead nigger. Earl was crying, telling him to stop, but Button wouldn't let up; all I remember was the slapping, the crack every time he whaled on Earl's face. He just kept hitting him, harder and harder.

I believe Button was going to kill him, right then and there; I could feel it. But then Button made a mistake….a *big* mistake. Fatal.

He told Earl he was going to take Lilly away and Earl would never, ever, see her again. And I remember *exactly* what he said; it was the only line I never forgot – like it was burned into my fucking brain:

*'Lilly and I are going way away, far away; you'll never, ever see her again, you stupid shit. And she'll forget all about you, like you never existed. I'm taking her **far away**."*

All of a sudden, Earl erupted; he jumped up from the bed and screamed at the top of his lungs:

'Don't you take my sister away!'

And Cord, I swear I couldn't see from under the bed, but Earl must have grabbed Button by the back of the shirt and the pants and launched him, like a little rag doll, like a fucking rocket, across the room. It all happened so fast, I couldn't believe it.

Button's head went clean through the sheetrock wall, his whole fucking head! Right to his shoulders, like he was decapitated. It was a heavy dull thud as he went through the wall, and then he just slumped, and didn't move. I thought he was dead; he *had* to have broken his neck.

For sure, that dude was dead; no one could survive that, right?

Earl probably didn't even see what happened; he was hysterical crying and after he launched him, he turned and ran out of the room, crying and yelling Lilly's name, calling her Bibby, like he does whenever he's scared. A second later, I heard the front door slam. And then everything was quiet, real quiet....too quiet. I really thought he was dead, man; broken neck or something - he just *had* to be.

I was frozen, couldn't move; I'm nine fucking years old! My heart was beating like it was coming out of my fucking chest. And I *didn't* move, not for awhile. It felt like hours; it wasn't, but it felt like it. It was kinda like time stopped for a bit; fucking weird.

It was a *long* time that Button didn't move, slumped against, Christ *in*, the fucking wall. He didn't move a bit, not an inch, or make a sound. And I didn't hear him breathing either; I didn't hear a fucking thing, except *me* breathing. For sure that dude was dead.

Then from nowhere, with no warning, I could hear him barely breathing, just a tiny bit. And I thought that was strange, because I couldn't hear him breath before, but now I could. His shoulders twitched at first, just a little; then he started to moan, a low muffled moan, from inside the wall. Christ, it didn't sound like him; it didn't even sound *human*, like some weird fucking animal. And I swear, in-between the moans, just once, I thought I heard him laugh, like some weird fucking high-pitched giggle. Fucking creepy.

And then he must have come to, and realized where he was, or maybe not, but either way, he started to try and pull his head out of the wall. And that's when I heard a blood-curdling scream. Apparently there was a nail, some kind of spiked end of a nail, in one of the wall studs, and it was pushed up against his right cheek; him moving his head was like pulling a fish hook out of your lip or something, but like trying to pull it *straight out*. And as he tried to pull his face out, the nail just dug deeper into his cheek.

Now, most people would feel that fucking nail and freeze, and not move, because the pain must have been fucking bad, *real bad*. But that mother-fucker, he pulled his face out of that wall anyway, *slowly*. And as he did, he sliced his own right cheek clear open, practically all the way into his mouth; it nearly cut the right side of his face in half, like he had a hinged jaw, and the hinge broke. I just caught a quick glimpse of his sliced face from under the bed, then I squeezed by eyes shut, and didn't look again. Dude, it looked like the jagged scar of the *Joker*. For real.

Cord, that mother didn't scream at all as he cut himself open; he just let out a steady, deep wail, some sort of rage, a bellow like I've never heard....it wasn't even human. I don't know how he did it, how he endured the pain, but he did. Then he stood up, put his hand over the gape in his face and quietly walked out the bedroom door. A moment later, the front door clicked shut.

And that was it; it was quiet again....dead quiet.

Man, there was blood *everywhere*, pooled on the floor and in the wall, all the way to the front door, like a trail. I know, because I cleaned it all up, *all* of it. I don't know how I did that, I was crying and shaking like a leaf, but I did; I didn't want Earl to get in trouble. But, thinking back, there really wasn't as much blood as you would think there would be, should be, considering how bad he was sliced open. Christ, he should have bled out. But at nine years old, I thought it was a lot of fucking blood. Oh, and the last thing, there was a long, wrinkled strip of white flesh coiled around the nail, in the wall....I saw it, it looked like a shriveled worm. That's how I know what happened to his face, in the wall. I flicked it with my finger, like a fucking bug, and the wormy thing fell inside the wall. Gone.

I never told *anyone* what happened; that was in 1997, nine years ago. Christ, that feels like a lifetime ago. Button left Town that night, and was gone for about a year, maybe more. Never told anyone where he was, or what he did, including Lilly, I think….just gone. Vanished. When he came back, word was he got in a fight and someone cut his cheek, with a knife or something, some bullshit story. He said he fucked the other guy up even worse. He hid the scar under a beard back then. But the scar wasn't nearly as bad as I remember that day, not nearly so; it was actually pretty small, and I remember thinking that maybe I exaggerated how bad he was sliced, you know, because I was just nine, and maybe I was in shock, or something, or just scared shitless. But strange enough, the scar, which was already smaller than I remembered, just disappeared over time, I mean gone; no trace at all. Man, his face was fucking disfigured, cut in two, *Joker*-style dude, and now, no trace….none? How's that happen? Strange. Maybe he got surgery or something, I don't know. But I don't think so; I think it just disappeared, on its own. I know I didn't imagine all that blood, and that long disgusting curl of skin that I flicked in the wall; no way. I'm sure it's still in there, got to be.

Cord looked at Buck intently.

"*No one* knows you were under the bed? You never told Earl? Button never found out?"

"No, never. No one ever knew, till you, till now. Earl had Marty fix the wall; he doesn't like to lie, so he told Marty not to ask him what happened, because Lilly would get mad, so Marty didn't – and that was that."

"What did Lilly do?"

"Nothing. I don't know what Button told her; like I said,
I'm sure it was some bullshit story, and she bought it,
like she always does when it comes to him."

Cord shook his head in disgust.

"I don't get Lilly."

"No one does, not when it's about Button."

"So when's he coming back?"

"Who knows, but I would guess soon. Lilly's been solo
since he left this last time, three years ago. I heard it had
something to do with the rich lady in the Lion House
[*Buck nodded toward L'antre du Lion*]; that's what I
heard, anyway. Not sure what, but not good – Lilly went
nuts. Anyway, Vinny's been spreading that you've been
banging Lilly hard since you got here and talking shit
about Button being a fucking pussy and that you'd kick
his ass if he ever dared to show his face in Town, stuff
like that."

Cord shook his head. Oh, the irony; if only the Lilly-
fuck stories were true; then at least dealing with this
jerk-off Button would be worth it – at least he would
have gotten some tail for the effort.

"What about the disk?"

C asked nonchalant.

"What? What disk?"

Buck said, confused.

"Nothing; never mind."

C said, dismissive.

"Listen, about the news article, about the seagulls, I told you Button kept it folded in a little black book, right? But I didn't tell you about the book, what that book is, did I?"

C stared hard at Buck, annoyed that yet another tale was in the offing.

"How many fucking stories do you have about this jerk-off?"

"Last one. But trust me, you *want* to know this one."

Buck whispered low.

"What about it."

C snorted, tiring of the topic.

"That little black book is a *Kill List*; Button *always* carries it on him, ever since he was a kid, like a fucking Bible. It lists every different type of animal kill he's made since he was, like, ten years old - when, how, what weapon…whatever. Brags about it all the time, waves it in your face. And that book is *full*, dude, full of kills of every way, shape and form – hundreds of butchered animals and the weapons he used to do it, including his bare hands. Creepy shit. Nothing matters more to Button than that *Kill List*….and the word about Town is, you're the next entry, just so you know."

"Really? I guess I should leave Town."

C said matter-of-fact sarcastic.

"Hey, I'm not saying you should do anything. But when he comes back, he aims to hurt you, and I'm sure, Earl too, just cause he knows you two have become some sort of buddies. Kind of icing on the cake, in his mind. You know, most people, even tough people, are afraid of something, you know, like afraid to go down a dark alley, you know, in some bad place, some bad part of town, because no matter how tough you are, there's *always* something scarier, that isn't afraid of you, that could be hiding, just ahead. But at some point, there can't be anything scarier; there has to be a *scariest*, right? Something that, in the end, doesn't give a fuck about anything, or anyone; the one everyone else should be the *most* scared of. In my book, that's Button Pierce, always has been….and he fucking knows it."

C looked at Buck and smiled, but it wasn't a good smile; it looked corrupt, maleficent, as he mimicked the words, in a hushed, ominous tone.

"You're right; at some point, there has to be a scariest."

CHAPTER 136 – CHICKEN LITTLE IT IS

Neither Buck nor Cord realized Earl entered the Park till he was almost upon them; he was carrying two bottles of *Vernors*, a bag of barbecue chips and a box of animal crackers…common fare for the big man.

"Why didn't you stop by this morning, C? I got animal crackers, and they *all* have heads! Lilly didn't get to them; hid 'em in my room! Hi Billy! Sorry, I didn't know you were here, only brought two bottles."

"Hey Earl, no problem; I don't want any, trust me."

Buck said, as he looked to C, smirking at the irony; Earl and food got him in just a bit of trouble the first go round.

Billy stood and patted Earl light on the back; he knew he was sitting on Earl's bench, and moved to let the big man sit next to C.

"Hey, what's in the bag?"

Earl asked.

"It's a surprise; look inside."

Earl bent over and squinted through the nylon mesh at the little gray ball of fur.

"Hey, that's a real kitten! Where'd you get it?!"

"A *cat*? There's been a cat sitting by the bench this whole time?"

Buck said, astonished, completely missing that boat for the past half hour or so.

"Found him at Carol's, under the neighbor's porch, you know, the house out back, after she left."

"Cool! What's its name? Is is a boy or a girl?"

Earl said excited.

"I don't know what it is; I assumed it was a boy, don't know why. Called it Columbo; I think its only got one eye."

"Can I look C? Can I? I promise I'll be careful; I was always real careful with Mr. Boeman's cats, upstairs, in your house."

"I know you were, but he's very tiny and scared, so be extra careful. And don't be afraid if it hisses at you or bites you, or something like that; he's used to me, but probably afraid of you."

Like a surgeon, Earl carefully zipped open the Sherpa bad and extracted Columbo, who greeted Earl with an immediate, deep purr, rubbing its face on Earl's immense hand.

"Yeah, watch out for that hiss and bite, Earl."

Buck said, sarcastically.

C just frowned, then smiled. Figures; who couldn't like Earl?

"She's purring, loud!"

Earl said ecstatic.

"I thought it was a boy; how do you know it's a girl, Earl?"

Buck said.

"I don't think it's a boy; she feels like a girl."

"That's crazy; how does she *feel* like a girl, Earl?"

C mocked.

"I don't know, she just does."

And with that, Earl unceremoniously lifted Columbo's tail, squinted and stuck his nose, close to the hairy tucker, for an inspection.

"Yep, a girl, no balls; and she's got a kink in the end of her tail!"

Earl said, as he ran his hand the length of her aborted tail.

"Get out of here!"

C said, and stuck his nose to her butt. Yep, no balls.

"Son of a bitch."

C whispered to himself; a girl indeed.

"What's her name again?"

Earl said, knowing it was Columbo.

"Well, it *was* Columbo, but I guess since it's a girl, you can rename her."

"Columbo's a nice name."

Earl said, rolling his eyes, mocking C.

"Thanks, buddy."

Cord said, answering in the same sarcastic tone. Then continued.

"Why don't you give her a nickname then."

Earl racked his brain, and stared into Columbo's single big green eye, scanning her brain. She was so tiny, engulfed in Earl's huge mitt. But she wasn't scared, not one bit. She started purring and looked skyward, wanting him to rub her chin.

And just like that, it came to Earl; the answer was obvious.

"*Chicken Little*! That's it!"

C smiled.

"Okay then, Chicken Little it is."

CHAPTER 137 – ALL WAS RIGHT WITH THE WORLD

"I love you Chicken."

Earl said, as he rubbed her ever-so-gently on the top of her tiny gray head. She couldn't get enough.

"Okay, Earl, you said that at least ten times now."

"But I do!"

Earl had placed Chicken on his massive chest, and she cuddled up and closed her eye, purring as she fell asleep. Earl was paralyzed, afraid to move, lest he disturb the new princess.

"C, my butt fell asleep; it's all tingly."

"Can't help you there, buddy."

Buck laughed.

"Hey, Cord, Earl, I'm gonna go; see you around."

Cord stood up and extended his hand, in friendship.

"Hey, seriously, thank you."

C said matter-of-fact.

Buck shook his hand and just smiled; for the first time, in a long time, he felt good about himself.

"Drop that Vinny-kid, he's no friend."

"I know he's an asshole, but I'll keep him close, with what's going on. I'll keep you posted."

"Thanks."

Ay said. And with that, Buck walked away. Surprisingly, Earl didn't ask about the exchange; he was still glowing about getting Chicken's second eye to open. He just gently rubbed it as she slept, and then, from nowhere, it just opened, like magic; a second giant green/yellow orb – much too big for her tiny face.

"Okay, Earl, enough; you got lucky with the eye thing."

C said, mildy annoyed that Earl somehow got that eye to open, when he couldn't.

Earl gently strained to kiss Chicken on the head; she never stirred, just closing both eyes, to take a nap.

"She loves me C, and I love her."

"I know you do, and I know she does. Less than twenty-four hours and I'm already replaced. I'm already shoved out before I was even in….typical."

C said, then stuck his head back into his newspaper, flipping to the comics.

"Hey Earl, look at the *Blondie* comic, you'll get a kick out of it!"

Cord handed him the newspaper and Earl scanned the panels.

"Louie!"

Earl yelped, but not too loud, lest he disturb Chicken.

"How'd Louie get in the paper?"

C smiled.

"Can you believe it? *Dagwood* is talking about *Louie The Smart-Alecky Lobster*; who knew *Dagwood* shopped at the Belvidere supermarket!"

"Louie's famous! I hope they let him stay in Belvidere; do you think they will C?"

"I'm sure they will."

"Good, I'd hate to see him get all famous and stuff, and leave. Plus, I don't trust that Dagwood guy; he might eat him, he eats everything on big sandwiches!"

Just then, from nowhere, a huge wasp circled Earl's head; the big man let out a girlish wimper.

Earl tucked his chin into his chest, and puts his hands over Chicken, to protect her from the wasp, which looked like a miniature, striped dirigible, slowly scoping out Earl.

"Will it hurt Chick?"

It was the first time Earl called her Chick.

"No. Let it alone, Earl; it's a *cicada killer wasp* – it won't hurt you, just let it be. Just be happy you're not a cicada though, then you'd be in *big* trouble. She'd drag you to her nest, underground, and lay a slimy egg on you; the egg hatches and the larvae eats you alive, for lunch *and* dinner.

Earl gasped, eyeing the wasp wary.

"But no worries; she's not looking for you. And if it's a guy, he doesn't do anything; can't even sting you, no stinger. All he does is eat and fuck; which is really not so bad. They are pretty big and scary looking though, huh….pretty cool."

 As quick as the wasp came, it darted away, gone.

"See, no worries."

But inside, C was plenty worried. He didn't need a fight, and he certainly didn't need a Button. *Maybe he should just fuck Lilly*, as if she was just waiting around for the taking. He huffed sarcastic to himself at the thought. But he could dream; fucking her would at least get him something for the confrontation that was already in motion, a train without brakes. His mind drifted to one of the many Lilly-fucks he had imagined, and jerked-off to, over the last three months; there were plenty to choose from.

He smiled as he settled into a favorite; nearby, Earl fell asleep on the bench, Chicken curled in a ball of content on his chest.

And for now, on a sky-blue Monday-morning, in the pocket Park fronting the Warren County Courthouse, surrounded by quiet churches and stately homes, in a forgotten corner called Belvidere, all was right with the world.

CHAPTER 138 - IT WAS THE BEST JAG, THE ONE TO END IT ALL

He expected her to come tonight.

It was appropriate; it felt right, which is why he was surprised it actually happened. It rarely worked that way; Jenny operated on her own schedule, the mechanics of which were never shared with him. One of the many mysteries he long since ceased to question; above his pay grade, so to speak.

There was never any predicting when she would visit, and there was certainly never any ignoring the call. But this was a very early knock, minutes past midnight. And just as he foreshadowed her visit this evening, he wasn't surprised at the early morning stopover. That too, in this instance, seemed to make sense.

He had been asleep for a short while, fitful, but out nonetheless; he laid on his right side, as she laid quiet next to him. It was at that point of dreaming when you're fuzzy; somewhat cognizant, ready to wake, but not quite yet. It wasn't a dream, rather it was in that ethereal slot, the opaque malleable time between sleep and wake, when Jenny would invariably visit.

And on this sad early morning, Jenny came for her visit….her verse, anyway, and he quietly sighed.

The words drifted, single file, through his mind, like the first day he laid eyes upon them, staring back from a tiny sheet of white paper, hung plainly on the museum wall:

Some days we wake and immediately begin to worry;
Nothing in particular is wrong;
It's just the growing sense that forces are aligning, quietly;
And there will be trouble.

He knew the words were wrong. That's not exactly what Ms. Holzer said, or wrote, so long ago; over the years the sentences slip and morph to something different with a faded memory. But the words were close, close enough, and the intent was the same, especially the last five.

He rolled onto his back, away from her, still half-drunk, stared at the stark white bedroom ceiling, now masked in shades of night-gray from moonlight sliding in a side window, and sighed a second time. She lay perfectly still in the bed beside him, not the slightest stir.

He was embarrassed that he woke with a hard-on; why he had one was a mystery. Maybe from some dream he didn't remember, since he never remembered a one. He lay beside her, where her husband normally laid, he was in his space, till the stiffness in his boxers disappeared, which thankfully happened fast enough. Then he slid quietly out of bed and drunk-stumbled down the hall, to her bathroom.

So the routine began.

He stood in the ceramic-tile stall and thought of nothing, simply feeling the near-scalding spray from the shower head run down the nape of his neck. His back turned crimson from the slow cook, trying to sober up, at least a bit. The routine warranted it, and he rarely performed same in a state other than alert.

Except this time; this time, in several respects, was already more than a bit different.

In his boxer briefs and crew neck tee-shirt, his skin still shower-red, he carefully removed the oblong cardboard box from the upper shelf in the closet, her closet, their closet, sliced open the tape, and peeled back the flaps.

He slowly removed the set of garments, remembering the last time he wore them, eight months prior. He dressed quietly, deliberately; faded jeans – his favorite, the light green button-down *Brooks Brothers* oxford, the familiar navy blue blazer. He sprinkled a bit of *Ammens* powder on his feet and slipped on the polished tassel-loafers, sans socks. His head had begun to clear.

He checked his look in the darkened bedroom mirror; turning on the light would be rude. He fastened the upper on his two-button sack jacket, straightened and pulled his collar and quietly walked away.

The sealed envelope he removed from the box was placed squarely, neatly, on the desk, at the far end of the bedroom. He removed the cell phone, slipped in the battery and hit the red *End* button, waiting for the march through a series of bucolic scenes, finishing with a lighthouse and a perky jingle, signaling the phone had awaken from an eight month slumber.

He hit *Speed Dial No. 2* and waited for the transfer to voice mail; that number was not meant to be answered, not when he called....ever.

"Hey, it's time; no word in a half-hour, you know what to do, but you need to do it fast – this one has unrelated complications – you'll know what I mean when you arrive....be good."

He flipped the phone shut and placed it gently by, and perpendicular to, the envelope on the desk. He fussed with them a bit, so they were aligned just right. That was important.

He peered into the box and removed the last item, for now, wrapped in a navy velvet sleeve. He slipped it free, held it in his hand, once again admiring its beauty, like he did every time – never tiring of the drill. He turned it slowly, marveling at the intricate carving in the ivory hand grip, the detailed engraving in the polished nickel on the cylinder, the barrel, the frame, painstaking, delicate artwork by caring Colt craftsmen. It was truly a piece of art, to be handled gently, lest it be damaged.

He smiled at the irony.

He swung open the cylinder and spied the single bullet in the chamber of the revolver – it had been eight months, and it had waited patiently, like it always did, for this day. He took his finger and ran a light circle around the end of the shell, flipped it shut and gave it a half-hearty spin; it rotated just shy of two turns.

'Seventeen percent.'

He whispered.

He placed the revolver on the table, barrel facing away, closed the box flaps neatly, settled in his seat, cracked his knuckles, one last time, exhaled deeply, slowly closed his eyes and began to ponder.

This was the best part, and it was the only time he allowed himself the luxury.

The end of his odyssey, his own road novel, finally coming to a close. His mind didn't race, it didn't agitate…it didn't fester. It was calm, and simply wandered on its own, like a lazy jag through a fallow field, taking him wherever his subconscious desired; it always ended this way, it always did.

And there was always water; inevitably, there was water.

First stop….*Cemil Topuzlu Park*, northeast of the *Olde City* and the *Ciragan Palace*, sitting on a grassy knoll, overlooking the greenish-blue Bosphorus, with its constant chop, Asia waiting on the far shore. The *Sesta*, a large wooden fisher, decked in faded blue and white, with rust stains – tiger stripes – streaking its curved hull, sat empty, moored to the dock; it was crusty, old and tired, waiting patient to fish again. The *Starway*, a monstrous cargo barge, plied the deep water behind her, on its way to ports unknown ringing the Black Sea.

A half dozen groups of local Turks barely noticed the river traffic, women in headdresses lost in conversation, picnicking on blankets, eating grilled, partially burnt corn cobs, scattered under trees throughout the park. An aged golden retriever, untethered, slept comfortably on the pier, beneath a small tree, no more than a dozen feet from the *Sesta*, its master dozing on a nearby bench, a sheathed red umbrella propped by his side. The dog never once expended the energy to raise its head as people strolled nearby, it simply moved its eyes to lazily track them, with scant interest, as they shuffled past.

A half-dozen fisherman, all locals, cast lines into the turquoise waters; discarded mussel shells, bait on the line, scattered on the dock amongst them.

He remembered that sunny day, the blades of course grass against the bareness of his legs, not so long ago, and smiled; he wasn't sure why it was the first memory to greet him on this early morning jaunt, but he was happy with the stint – Istanbul was more pleasant than not.

Next stop, the Mississippi, in St. Louis, under the night sky, walking below Eads Bridge, drunk, his brother ahead of him, in silence. The moonlight gilding the stainless sheath of the Arch. The water was ink, with silvery highlights, carrying massive, orphaned logs silently past, bobbing slow, marking their long journey south to the Gulf. He remembered the soothing, gentle sound of water lapping the oversized granite cobblestones which extended to the waters edge and disappeared into the blackness of the river.

Just as the puppet shaped his youth, upon this mighty shore he became the man he was, for better or worse. Mostly worse. The Mississippi in Missouri, it was part of him, it always would be.   And this dream weave inevitably took him back to this place, at least for a short while. He didn't smile at this memory.

Onto the Gulf of Panama, the pelicans and the cormorants – preening, fishing, sleeping, sleeping…and more sleeping. *Bocas Del Toro*, with the john-boats puttering by his over-water hut, while he swung like a metronome in the hammock. It would always be his favorite retreat, *the* retreat. He spent most of the jag here, reflecting, remembering, all those mindless rocks in the hammock, drinking in the sounds around him, the roof thatch twitching in the gentlest of afternoon breezes. Lobsters in the distance, hiding in the thicket of mangroves, and the little blue fish, and the lonely coral outcrop it endlessly circled, in the shallow turquoise water below his hammock.

To this, he smiled; it was a good smile.

The jag moved to an early morning solo walk along a lonely stretch of beach, in *Puerto Morelos*, Riviera Maya, in the Yucatan. Two vultures, one turkey, one black, lay ahead, hopping clumsily amongst the detritus high on the beach, his beach, searching for that unfortunate soul washed up in the prior nights storm. They pay him little heed, simply watching him pass with black, dead eyes. He knows those eyes, and he knows the place, all too well. The morning sun glints off the surface of the sea, barely above the horizon; the milky path crosses the open ocean, a silvery ribbon of carpet, ending at his feet. It follows him, walks with him, a companion to saddle alongside as he threads the high tide line, half-heartedly dodging the frothy surf. The hiss of air and retreating seawater seeping through the sand, and the steady, sonorous clap of wave breaks, fill his ears. The beginning of a new day, filled with hope? With promise? Not in this place; never in this place.

He creased a sad smile.

How many times do you get to start over, till you aren't allowed to start over anymore? A lifetime of do-overs spent, your credit line maxed. But he was long past maxed, and the game played on. And he was tired.

He bent and picked a non-descript fragment of a white shell, barely the size of his thumbnail, slowly being ground by the pound of the surf into sand. It had been whole at one time, long ago, but now just a bit of what it once was. No respectable beachcomber would eye it, let alone save it; a sorry substitute for a memento. A real pass-by.

So why does he pick it up?

Did he grant the fragment, the broken shell, a favor? Giving attention to something that deserves none. Perhaps it should simply be left alone, to disappear into grains of nothing. Perhaps that is what it wants, perhaps that is its destiny. But he pockets the quarry, and it is doomed to a life spent with him, with no say in the matter. And he realizes that shell is him; he *is* the shell; always has been, picked up by others and saved, and doomed, both at once. Forever.

This journey was cut short, shorter than normal, for he found himself, once again, at the lake. He usually didn't arrive here quite so fast. Maybe this time, the players were a bit impatient.

Twelve years old, innocence, before the puppet, the crickets and the flies, laying on a beach towel spread atop the concrete swimming dock, all alone, warming up in the early morning summer sun, looking at the lake below. Quietly slipping into the cool water, before eight am, always before eight am, mask on, bread in hand, and letting out air, to slowly sink to the gravelly bottom. It was only eight feet of water, but it was another world. There he would sit, waiting for the locals to arrive from the murky edges of his ken.

Invariably they would come.

Dozens of sunfish, perch, catfish, the occasional bass, soon swarmed him; but it was mostly the sunnies who came, to grab the next quid of bread from his hands, his toes, or from a piece he would shove into the front grill of his mask, to greet them, eye to eye. He felt solace in the water, peace, and he felt special, encircled by dozens of fish. They felt safe around him, trusted him not to hurt them, and thereby granted him membership into their secret world. That's how it felt to a twelve-year-old, anyway. He never fed the fish with anyone else, it was just him, his special place to go, to see friends he only had. God, it was like yesterday. He wished he could hold his breath forever, and stay down with them, forever.

But that was a different life; that twelve-year-old did not grow to be the man he now was. He missed that little boy.

After the fish were fed, he would lay on the grass near the diving board, looking up at the summer sky. He never mastered a forward flip, although he spent many summers trying. Then there was the adjacent *Girl's Camp*, where he and his friends forever trespassed, sneaking peaks at the girl counselors and crawling through the underbrush to that one spot where you could climb onto the counselor's dorm roof, scamper across, and jump off the second-story hipped peak, into the lake far below. It was so high, and half the kids never dared make the leap. It took him two summers to muster the courage to jump; but once he did, he was quick to endlessly mock those too scared to follow.

Later, fighting and guarding against the onslaught of other neighborhood kids to wear the crown as *King Of The Raft*, a title that meant the world to a twelve-year old boy. Rag-tag played for hours on end, diving and hiding in the beds of seaweed, to avoid being *it*. The State Park, on the distant shore, with the City-blacks and

Hispanics bussed in by the hundreds to wade knee-high in the cool fresh water; they rarely swam, because most didn't know how. African bongo drums marked their annual arrival. It was here, this Park, mere months later, as winter approached, that he first met the puppet. But now, such thoughts didn't exist. He remembered sleeping on the concrete dock in the mid-day sun, exhausted, till the next group of kids on the block, from Boomer Avenue, and from way down on Stone Avenue, made their way to the swimming dock, late to the daily party, and the whole routine of games began once again. By late afternoon, hungry, it was time to walk the three long blocks home, young feet dodging the gravel chips on the narrow oiled roads, the tar crazy-hot from baking all day in the summer sun.

Till you did it all over again the next morning.

That was a nice part of this jag; he was always glad when those memories came back to share some time with him. A tease of simple times.

Twelve years old; what was he thinking back then, when his mind idly wandered? What occupied his brain, before the puppet corrupted him? A long life ahead? Planning and re-planning where we would go, what he would become?

No, probably not. What twelve year old does? Girls? Probably yes; in the end, it was always girls.

He wished he could remember; to get back inside that young boy's brain, to have a clean slate. My God, how did he get here from there?

Of course he knew that answer, and he knew what came next.

The swimming dock always morphed to sitting in silence with his mother and father at the round dining room table, stained a dark walnut, Colonial-style, reading the

Sunday morning papers and eating oversized crumb cakes, sipping tea, with extra milk and sugar, after they attended church. They would read, then trade, various sections of the papers, occasionally breaking the silent pact to discuss an interesting story at hand, or a comic that made one think, or just smile. His mother silently writing letters to friends or relatives, or paying bills, head down, lost in thought, while he and his father continued to read, and read, and then read some more.

It would go on for hours every Sunday, with nary a word spoken. It was his next-favorite memory, and his best memory so far on this latest walk in the woods. And although he couldn't say he missed his parents like most people miss their parents, he didn't have an aching, longing desire to see and speak to them again, in this particular way, he did. He didn't miss much, but he did miss that....the Sunday morning routine at the dining room table, sans words; words simply weren't necessary.

The dining room table on a Sunday morning, it was always the next-to-last memory; it came whenever it came, and now it had come, and now it had gone.

So, with its fade, he was onto the very last trip back; it was always the last, and it was the best jag, the one to end it all.

CHAPTER 139 – HOPING THE LONG RIDE WOULD FINALLY END

It was September, 1974.

He sat straight-backed, anxious, on the after-school bus, waiting to go home, the first day of sixth grade behind him. The bus driver, Mrs. Betty, was a battle-ax, thick and grizzled from the head down, with a mop of bed-head hair, overpowering body odor and a distinctive black mustache she never pretended to hide. He had already been herded into row three, on the right side of the bus, the two-seater side. He's not sure why he was already sitting in that seat; that part he couldn't remember, but he knew Mrs. Betty made him sit there; she assigned all the seats.

Looking out the window, he gawked at the queue of kids waiting to board, hunkered while Mrs. Betty barked and spat seat assignments from the top step of the bus, with venom:

> *'Left, left, left, right, right;*
> *Next aisle, left, left, left; come on, move it!*
> *Remember your seats!*
> *The rest of the year – same seat! No talking!*
> *Right, right....'*

Sitting at her desk in the darkened bedroom, as his mind slowly reopened that long dormant file drawer, tears welled behind the lids of his closed eyes.

There, six back in the queue, he first laid eyes upon a girl he had *never* seen before, a little blonde-haired girl, the one he fell in love with right then and there; her long, straight hair, upturned button nose, the cutest, knobby eleven-year old knees.

She was beautiful.

He quickly ran the formation in his head, trying to figure in what seat the little blonde-haired girl would be assigned, his mind racing, trying to out-think Mrs. Betty, ready to change his seat if necessary, and risk annihilation by her iron hand.

It would be worth it.

His heart raced as the tiny blonde swayed in line, oblivious to his machinations, talking and laughing with her friends, wholly ignoring Mrs. Betty's bloviation; her place in line blurred by her restless feet and the amorphous queue of sixth-graders, who simply couldn't keep a straight line.

The count continued as she edged closer to the folding bus doors, mindless to the tension she was creating in row three, in his frantic brain.

But wait, adrenaline fueled by desperation quickly turned to warmth, to a feeling of utter content, which blanketed his body. It couldn't be, it *never* happened that way; but in this case, it did. Her assigned seat would be the empty slot in his own two-seater!

He held his breath as she boarded the bus; Mrs. Betty's meaty finger pointed right at the empty piece of cracked, green vinyl next to him.

'To the right....'

She barked, unaware she had changed a little blonde-haired boy's life....forever.

And just like that, down she sat, fumbling with a sloppy pile of first-day books and loose papers. She fussed with them, a half-attempt to straighten the pile, before she gave up and plopped them haphazard on the floor by her feet, where they fell in disarray.

She let out a huff, looked around, and for the first time, realized someone was sitting beside her. She smiled a white toothy grin, with slightly over-sized, picket-straight teeth and warm slate-blue eyes. And he'd never forget the first words she ever spoke to him:

"Hi, my name's Kristine...."

And for the first time in his life, his little heart felt that pang, the one that makes little boys, and the grown men they become, do things they probably shouldn't do.

He had just met the girl he would love for the rest of his life.

They became fast friends, and then they dated, which, for two eleven-year olds, meant mainly talking for hours on the phone, or just listening to each other breath into the receiver when you ran out of things to say, but don't want to hang up, you *never* wanted the call to end; passing notes in class and on the bus – written in cryptic code only the two of you shared; endlessly writing each other's names on just about anything a pencil would stick to; and kissing, yes kissing, on the lips, mostly when playing spin-the-bottle in her parent's basement. He sure loved to kiss Kristine.

Life was good, life was grand, until she did what little girls you fall in love with do; she dumped him for a twelve-year old, and then moved away....far, far away. And he never saw nor spoke to Kristine again; she simply disappeared.

His first heartbreak, the one he could never forget, no matter what parade of females followed in the thirty-two years thereafter.

God, what ever became of her? Where did she end up? Was she happy? Would she even remember him, the little blonde-haired boy who sat next to her on the bus, in 1974?

He would have liked to try and find her; he thought of doing it often, too often, but in the end never really tried…in fact, he never tried at all.

And now, sitting at her desk, in the darkened bedroom, he regretted that. He always had regret when he arrived here.

Somehow, he always felt his life would have veered in a different direction, a better direction, if he had just found Kristine. Somehow, he thought, she might have made a difference, *the difference*, and he wouldn't be sitting at this darkened desk, right here, right now, looking back at the slash and burn that was his life….a real fucking mess. He always felt she would have saved him somehow, that she was the difference he never had by his side.

And for that, he was truly sad.

He loved that little blonde-haired girl, he did, and always would, till the day he died. He smiled at the thought….and it was a good smile.

He picked up the revolver and placed it lightly against his right temple, the end of the steel barrel a cold kiss. It felt good. He closed his eyes and reset his brain, a rewind back to when that little blonde-haired girl first sat next to him on the afternoon school bus, smiling at him with that beautiful face, when he felt like the luckiest guy ever, long before the puppet, the crickets and the flies, when all was good and right in the world for a little eleven-year old boy.

He half-smiled and gently whispered *Kristine* as his finger squeezed the trigger, hoping the long ride would finally end.

CHAPTER 140 – IT WAS TIME FOR A TURN OF THE WORM

A week prior and a world away.

He fully expected a confrontational meeting, between two people who neither liked nor trusted the other; but at least it would be manageable, controllable - a dialogue between two.

What he *didn't* expect was seven cotton-pickers to come through the warehouse door.

He wasn't prepared for that, although he should have known better, and expected as much; and for that, he was disappointed in himself. Very.

And as a Marine, it was unconscionable.

Button quickly found himself standing inside a loose semi-circle, which was slowly closing in, the tightening of a noose. He was tense, keeping a wary eye on the string of men before him: the Kreme-King, Mr. Chills, Black Dog, Burr, Bogs and two nameless skinny-ass recruits he never saw before, kids, each fourteen-years old, tops.

But he focused his attention on Black Dog; he was the reason they were here, and the topic at hand was Billy Bones, the white boy standing wary in the center of this quickly closing circle.

Button was surrounded by a sea of *Billy Reubens*; he hated niggers, above all stupid niggers, and this was an especially stupid bunch of monkeys – foot soldiers and captains for Dr. Pool....myrmidons.

Dr. Pool, now *that* was a black man he could respect, and trust; one of the few, actually the only moolie to which he laid that claim. But he always saw Dr. Pool as a Marine, not a nigger, and that was the difference. And

Dr. Pool was why he now found himself surrounded by the stench of the darkie.

Billy Bones stared down Black Dog, and the disgust must have shown on his face, for the big black man's wide nostrils flared, like an enraged bull.

"He's *mad-dogging*, dog! Fuck the Cracker up!"

Mr. Chills yelled to Black Dog, egging him to start a beat-down, his voice echoing in the cavernous, empty warehouse.

Button rocked back a half-step, and clenched his fists; this was going to be real bad, and there was no easy way out. He figured he'd try to buy some time, anything, to plan an escape.

"I'm not dogging, man, I just want to know why we're…."

Billy never finished the sentence.

And he never saw it coming; he should have, but he didn't. That fat nigger was quick.

The answer came in a lightening-fast blow, which hit Button like a lead pipe, dead center to the chest. Black Dog's fist, encased in a heavy set of gold-plated brass knuckles, crushed Billy's rib-cage in one telling blow. It knocked the wind out of him, and Billy staggered for a bit, fell to his knees and blacked out, falling backward, still kneeling, smacking his head lightly on the concrete floor.

One shot; he was out cold.

He wasn't sure for how long, but it wasn't too; a brutal kick to side brought him back quick enough.

He opened both eyes in a fog; the acrid smell of urine filled his nostrils. Beside him was a puddle of warm piss, which ran slowly across the oil-stained warehouse floor, toward his right cheek, inches away. He tightened his stomach to lift himself upright, and was greeted by an intense stab of pain, a hot poker shoved in his chest. He was pretty sure at least one rib was broken, maybe more. But all he did was wince; he never let out more than a muffled wheeze. He wasn't going to give them the satisfaction.

"Yo nigger, stuff like that, mad easy, to whitie! Fuckin' Cracker!"

Mr. Chills yelled, pounding his chest, his big cock still hanging from his boxers, to be sure Billy knew who pissed. Then he bull-charged Button, still hunched over on his knees, stopping just short of the fallen white boy.

"Shut the fuck up dog, and step back!"

Black Dog barked at Mr. Chills.

"And put your fucking dick away! I don't wanna see your damn cock."

The last part Black Dog spat, as he slowly shook his head in disgust.

And with that, Mr. Chills retreated.

"The Devil here is mine, to *interrogate*."

Black Dog said softly, as he knelt on one meaty knee, saddling up comfortably beside Billy Bones, showing him no fear.

"Say yo...."

"Those is...."

"The shit...."

Chimed a low chorus from the men standing behind Black Dog; then it was silent, and Black Dog spoke lightly, gently, to Billy Bones.

"Truth is, don't know why your ditch-pig ass isn't already cooked. Dr. Pool, he and I go *way back*, dog, kids in the hood, *kings* of the hood; homies, associates, business partners....*survived* together, even when we shouldn't have....*busted 'em up* together, *brothers*....no one I trust more than that blood. And for some fucking reason, he trusts a fucking Hillbilly Cracker, and *that's* why I stopped him from pissing on your face, in your fucking mouth *[pointing to Mr. Chills]*, cause that's what he wanted to do. But Dr. Pool wouldn't look kindly on that....disrespectful. And I don't disrespect the Dr."

Black Dog slowly stood up, towering over Billy.

"But bringing you in, and sneaking shit around me?   I don't get it. And now, those is, you involved in some sort of *new* shit, shit *I* don't know about; and that shit, *that* shit, don't fly dog."

His senses back, Button went to right himself, and stand erect. Black Dog put his big fleshy mitt on Billy's shoulder and shoved him back down, hard.

"The man stays down whiles I'm talking."

Button obliged. He knew they were all itching for a beat-in, and looking for any excuse to bust him up; killing him would be a bonus.

"Now, since Dr. Pool hasn't told me, *you will*, mother-fucker. And if the....the shit you gotta spit is....some Opie-shit, well, I'll hafta explain to the Dr. the unfortunate accident you had."

Button stayed down, but had shifted to one knee. He had a killer throb in his chest, taking shallow breaths to lessen the knife in his rib-cage. The adrenaline pumping furious through his veins was the prop he needed, and it was the only reason he hadn't passed out again.

In a way, the pain helped, it focused him, and Button excelled in crisis mode. He always thought fast, and smart, especially when he was cornered, like a dog, with the odds against him.

Button spoke in a slow, halted manner, taking short breaths between broken phrases to lessen the pain in his ribs, and to buy time, to recover.

"Dr. Pool sees me as a….valuable resource….a different kind of business partner….who brings new faces….new areas of commerce….to the table….beyond what you've been involved in. And those opportunities require certain contacts….ones *I* have….that he doesn't….*won't ever* have….and for that….he sees opportunity in me for him….and you….and everyone, right down to the foot soldiers….*can you understand that?*"

And Button made the statement to Black Dog in a polite, calm and respectful manner, most of it anyway. He simply couldn't finish it politely; those last four words, he just couldn't say them without adding a thick, superior, sarcastic air. He wanted to end the sentence with *you stupid fucking monkey*, but he didn't; he thought better of it.

It didn't matter; the damage was already done.

Button saw the next slug coming, a real roundhouse, and turned his head just quick enough to have the metal knuckles glance off the side of his temple. If it had hit him square, it surely would have caved in the side of his head, and he would have been done.

He was *that* close to being done. But the half-head turn saved him.

Even the partial blow was heavy; it split open the brow above his eye, ripping a deep gash, like a knife in a melon. Blood exploded like a bomb; a thick, steady stream of red gushed down the side of Billy's face from the deep slice in his head, a portion pooling into his left eye, blurring his vision.

The Kreme-King let out a bellowing laugh, followed by riotous howling and histrionic hand gestures and fist pumps from the others. Mr. Chills bull-charged Billy Bones a second time, stopping just short of the fallen figure.

"You understand **that** Elvis? You cow-fuck mother-fucker....dried piece of shit. You disrespect me again, and I'll cut your fucking head clean off, piss down your fucking neck."

Black Dog was spitting as he yelled at Billy, turning hoarse with anger.

Button felt the blood run heavy down his face, and spill onto the concrete floor beside him; it was a big pool of red, and it was growing. But he didn't attempt to touch his face, he just let it flow. He closed his eyes; his head was cloudy, and spinning, and it took all his concentration to stay focused, and not pass out.

Silence followed the blow; they all just watched the blood run steady off Button's face, forming a large puddle of crimson on the floor. Billy Bones was in a bad way; a couple of them thought the white boy was done, for sure.

Black Dog regained his composure, and spoke plainly, and calmly, slowly shaking his head.

"Billy Bones, can you hear me? Dr. Pool isn't here to help you, you can only help yourself; now don't disrespect me no more, and tell me....what *opportunities*?"

There was silence for a bit; and that bit was too long of a wait for Black Dog.

But just then, Billy spoke. His eyes were closed, so he didn't see that Black Dog was winding up to smash his face with the heavy knuckles one more time, square between the eyes, likely for the last time in Button's life. He beat it by a mere moment; for a second time, Billy Bones came *that* close to checking out, for good. And oh, how the whole story would have changed. But they simply wouldn't have it that way, so Billy beat it, and so the story didn't, and the game played on.

"Lose the posse, and I'll tell you; it's confidential, straight from the Dr."

Black Dog dropped his fist mid-cock and eyed the broken man cautiously, calculating what to do, determining if it was some sort of whitie-trap, then figuring it couldn't be; the risk was low, with nothing but a bloody lump of flesh on the floor before him. He turned to the dogs, telling them to disperse, which they did, without a word of dissent. And just like that, the two of them were alone in the cavernous space. And with that, Black Dog's demeanor changed; he got down on one knee again, and was face-level with Billy, who half-opened a single eye to greet him.

Black Dog spoke softly.

"Yo, be bustin' my ass for Dr. Pool twenty-five years, bro; it's okay, it's who I be. He's got the brains, lots....me, not so much. But that's okay, I got the muscle. You need that....the muscle. I'm thirty-three and never expected to see it....*never*. Dead in my teens, twenties maybe, but make thirties? Never. But here I am, still standing. And I'm still here because of him, but he's still here because of *me*. What I got is respect, and fear, from my captains, my soldiers....and because of that *I'm* the ranking member to the O.G.! And you be buggin', with no cred, no beat-in, no history....whatever; that shit don't fly, not with me. Now I know you must got some mighty shit for the Dr; you're a fuckin' Cracker and he don't dance with *any* whities – don't trust 'em. So why does he trust *you*? He told me about you, in the Service; said you freed him from a *big* jam. Don't know what, but must have been big, *real fucking big!* So I know you're around, for awhile anyway, and I gotta live with your sorry ass, but I don't like it, and I don't like you....and I don't trust your *Memphis* ass as far as I can toss it....straight?"

Button nodded silently in agreement.

"Now, what *opportunities* is the Dr. looking at, and what's it mean to me?"

"Can I stand up?"

Black Dog nodded once in the affirmative, happy the Cracker was asking permission, begging permission.

And with that, Billy Bones slowly stood, on wobbly legs, the blood, partially coagulated above his eye, began to seal the pulpy, oozing gash, which had swollen to the size of small plum. The red smear on the left side of his face was crusting over; it cracked as his cheeks moved.

Button looked like he weathered a war, and he survived the assault.   And through the fog of blood and pain, Billy Bones began to weave a too-tall tale; it was time for a turn of the worm.

CHAPTER 141 – A QUIET, EVIL SEETHE

"The Dr. is setting up a whole new division, no drugs. Stolen art...museum-quality, but second tier - very lucrative; human trafficking – sex slaves, but also high-high-end whores....Asian and white mostly, Russian, former Soviet Republics – the Dr. is hot on that one. Stolen art alone is *six billion dollars* a year, most of it never recovered or prosecuted, and second tier shit can always sell on the black market. Counterfeiting, low-end ink-jet runs, but even that stuff is high quality shit! Easy enough to pass; *sixty million bucks* in circulation stateside last year alone – and the Feds don't give a shit about tiny Mickey Mouse operations – although ours would be a web of them, all connected, one big fucking mouse....a huge fucking rat! And new recruitment, suburban, easy pickings - stupid, angry and easily molded. And it will all be under the umbrella of a brand new partnership, with my *Aryan* friends; a whole new set of Charters and By-Laws, new colors, new name....all new. And the roll-out is coming soon....*real soon*."

Now all that was true, Billy didn't lie a bit.

And he bothered telling the ham-bone because he knew Black Dog understood almost nothing of what he just said, and probably forgot most of it before Button even finished the sentence; he was a big, stupid piece of leftover dark-meat.

And he knew *exactly* what Black Dog's first question would be. Of all the right questions he could ask, *should* ask:

- How would the sex trade work? Are we shipping them overseas, or domestic?
- Art? Where do you get it? How do you offload it?
- Ink-jet cash? What a fucking idea!
- Who are our partners? Organized crime?

- Where do I fit in? What's my role? How can I help make it happen?

Of all the myriad possibilities, of all the intelligent questions Black Dog *could* have asked Billy Bones, to show he had the slightest clue, and could offer something, *anything*, constructive, the big man came up with *the* one question, the one Button knew would cut right to the heart of it. Even in pain, Billy smiled as the words fell from Black Dog's puffy-ass lips.

"New colors? What are the new colors?"

And *that* was why Dr. Pool was looking for new opportunities, and turned to whitie.

"Deep purple, almost black. And the new name? *The Drin.*"

Button figured he would answer Question No. 2.

"Purple? Cool! Pretty cool, dog."

Button smiled, and then he started to lie.

"Dr. P. thought you'd like the color. He wanted me to bring you up to speed on all this anyway in the next couple days; he knew you were itching, you just beat me to it."

"Yo, dog, sorry for the beat-down; had to place you, gotta say, it's like….you know."

"Understood. Listen, while it's fresh, let's get you fully up to speed; the Dr. says you get final say, he wants your full buy in. He said: *it doesn't happen if the Dog isn't on board*; you're too important to the organization."

And it wasn't until that moment that Black Dog finally relaxed, letting out a long, grateful breath, and shaking his head slow, in the affirmative.

Truth be told, Eugene Henry, Black Dog to the street and crew, was scared of Billy Bones – scared to death. And lately, his mind was racing, nervous, all the time. Eugene knew he wasn't that smart, although he tried to be, he really did; it just didn't come easy for him. So he relied on what he knew - the streets and intimidation - to get along. On the other hand, Tyrone Jones, Dr. Pool, Eugene's best friend since they were eight years old, friends for life, was super-smart, and Tyrone carried Eugene as he rose up the ghetto food chain, out of loyalty, for the history of bad times, hard times, they shared.

In return, Black Dog was the muscle, the enforcer; that had always been his role. But Eugene knew it was always easy to find new muscle, younger studs who were tougher, hungrier than a thirty-three-year old who felt a hell of a lot older. But muscle alone couldn't take the place of loyalty and trust, and that loyalty and trust was Eugene's ticket to stay No. 2, the Ranking Member to the Dr; no one had the history he had with Tyrone....no one. Eugene banked on that; it was his most valuable insurance policy.

But Black Dog was consumed with the fear that Billy Bones was making a play for No 2, and he knew the potential was real; the Dr. trusted the white boy. They had a different history, in the Marines, and whatever that history was, it meant a great deal to Tyrone; he never talked about it with Black Dog....never. But he knew it must be real big.

And the trust and loyalty between the Dr and Billy seemed to be growing, and Eugene was worried sick. He knew Billy was smart, smarter than him anyway, and the Dr. and Billy talked more and more about things he didn't understand. Shit, they made enough money at what they did; why did the Dr. need more? Life was good enough; why did they even need the fucking Cracker and the more money that came with whitie strings? He didn't get it, he just didn't.

He knew giving Billy a heavy beating was real risky, but Black Dog sensed a change was coming, and soon….so he panicked. But now, in the end, it looked as if his gamble paid off; it looked like Black Dog was safe, and Billy was put in his place.   So Eugene let his guard down.

"Cool, nigger; when do I get it, the details….so's I's can say, you know, yes or no?"

Eugene said excited, as if talking to a new best friend. Button whispered his response.

"How 'bout tonight? But no posse – this info's strict – just you, me and the Dr. I'll give him the heads-up; and don't tell him about this impromptu, dog, this little meeting you called. He doesn't know about it, right?"

Black Dog shook his head in the negative.

"Good. I was supposed to let him know first, you know, when I, we, spilled the good news; he wanted to be there to see your face….knew you'd be cool. You're gonna be the Ranking Member of a *large* organization, dog, congrats. I'm just a….facilitator, on the sidelines; a go-between to some of the new suburban partners, is all. You know, to smooth the way."

"Who I be nigger....**Yo!**"

Black Dog cracked a big-ass grin, his first smile, throwing Billy the gang's hand sign, pumping it in the air for emphasis, along with the requisite nods.

"Where and when?"

"Let's say….1:00 am, nah, make it 2:00 am, Jersey side, about a half-hour north of the junkyard drop in Dope City. Remember that woods drop just below the Tacony-Palmyra Bridge we used about six months ago, right when you get off?"

"Yeah, yeah, I remember....yeah, cool *[Black Dog didn't really remember, but did a play-pretend, so as not to look dumb in front of Billy. Button could see he didn't remember, the stupid fucking nigger, but he played along that he did]*."

"Good. We'll don't meet right there; take a cab, solo....and stop a couple blocks, I think it's two blocks, off the end of the bridge, at Market and Madison. There's a kid's playground with a basketball court on the corner, meet me there. We'll drive back to the drop in my truck, off the end of the bridge. Dr P. likes to use that spot when he meets the *Aryans*; there's a soft spot in the woods that's secure, way off the road, there's an old house, abandoned shit-box, but we got it fixed with a few lights....a hidden generator. A safe house. Bring a flashlight and your hiking boots, it can a bit muddy on the walk in, down by the river. But first, you gotta make that delivery tonight, right?"

"Yeah, but two is cool; be done with Mr. Chills and Bogs and be there; say yo....no problem."

"Remember, *solo* dog, no one can know about this yet, or the Dr. will have *both* our heads. Cool?"

"Solo, got it; how's the Dr. traveling?"

"He don't even know about this meeting yet, but he'll be there....he wants to see your face dog! He's got other business that I ain't part of tonight, but he should be done and should be able to meet us by two; if not, I'll call you. Remember, no call, and the two am meet is *on*....cool?"

"Cool."

Black Dog said, as he offered his clenched fist, to lightly bump Billy's fist, which Billy did. They both smiled.

"Yo, you be cool, dog?"

"We're cool."

Billy replied, never losing his Plasticine smile.

And with that, Black Dog turned and headed out of the warehouse, a lively bounce in his step. Ten seconds later, he was gone, and Billy stood alone in the gray, cavernous space.

And his smile was long gone.

It was only then that Button lightly touched the blood-crusted, pulpy flesh above his left eye, shaking his head left and right and squeezing his right fist so tight that the muscles in his arm burned with lactic acid. And he stared out into nothing, beyond the broken windows of the abandoned building in which he stood, as he breathed heavy through clenched teeth, in a quiet, evil seethe.

CHAPTER 142 – DRAW THE CURTAINS AND LET THE MONKEYS OUT OF THE CAGE

Black Dog paced the basketball court, on the fringe of broken, alligator-checked pavement, just outside the orb of dull yellow light from a nearby streetlamp. Eugene blended into the night; only the occasional soft sound of his shuffle on the asphalt belied his presence.

It was 2:13 am; as usual, Billy Bones was late.

Black Dog had been having second and third thoughts about this meeting from the moment he left Billy at the warehouse. The insistence on coming solo, the remote meet, away from the safety of the hood, his soldiers, in *Aryan* territory, all from a flat-ass that he nearly beat to death hours before….a dog-fucker he didn't, and shouldn't, trust.

But Black Dog was a survivor, and when it came to safety and caution, and his own hide, he was smart; Eugene was smart about stuff like that.

So he stuck his lucky Glock in the rear waistband of his baggy blue jeans, under his wife-beater. He also brought along his best captain, Mr. Chills, and he got to the meet early, *way early*; he had been waiting with Mr. Chills in the shadows at the court for the better part of two hours, just to be sure there was no plant, no ambush….no retribution from the *helo* for the warehouse matter.

Black Dog was smart that way.

Mr. Chills stood alone in a fringe of shrubs beyond the metal backboard, leaning against a tree and kicking the dirt by his feet….bored. But the thought of catching Billy Bones in a set-up was worth the wait; Black Dog gave him the green to waste the mother-fucker if there was any *shit not right*, and he could do as he pleased to the hick-bastard before he killed him.

That alone was worth waiting all night.

Mr. Chills hated Billy Bones more than he hated anything, and he didn't like much. To end that redneck would be a fucking highlight like no other, and he kept running through his brain the best way to do it, the way to inflict the most humiliation and pain, before he cut his throat. That was Mr. Chills signature - an ear-to-ear neck-slice and bleed-out, using a black-handled, five and a half-inch, double-edged Bowie knife he lifted years ago.

Mr. Chills felt like a fucking cowboy whenever he used it, and would howl like an Indian, shaking his dreadlocks in a ritual frenzy. He sliced four throats with it to date, and sticking the point of that steel into Billy Bones and watching the white boy bleed out would be such a sweet number five.

Mr. Chills smiled to himself at the thought, as he kicked the dirt by his feet, leaning lazily against the tree.

Billy had waited for the flush in his face to fade, but he was still sweating from the labor. He wiped his cheeks and forehead clean with a cotton rag on the seat next to him, but perspiration kept beading on his brow - not from fear, he felt cool and relaxed, like he always did in these situations - it was just the exertion and fucking heat of the night; two am and it was still too God-damn hot, especially down by the river, swatting skeets in the lamp-light.

The hard knuckle above his left eye had reduced to the size of a walnut; two butterflies helped close the gash tight. He knew the swelling would drop quick; it always did – good genes. He had wrapped his rib-cage hard and tight with gauze and medical adhesive, like a mummy, which made it just about impossible to suck in a full breath. He thought they might not be broken after all; he could have never done what he did with broken ribs, but they were still bruised bad for sure, and sore as a mother-fucker. But the combination of adrenaline and sheer, fucking hatred permitted him to finish the task at hand, through the excruciating pain.

But the preparation was done, and Button was ready to go fishing. He lit a cigarette and sucked in a long, slow drag, savoring the nicotine. He exhaled satisfied, the smoke circled his head and rose lazy in the heavy summer air, dissipating into the night sky. Three more drags, and he flicked the burning butt; it disappeared into the blackness beside him.

Billy hopped into the pick-up, and slowly made his way out of the woods, his grip hard on the steering wheel of the short-bed Dodge. The anticipation hung thick, and the payoff was going to taste *oh-so-sweet*. The diesel growled low as he crawled down the darkened street, a hound on the hunt. He slowly made his way to the intersection of Madison and Market.

And he saw the faint outline of Black Dog, skulking in the shadows; Billy smiled wryly and whispered aloud:

> *Draw the curtains,*
> *and let the monkeys out of the cage.*

CHAPTER 143 – STUCK IN HIS FAT FINGER
AND SPLIT HER OPEN

The Ram pulled up and idled courtside, but Black Dog had disappeared into the shadows. Billy knew he was eyeing the truck, and he knew at least one other guy was nearby, probably Mr. Chills. If Black Dog was smart, he would have brought more, but Button figured he was dealing with a two-some, and he was sure Mr. Chills got the nod; he always did in these situations.

The truck idled, burping diesel in the early morning air; nothing happened….no one moved. Billy sighed, pulled out his cell phone and hit speed dial No. 1; the phone rang just once.

"Yeah."

The voice on the other end was clearly annoyed.

"I told ya; yeah, hold on, I'll put him on."

Button straightened his arm and held the phone out of the window, and spoke plainly, without emotion, into the darkness.

"It's the Dr.; he wants to talk to you, now."

Button waited a bit, but still no bite.

Billy placed the phone to his ear.

"Can't flush the dog out of the bush."

"Mother-fucker! Are you kidding me? Just say *718 Brodhead!*"

Button did, and with that, Black Dog emerged, slowly, from the shadows.

"Must be the magic words; and here he is, *come on down!*"

Button said game-show sarcastic to the Dr., as he handed Eugene his cell phone.

Black Dog didn't say a word, he just placed the phone tightly against his ear, to try and block Billy from listening, but it was useless. Billy smiled as he heard Tyrone rip Eugene a new ass.

"Okay, okay; yeah….Mr. Chills.   Okay, *okay*! Sorry….okay."

And with that, Black Dog flipped the phone shut, and handed Billy the Glock from the back of his pants; Eugene had his head down, beaten.

Button looked at him and shook his head.

"Not a good way to be introduced into the *new new*, my man. Now, you can tell Mr. Chills to give up the Bowie, and whatever else he's got shoved down his pants, and to sit tight and stay out of trouble; I'll come back to get him in awhile, after we talk shop, so he can see the digs and you can show him your handiwork."

"What's that mean?"

Black Dog sniped, still pissed he was ass-chewed in front of Billy by the Dr.

"Didn't the Dr. tell you about the Salvadoran?"

"He didn't tell me *shit*, except to shut-the-fuck-up and do what you said, and that he was okay with it, and would be here later; he got held up."

"Cool, he wants me to surprise you….very cool."

Billy said, with the sound of genuine. And with that, Black Dog turned and walked back over to the basketball court; sure as shit, Mr. Chills emerged from behind a tree, skulking.

This was too good to be true, Button figured….way too good.

A moment later, Black Dog was back at the Ram, holding Mr. Chill's Bowie and a 9 mm Hi-Point, black. Button took them, along with the Glock, and threw them in a satchel, stashed behind the driver's seat, next to the bow.

"Did you tell him to sit tight? *[Black Dog nodded a single yes]* Good. Now get in, it'll only be a couple minutes."

The two traveled in silence ten blocks, in what seemed a random zig-zag through a mixed neighborhood, residential and commercial; it looked fairly clean.

"Gotta cross 73, it's fucking divided; this is the quickest way."

Billy preempted, sensing an uncomfortable squirm by Eugene in the seat next to him.

They finally crossed Route 73, turned right onto a lonely, divided service road heading toward the bridge access ramp, and after a minute, veered left onto a single-lane ribbon of overgrown, unpaved dirt, which quickly tunneled into the darkened thicket of dense trees and under-story that ran along the east bank of the wooded Delaware River. The river water here, flowing lazy beneath the Tacony-Palmyra bridge, probably ran past Belvidere, ninety miles upstream, about three days prior; hard to believe it was the same river, the same water, that swam past the Belvidere boat ramp, forever away from this alien patch of wood.

The Ram created a shallow groove of tracks in the warm summer mud, the only tire treads on the road were from Billy's trip earlier that night. They drove in silence a couple football fields into the ink, the only sounds being the belch of the diesel, the claw and fillip of branches scratching like fingernails along the side panels and windows, and the slosh of water in a big carboy jug in the truck bed, as their ride gently rocked to and fro, delving deeper into the brush.

"What's the water for?"

Billy half-turned his head and spit an answer at Black Dog; the mood had clearly shifted south.

"Don't worry about the fucking water."

And that was that; silence returned, as the diesel tunneled deeper into the thicket. A small clearing ahead signaled the destination, and Billy turned to Eugene and smiled plastic.

"Almost there."

Black Dog didn't respond, but his mind was racing, and he was scared. It must be okay, 'cause the Dr. told him so; *it must be okay* - the phrase kept ringing his head, as he tried to feel comfort in the words. But it wasn't working. He lost his Glock, but he still had his brass knuckles, he still had them; he quietly stuck his hand in his pocket and fingered them, for comfort.

They hopped out of the truck. A muffled percussion of some sort hummed in the distance; Black Dog couldn't make out where it was, hidden behind a curtain of thick vegetation, colored in various shades of dark gray, melding to soot. Off to the right, almost beyond view, Eugene could make out the faint outline of what looked like a small abandoned shack, or maybe it was just a woodshed; it was jet-black.

"What the fuck is that noise?"

The hair on Eugene's arm rose.

"A generator shithead; needed some lights. Relax, didn't you ever camp as a kid?"

"No, I never fucking *camped* in Camden, asshole."

Button just looked at him and chuckled, mostly to himself. It didn't make Black Dog feel any better; it wasn't a good chuckle, it didn't even sound like Billy....it was a creepy-clown snigger. And as quick as it came, it was gone.

Listen, stay here, but watch out for the bears."

With Button's words, the whites of Eugene's eyes grew to saucers.

"Jesus, man, I'm just kidding *[Button forced a laugh]."*

"Look, I'm gonna go get our little friend from the shack, the Salvadoran. Remember the scout from MS13, the mother-fuckers trying to move into our ward on the north side? Well I *got him*; he's gift-wrapped, hog-tied, and the Dr. wants you to interrogate him a bit before offing him, as a kind of kick-off to *The Drin*. His idea; his gift to you, the enforcer."

"Really? Bring it on, dog!"

And all-of-a-sudden, Black Dog found his courage again, as he fished his hand in his front pocket to finger the brass knuckles....his lucky charm. Suddenly, just like that, everything was gonna be okay.

He smiled, ashamed at being spooked; *fucking bears*, he laughed to himself. Now it was time to take his frustration out on the little Mexican. To Black Dog, all the Latinos, Central Americans, whatever, they were all greasy fucking Mexicans, lumped together, wetbacks; almost as bad as whitie….maybe worse. *This,* he was going to enjoy.

As Button walked into the darkness, he stopped and turned to Black Dog.

"Hey, follow the sound of the generator. There's a little path in front of you; you'll see a light on a tripod, and a pit. There's a note on the generator, it's sealed, from Dr. P to you; directions on what he wants done. Read it, and I'll be right there."

Black Dog raised his hand in recognition, but Billy had already turned and melted into the night. Eugene spun slow to look for the path, which he found in short order.

This camping stuff is easy he thought to himself.

Eugene pushed his way roughly through the brush, making ample noise along the way. He ran smack into a patch of barberry and wild rose, quickly getting stuck in a thicket of sharp thorns, which tore into his skin, drawing blood.

"Ow, shit; mother-fucker!"

He stopped and tried to unhooked the barbs from his arms, re-hooking himself more than not. Finally, pissed, he just bulled through, ripping his skin along the way.

"Fuck!"

He soon found himself in another clearing, illuminated by a single light, set on a tripod; a small portable gas generator hummed nearby. His eyes acclimated to the scene, and he made out, to his right, a pit dug in the moist, silty sand, about seven foot square, and about five feet deep. A pile of fresh soil set beside the hole, with a brand new shovel spiked into the top. A gallon can of gasoline and little butane torch sat by the edge of the pit, along with a clear plastic bag full of white balls. Black Dog walked over to the pit and bent down to look closer; they were marshmallows.

What the fuck is this, a cookout? he thought, then quickly spun around, a shot of adrenaline spiked his spine, thinking he heard something. He continued to slowly spin, full circle, then another half, eyeing the edges of dark, just beyond the glow from the single dim bulb, but there was nothing, just the flicker of the light and the staccato burp of the generator. He couldn't hear anything else. And the thought of bears came roaring back.

"Billy?"

He threw the word into the darkness, in a voice just an octave above a whisper.

No answer.

The leaves rustled in a half-breath of early morning breeze; it must be close to 2:30 am by now, he thought. The chill came back, and the hair on his arms rose. But he heard nothing more, just the leaves and the generator; no bears, no monsters....nothing. And the scare once again drained away.

That's when he first saw the plain white envelope, propped atop the generator. He walked over and quietly retrieved it. The outside was simply addressed:

Eugene

That was strange; no Black Dog, or just Dog, but Eugene. He couldn't remember the last time the Dr. called him that. This must be really serious stuff. He looked around again; nothing, just the cough, percussion and burp of the generator he stood beside, all alone.

Eugene flipped the envelope to the backside, stuck in his fat finger and split her open.

1274

CHAPTER 144 – WHOA, THAT WAS ONE BAD MELON

It was a single sheet of folded white paper, printed out from a computer. A short, simple note.

To: *Eugene*

From: *Tyrone*

Hey buddy, just want you to know that you and I go back a long time, way back, to when we were kids. We have a lot of history, mostly cracking heads and hating Whitie.

Hey, see that pit over there? Billy dug it all by himself; he did it even though you probably broke his ribs today.

He's a good man.

He figured he'd make a barbecue pit, cook some dog meat.

You know this new deal, it's really gonna be the fucking nuts for me! New fucking car – two of them! New house, a shit load of cash – more than I can fucking spend, guns....anything I want, including lots of pussy - black, white, Bacardis, whatever....pussy out the fucking ass, and you know how much I love pussy! You can never get enough.

But there's just one catch; damn Whitie, they always have a catch, don't they?

All that history, you watching my back, all that loyalty and trust you gave me all these years, our friendship, it don't mean shit to me now, you stupid fucking monkey.

Eugene went numb, his fingers tingling, like they used to do, when he was a fat little kid, looking for presents under the skinny tree on Christmas morning. But this was no Christmas.

He slowly pulled the paper closer to his face, examining the words, a careful re-read of the end, to be sure the first read was read right. He just started to say *Shit*, but the word never fully left his lips.

The thick, extra-long baseball bat, with an end chock-full of razor-sharp hobnails and longer iron spikes – carefully, skillfully hammered around the circumference years ago by Billy Bones, a medieval hybrid – part trench club, part morning star – smashed hard and square into Eugene's face, crushing it into an unrecognizable pulp in a single lightning blow.

And just like that, that quick, Black Dog's head was flattened; he had no nose, no mouth, no face....just a jagged crater of caved skin, teeth and bone. Blood exploded into the air, like the burst of a Roman candle.

Eugene never had time to make a single sound - not a scream, a yelp or a whimper. Nothing. He *was*, and then he simply *wasn't*.

His head whiplashed and his neck snapped in a single, sickening crack; the top of his cranium flew off and landed in the sand, about eight feet away, a curved plate of bone about the size of a hefty pork chop. The hair and part of Eugene's brain that still stuck to the bone were covered in a fine coating of Delaware River-side sand; shake and bake.

The body slowly crumpled to the ground in a sad heap, the remaining half-head still skewered to the jagged nails and spikes in the club-end. The piece of note paper had jammed deep into the wet hole that used to be Black Dog's face.

Billy, standing naked, the gauze and medical tape that had wrapped his chest removed, was covered in a fine spray of blood, brain and body fluids.

He carefully placed his bare foot on Eugene's fat neck and wrenched the weapon from what was left of Black Dog's head, tilting the back back and forth to dislodge the long spikes from the mess of paper, bone and gray matter. Billy winced from the pain in his side….fucking ribs.

He gently placed the soiled blackjack on the ground, small bits of Eugene still stuck to the morning star spikes, and let out a delayed wince from the windmill swing and subsequent club-pry off the remains of Eugene's frontal. The adrenaline largely masked the pain he knew would come from that swing-for-the-fences.

He went down on one knee, to get a closer look at his work, at what used to be a Eugene; he wasn't sure what to call it now.

"Dead men don't bite; *Treasure Island*, mother-fucker."

Billy Bones said to Black Dog, smiling at how clever he was.

He slowly scanned the inside of Eugene's head, the little that was left of it, carefully leaning in and concentrating, like one views and digests a piece of art hung on a museum wall, amazed at the destruction wrought from a single blow, and how the note paper had been mashed into his monkey brain.

Then he leaned away from the pulpy mess and chuckled to himself.

"Whoa, that was one bad melon."

CHAPTER 145 – 2 MONKEYS – AGE 45:
MORNING STAR & GUT HOOK

Billy grabbed Black Dog's right sneaker and dragged the corpse over to the long side of the pit; Christ, that *groid* was heavy. His ribs ached from the exertion, a steady, dull throb, as he knelt beside the body.

Billy grimaced as he rifled through Black Dog's pockets: he snagged the brass knuckles, a memento, from one; the other pocket held a neat, folded wad of Franklins. Button did a quick count – twenty-six bills.

Button stood slow, like an old man, and gazed at the lifeless body in silence. He kicked it lightly in the back, just enough to tip Black Dog over the edge, into the grave. He landed face down; from the back, the body looked pretty normal. He tossed the pork chop-sized piece of Eugene's head in the pit; it landed on the small of the nigger's back.

Billy placed the wad on the soft soil and grabbed a handful of kindling he gathered earlier and threw it in the pit, atop the shit-skin, followed by dousing the *olla podrida* with a healthy marinade of gasoline. He lit a match and tossed it into the dog-stew, watching it ignite. The broth hissed and popped as Eugene's liquids, mixed with petrol, began to vaporize, the meat set for well done.

Fire in the hole he whispered, chuckling to himself.

Billy snagged the telescoping camping fork he set beside the pit, pulled open the marshmallows and skewered a soft, fat one, crouched down on one knee, and tilted the mallow toward the flames, till the white sugary treat turned a healthy tan. He was smiling the whole time he slowly rotated the ball and stick above the flame, squinting as the waves of heat buffeted his face; the sear reddened his cheeks. The awful stink of the pit-stew wafted around him, but he paid it no heed.

"You stupid fucking monkey; that little stunt today cost you two weeks – life cut short. You were dead anyway, but you had some more time, and you wasted it....fucking moron. You're all alike; stupid, shit-for-brains niggers."

Button talked with his mouth open, chewing the marshmallow like a cow chews a cud.

"Least it was quick; you're welcome, by the way. Count yourself lucky; Mr. Chills....not so lucky."

And the smile left Billy Bone's face, as he set his jaw hard, and his eyes went dead.

"Time for shoe-shine number two."

Billy slowly stood, grabbed the wad of cash, and quietly walked back to the truck, still naked, and washed himself down with the water in the carboy. He cleaned himself up real pretty, got dressed, and shimmied behind the wheel of the truck, ready to pick up the next load of livestock.

The dull throb in his ribs was gone; he always recovered quick....too quick.

Mr. Chills heard the Ram before he saw it; in no time, it saddled up to the empty basketball court, ready to take him into the woods. Mr. Chills peered in the cab, wary.

"You bugging; where's Black Dog?"

"Ready to have a low-rider weenie roast; come on man, get in - the Dog doesn't want you to miss it! I picked up that Salvadoran we saw by the docks yesterday; Mr. Black has been interrogating him. You thought he beat *me* bad? Shit man, this dude is *fucked up*! Anyway, he's ready to throw him in a fire pit, *for real*, and watch him cook. He wants to see if you want the honors, you know, to set this little-shit crank on fire!"

"Are you fucking kidding me?! Be like, shit you gotta spit!"

Mr. Chills hopped excited in the truck.

"That little Mo? You got him? How cool is that dog? **Mess**! Why didn't you say something? When did you pick him up? Where'd you stash the greaser?"

"Hey dick, shut your fucking hole with the fucking questions! You're not even supposed to be here; you're lucky the Dr. doesn't fuck you and the Dog up for you even coming - be happy he's cool about it."

Mr. Chills frowned; it was hard to stomach taking any shit from Billy, but he bought the story.

"Say yo, hurry up then, fucking milk-head!"

Mr. Chills said, getting the last word in. Billy just turned to him and smiled with vacuous eyes, talking in his best nigger-slave accent.

"Doing the best I can….boss!"

And then Billy cackled, loudly, a forced guffaw; a real creepy laugh that just didn't sound….right.

Mr Chills didn't laugh, and the hair on his arms tingled a bit. He just stared at Billy with suspicious eyes, like one does at an animal, waiting for it to leap, jump, attack, to do something, anything, when you least expect it. He was sure whitie was some fucked-in-the-head burn-out; the guy was just….*off.*

Mr. Chills kept a guarded eye on Billy Bones; for the rest of the trip, the two rode in silence. The creepy-doll smirk never left Button's face as he stared into the blackness beyond the windshield.

The Ram nosed onto the thin, rutted dirt road, passing through the close thicket, idling to a slow stop in the same lonely clearing as before. Mr. Chills quickly exited the cab, mainly to get away from Billy; he didn't like sitting so close to psychotic whitie. Once he was safe away, he barked baritone at Button, like a man in charge.

"Yo, where they be?!"

"Hear the generator stupid *[Billy put his finger to his ear]*? Just follow the sound, you'll find the cookout."

Mr. Chills jogged about fifteen yards, toward the thicket of shrubbery illuminated by the truck high-beams, but stopped mid-step and looked back, when he realized Billy wasn't in tow. Button was standing statue by the open door of the truck, smiling - that same creepy smile.

"Why you standing there, *Ric*? Yo, let's go! You still work for Dog and the Man, *and me,* asshole. And besides, hey, give me back my fucking knife and *Hi-Point*, mother-fucker!"

"Okay."

Button said calmly, with no inflection in his voice, staring through Mr. Chills with utter indifference. The smile had washed from his face.

And with that, Billy reached behind the seat and pulled out his *Predator* crossbow, loaded with a twenty-inch bolt, a sixteen-inch power stroke, cocked and ready. Billy flicked on the scope and lasered the red-dot, centered square on the nigger's midsection.

Mr. Chills looked down and saw the diode glowing blood-bright on his white muscle-tee, square in the middle of his washboard gut.

Billy slowly, cautiously walked toward Mr. Chills, his finger on the trigger, expecting a rabbit. But the black man froze, unsure what to do….a deer in headlights.

"Woah, woah, dog."

Mr. Chills said, taking a single step back. That's as much as he spoke, and as far as he got.

Without a word, and without warning, Billy pulled the trigger and launched the razor sharp stainless steel broadhead bolt-cutter, a mean fucking arrow, hissing at two-hundred-fifty miles per hour, straight into the gut of Mr. Chills, which knocked him clear off his feet. The end of the tip emerged from Mr. Chills back, skewered straight through, a dark meat shish kabob.

Mr. Chills gasped a long, muffled groan, as he squirmed on the ground, a worm on a hook, his hand wrapped around the end of the bolt shaft, too dazed to pull it out, to do anything, other than tightly grip the stainless rod. His hands were shaking uncontrollably as he curled fetal, his brow already beaded with sweat. His whole body felt on fire.

Billy quickly reloaded the crossbow and stared hard at Mr. Chills, who was still squirming, incoherent, eyes shut; waves of excruciating pain rippled hot through his midsection. It felt a thousand degrees in his belly.

"*Vale tudo*, mother-fucker."

Button calmly rustled behind the truck cab seat and grabbed a little black nylon satchel, along with a molded plastic side carrying case. He strolled over to Mr. Chills and pointed the arrow at the side of his head, the end of the arrow tip jabbed into his ear canal. But Mr. Chills eyes were squeezed shut in pain, and it looked as if he was about to pass out.

"Hey! Monkey! Wake up; stay focused. Hey! Open your eyes!"

Button yelled, spraying spit as he drop-kicked Mr. Chills in the lower back of the head with his steel-toed work boot, a crushing blow, just above the neck. The black man opened his eyes and stared blankly, in a fog, drool spilling from his open mouth. He looked like a fish, coughing up a hook.

"Hey! Come on, hands behind your back!"

But it was no use, the man simply wasn't paying attention, writhing in pain, gummed to the bolt in a death-grip.

"Jesus, you're a fucking pussy."

Button stepped back, shaking his head in disgust.

"Let go of the bolt."

Billy said as calm as can be, repeating the phrase as he swiftly kicked Mr. Chills in the small of the back; by the third heavy boot blow, and third repeat, Mr. Chills obliged, still moaning in agony....eyes closed once again.

Button had expected a fighter; he figured at least two bolts would be necessary to subdue Mr. Chills, and even then, he figured he would scrap and claw.

Instead he got a fucking nigger-wimp, who simply gave up. It always the tough-talking ones, when they have the weapons and the upper hand, who turn out to be the biggest chicken-shits.

Always.

Billy grabbed Mr. Chills' hands and held them behind his back; the butter didn't fight a bit, still moaning like a girl, taking half-labored breaths. Button simply stared at his mouth, as it opened and closed, a fish gasping for oxygen. He smiled at the spectacle.

In short order, Button had the leather hog-tie cinched and secure; the snaffle-hooks and D-rings were locked tight on Mr. Chills wrists and ankles, both bent and folded behind his back. He was bound, stretched and tied taut; a fly fixed tight in a spider's web.

Billy bent down, his face close to Mr. Chills; he grabbed the stainless steel rod of the bolt and shimmied it back and forth as he drove the shaft deeper into his gut, the point now protruding a good half inch further out his back.

Mr. Chills let out a guttural cry. Button simply laughed.

"You know, this hog-tie, I used it on my girlfriend for years; she loves bondage, being restrained, while I violate her up the ass. Too bad I have to retire it; can't use it now, with your nigger-stench on it. But it's still missing the best part; she just *loved* this little piece. Don't know why; it's fucking disgusting, the thought of it, but she just couldn't get enough, know what I mean?"

And with that, Billy Bones reached into the black nylon bag and pulled out an inflatable, rubber ball gag, jet-black, in the shape of a thick, curved cock. He roughly slung the rubber head-strap around Mr. Chill's noggin and told him to open his mouth. Surprisingly, he resisted, pursing his lips in defiance.

"Well, it's a bit late for that isn't it? I mean, don't you think you should have grown a set, put up just a bit of fight, *before* I tied you up, moron? You never were too bright, you stupid, fucking coon."

"Fuck you; I'm gonna fuckin' kill you!"

Mr. Chills first words, eked out through clenched teeth and spittle.

"Uh huh, I'll keep that in mind."

Button just stared down at the bound, helpless man; the piece of black cock-rubber was lightly touching Mr. Chills lips. Then Billy spoke, in an even, emotionless whisper.

"Every man has a plan, till they get punched in the face, or shot through the gut with a bolt *[Billy cracked a half-smile, impressed with himself]*."

Button's eyes searched for a reaction, any reaction, but got none, just short labored breaths and high-pitched groans from Mr. Chills, who was doing a poor job managing the pain.

"Know who said that Bojangles? Huh? *[Button lightly kicked his head, more of a nudge, with the tip of his boot]*. None other than the used-to-be ultimate black man, Iron Mike Tyson; can you believe it? Me, quoting a moolie? Funny. Of course, I ab-libbed the ending."

Button thought he was pretty clever, but Mr. Chills simply wasn't paying attention. The spider knelt beside the fly, and whispered.

"Know what? I don't think you've got a plan; not now, not ever. But *I* do; I got a *real good one*....you'll see."

Button smiled, showing his teeth in an exaggerated, watermelon grin, his best take on a genuine nigger shine. But Mr. Chills never saw it, his face was shaking wild, beads of sweat running off his brow. Button never saw a man sweat so much, so fast. The black rubber dick pushing gently against his lips, and his chin.

And just like that, the smile left Billy's lips, and he got serious.

"Okay, no more fucking around. I'll give you a choice; either you suck *this* black cock *[Billy pointed to the piece of curved rubber pressed against Mr. Chills lips]* or you get a stainless steel bolt through *your* black cock, the one you were waving around today in the warehouse…a nasty arrow right through your fucking ball-sack, and then you can kiss that cock goodbye, my friend. I could give a shit either way; you got three seconds to decide."

And Button picked up the crossbow, flicked the diode on, and placed the end of the razor sharp arrow head on Mr. Chills crotch.

"Three…."

The nigger's mouth immediately opened, before the number *two* was ever heard, and in slipped the black rubber cock, easy peasy.

"Good Chango."

Button said, as he lightly patted Mr. Chills on the head, like a lap dog. He grabbed the pump and inflated the rubber appendage till Mr. Chills started to squirm and gag, his mouth grotesquely distended. Button eased a bit of air out, just enough for Mr. Chills to get enough oxygen to survive, but not a sound was uttered.

Billy stood tall over the hogtie.

"You get a real fucking kick out of calling me a *Cracker*, don't ya? Well, maybe I'll be one, all authentic, just for you; maybe I should flip you on your belly and pull down those baggy-ass pants of yours, make you squeal like a fucking sow. Would you like that?"

Billy took the razor tip of the arrow and placed it on Mr. Chills ass, pushing it gently until the point pierced and ripped the denim rump; the tip slid into his pants. A second later, the nigger flinched, when it was clear the blade was pushed against his colon. A simple pull of the trigger and he would bleed out, sodomized by a stainless steel bolt.

Mr. Chills froze; he didn't move a muscle, his ass muscles pinched tight.

"Let me hear you squeal like a pig boy; *squeal! Squeal!*"

Button pushed the bolt in a quick mini-thrust, slicing into Mr. Chill's ass; he could see the black man try to scream, the sound muffled to nothing but a whimper around the rubber cock gag.

Billy Bones smiled.

"Can't hear ya; did you say you want another? Was that as good for you as it was for me?"

Billy thrust the bolt into his ass again, this time *much* deeper. Mr. Chills writhed in pain. Billy yanked the bolt from of his pants; the arrow tip and shaft were enameled in blood.

Button laughed and mocked the craw.

"Say you want it! Say you want my *Cracker* cock instead of this big bad bolt! Come on, spit it out!"

Mr. Chills screamed, his face contorted in the effort; not a word emerged.

"Hey shithead, I can't hear you with that cock in your mouth."

Billy kicked him again, this time in the right cheekbone, caving it in, the bone shattered.

Button went down on one knee and whispered.

"Okay, okay, we'll leave your nigger-hole alone for awhile; we'll come back to that, later."

Billy again patted Mr. Chills on the head.

"Breathe easy boy, you're doing good; hang in there, the night is not nearly over, for you. Are you comfortable? Good, now hold on; we're going for a little ride."

And with that, Button tightly cinched a handful of Mr. Chills braided dreadlocks and proceeded to drag the bound and gagged Mandingo across the ground on his side, the point of the bolt jumping and scratching a jagged line in the sand, catching on rocks and roots along the way. Billy looked back and could see Mr. Chills trying to scream, his eyes watering a steady stream of tears. Button smirked at the spectacle, and spoke slave.

"Having fun yet boss?"

As he dragged the body through the scrub, Billy purposely walked alongside the dense thicket of barberry and wild roses, pulling Mr. Chills through the nest of thorns, which ripped his body to shreds. Every time he hung up on the branches of thorns, Button would yank harder, ripping handfuls of braids from his head, large patches of fleshy scalp tearing off. Billy would just grab another handful of braids, and start to pull again. Mr. Chills head was covered in blood, which soaked into the fine silty sand he picked up along his drag through the brush.

"Almost there wanker."

Billy dragged Mr. Chills right up to the edge of the pit. The fire had died down and now glowed a dull red; Eugene was indistinguishable in the bottom of the hole, an amorphous black crisp, mixed with kindling ash. The smell of gasoline, burnt hair and flesh was overpowering, but it didn't seem to faze Button in the least.

"Say hi to Black Dog."

Billy said without emotion, pointing into the smoldering fire-pit. Mr. Chills eyes were wide open, full of terror; he couldn't blink. He shook his head, trying to get away from the stink of burnt meat.

"That woke you up, huh? That campfire smell of cooked dog?"

Billy stuck his hand in his pocket and pulled out a pack of cigarettes, knocked a stick free and lit it, taking a long, leisurely drag. He knelt down and exhaled, slowly blowing the smoke into Mr. Chills' face.

Mr. Chills lay rigid, afraid to move, afraid to do anything that may trigger more torture, more pain. He was still alive, only alive, on adrenaline, nothing more; he just wanted it to end.

Billy just knelt there, in silence, staring blankly into the eyes of the bound man, amazed at the size of the whites, just toking and slowly blowing smoke at his prey. Mr. Chills' face was distorted, swollen and caved-in, all-at-once; it already didn't look human, and Billy was just getting started.

Minutes seemed like hours, until Button finally spoke, in a low, soothing whisper.

"I know you're scared; you're not angry anymore, just plain scared, hoping that all this would just end. But it's not, not by a *long* shot. And you're gonna be scared for a while longer, and I ain't gonna lie, it's gonna get *real bad* for you in a little bit, and you're gonna want it to end; but trust me, it won't. That's what torture is all about....*not* ending. It's a beautiful thing, at least from my seat. From *your* seat? Not so much."

Billy got a little closer to Mr. Chills' face.

"The game is only gonna end, the thrill of the kill, when I see it in those big white eyes of yours, when they look at me, and become quiet, helpless, asking for mercy from the very man who's inflicting all that pain. And in *that* moment, when your life is at its very end, about to flicker away, when your body and mind finally give in, and give up….when you surrender unconditional - *that's* the ultimate rush. It's *intoxicating*, like a fucking drug you just can't get enough of, the *best* fucking drug ever invented....and it's free for the taking! You can't beat that with a stick. And only when we get there, together, only *then* will I let the game end….and you'll thank me."

Mr. Chills was still frozen, his eyes fixed on Button's, on his thick, dark eyebrows, on the wrinkles around his dead, blue eyes, squinted into thin lines.

Billy stood up and tossed his cigarette in the fire pit, letting out the last lung of smoke. He looked down at Mr. Chills, speaking in a mocking, serious tone.

"Have you ever pondered the ordinary man's capacity for evil?"

Then Billy laughed.

"I read that once in the newspaper; can't remember who said it, I guess somebody; who gives a shit, really. Anyway, I always wanted to say it to someone, out loud, when it made sense; sounds kinda cool. And I think in this situation, here, it makes a whole lotta sense, agreed?"

Billy stepped away from Mr. Chills, about ten feet to the left, and slowly started to disrobe….first his shirt, then his tee-shirt. As he peeled the tee, his torso revealed an intricate tattoo, spread across his chest and extending onto his deltoids and upper arms. It was best described as beautiful; a series of doves and songbirds intertwined in flower garlands, circled by butterflies. A large carp framed the edge, all set in a mural of red and blue hues....mainly blue. The name *Lillian* was weaved into the design, along with the name *Carol*. *Lillian* crawled across the back side of his left shoulder; it looked out-of-place, almost an afterthought. *Carol* was integral, an intertwined band across his chest, clutching, squeezing his heart.

Mr. Chills stared blankly at the inked art; shock had finally settled in.

"Like it? The Dr. always called me a fag, thought it was girlie, with butterflies and shit; what do you think, faggie? Fuck it, I like it....shows my sensitive side."

Button undid his pants, and, standing over Mr. Chills, pulled out his cock, shaking it once or twice, till the stream began. Then he redirected it, arching it through the air, landing on the nigger's head, spraying over his face, his distended mouth, his neck, pissing in his ear, peppering the ground nearby. Billy spoke in what he thought was a damn good Clint Eastwood accent, as he urinated on Mr. Chills.

"You see, in this world, there are two kinds of people, my friend, those with loaded guns, and those who dig....you dig."

Billy chuckled to himself.

"*That one*....that one is from one of my *favorite* movies, *The Good, The Bad And The Ugly*. Clint Eastwood says that to....what the fuck is his name? *[Button thought for a bit, trying to remember]* Eli Wallach - that's it! Right before he makes him dig up the buried gold coins, remember that? Just before he puts a noose around his neck to kill him, hang him from a tree. But Clint, the good guy that he is, saves Eli in the end, shoots the rope to break it. I woulda never shot it; fuck Eli, let him hang....take his gold too. Remember that movie? You should really rent it....classic!"

Button talked excitedly about the movie as he wiggled his dick, the final drips landing lazy on Mr. Chill's forehead, like a slow leak. The urine beaded here and there on Mr. Chills' face, with the remnants of streaks running down his silt-covered cheeks, like face paint.

Billy continued to disrobe, removing his shoes, socks, pants, and finally his boxers. He folded his clothes neatly in a pile, a good distance from Mr. Chills, a safe distance, well outside the spray zone. He stuck his hand in his pants pocket and pulled out the brass knuckles....Black Dog's brass knuckles.

He walked back and crouched next to Mr. Chills.

Within sight, Billy slowly fitted the brass knuckles on his left hand; they were a bit loose. While fidgeting with them, without warning, he unleashed a wicked blow, square in the middle of Mr. Chill's face, a dull thud marked the breaking of his nose and left cheekbone. A spray of red splattered across Billy's body; a fresh stream of blood gushed from Mr. Chill's nose, mixing with the urine and blood from his pocked scalp. His face was all but indistinguishable.

Billy looked close at him, and saw that he was still breathing, barely.

"Hey, don't die on me yet."

Billy whispered, as he stood and shook his left hand; that blow cracked his fingers, but good. He tossed the brass knuckles in the fire pit. He turned back to Mr. Chills, who was drifting in and out of consciousness, a state of fog.

"You know, in the Marines, the Dr. and I had a buddy, Jimmy Springs, Jimbo, a good ol' boy from the scrub-brush country....West Texas. Anyway, this boy used to wear a baseball cap with the longest fucking saying on it; how it fit on that fucking hat I'll never know. It used to wrap all the way around his head, but it said something like this; actually it said *exactly* this:

God said unto them, be fruitful and multiply and replenish the Earth and subdue it, and have dominion over the fish of the sea, and over the fowl of the air, and over every living thing that moveth upon the earth.

And you know what? That includes fucking monkeys like you. To be *the man*, you've got to beat *the man*, and you simply don't got the 'nads, my friend, never did, never will....you, or any of your nigger herd. That's just the way it is."

 Button stared hard at Mr. Chills.

"Okay, you look a bit sleepy, so it's decision time. You get to choose Door No. 1, or I get to choose Door No. 2."

Billy looked at him intently.

"You ready?"

A strange wave of consciousness came over Mr. Chills, and he suddenly seemed alert. Where that came from, who knows. He tried to speak, but nothing came out around the ball gag. His jaw was broken anyway. Billy grabbed the bolt and slowly wiggled it. Mr. Chills arched and tried to scream, but no sound emerged, his eyes streaming tears.

Billy asked again.

"Stupid, you can't talk, just shake your head....you ready?"

Somehow, for some reason, Mr. Chills engaged, and slowly shook his head yes. Billy smiled, happy for the reprieve.

He walked over to a stash of camping gear piled about twenty feet from them, along the edge of the clearing, and brought back a small butane torch and the marshmallow fork. Then he pulled Mr. Chill's Bowie knife out of the black nylon bag. He clicked on the torch, and slowly heated up the two prongs of the rotisserie fork, till they turned sooty black, followed by a dull vermilion glow.

"Okay, you see this fork? I'm gonna use it to puncture your right eye - stick it in quick and deep, like skewering a slippery meatball *[Button thrust the fork at Mr. Chills, stopping just short of his eye, and pumped it staccato right up to his eyeball, in a mock attack]*. The heat will sizzle the liquid in your eye and make that puppy swell up quick, and it's gonna hurt like a mother-fucker, pain like you *never* felt before, till it pops and oozes all over your face. Then I'll twist what's left of it, like looping a fork in a bowl of fucking spaghetti, and yank it clear out of your head, entrails and all. Now, I'm not gonna lie, that right eye's gonna hurt like a mother, especially when I twist what's left of it out of your head. But, it is not gonna hurt nearly as bad as the left eye, because now you'll know that hot forks a-coming, and you'll know the fucking pain is coming again. And the second time around, knowing what's coming, it's *always* worse, And I'm gonna fuck with your head; I'm gonna keep fake-jabbing the fork right up to your left eye, five, six times, maybe more, while I'm laughing, and you're not gonna know which one is gonna be the one that I stick in.....*deep*, till you feel that hot steel spike skewer your eyeball, and drive into that tiny brain of yours."

Mr. Chills got a burst of adrenaline and tried to scream, as he rocked his body violently, trying to get away.

Billy just laughed.

"Please, you look like a fucking turtle; just stay still….you *really* need to pay attention."

Mr. Chills was hysterical, rolling closer to the edge of the fire pit.

"Whoa! You don't want to go in there; not yet anyway."

Billy got up and pushed him away from the edge with his foot.

"Now calm down, or the fork's going in right now! *[Button fell to his knees, quickly mounted Mr. Chills like a horse and started to fake jab the skewer within a sliver of his saucer eye]*"

Mr. Chills stopped squirming, but his body was trembling uncontrollable.

"Now stop interrupting, let me finish the story, for Christ sake. Anyway, now that both eyes are history, you can't see what's gonna happen next, which, trust me, is good for you. And I'm gonna make you wait, knowing it's coming, and soon. When I let out that stupid fucking Indian scream of yours, you'll know I'm gonna slice your throat deep with that Bowie, ear to ear, just like you do to all those poor niggers and wetbacks you killed. And I'm gonna do you with your own fucking knife. And I'm gonna slice *real* slow. I figure if you bleed out in a couple minutes, tops, the whole messy ordeal, eyes and all, will be over in under five minutes; not too bad for you, in a sense, because dead in five minutes is *way better* than what waits for you behind Door No. 2….*trust me* on that."

Button off-mounted the nigger, who's whole body was still shaking.

He turned his back on Mr. Chills, crouched down, and re-lit the fork tines in the butane flame, slowly turning them left and right across and through the flame, till they, once again, throbbed the dangerous dull red of an oven element. And as Billy slowly seared the steel, his back to Mr. Chills, he spoke.

"Here's something to think about; I bet you didn't figure, when you rolled out of bed this morning, that you were never gonna brush your teeth again, huh? Or see yourself in the mirror, or suck on a fucking watermelon, you stupid nigger. Never thought you were gonna fucking die today, in the same pants you pulled on this morning, did you? That's the bitch of it, you never knew, never figured, that today was *your* day to die."

And now Billy turned to face the fly.

"And to die in a *real bad* way to boot, at the hands of your favorite Cracker; overall, a pretty shitty day for you. So what do you say? Do you want Door No. 1? Painful, but quick!   Or Door No. 2....a mystery you don't want to solve, trust me. You got five seconds to decide; I'm *ready to go [Button remounted and throttled Mr. Chills throat with one hand, and held the fork high, ready to plunge it into the right eyeball]*"

Mr. Chills just rocked hysterically back and forth; he couldn't do much else.

"No?   That looks like a no to me.   Are you sure? Because Door No. 2 is *much* worse."

Billy dismounted and stood up, resigned.

"I didn't think Door No. 1 had much of a shot anyway; too bad for you."

He kicked a bare foot scuff of river silt into Mr. Chills face in disgust. Then he stared hard at the lump of bloody meat lying beside him.

"Hey, trust me, that whole *not-seeing-yourself-ever-again-in-a-mirror thing,* it's a good thing, for you. I don't think you wanna see yourself in a mirror anyway; you're not looking too good my friend….a bit pulpy."

Billy speared the molten fork hard into the sand, an inch from the face of his quarry, and walked out of Mr. Chill's view. He heard him wrestling around with something metallic, and what sounded like the friction-zip of a rope being pulled out of the nylon satchel. A few moments later he walked behind Mr. Chills and grabbed him by the braids, the few that were left, dragging him fifteen feet away, to the edge of the clearing, next to a large maple tree. Mr. Chills was rocking violently, trying to see what was happening behind him.

Button raised his arm slowly, concentrating hard as he came down in a powerful, swift arch – a tee off a long par five.

Suddenly, a bolt of excruciating pain shot through Mr. Chills, and the lower half of his body tingled for a split-second, then quickly went numb. Button had driven a rusted meat hook from the slaughterhouse into his upper back, the spike punching deep, right beside his spinal cord – a real worm on a fishhook. Mr. Chills' upper body writhed violently in pain, his lower body went still, dead in the sand.

Button threw the rope over a low branch of the maple and hoisted Mr. Chills off the ground, like a pig carcass, his weight drove the spike deeper into his back, and the flesh and muscle strained and ripped under the weight of his body. Button winced as he hoisted the black man off the ground; his ribs throbbing.

"Mother fucker! Jesus!"

Button griped, amazed at how hard it was to hoist the slab of dark meat….dead weight. He tied him off, and walked around to face Mr. Chills, who looked ever-close to punching out.

"Fuck, don't die on me yet, we still got things to do."

Button retrieved the fork and, for the third time, singed the tines in the butane flame till they were molten red.

In a quick spin and stick, he sunk them deep into Mr. Chills' left thigh.

Nothing happened.

No reaction from the carcass, save a long creak from the slow, silent counterclockwise rotation and stretch of the jute rope, straining against the maple bark.

"Fuck!"

Button kicked the ground in disgust; he fucked up, and he knew it. Immediately.

He hooked the bastard too deep and close to the spine. Button yanked out the marshmallow-fork in disdain; blood poured from Mr. Chills' leg, saturating his jeans in an expanding blot of ink. It quickly pooled at his bent knee and soaked through the denim; a thin, steady stream of red fluid disappeared into the sand below him, a faucet at quarter-turn.

Button held the rotisserie aloft, like a spear, and carefully scanned Mr. Chills' body, a surgeon picking an entry, and plunged the tines deep into his upper chest, just below his shoulder. Mr. Chills arched half-heartedly on the meat hook.

"Shit."

Was all Button whispered to himself, shaking his head in a quiet anger, as he watched the distorted body slowly spin in a half-rotation on the metal hook. Mr. Chills' eyes were closed, but he was still breathing, lightly, the marshmallow-fork sticking from his chest.

Button just stood in front of the body, watching it lazily swing from the tree branch, a tire swing in the summer. The blood was still draining steady from the pocket of liquid trapped in his jeans, at the knee. His broken nose still bled a trickle of red, down the side of his face, both cheeks crushed and his face a distorted mess of meat.

"Fuck."

He whispered even lower to himself, pounding his fist into his thigh in frustration.

The nigger was a fish who lost its fight on the line; he probably had minutes left to live, and not much more. Not nearly enough time. And more than half his body couldn't feel the pain he still wanted to inflict, to still heap on top.

Billy Bones had this whole palmistry thing planned for Door No. 2. He was going to sever Mr. Chill's arm at the elbow with the bone saw from the field dress kit he brought along; it would dismember that skinny nigger arm in three quick strokes, like butter. He would cauterize the stump with the torch. He would hold up Mr. Chills' severed arm, like show-and-tell, slap him stupid in the face a few times with his own nigger-hand, and talk to the shit-skin about his *head line*, and how short it was, indicating how stupid the monkey was, and joke about his *fate line* and *line of fortune,* and how lucky he was to have such good lines on his palm, indicating he would lead a long life. It was going to be a good joke, and he thought of some witty lines, but now, there simply wasn't time for the show. And he certainly didn't have time for the Door No. 2 *coup de grace* - to slowly, carefully, as he hung from the tree like captured game, flay him - skin him alive, for at least as long as he could keep him alive. That was the goal, to keep him breathing, in unspeakable pain, as he slowly banana-peeled that shit-black skin, to literally strip the *nigger* right off him, right out of him, piece by piece. But that desire would take time, time he simply didn't have.

And now all that, the dismemberment and flaying, it wasn't worth the chance that Mr. Chills would simply, quietly, flame out before he got very far. So he had to forego the bone saw and filet knife, and for that, Billy was pissed.

Button sighed in resignation, bent over and pulled the shiny, fixed blade skinner knife, with a gut hook, out of the plastic field case. He walked over to face Mr. Chills, and gently poked the blade into the base of his neck, just below his throat. The razor tip broke the skin and a trickle of blood lined his exterior, disappearing into his tee-shirt, long-since tie-dyed with silt, blood and urine.

Mr. Chills didn't even flinch; he just opened his eyes slowly, looking down at Billy. His orbs were empty eggs, helpless, and the fear was gone; it was clear the lights were just about out. Billy was surprised he was still holding on. Dried tracks of tears stained what was left of his dark cheek, but no tears flowed.

Mr. Chills had given up; whatever little fight he had in him was gone. He simply surrendered to Billy Bones, to do as he wished....at his mercy.

Button nodded once at the surrender, and slid the tip of the blade down a bit, hooked the cotton of his shirt, and slowly pulled the gut hook down, side-stepping the bolt, and shredding the tee-shirt in two, exposing Mr. Chills' chest and belly. He stopped right above the waistline of his pants, spun the blade vertical and pushed lightly on the handle, till the point punctured the skin below his navel. A fresh trickle of blood emerged.

Billy peered deep into Mr. Chills' eyes; the black man blinked, slowly, just once. And Billy smiled.

"It's a bitch not being at the top of the food chain."

As the last word left Button's lips, he drove the gut-hook deep into Mr. Chills, who wriggled on the line herky-jerk, the last gasp of a spent fish.

In one quick motion, Button sliced his abdomen open, like a zipper, clear up to his rib cage. Mr. Chills threw back his head, his eyes rolling north, till they were nothing but white orbs. He pissed himself and defecated; the last things he ever did.

His intestines hesitated for a split second, then quickly unraveled, his entrails falling onto the ground like links of sausage, in a chaotic stream of blood and milky fluids. In seconds, his abdomen cavity was empty, the contents on the ground below him, with the last section of intestine still tethered to his ass.

Billy stood back to study his splayed work, and gave a half-frown; it all happened much too quick, and was not nearly as satisfying as he thought it would be. He was disappointed in himself. He had much higher hopes; the affair was, in toto, anti-climactic. He thought about it, and silently gave himself a D, at best a D; and he didn't get D's, not in affairs such as this - things that mattered to him.

Next time, he insisted to himself, he would have to plan better, not be so brutal, so lethal, so quick; it showed a lack of discipline on his part. A Marine doesn't do that. The goal was to keep them alive, and alert….longer. He fully expected the will to live, the resistance to surrender, to be much stronger. Instead, the nigger gave up early, without much of a fight, but then just hung on, like a limp dick – where's the challenge in that? He shook his head in disgust at the missed opportunities.

Mr. Chills didn't suffer nearly enough, and that would never happen again, not on Billy's watch.

The dead nigger spun slowly on the hook, his lifeless eyes wide open, blood still dripping from the knee of his jeans; a busted pinata. The smell of innards wafted over Button; blood, sputum, urine, diarrhea and bile - the repulsive mix of fluids and stool drifted about the clearing.

But Billy Bones hardly noticed.

He lit a cigarette and went down on one knee, which made a small indent in the cool night sand, and exhaled a heavy sigh. It was a long day, and, all told, things went off fairly well. Regardless of the disappointment with Mr. Chills, both gars were dead, with the blessing of the Dr. no less. And he was new No. 2; prosperous times lay ahead, and Lilly would be back in the picture, hanging on his arm like she always would, obeying, like she always did, and making him gobs of money. Things were moving in the right direction again, and he half-smiled at the prospect.

And thoughts of Lilly inevitably led to thoughts of Carol, and his smile grew wider. Button slowly turned over his right hand and studied his palm, the same palm Carol used to gently hold, and gently kiss, when they joined for long, solo walks in the woods.

Many walks.

God, 1979, seventeen years ago; it felt like yesterday. It felt as if he should just be able to go home, knock on the Fourth Street door, and see her beautiful face again, standing sexy in those short, tight little dresses she liked to show off in, especially that naughty black one....*that* was his favorite.

He took his left pointer and ran it in a soft, peaceful manner along his *life line*; she always told him it was so long, and that he would surely live forever. She never said she would; he remembered that now.

She would kiss the *bracelet lines* around his wrist, telling him how lucky he was to have so many; he remembered thinking how lucky he was to have her. And the *heart line,* that was her favorite; she would run her tongue along it, barely touching his skin, then rest her head in his hand, while he ran his fingers back and forth through her long blonde hair. Lilly loved when Button ran his hands through her hair; she always told him it was the most gentle and heartfelt thing he ever did. It was her favorite; it made Lilly feel special.

Button only ever did it thinking about her mother.

Carol would swear palmistry was real; she read about it and was convinced....how one's destiny, one's fate, was set in the lines in your hand. He always thought it was a crock of shit, but never told her that; he would talk it up with her – he loved talking to her about it....about anything.

She first held his hand, and first read his palm, on that last walk in the woods before he boarded the bus to boot camp in '79. He was almost nineteen and cocky, but he always felt like a little kid around her, goofy and unsure of himself. She rattled him, but in a way that made him feel good, made him feel alive, and worth something.

She was the only woman he ever truly loved; to this day, it was still true.

And to this day, no one ever knew what happened after that first palm read in the woods, after picking up trinkets along the wood path, to bring back to Lilly. And no one ever knew what it led to, over and over and over again. Insatiable.

No one, but Carol and Button.

That day, and the dozens of days over the next two years, when he secretly came home on leave from the Marines, trysts, their secret secure right up to the morning of April 7, 1981, the last day he saw her, the last time they spoke....the same day she died.

Button set his jaw hard at the memory's end; he rarely went down that bitter road.

He stood up, spat and flicked his cigarette into the fire pit, putting the thought of Carol out of his mind.

He walked over to his neat pile of clothes, and pulled out his little black leather notebook, with the attached black pen. He flipped open to the last page and noted the entry in carefully laid print:

No. 89: 2 Monkeys - Age 45 - Morning Star & Gut Hook

"Yeah, yeah, both buggers went quick and painless, single shots, just like we discussed. That's right dude, I keep my promises. Yeah, we both called it; knew he would bring his boy along, but it all worked out in the end. But I gotta tell ya, Mr. Chills, what a pussy. Yeah, all cleaned up, done. I'll be out of here and back down in about an hour; I gotta get out of here before the sun comes up; let me go."

Button listened as the Dr. talked and talked on the other end; after a bit he held the phone from his ear in mock disgust.

"Dude, you gab like a fucking girl! They're dead for Christ's sake, it doesn't matter how; yeah, yeah, quick and painless. I *already* told you, one shot each, just like we said, just like we agreed. No they didn't say shit! We didn't have a fucking conversation - just one and done. Jesus, shut up already and let me go. Hey, forgot to tell you, next week, I need to blow for a couple weeks or so; got to go north and take care of *that* business, you know. Plus, when I'm up there, I'll shore up those contacts we discussed, you know, local; some safe house shit and other stuff, you know, with my boys."

Button listened some more, getting annoyed, dragging deep on a fresh cigarette.

"Listen, I still gotta get her on board, and I need a little face time for that; it's been three years, you know, I can't dump *that* in the first conversation, *capiche*? Trust me, it *will* be worth it, you'll see, firsthand, I guess. Once you taste a piece of her dude, there's no going *anywhere* else; but just *one* taste for you, you fucking dog *[Button laughed]*! Plus, I got that other issue I really need to address; just a fly that needs swatting, nothing crazy."

Button rolled his eyes.

"Listen, I've been hearing a rash of shit about this schmuck and I told you I have to address it, no choice, no discussion. It won't be a big deal, but it *will* be if I don't squash it. Yeah, yeah; well I'm not leaving for a couple days, so we got time to reestablish things, you know, with the crew. You **need** to be there tomorrow during the announcement, bro; you need to *make* the announcement. And any dissent - Kreme-King, Burr, Bogs – you gotta crush it, and quick! We need to take care of this swiftly, you got it? I need to show solidarity and commitment to my *other* boys, the big boys. Yeah….they think you and I don't have our shit together, that we're not united, not real, just a bunch of pretenders; we need to show them the organization, *The Drin,* is solid. Yeah, okay, let me get outta here, before it gets light."

Button listened, took a long toke, and dropped the butt, crushing it with his heel. He dug a little grave for it, kicked it in, and smoothed over the soil with the side of his boot.

"Thanks, but no, I can handle it solo – *need* to handle it solo. I don't know, some jerk-off from somewhere, somewhere, shooting off his mouth; nobody I know. Trust me, it won't be a problem; he'll be dealt with, and he'll be gone. You wouldn't know him, some nobody whitebread from somewhere else. No! His name is….what the fuck is it? I can't remember; who the fuck cares?"

Dr. Pool cut him off; Button gripped the phone hard, kicking the sand, getting more impatient.

"I know! Listen, I can't remember the stupid fucking name, okay?!"

Then Button's nose flared and his lips curled in disgust; he remembered.

"*Brin*, that's it….Cord fucking *Brin*."

CHAPTER 147 – SHE WAS SMILING, JUST A BIT

Monday, July 10th; early evening in Belvidere – day eighty-two. Two hours south, Black Dog and Mr. Chills have been stacked below ground in a slow, cooked rot; have been for a week.

C stood in the shower, stiff-armed against the wall, holding himself up; the scalding water cascaded over his down-turned head. He took an evening shower to try and relax….reset.

His eyes were lightly closed and he breathed calmly. But his mind raced; a freight train that simply wouldn't slow.

Thoughts streamed, came and went, in no particular order or level of import; he weaved a jagged path.

- Lilly was first-up - thinking about her tight little ass, and how much he wanted that ass, to see it – rather, for her to *want* to show it – that's what he *really* wanted. For her to lift that little black skirt, sans panties, wearing those sexy black pumps she had. He thought about drilling her in the ass, and his cock responded. He started to jerk-off; thoughts of tapping her slow and steady in the butt, with her dress pushed up and pumps on, moaning, low and long. God, that was some good stuff.
- Yet somehow, involuntarily, that morphed into Button fucking her, since he knew that's what she *really* wanted. How could she pick that fucking jerk-off over him? His cock shriveled in his hand, and he dropped it in disgust….motherfucker.
- He switched gears; Earl was next, both of them looping the Park. He thought about how much easier it had become; he opened his eyes and looked at his stomach, which was flatter than it had been in years. The upper rows started to

show, very cool; he wondered how it compared to Button, how strong he was, how ripped he was, and could C compete in the body department when it came to Lilly. Probably not, not yet, probably not, but maybe soon - he had to keep working on it. Fuck, looking down, suddenly his stomach maybe didn't look as good as he thought, likely nowhere near as good as that asshole's. Mother fucker.

- He shook his head to reset, to get off the subject of that asshole, to think of something good. Up popped Panama and snorkeling with Earl, and finding the *other* Earl – the little blue fish – and the big lobsters hiding in the coral outcrops, and how happy Earl would be; C smiled to himself.
- To the deeply cracked skin on his left heel, and how he could feel the dull throb of pain as he pushed his foot into the pooled water, waiting to exit the shower pan drain.
- To work and fruit inventory, tomorrow's order, including replacing last weeks bad batch of *carambola*....disappointing.
- To Mae, and fucking Mae doggie-style *tonight;* he was in the mood to fuck her good and hard. He would think about Samantha, her neighbor's niece, in that little Catholic–school dress, like he had been almost every time he fucked Mae, recently anyway. His dick paid attention, and started up again; he got hard thinking about pumping that little college sweetie in the shower, her firm, tiny tits pressed hard against the stall, moaning, stripped of her school dress, with black panties looped around one ankle. But just like that, Samantha dissolved into Lilly, and C morphed into Button, and his dick went soft a second time. And that got him pissed; he'd have to kill that fucker for *this* nonsense alone.
- Work....think about work.
- Which dissolved into the Georgia-Pacific Brownfield parcel, and running some initial pro-

forma calculations and end-user options, and discussing it with Carol.

- Carol; he just thought about Carol in general. He was pretty good, pretty disciplined, at avoiding mind-fucking her; it just felt wrong, for Earl's sake.
- To Lilly again - nothing in particular, just an image of her, her face, sporting that pirate smile she would sometimes cast his direction – he loved when she flashed that smile....he felt special.
- To Selena, and invariably, to London, outside London. Fucking London....Jesus, he didn't like to think about that – he rarely did. Where did that come from?
- To Kansas, the farm, to her, the bad ending, the darts. He quickly switched gears.
- Back to Earl, nothing in particular came to mind.
- And to Button; the road always seem to end with that shit-head. Where the fuck was this pussy anyway, besides constantly crawling around in his head?

He stepped toward the shower wall and lightly rapped his head against the stall. It was going to happen soon, he could feel it. He'd meet that jerk-off and it would end badly, like it always did. There was *always* a new jerk-off to meet.

He reset and tried to think of something better, something to jerk off to. Lilly? Mae? Samantha? He stroked his cock while he decided what offered the best shot. He was semi-hard at best, half-trying to get stiff, but he couldn't get the thought of Button out of his head. He looked down and the half-interest shrank to none....*fucking asshole*.

He gave up.

If he was going to Mae's, wasting a shot in the shower was a dumb move anyway; he needed all the stamina he could muster for her marathons, especially since she was still *quasi-punishing* him, got in another funk, and didn't give it up *once* last week, the first time she held out that long, and he knew she likely wouldn't go a second week dry. Her ploy worked too, because C wanted that senior pussy in the worst way, even if it would be wearing Samantha's skirt in his head.

The water running over his ears had muffled the sound, till Earl finally opened the bathroom door and yelled.

"C, come on! We're gonna be late for class! Lilly will be *really* mad; she hates when people are late! Then she makes the class even harder, *real hard,* even hard for me!"

C was annoyed.

"What's that mean? *Even hard for you* means what - fucking impossible for me?"

Earl didn't answer, he just put his head down. Like usual, Chicken, eyes already closed, was wrapped around his shoulders, like a scarf. Whenever Earl came into C's apartment, Chick came running, her tail shaking wild in excitement, so he could scoop her up onto his shoulders, where she would sit, or lay, for as long as Earl would stay, watching the world from her favorite perch.

"Sorry C."

Cord frowned, mad at himself for snapping at his friend, who was simply telling the truth.

"No, I'm sorry; I'm just in a bad mood. You're right, can't be late; I'll be ready in a minute."

Earl was wearing his bright purple *Rican* spandex shorts, which accentuated each sinew in his massive legs; he had on a white tee-shirt, an extra-extra-large, and it was still too small. Cord wore his black biker shorts, along with a blue guinea-tee; he saw himself in the mirror and looked like a junior-high-schooler standing next to Earl, pre-puberty. That didn't help his mood.

"Can I bring Chicken?"

"No, Earl, let Chick stay here; you can come back over and visit her later."

Chicken stretched and yawned on Earl's shoulders, then stood up and placed her paw on his ear.

He laughed, since it tickled, and cradled his big mitt around her belly, placing her gently on the floor; she stayed and rubbed on his leg….hoping to get a ride up the elevator once again.

"Who's cat is that anyway? Apparently not mine."

"She loves both of us, C."

"Yeah, whatever."

C said, annoyed at Chicken ignoring him.

"Bye, Chicken *Teriyaki;* bye Chicken *Chimichanga.*"

Earl said, waving to the cat as they headed for the door; Chicken just sat motionless, blinking her saucer eyes once or twice, stoic, watching the two of them leave, not a care in the world.

The walk over to the Red Mill was quiet. Cord was brooding, and Earl knew not to talk when C got like that. Head down, Earl dodged stones and twigs, trying to walk quietly. Soon it became a game, and he was hop-scotching alongside C, like a little girl.

C looked at his friend and smiled small to himself, but he didn't say a word. Soon enough, the darkness passed, and Cord was better again.

A poster on the bulletin board listed times for cardio classes, floor and step aerobics, circuit training and intervals. The strength classes - free weights, tubing and *Bosu* Balls, all had slots open.

"What the fuck is a *Bosu* Ball?"

C asked Earl, who was stretching next to him, in the hallway.

"*Both sides up.*"

Came a demure voice from behind Ay, off his right shoulder.

C turned to see a waifish women, about his age, but with the classic lines and muscularity of a long black cat. Her retro-hair was thin and arrow-straight, obsidian, dropping to six inches below her tiny shoulders. Her skin shone porcelain, and revealed not a blemish. It was almost too-white, pent-up white, effaced of all detail. She seemed frail. C felt he had to speak in a hushed tone, as if a raised voice would somehow damage her.

"Oh, sorry. Thank you, thanks."

C actually got a bit flustered.

Her eyes were dark brown, slightly inset, and penetrated him with a soulful gaze. How did he never catch wind of this one in the three months he had been tooling about Town?

"It's an inflatable rubber ball, half ball, actually; it helps with balance and strength training. It's pretty easy, once you get the hang of it. Lots of skiers and snow-boarders use them; do you snowboard?"

Earl snickered.

C glared at him, annoyed at the mock.

No, not a snowboarder."

C responded sarcastic, directed at Earl.

"He does push-ups and sit-ups and leg lifts *every* day! He did forty-seven today!"

Earl gushed, bragging about C's exercises, not realizing how pathetic and embarrassing the statement really was, especially to someone clearly as athletic as the woman standing before him.

"Earl, stop helping, please. I'm cycling up, and, well, you know...."

C's voice trailed off.

"No problem, I get it; I do the same thing every day....*Cord*. My name's Margery."

He looked at her cocked, wondering how she knew his name. She responded to the blank gaze.

"I assumed you were him, you fit the description. I hear quite a few stories about you from Lillian."

"Good God, that's all I need; should I leave now?"

She laughed and tilted her head at him, like one does when they are comfortable, and want to show it.

C couldn't take his eyes off her, her pouty lips, thin eyelashes and light, wispy eyebrows. She had forever long legs, with slightly knocked knees. Her hands, her fingers, were long, and delicate. She had a classic beauty, yet she wore a tired face. She had the look, the feel, of a ballet dancer, which C later learned she once was....long ago.

His eyes dropped and he stared at her small breasts, pancaked under her tights; he looked, but couldn't see the outline of her nipples. She saw his not-so-subtle stare, and ignored it, letting him graze as long as he wanted. And that complicit gesture wasn't lost on Cord.

"Actually, Lillian compliments you, at times anyway. With her, any compliment is a endorsement."

"Really? Compliments? Maybe I should sit down."

C said sarcastic, to which Margery smiled again.

"Well it wasn't always that way; you got pretty pummeled early on, still do, on occasion. But for the most part, I think she likes you."

"Jesus Margery, I don't *like* him; he's usually an asshole. And he's gonna get *punished* tonight!"

Lilly pushed by C, purposely knocking Ay's shoulder as she passed between the two of them, making her way into the large exercise room.

"C, stop flirting with Margie and get your butt in here. Earl, you too! Let's go!"

And with that, Lilly donned her game face. *Lilly The Instructor;* a little power in Lilly's hands was always dangerous.

Margery held out her hand to shake C's.

"Well, I'll let you get ready for class; Lillian is a tough instructor, right Earl?"

Earl shook his head emphatically. He was usually too scared to even look at Margery, but with C nearby, he was okay.

"Why are you here so late? Do you teach along with Lilly?"

"No *[she chuckled light]*. Lilly is pretty much a drill sergeant in her classes; it's best to let her be alpha. Since we're open late anyway, I like to come down and stretch, prepare mentally, when I do my routine: *passé, releve, plie*….you know."

It was clear in his eyes that C really didn't know what she was talking about.

"They're different movements of the feet and knees, in ballet, lifting onto your toes and such….boring perhaps, but therapeutic. I also work out new routines for some of the classes *I* run: pilates, yoga and ballet. They're more my speed; Lillian is into the rougher stuff: kick-boxing and Tae Bo….that's not me. I let her run with it; the two of us get along pretty well, as I'm sure she's told you."

Actually, Lilly had *never* mentioned Margery to Cord, not once, not ever, since the day he came to Town three months ago.

"Yeah."

Cord lied.

"Well, nice to finally meet you; have a good workout, and be sure to…."

"Hey! Ass-Munch! The class is starting! Don't walk in here after I start!"

Lilly barked to Cord and Earl, over Margie.

With that, Margery laughed and turned to walk down the hall, ducking into a small workout room. C watched the entire stroll, until she disappeared into the room.

"Hey! Last call! Earl, grab your girlfriend and get in here!"

C and Earl jogged into the room and stood in the back row.

The students, about twenty of them in toto, including the two boys, milled about in three loose lines, stretching and jogging in place, waiting for the drill instructor to begin. The class consisted of mostly thick-set, loose-bottomed, middle-aged women, with a couple college-aged girls sprinkled in. They had big asses too. This must have been the big-ass class.

Earl and Cord were the only males, except for a super-slim, toned twenty-something in the front row, front and center, directly in front of Lilly. He rounded the male contingent.

Earl didn't notice the other man at first, but his jaw dropped when he did.

"Oh boy C, we're in *big trouble;* Harvey's here."

"Harvey? Harvey who? So what?"

Earl pointed to the front row, at the back of Harvey's head; the man was switching between stretching and rapid-fire shadow boxing.

"Harvey's in the best shape ever! Even *better* than Lilly! *[Earl whispered the last part; no way did he want Lilly to ever hear him say that]* Whenever he comes, Lilly tries to make the workout harder, to get him tired, but it never works! Harvey just laughs at her, and she gets mad, and makes it even harder. And then he laughs more! Nobody can ever keep up with him! Oh boy, this isn't good C, not good at all. We're in *big* trouble!"

"Great."

Was all C could get out when Lilly commanded the floor.

She looked ahead and ignored Harvey completely; she definitely had her game face on.

"Okay girls, and Earl, were gonna go hard tonight, good workout, lots of blood pumping….no mercy."

"You go girl! *Ow!*"

Harvey said in an overly effeminate tone, pointing his finger teasingly at Lilly, partly to mock her, and partly because that was who he was, and how he spoke; he apologized to no one for it. He was an opinionated, outspoken and supremely self-confident young man, who just happened to be *uber*-gay.

"Hey Fuck-Nuts, if you don't keep quiet, I'm throwing you out! Understand?"

Harvey smiled at her.

"Oh, gut shot *[Harvey faked being shot]*! Okay girls, *and Earl,* let's get it *on!*"

Harvey chanted as he turned around to look at the back row of women; that's when he first saw C, standing next to Earl.

"Oh sorry, didn't see you two; hey Earl, who's your little friend?"

Harvey purred the end of the sentence. Earl put his head down and didn't answer; Harvey made him nervous.

C ignored the inference, like he always did. Gay men, and street beggars, always called him out as a mark, regardless of how many people passed by. He never considered himself approachable, he rarely spoke, usually wore a scowl and never made eye contact; how did that signal he was an easy target to dig in his pocket for loose change? He never got it. The gays, same thing; he always got the eye and shitty grin – why, he never knew. He certainly didn't lean in that direction; C was lots of things, but gay wasn't one of them. Maybe it was the bald head and bare ankles.

Harvey cocked a devilish grin and turned back toward Lilly, while talking to Earl, behind him.

"I'm gonna *try* and keep up with your sister, Earl, she's a real…."

Lilly cut him short.

"If you don't shut up, you are *so gone* Harvey, out of here, fucking tossed.   And I'm so gonna so crush you tonight….humiliation!"

The girls in the class laughed at the banter; Cord and Earl looked scared.

"Ow! Bring it on girl!"

Harvey put both his hands on his hips and gave her a hearty pelvic thrust, an exclamation on the taunt.

And with that, the kickboxing class began.

C took a deep breath:

"Pace yourself, pace yourself; you can do this."

He whispered; it was all the advise he could muster for himself. He wanted to show Lilly he was in good shape, that he wasn't an old man. The gut that stepped off the bus with him in April was largely gone, and running with Earl had actually become enjoyable; he could talk and run at the same time, and he was generally feeling better about himself. Maybe he would surprise Lilly and keep up; maybe she would be impressed, for once.

That was the plan anyway.

The warm-up was abbreviated. Lilly was fired up, ready to deal with Harvey; she invariably would try to break him, and would never succeed. That little queer was in amazing shape, better than Lilly, and the harder Lilly ramped the workout, the more he reveled in it, breathing lightly, laughing, and taunting her the whole time. And she *knew* he was in better shape, and she hated that feeling. At *half* the taunts, any other man would have gotten his nut-sack kicked-in long ago, but Lilly tolerated Harvey, and even though she treated him with utter disdain, and even though she would never admit it, Lilly actually liked him….one of the few men she did.

Why, neither one really knew.

Less than five minutes in, the pace was already killer. They had already cycled through a series of front-side semi-circular roundhouse kicks, spinning sidekicks, jumping back-kicks, spinning hook-kicks and crescent kicks.

C was utterly lost; this was no class for beginners. It didn't help he couldn't lift his leg much above thigh height; flexibility was always a problem. He tried to hide it, but he needed more oxygen, much more oxygen; his cheeks were flushed and his thighs cramping.

They were only five minutes in; the class was an hour.

By the eight-minute mark, C was spent, gasping for air; and the worse part was, he really thought he was in shape. He was pissed, but too busy breathing to show it.

Earl was smiling, a walk in the park. Harvey was still in first gear, chatting away with the girls to his left and right; it looked as if he was wondering when the class was going to start.

Fucking bastard C thought to himself, his face the color of an apple. He kept looking up at the clock on the workout room wall; he swore it clicked backwards.

At ten minutes, C was done, winded, dizzy and cramped. He stumbled out of line and crumpled against the wall; the very first casualty in dodge-ball. He didn't even look up; he simply wanted to leave, mortified with his performance, or lack thereof. He grabbed a pinch of skin on his stomach and squeezed hard, mad at himself....fucking stomach.

Normally, Lilly would have had a wisecrack lined up; he was waiting for it. But she barely noticed Cord's departure; she was focused on the lithe competition facing her, and his ignominious exit was met with silence. Come to think of it, that was probably worse; an insult from her was better than nothing. How pathetic was that?

Lilly couldn't be bothered with all that, not tonight; tonight winning mattered much more than taunting C....*much* more.

The second victim went down at the fifteen minute mark, quickly followed by three more.

With a quarter of the class sitting against the wall, most instructors would crank it down, take a short breather, water break, whatever, and re-inject the stragglers into the workout – rattle off a group *high-five* for effort; everyone's a winner.

Not Lilly; not this class. No chance.

This was Lilly's world; there was no pity. And if you kick-boxed with her, you knew what to expect. And when Harvey showed up, it was nothing more than a dual, a two-some, with the rest of the class hanging on for dear life, while the playground round-about spun faster and faster still.

Earl was still in good shape, lowly whistling *Neighbors* tunes while jogging in place, reeling off diagonal kicks, mixed with short-straights and spinning back-fists, one after another, a gazelle the size of a dinosaur.

Harvey was in a particularly mischievous mood, tossing dangerous digs at Lilly with abandon, ignoring completely the bomb he was fiddling with. Earl was smart enough to enjoy the teasing from the relative safety of the back row; he was no dummy.

Prompted by Harvey's antics, the *Oh Say, Can You Say, Polite Things All Day* newspaper article popped in Earl's head, the one-liners from the self-help list Carol sent him for Lilly, along with that October invitation to the *Indian Summer Bacchanalia,* the *best* invitation he ever got, even if it was really the only one he ever got. But if he ever got another one, Carol's would still be the best; he was sure of it. Earl smiled thinking about it, and Carol; he couldn't wait to go. Carol was so pretty, and she always smelled *really* good, like flowers. And her teeth were really straight and white, and she had the coolest little tiny gap in her front teeth; he bet that would be the best gap ever for whistling. Maybe she would whistle *Neighbors* tunes with him! October 7th was his birthday, his *fortieth,* and Carol's party was October 14th; October was going to be the best month *ever!* He started counting the days in his head until the party; the last time he checked it was one-hundred-twelve. It has to be less now; it just *has* to be! How many days were there in July? He was getting flustered, trying to count the days, to figure the math in his head; then he heard the familiar screech.

"Earl! Pay attention! We're on stick-kicks! *Stick-kicks!* **Come on, keep up!"**

Lilly jolted him back to reality, and he was mad she ruined his Carol daydream, and messed up his math.

"Stop being a cranky pants!"

Earl yelled from the back row; that was his mom's favorite line to throw at Lillian when she acted up. And as long as Earl was talking directly to his sister, he wasn't nervous speaking in front of all these people; at least not *as* nervous.

The row of drop-outs along the back wall laughed at Earl's retort to Lillian, which stoked an already enraged Lilly.

"I'm sorry, are you talking to me?"

Lilly barked sarcastically, never missing a beat in her stick-kicks.

Okay, this was war; Lilly messed up his math, and his Carol daydream, and that just wasn't very nice. So Earl reached for his best, but also his most dangerous, weapon against his sister....Carol. He rarely reached for that loaded gun. But he pulled Carol from the holster anyway.

Earl had memorized all one hundred *Polite Things* to say....all of them. He scanned the list in his brain, loaded the chamber and started firing.

"No. 98 – I appreciate your kindness!"

Earl yelled from the back row.

Lilly shot him a wicked glare; she knew exactly was he was doing, what he was reciting, and the Carol reference infuriated her. She threw in agitated straight knee thrusts, one after another.

"Keep it up Earl; just keep it up!"

Lilly growled through pursed lips.

"No. 85 – What a great smile you have!"

Lilly stared hard at Earl; she wasn't kidding.

"One more Earl, just one more and you are gonna regret it."

"No. 21 – I'm sorry."

He said to himself, barely above a whisper.

Lilly saw his lips move.

"What did you say?!"

Lilly snarled. Then Harvey jumped in the pool.

"Is this workout gonna start or what; when's the warm-up over?"

Lilly went ballistic.

"Hey jackass, and you too Earl, No. 200 – The Roundhouse Nut-Crunch is coming next, so both of you shut the fuck up!"

Harvey laughed and thrust his pelvis toward Lilly, taunting her to take a free swing. Earl instinctively took two steps back; he knew better – let Harvey take the fall – he could always apologize later. Earl was a survivor.

The burst of angry adrenaline juiced Lilly and a furious round of jabs and kicks ensued; the hangers-on dropped like flies.

By the twenty-five minute mark, the pace increased yet again, Lilly was trying to shake Harvey, with no luck. The class of twenty had dwindled to four, two college-age Tae-Bo fanatics, Earl and, of course, Harvey.

The rest of the class huddled against the back wall, sucking oxygen and cheering for their favorite survivors.

The pace was finally getting to Earl; no more *Neighbors* whistling or *Polite* recital games. He was breathing heavy, his giant chest heaving, searching for any air it could suck in. One of the Tae-Bo girls dropped, kicking the mat in disgust. The crowd around the perimeter cheered her effort.

Now it was down to just three....and Lilly.

That's when Harvey chimed up, this time in a no-nonsense tone, in as masculine a baritone his effeminate pipes could muster. He pointed ominous at Lillian as he spoke.

"Okay, gloves off, you follow *my* pace, until I drop you bitch, like a bad habit. I **own** you girl, always have."

A spontaneous cheer erupted from the sidelines; a cacophony of whoops and calls for Lilly, Earl, Tae-Bo Stephanie and Harvey, each with a fan base. The raucous stirred Margery from down the hall.

Lilly was zoned, her eyes scary wild. She answered terse, sans emotion....two words were all she needed to say.

"Bring it."

The gauntlet was laid, and the room again went wild.

Only Lilly and Harvey could really survive the onslaught that was about to begin; for Stephanie and Earl, it was simply a fight for the bronze. Stephanie smiled at Earl and punched him lightly in the shoulder; he actually made eye contact and smiled, which meant more to Steph than anything else....she knew Earl rarely handed those out.

And so it began.

Lilly graciously passed the head of the class to Harvey, but she nary cracked a smile in the process, strictly game face, intense….focused. Harvey took front and center, with Lilly sliding into the front row. That alone was unheard of. Inside, Lilly seethed, waiting patiently for the fly to hit the web.

Like the peg of the tachometer tapping to red, the pace immediately exploded. Earl and Stephanie lasted just a shade over a minute; Earl could have gone longer, but he saw Steph fading fast, so he pretended to be too tired to continue, stumbled clumsily, and stopped before she did. Stephanie's girlfriends wildly cheered her win, and before Earl knew what happened, Steph bounded over to him and planted a big dry peck on his cheek; she had to jump up to reach.

The room went crazy cheering, and Earl froze, like he was shot. Then he smiled sheepishly, head down, and walked to the back of the room, his cheeks blushed.

A whisper came from behind C, who was now standing, leaning alone against the wall.

"He faked it."

It was Margery.

"I know."

Cord said, smiling wryly.

"That's what makes Earl….Earl."

Margery nodded in agreement, a thin smile creased her lips.

C turned to face her. She had slipped on a gray, oversized sweatshirt and black exercise pants atop her body suit, but she still looked thin, with a forever-long alabaster neck….a classic silhouette.

C's eyes wandered to her pussy, and he had the sudden urge to rip off her spandex, cut the crotch a la *Clockwork Orange,* and fuck her hard, violent, doggie-style, against her will. But, of course, she would quickly succumb, start moaning in wild pleasure and want it more, harder. They always do in a guy's mind; they always come to realize how much they want it, and need it, and how good a fuck he really is. Where had he been all her life? That's the conclusion the guy invariably comes too; that's why they call it a fantasy.

C's digression was cut short, snapped back to reality as Earl bumped him, slumping down to the floor, parking his ass against the wall.

"Good job buddy."

Cord said; Earl just smiled at his best friend. Margery patted him lightly on the back.

"But you better not tell Carol about that kiss from that little sweetie though; she could get jealous!"

C taunted. Earl looked positively horrified.

"I didn't know she was going to do that! I swear!"

C just smiled.

"Relax, your little secret is safe with me."

He looked up at Margery, who quickly crossed her chest.

"Me too, promise."

Earl let out a sigh of relief, and then whispered.

"Her lips are chapped, kinda crackly."

Both C and Margery chuckled.

The duel extended past two-and-a-half minutes, and neither was giving any ground, Lilly matching Harvey kick for kick, punch for punch. But it was clear Lilly was deep in the zone; her eyes were steel.

Without warning, at the four minute mark, she yelled aloud.

"Non-stop jumping side-kicks, till one drops! **Now!**"

And she proceeded to leap vertical and aggressively side kick the air, one after another, with Harvey in tow. Lilian picked Harvey's best exercise, the move he bragged about, the move he owned, above all others. No one beat Harvey in anything, but especially jumping side-kicks. He owned them.

The count-aloud from the crowd against the back wall quickly hit five, then ten….thirteen….seventeen; Lillian was a machine. But Harvey matched her kick for kick; she wasn't shaking him, certainly not in his signature move.

"Nineteen! Twenty! Twenty-one!"

And something strange began to happen.

Harvey was starting to breath heavy, sporting a thin wince with each thrust; the first chink that anyone had *ever* seen. He kept a brave face, but it was clear the workout was slowly taking its toll. Lilly was simply automaton, eyes a blank stare….her mind somewhere else.

"Twenty-two! Twenty-three!"

The crowd yelled in unison, each number shouted louder than the one before.

"Twenty-six! Twenty-seven! Twenty-eight!"

Finally, at an incredible twenty-nine non-stop jumping side-kicks, Harvey, legs numb, started to stumble sideways, and it was clear the building was going down; he tottered briefly, then fell ignominious to the mat; a clean knockout.

The room erupted in cheers; Harvey, sitting on his ass, knees pulled up to his chest like a girl, breathing heavy, and smiling. There were even small beads of sweat on his brow.

"Wow."

Was all he said, sans sarcasm. The man who couldn't shut up was at a loss for words. His first defeat, ever; *no one* out-kicked Harvey....no one except Lillian.

Lilly was so zoned, she still wasn't smiling; her hands clenched in tight fists by her sides.

Harvey quickly hopped up, already recovered, and started clapping, his hands raised high above his head. Everyone spontaneously joined in, the whole room pulsating to a rhythmic thunderous clap, with hoots and hollers thrown in, calling out, chanting, Lilly's name in victory.

Earl ran to the front of the room and kissed his big sister on the cheek, grabbed her by the hips, and like lifting a feather, hoisted her high in the air, well over his head, showing her off like a trophy....a proud brother. The proudest brother ever.

As he held her aloft, he gazed up at her and smiled, amidst the cacophony of cheers and applause.

Lillian's fists were finally unclenched, and she was smiling, just a bit.

CHAPTER 148 – INTO THE POWER RACK THEY WENT

"What was that about?"

Buck said, leaning over C, hand on his shoulder, catching the die-down of the applause, a group of attendees still circling Lilly, like a rock star.

"How long have you been here?"

"Just walked in; you said nine right? A little early."

Buck pulled out his cell phone to confirm the time.

"It's was all about Lilly being Lilly."

C said.

"She *always* wins when she *really* wants to; she did that 'cause you were here."

Earl whispered; Buck shook his head in agreement.

C frowned in disbelief.

"It's true man, trust me, I can tell; she likes you."

"I told you!"

Earl yelped.

"Yeah, the girl who called me an ass-munch, but in an *affectionate* way."

C said sarcastically, and followed himself.

"Just drop it."

Cord wanted to believe them, but Lilly ran so hot and cold, he stopped trying long ago to figure her out. And then there was always the back issue of Button; if that guy showed up, when that guy showed up, he knew he'd be forgotten, dropped in a heartbeat. Maybe, just *maybe*, Lilly might remember C's name, that's about it. Cord was feeling sorry for himself, and got pissed that she had that grip on him, and he really couldn't do anything about it. That's usually how love works, and as much as he wouldn't admit it aloud, C was stone in love with Lillian Liddell, had been from day one at Sam's.

Buck spoke up.

"Listen, here's the deal with her; if Lilly doesn't give a shit about you, which is, like, ninety-eight percent of the guys out there, she ignores you, completely. If she likes you, which is one percent, she treats you like shit; and since you're the current shit-burger, she likes you….trust me."

"Yeah, and what about the other one percent?"

Before he asked, Cord knew the answer, and was pissed he even put the question out there, public.

"That's Button, and there's no competing with that, ever, not with her, anyway. Sorry man."

Buck slapped C on the back.

"What are you sorry for? I'm not competing with that guy."

C said, but no one believed it.

"Jerk-face."

Earl muttered to himself. And then the subject changed.

"So why am I here, wearing these ugly shorts? What are we doing?"

Buck pushed on C's shoulder.

"Well, it was *supposed* to be a little experiment, but now that Lilly went crazy in class and spent Earl, I doubt it will be much of a show."

Harvey had gathered his belongings, said his goodbyes, gave cheek-kisses all around, and exited; the main event was over. Lillian resumed the class, at a slow pace, for the early drop-outs who wanted to get a bit more work in. Everyone was chatting rapidly about *The Duel*, as it quickly came to be known, laughing and talking over one another. For once, Lilly let the idle talk go on; she was still in a good mood with her victory, soaking up the adulation.

"What kind of experiment?"

Buck asked.

C looked at Earl and placed his hand flat on his broad chest.

"Hey, you spent? Or you want to try a little bit of that squatting stuff I told you about?"

"I'm okay! I promise! I'd like to try Ay; I'm okay, I'm okay….promise."

Earl *was* spent, and he wasn't really that okay, but he liked to try anything new, as long as it was with C, so he fibbed, just a little.

"Okay, okay; were gonna do a little squat workout."

Cord turned to Buck.

"You want to lift too? See what you can do?"

"Of course! How do you think I got these massive trunks!"

Buck pulled up his extra-long baggy shorts, two-sizes too big, and flexed his skinny, bony leg; Earl snickered.

"Hey!"

Billy mocked insult.

"Cool. I got a hunch about Earl, although after that stupid workout with Lilly, we'll probably go light….lighter anyway."

Margery had left the room earlier, missing the Lilly/Harvey finale. She was at her desk, staring blankly at the wall in front of her, deep in thought, when the three of them passed on their way to the gym, in the basement of the old mill.

"Hey, were going down to the gym….wanna come?"

C proffered.

Margery shook out of her trance; after a pause, she answered, in an upbeat tone.

"Sure."

And with that, the four of them made their way downstairs.

C turned the corner and was caught off-guard. The set-up was surprisingly hardcore; free weights, tons of Olympic plates neatly set on weight-trees, including, it must be, at least ten hundred-pounders at a quick glance, along with a rubber-padded deadlift platform, a competition-grade flat bench for pressing and a beefy power rack for squatting. It was the kind of equipment you only see in real power-lifting gyms.

"Holy shit, pretty impressive; does anybody use this place? *[C turned to Margery]* I mean, this is a serious set-up – competition quality stuff, not some candy-ass gym."

"My fiancé is a pretty serious lifter; we, well me really, bought this stuff mainly for him and his lifting buddies. Anybody can use it, with their membership, but you're right, most don't; they're looking for Smith machines, and universals, that stuff is in the room next door. Anybody lifting is lifting in there, for the most part; this stuff scares 'em. This stuff is really for him and his muscle-head friends."

The only thing C heard in that soliloquy was *fiancé*, the rest of it blurred into background static. Fuck! Figures she has a boyfriend; why wouldn't she? Immediately, his interest in learning more about Margery, and engaging in a series of playful banter, to see how far he could get with her, innuendo and not-so-accidental body contact, which was the plan swirling in his head just seconds before, withered on the vine.

He was so fucking shallow; he knew it, and didn't care one lick.

But that immediate withdrawal reaction was always short term. Actually, fiancé and husband were words C longed to hear; he always went for the women who were attached. And the stronger her relationship was, the stronger his desire to let out line and troll, to wait for a nibble. The challenge of taking another man's squeeze, the power in doing someone else's girlfriend, someone's wife, was intoxicating. It was the ultimate power trip, the ultimate measure of control; ownership in something he shouldn't own.

He really had no long-term interest in any of them, not a lick. And since he was always on his way somewhere else, long-term interest didn't make sense, on any level. But to get a women who was crazy in love, who was happy, a woman not on the prowl, a woman who hadn't an unfaithful thought in her head - to get *that* woman to stray, to suck his cock, to open her legs....it was an opiate.

He wouldn't trade that *game* for anything; it was simply too much fun to know he was doing some other guys' girl. And for a man with little patience, his patience was unending in this regard. He was like the incoming tide; tiny, imperceptible advances, casual lines continually crossed, which over time morphed into her looking forward to the attention, enjoying the attention, her own secret narcotic, all the while her rationalizing, the technicalities cited over and again, as to how this really didn't count, while C rubbed her shoulders, gently ran his fingers, light as a feather, down her spine, and kissed the back of her neck.

If he befriended the guy, hung out, played poker, drank together – talked about fucking girls – asking if his wife was a good fuck – telling him how *oh-so-lucky* he was to have such a lovely wife, such a faithful wife, that was simply sugar on top.

And C was a guy's kind of guy; invariably, awash in ignorance, the husband, the boyfriend, whoever they were, they always liked him; Cord was just a likeable guy. And he was always amazed at how gullible these schmucks really were.

And in the beginning, in the middle, and in the end, he felt no tinge of regret, no sorrow, no sympathy....nothing.

Cord was a dog, plain and simple. And he didn't give a rat's ass that he was, or about what he was doing, or who he hurt in the process. In that regard, amongst many others, C was a fucking bastard....a real prick.

He smiled to himself at the thought, and turned his attention back to the stack of weights before them, and the new challenge standing beside him.

"Okay, big guy, I don't think you need to stretch, but I do, since I didn't last too long at the Lilly-fest upstairs. Buck, you should stretch too. Hey Margery, are you gonna try? Have you ever squatted?"

"Walt is always trying to get me under the bar; no interest. But I'll stretch with you guys; I like to stretch. I'll do it down here sometimes when Walt and the boys lift."

Walt? C tried to picture a 'Walt' as a musclehead lifting in this gym. 'Walt' didn't seem to fit the image. He wondered what numbers he pushed; guys always focus on other guys' numbers, and no matter the number, they always figure they're lying about them, inflating the weights. That's just what guys do.

C's mind wandered from pumping weights to picturing Walt pumping Margery's pussy on the flat bench, right next to where she was stretching. He figured she must have gotten nailed down here at least once, probably dozens of times; he knows he would have done her here if she came down to stretch while he lifted. C was sure that pussy hair was dark black, but shaved to a landing strip, or less; he just knew it. A ballet dancer with a full bush? No way, and he was disappointed in that fact. He should be pumping Margery, not that guy; he should have Jessie's Girl. He knew he could get her to spread if he tried. He figured she liked him; why else would she have followed them down to the gym? That was good enough for him; maybe he would pursue her....give it a shot.

That whole sequence passed through C's head in about three seconds, like a car passing by, it came and went. If Margery only knew how Cord's mind raced in circles, shifting gears, fits and starts, weaving out of control, and fucking her along the way.

But Margery knew none of that; instead of that jumbled mess of carnal thoughts ricocheting between C's ears, all Margery heard was this:

"Not me, stretching is worse than lifting; flexible I'm not."

C said as he grimaced, trying to stretch his hamstrings.

Margery looked at Cord's bad attempt at stretching and cracked a slight grin; he wasn't anything like Lilly described. He seemed likable enough, harmless….a real nice guy.

Earl joined them anyway, and the four sat and chatted while they stretched, a fluid display of extended arms and spread legs, accompanied by grunts and groans from male tendons which simply wouldn't cooperate. Margery smiled at the spectacle, bent like a pretzel.

And the more C looked at her, the more he wanted to bang her. She seemed so nice, easygoing, laid back and self-assured, a real pleasure to talk to. He had no worry about saying the wrong thing and getting a kick to the groin to mark the mistake.

And man, was she *flexible*. Walt, that bastard, was a lucky man. And, for just a second, he forgot all about Lilly.

"What are you doing down here Margie? You don't *lift*; don't think Walt would like you down here flirting with my brother and….and...."

Lilly was going to call Buck and C his *girlfriends*, but she used that tired one-liner too many times, and she hadn't come up with a quick replacement, so she sputtered at the punchline.

"What, running short on insults? It's typically *girlfriend*, in case you forgot."

C said, trying like hell to touch his toes. Margery chuckled and didn't answer Lilly's question, but rather asked her own.

"Everyone left; done early?"

They kept yapping and weren't doing anything I told them anyway, so I pulled the plug. They didn't care; they're happy, especially since I put that little-shit Harvey in his place."

Margery didn't even ask for an explanation of that one.

Lilly sloughed it off and straddled the bench next to Margery, who didn't seem too bothered that Lilly ended her class early and barged in on the party. Maybe she wasn't interested after all. If she was, C would have expected just a little attitude; she gave none. Maybe she *did* just want to stretch....and maybe she was mad in love with Walt. Shit, another fantasy shuffled to the back burner....for now.

C gave up on any more muscle-coaxing.

"Okay, let's start. I'll go first, just the bar, to show you how to do it Earl, and you too Buck, unless you've done it before."

"A little bit, in school, but not really."

Buck said sheepish.

"Are you gonna lift?"

C looked over at Lillian. She laughed mockingly.

"No, I'm here solely for the entertainment factor; I hope you lift better than you kick-box."

Margery smiled at the banter, flipped on the radio and played with the dial, till she found a familiar voice.

Money For Nothing was just starting, and into the power rack they went.

CHAPTER 149 – AM I GONNA BE SORE TOMORROW?

The squat flight went Buck, Cord, then Earl. The first set of ten reps was simply the empty power bar across their shoulders, all of forty-five pounds.

45 X 10

It was simply meant to get the blood flowing, to practice form and to get pointers from C - how to grip the bar, where it should sit across the shoulders, setting your feet, setting the height of the power rack pins mid-chest, ensuring knees didn't lean forward, squatting till your hips break parallel, taking in air and holding it for the rep, head up, chest up, racking the bar; the whole works.

Earl and Buck gave a joint look of bewilderment; it seemed like an awful lot of rules and things to remember just to bend down and stand up again with some weight across your shoulders. Sounded pretty simple.

C saw the skeptical look from the both of them, and responded to the silence.

"Hey, when it gets heavy, all that stuff is gonna matter, or you'll only end up squatting in one direction – *down*, with no up. That weight will fold you in half and plant you in the floor if you're not careful; trust me, been there."

From there it went to a set at one hundred pounds; a twenty-five pounder on each side, along with the two-and-a-half pound snap-clamps, to hold the weights in place.

100 X 10

Again ten reps at a low weight, mostly to work on their form....slow steady reps. Easy stuff.

Lilly was already bored; time to stir the pot.

"Wow, that's pretty impressive lifting; I'm sure Walt would run scared when you animals show up at the gym."

C sighed long.

"You know, it was pleasant down here till you came, the three of us and Margery, all having a nice talk, no snide remarks, no sarcasm, nothing; don't you have something to do?"

"Yeah, watch this comedy routine. What do you think Margery; animals, aren't they?"

"They're just warming up Lilly."

Lilly shot her a condescending look and said, sarcastically, not caring a lick that the disdain was aimed at her boss.

"Oh, sorry."

Cord smiled.

"Thanks Margie."

"Hey, you don't get to call her that, only Walt does."

"*You* call her Margie."

C said sarcastically.

"Well, Walt and me, then, but not *you*."

And with that, Margery went from smiling to visibly annoyed….at Lilly. Whenever Lilly entered a room, she had to be the center of attention, and it got tiring, especially for Margery, who was simply looking for some quiet downtime with new-found friends.

"I'm staying out of this; I gotta finish up my paperwork anyway. Have a good workout guys."

And just like that, she turned and disappeared.

"Nice, Lilly…thanks."

C said, annoyed. Buck and Earl didn't say a word, not risking a poke of the hornets nest.

"You're welcome….asshole."

"*Asshole?!* Why am I an asshole? You are unfucking believable; only you can walk in a room, fuck things up, and then blame someone else."

"What did I fuck up? Are you trying to date her? Fuck her? Walt will crush you like an ant!"

C's face immediately started to flush and he squeezed both hands into angry fists; he wanted to go over and just choke her, he really did. But he kept his cool, for once, and let out a long, steady snort of air from flared nostrils.

"I'm not buying in Lilly, not today, say whatever you want, talk to my back, I'm done debating. We're gonna lift, and that's it."

Without waiting for her to answer, C turned away, and summarily ignored her. He didn't hear her snort back, but she did.

"Okay, now were going to drop down and start with work sets of five, just to see how you do. Buck, what do you weigh, about one-sixty?"

"One-seventy-five."

"Really? Okay, you're going to top out around two-fifty or so, maybe two-seventy-five for a single. Just a gauge; we'll see how you do as we go up; two-seventy-five might be too much."

"What am I gonna top out at?"

Earl yelped like a little kid; he was so excited.

"That, my friend, is what we are here to find out *[Cord patted the big man on his chest]*. Safe to say it'll be north of two-seventy-five."

The first real set, with a single forty-five pound plate and lock-collar on each side, was scrawled by C on the chalkboard, by the power rack.

140 X 5

C punched out an easy five, as did Buck, trying to remember all the steps to follow. He ended up holding his breath for the entire set, and his face was apple-red at the end. Even though it was pretty easy, Buck was a bit wobbly with the mechanics, too much to remember. Earl was slow and methodical, his form perfect, even though he did his first squat of his life, at thirty-nine years old, about five minutes before. Since Earl was almost a foot taller than Cord, he had to hunch over quite a bit to get under the bar.

C scrolled the next set on the board.

190 X 5

The five reps looked decidedly tougher for Buck; the extra fifty pounds bowed his legs in a bit, knock-kneed, with his back starting to round out. C and Earl did perfunctory sets; again, Earl moving the weight in slow motion….effortless.

"Okay, let's move up a bit."

C said, unclamping one end of the bar and reaching for another forty-five pounder.

230 X 5

The strain was quickly showing on Buck; C saw it at the bar un-rack, when he had a tough time stabilizing his footing, shuffling around, trying to find what felt right….an awkward two-step.

"Hey, don't do five; just try two or three reps. Stay tight, take a deep breath of air and hold it - that's it. Down….head up!"

And with that, Buck went down and up, his knees caving on the upstroke, and his back rounding. He racked it at two reps and put his head down, sucking oxygen.

"Wow, I know I've done more than that before; that was fucking heavy!"

"Yeah, but you probably never did it right. You're going deep, man….breaking parallel with your hips - that makes all the difference in the world. Anybody can do big weights in a quarter or half-squat, making all sorts of grunts and noise, but not really doing the work. The key is to break parallel, that's the right way, and it'll knock serious pounds off what people think they can do.

1345

Most clowns in a gym don't come close to doing a real squat; it's always easy to pack more weight on the bar and cut the rep; the bar looks better in the gym mirror….that's all that matters to most guys."

Buck sat down, dejected, on the flat bench.

"I gotta get out here more often; this is pathetic."

He said, pinching the muscle on his scrawny thighs, milquetoast skin to boot.

C and Earl punched out five each, easy. Earl could have done them all day long.

Between their sets, C and the boys had to unload the weight, and put the rack-pins up three hole settings, since Earl was a foot taller. Back down the pins came after Earl was done; otherwise C would never be able to unrack the weight. The whole process added a full five minutes to the time between each guy's set, loading and unloading the bar, and moving the pins up and down, over and again. Moving the pins like this basically sucked; it was a workout in itself, the curse of short and tall guys lifting together, especially when the weights got heavy.

Cord let out a big breath of air.

"Okay, let's try a single at two-hundred-fifty pounds Buck; you should get it, after a bit of a rest. Earl, you and I are going straight to three plates; three-hundred-twenty, with the collars."

Buck – 250 X 1

With the bar loaded, and knowing he had to punch out just one, Buck gave a throaty grunt, got a quasi-adrenaline rush and on those spindly white-boy legs, surprisingly cranked the two-hundred-fifty slow and steady. When he finished the rep successfully, he racked the weight hard, and gave a bit of a hoot, pleased with himself, smiling wide.

The display prompted a question from C.

"That was great; was hoping you had it, and you did. It was good, but it was slow. Do you think you got another heavy in ya, or want to end on a good note, and close the books today at two-fifty?"

Buck thought a bit, but not for long; the testosterone in the room was thick, and there really was no doubt.

"Fucking-A! Let's do it; two-seventy-five!"

The bar was quickly loaded so Buck could follow himself; he sat on the press bench, resting, head down, eyes closed, hands covering his ears….getting psyched for the next rep.

Buck – 275 X 1

"Since you're gonna follow yourself, give yourself time, no rush; you tell us when you're ready. Come on man, get into it!"

The three sat in silence, Buck looking down at his sneakers, deep in concentration; he was slowly rocking back and forth on the bench. That's when C first noticed Lilly was gone. He turned to Earl.

"When did she leave?"

"Right after you turned your back on her; she wasn't happy, Ay."

"You know what Earl, too fucking bad. This is about us lifting tonight; not everything, all the time, is about her. Are you fucking ready man? **Let's go!**"

Cord slapped his hands together hard and turned and yelled over at Buck. Buck shot off the bench, clapped his hands and set himself under the bar, making all sorts of noise, barking and yelling, one word expletives and general static.

He took in a big air, and pulled off the weight. C could see his knees buckle a bit, and knew this was probably gonna bury him; all the self-pump in the world wasn't going to finish this rep. Cord quickly saddled up behind Billy, and as he went down, C mirrored the squat motion behind him, as a spot. As suspected, Buck struggled with the weight, fighting it on the way down, trying to control it. When he hit bottom, and tried to push up, he had nothing left, and his ass immediately went up in the air while the rest of him stayed down, quickly leveling to a ninety-degree angle, with two-hundred-seventy-five pounds of trouble laying heavy on the base of his neck. C firmly placed his hands around him and cupped his chest, pulling him back gently, and guiding him up, still making him work through the rep, even though C was doing the lion's share of the lift.

It was a long, slow ascent; Billy grimaced the whole trip, veins protruding from his crimson face and neck. He racked the weight, exhausted, legs wobbly and light-headed, with white stars flashing around his head. He grabbed the rack for stability, till his legs returned.

C clapped in encouragement.

"At least you didn't dump it; you came up, with a *little* help *[C smiled as he put his fingers together, depicting a 'little'; they both knew he was a liar]*. Well, now you at least know where you are, somewhere between two-fifty and two-seventy-five; we'll hit two-fifty-five next time and work from there, if you still want to lift, that is."

"Fuck yeah! God-damn it!"

Billy said, as he slapped the power rack in disgust.

"If you guys are gonna keep lifting, after today, I mean, I'm in. No way am I gonna end on *that;* that two-fifty was harder than it looked and my back was already in a knot; I shoulda waited longer till I tried the two-seventy-five. Next time, I think I could, maybe....I could get that."

Buck sat down, dejected, on the flat bench and tried to sit up straight, to stretch away the knot; no luck, it was hard as a rock. And even though C told him pushing that much on a first workout was nothing to be ashamed of, especially doing it right, going deep, it didn't help. He still felt like a loser, a weak loser; two-hundred-fifty? Really? Two-hundred-seventy-five shouldn't have been that hard; he should be knocking at three-hundred, not two-fifty....pathetic. Buck sat and brooded, shifting his ass to relieve the pain from the pretzel throbbing in his lower back.

C squeezed Buck's shoulder lightly in encouragement, then delivered the bad news.

"You think that's bad? Wait till tomorrow and the next day, that's when the sore *really* sets in."

C smiled; Buck just rolled his eyes and frowned.

"Okay, Earl, just you and me. Pull off all the small stuff and throw on another forty-five, the big plate, and the orange clamp - that's three-twenty. After this, let's drop to one to three reps each, to save strength, and see where we can go."

C scrolled sloppily on the chalkboard:

320 X 5

1349

C had been working out pretty regularly before coming to Belvidere, but for the last three months, since he stepped off that bus, he had been idle.   And he lost a bunch of weight to boot.   And he was curious how badly the combination would affect his strength. He was about to find out; this next set would be the first real test.

George Thorogood was lighting up the radio with *Who Do You Love:*

> *I've got a tombstone hand and a graveyard mind;*
>   *I'm just twenty-two and I don't mind dying.*

C exhaled hard, dipped under the bar, wrapping his middle finger on the ring amidst the burly knurling. He rubbed the steel bar back and forth on his back, finding that groove where it felt best, sucked in a lungful of air and held his breath as he stood up and took the weight off the pins. He shuffled back in a quick three-step to set his feet, looked skyward and dipped down, a deep rep.

> *Who do you love?*
> *Who do you love?*

The weight felt pretty good, no problems. He went down for four more; no strains, no sticking points, nothing to note. He held his breath for the first three reps, then exhaled and re-gulped for the last two. Ay stepped in and racked the bar; he exhaled deeply, hands still gripping the steel rod. He looked at himself in the mirror, his face flush with blood.

"That felt good, pretty good, better than I thought."

He said aloud, mostly to himself.

Earl smiled and got under the bar, imitating C to a tee. He held his breath for all five reps, which were embarrassingly easy. He looked to C for guidance, and approval. C shook his head and mockingly laughed.

"What? What do you want me to say? That the weight's a joke? I know it is, for you; but wait till we get some real weight on your shoulders!"

"Okay, what's next?"

C asked himself.

"Throw another forty-five on each side, that gives us four-o-five, four-ten with the collars. Let's just drop to single reps, Earl, just to see where we are, me mainly, this is still joke weight for you. Never mind no one goes near these numbers in a regular gym, raw to boot, and were not even using a belt."

Earl was just listening; he had no idea what raw meant, and what belts did, but he was ready to do whatever C said.

410 X 1

They both pumped out a single.

But with this rep, Cord first felt the weight lay heavy on his upper back; four-ten was a respectable number, especially for a guy his size. He had to be pretty well under two hundred pounds by now; he figured he'd find a scale at the gym tonight, depending how the rest of his lifting went. He hadn't weighed himself since he got to Town three months ago.

Earl went down and up with the four-hundred-ten pounds in quasi-slow motion, being extra cautious. Yet the four-hundred-ten pound rep looked exactly the same as the ones before; perfect form and no struggle whatsoever, going through the motions as if he had nothing more than a broomstick on his back.

C shook his head in awe at the spectacle and looked over at Buck, who nodded in agreement; Earl was fucking-scary strong.

Cord stood alongside the power rack and pondered, wondering if he should go up another full plate. That was a serious jump for him, and that four-ten wasn't easy, wasn't easy at all.

He didn't think long.

He was feeling the competitive pressure from Earl, even though Earl wasn't acting competitive at all.

"Fuck-it! Throw on another plate; that makes it five-hundred even; fucking five-hundred!"

C clapped his hands long and hard, clapping louder as he went, in self-induced psyche–session. Buck and Earl quickly loaded the bar.

500 X 1

There was a floor-mounted stainless stand, topped by a tazza, holding a thick block of white chalk, off to the side of the rack. Power lifters use it to coat their hands and upper back, to help the bar bite the skin and fabric, lessen slippage. C and Earl hadn't used any to date, and Cord wasn't dipping into it now. No belt, no chalk, no wraps, no nothing, just him and the weight; either he was gonna get it, or not. One or the other.

Cord let out a loud grunt as he pumped his fists in the air and aggressively approached the bar….attack mode. The radio had been playing in the background the whole time, mostly a bunch of forgettable tunes. But when C began his walk to challenge the five hundred pounds, waiting patiently, silently for him, just when Buck and Earl finished loading it on the bar and snapped the last collar shut, like it was on queue, *the* song, his song, began. Everyone has *that* song, the go-to that gets them over the hump, gives the arm-shot of adrenaline they need, the song that just does it for them.

For C, that song was just beginning, right when he needed it most.

Time

Pink Floyd. A cacophony of clock alarms resonated from the radio, filling the silent gym, bouncing off the walls, until they slowly fizzled into the solemn, single chime of a lonely bell.

The hair on the back of C's neck tingled.

He just needed to hear the first bell and that song rocketed him back to high school; in a fraction of a second he was there, all one-hundred-thirty five pounds of him, lean, sinewy and strong, standing in line, one away from stepping atop the platform, his coach hunched over, studying the balance bar on the scale with the furrowed brow and crazed concentration of a mad scientist, ticking the counterweight to the left; another little tick, tick, tick….till the arm rested still and he barked out the weight for all in line to hear.

And you had better not be overweight, because that's when a hellish session became worse for you….much worse.

Varsity wrestling practice; locker room weigh-ins before hitting the mats, laid out in the cafeteria after school.

C didn't know why, but that song, playing while he stood perfectly still in line, eyes forward, in complete silence along with the rest of the grapplers on the team, on a non-descript practice day, no different from any other, always stuck with him. And it made an indelible impression on a fifteen-year old kid with feathered blonde hair. When he heard it, no matter where he was, even twenty-eight years and sixty-odd pounds later, he got a hot jolt of adrenaline, and briefly lassoed that feeling a man sometimes gets, not nearly often enough, when he feels he can do just about anything.

No song, *none,* could have been better to walk beside him on his way to wrestle five-hundred pounds in the power rack. It was the juice he needed.

C had to rush, to take advantage of the serendipity. He quickly grabbed the bar, rolled it forward on the pins, ducked under and rubbed the knurled steel grip on his back, set the groove and sucked in his air deep, lifted the bar and stepped back. The steel dug heavy into his skin; he could feel the dead weight travel the length of his body, and settle in his heels, like molten lead, making it hard to set himself for the lift. The plates, the bar - they weren't going to give this rep away, no way; they were going to make C earn every single pound.

His eyes tilted skyward just as the first deep cord and background drums began to fill the room.

C went down and the leaden force fought him the whole way, and doubt entered his mind, doubt that he could beat this weight. The deeper he went, the more bold the bar became; it had the advantage, and it knew it.

Cord bottomed-out and knew he needed to keep his head up; if he looked down, if he rounded his back, even just a bit, he was done - a dump of the weight - and the plates would laugh at his failure.

And right at that moment, without thinking, without planning, his insides, and the residents lying therein, peeled back the curtain and peaked from his brain; they were laughing at him.

Laughing.

And the utter indifference, the numbness, he felt most of the twenty-four hours each day irrupted into a pyre of anger, a blaze of defiance. And they realized, at least for now, that they lost this little battle.

C pushed off the bottom and began a slow, steady ascent; a long, glorious growl emerged from this throat, from a man who knew he was going one way – *up* - with the weight. It was going to be slow, and tough, but there was no doubt the weight, the rep, five-hundred fucking pounds, was in the God-damn bag. He was done and the weight was ready to be re-racked before the first verse of the song even began.

"Yeah!"

C barked in a full-throttle howl at himself into the mirror, as he slammed the bar hard back into the rack. He rarely displayed such histrionics, but it felt too good, and the curtain fell back in place, the characters receded, and Cord's head was quiet once again. Little did he know they gave no-shit about the weight; their peek was simply a tease for the future battle they were about to win, and they couldn't contain their glee, to revel in his soon-to-be misery. And it was oh-so-close.

But enough about that, for now.

Cord's face was flush, beet red. A small trickle of blood exited his right nostril; he smiled to himself at the irony, and discretely wiped it away, with indifference, thinking about his ass. A not-so-subtle calling card from within; a reminder *it* wasn't going away.

C sat next to Billy; he was spent.

"You fucking gutted that one dude – amazing; that was fucking great!"

Billy tapped C lightly on the leg.

"Thanks man. Earl, you're up; again, this should be joke weight for you, just do one, and try to make it look easier than mine."

And he did, with bells. Earl finished the joke rep and gently racked the five-hundred pounds, as if he was setting a delicate vase on a table. Ay just shook his head in disbelief.

"Okay Earl, obviously it's you solo from here on in. Now I would never suggest this to anyone else, ever, but this workout has been a joke for you so far. So what do you say we make a big bump for you, to see if we can even get you to struggle, even a little."

"Okay."

Was all Earl said, nonchalant.

"Buck, let's strip off the five forty-fives, raise the pins up again, and put on a hundred-pounder on each side, then put all five forty-fives back on; that brings us to seven-hundred fucking pounds; getting scary huh?"

"It was scary at two-seventy-five!"

Buck said, and they both smiled.

Earl just sat on the flat bench watching; he could have easily been sitting on the bench staring at Carol's house, he had on the same blank expression, like a dog staring at the door.

"Okay Earl, bars loaded, whenever you're ready. Now listen, when you unrack this, if it feels heavy, or unsteady, or anything, just rack it again, don't even try it, okay? This is some serious, serious weight, and you're too tall for me to really spot you, okay? You understand?"

"Yeah C, no problem."

And with the same methodical approach, learned an hour earlier, Earl stepped into the rack, with no pre-lift drama or hollering, no clapping or bellowing....nothing. He just quietly, almost gingerly, dipped under the bar, and gently lifted it off the pins, as if he was carefully handling a raw egg.

And just like that, he dipped down, sunk his ass deep, below his hips, and slowly, methodically, stood up. C thought he might have seen the slightest resistance on the way up; but then again, maybe it was his imagination.

"Well? Looked pretty fucking easy."

C said in disbelief, shaking his head. Earl just smiled weakly; that was as close to bragging as he ever got.

"God-damn Earl, you are *unbelievable;* you have absolutely no idea how heavy this really is, do you? Do you know how many people could walk into a gym and, never, *ever* squatting before, put *seven-hundred pounds* on the bar and do a perfect rep like they were bending down to pick up a fucking stick? After a killer kick-boxing workout to boot? I would venture to say a big fat zero. Scary, Earl, very scary, especially with those ridiculous purple shorts on."

"Sorry C, should I try to *make* it look hard?"

Earl was serious. Both Buck and Cord smiled at him.

"Okay, Earl, one more rep…and then we'll call it a day. Christ, I can't imagine what you'd be doing if you *didn't* kick-box. Okay, let's strip it down to the hundred, then add another hundred, then four forty-fives *[C was concentrating, doing the math in his head]*, a ten, and a trinket, a two-and-a-half; that should do it *[four-hundred-forty-five, plus three-hundred-sixty, is eight-hundred-five, plus twenty-five, equals, eight-hundred-thirty pounds]*. Yeah, that's it; we're set."

Earl – 830 X 1

"Earl, whenever you're ready."

C pointed to the loaded bar, then he whispered something in Buck's ear.

Earl didn't hesitate, he simply rose from the bench and calmly walked over to the rack, quietly ducked under the bar, just he did for each of the prior sets, grabbed the bar with his oversized mitts, and slowly lifted the bar off the pins. The power bar arched and strained across his back from the nearly half-ton of weight, but Earl was rock steady. He took a full breath to expand his massive chest, and in a fluid motion, just a hair faster than the previous dips, he traveled down and back up, with the faintest hint of strain, but it might have just been him clearing his throat.

He racked it gently, and turned to look at the two of them, standing shyly in his *Rican* spandex and ghost-white tee-shirt.

"Was that good?"

C just shook his head left to right, mouth open, to signal awe, and nothing else. Then he broke into a wide grin and extended his right hand toward the big man.

"Congratulations young man, *eight-hundred-thirty pounds,* in your first workout, *after* kick-boxing class to boot. You're famous; you now, unofficially, own the new record for a raw squat fucking *world record,* by the way. No belt, no wraps, no chalk, no nothing, just you and the weight....fucking amazing. Over three billion people crawling around, and the best of the best is standing in Margery's basement in bum-fuck Belvidere, New Jersey, and no one in the world knows it but us three....go figure. You're famous Earl, all the girls will be after you, groupies, thousands of them, throwing their damp panties at you; you'll have to beat 'em off with a stick! Maybe Billy can give you a hand with that one."

Famous? Throngs of girls? Damp panties?

Earl just stood there, dumbstruck; he didn't know what to say, absorbing the moment. So Earl said the very first thing that came to the mind of a new world champion, the best of the best, the very best in the entire world.

"Am I gonna be sore tomorrow, C? Like Billy?"

"I very much doubt it."

C said, as he shook his head and smiled at his best friend, chuckling as he repeated Earl's line.

"Am I gonna be sore tomorrow?"

CHAPTER 150 – CATCHING DAMP PANTIES AND THE GROUPIES

The three of them spent the next twenty minutes reliving the events that just transpired, with Cord and Billy laughing, joking and shaking their heads in awe at the spectacle called Earl, all while stripping and racking eight-hundred plus pounds of weights, which were strewn about the power rack. And as they cleaned up the gym area, the whole time, Earl was preoccupied – fretting and mumbling to himself, saddled by a troubled mind.

Finally, C broke down, confronting the worry on Earl's face.

"Okay, what's the matter?"

That was all it took to yank the finger from the dike; Earl spilled, in rapid fire.

"I don't wanna be famous! I don't want any groupies; I don't even know what they are! And I don't want *any* panties; I don't even like to look at Lilly's when she leaves them all over the house! Too many panties already; she leaves them *everywhere*! And if I'm famous, I'm gonna have to go away and leave Belvidere; they'll take me away and make me do all that famous world champion stuff, like *head-up, chest-up, hold your breath and break parallel* and probably other stuff I don't even know about, but it can't be good, I can tell you that! And I'll be all alone, away from home, and I won't see you or Billy, or Lilly or Carol *ever again!*"

Earl hesitated, then he blurted aloud, as if he forgot the most important part.

"**Or Chicken!** I'll never see Chick again! No more Chicken *Chimichanga!*"

"Whoa, whoa, whoa!"

C said, trying to brake the panic, but before he could finish, Earl yelped over him.

"I should've dropped that stupid weight! I should have never done it! Can I do a take-back? A do-over? I'll do it again and mess it up big-time, I promise….I know I can! Let me do another one C, so I can drop it! Please C, don't let them take me away and make me famous!"

C put his hand on Earl's arm, led him over to the bench, and guided him down. Earl's huge chest was heaving, tears welled in his eyes, and he was trembling like a little kid.

"Hey, hey, listen; no one has to know you did eight-hundred-thirty pounds, just us. And we won't tell *anybody,* promise; right Buck *[he nodded a quick yes]*? No one's going anywhere, promise; you can stay here with Chicken forever. Chick would never let you go; she couldn't live without you. Me? Yeah, she could live without me in a heartbeat, the little bitch; but you, *never.*"

Billy shook his head in agreement and put his hand gently on Earl's chest; the hyperventilation was slowing, just a bit. Earl sniffled as he spoke.

"*Really?* You won't tell? And I won't catch damp panties or the groupies?"

"It's not a disease, Earl. And that was a bit of an exaggeration anyway; powerlifting guys get about as many groupies as badminton champions, I suppose, probably less. So no worries about wet, flying underwear….sorry Buck. But just to save you from that lone weightlifting groupie hiding out there, ready to rip off her panties and tie 'em around your chin, like a babushka, your secret is safe with us, okay? Seriously, no worries; we won't even tell Margery."

Earl wiped his wet eyes with his bare right arm, sniffled one last time, and let out a big air of relief; that was way more stressful than any of his lifts.

"I would miss everybody, *especially Chicken.* I think she would miss me too C, I think she *really* does love me; she likes sleeping on my shoulders, and everything."

Earl donned a weak smile, talking in a raspy, halting voice, like the kind that follows a good cry. He cleared his throat and ended by setting the record straight, once and for all.

"And there was no way I was doing it C, no matter what you said, just saying. No way I was catching damp panties and the groupies."

CHAPTER 151 – HOPING THE HIGH WOULD LAST

They were just about done re-racking all the weight; Earl exited for a trip to the men's room, which prompted Billy.

"Hey man, guess what I heard?"

C shrugged his *I-don't-know* shoulders, half-listening.

"Button's *not* coming back, dude; the whole story was bullshit!"

Now Cord was listening, and turned to Billy.

"How do you know that?"

"Vinny was just trying to stir-up shit, like he always does, starting a rumor, trying to get you scared. He doesn't even *know* Button; he's a friend of a friend of a maybe-friend - I wondered how that douche-bag would be the one to know about how to get a hold of him to begin with, since no one else can. Anyway, no worries; pretty cool, huh?"

"I wasn't worried."

C said, matter-of-fact. But truth be told, C was relieved; not for any fear, but for the chance to avoid conflict. Invariably his life revolved around conflict - it was centric; less conflict, less mess, for once, was a good thing.

"Where is he?"

C asked.

"Who knows, who cares, as long as he's not coming back here *[Buck dropped a forty-five pound plate back on the weight tree]*. All that would spell is trouble, for

Earl, Lilly, you and anyone else who looks at him the wrong way; fucking psycho.”

Earl bounded back into the room; Margery wasn’t far behind.

“Whatcha talking about?”

Earl asked, chipper, all his worry long-since drained away.

“Nothing important.”

C said, as he racked the last ten-pounder.

“Good workout?”

Margery sported a relaxed smile.

“Yeah. Hey, sorry about that whole Lilly thing; she tends to ride me, sucked you up in the nonsense.”

“I know. She came by and sorta-apologized, as close as Lilly will get to one, anyway. It was good enough for me; then we just talked, girl talk; she really likes you, Cord, by the way.”

“Yeah, that seems to be the word; not buying it.”

“The place looks great - nice and neat, better than when Walt cleans up; maybe I should hire you guys.”

All three boys grinned.

“Well, anytime you want to come lift, feel free, no charge, it’s on me; nice to see someone besides Walt and his buddies use it, and always leave it for me to clean up.”

C wondered if that invitation was to all of them, or primarily to him; was it just an excuse for him to come see her again? Guys always think it's all about them. Once again, his brain started scanning her body, and he liked what he saw.

Suddenly, without warning, he found himself in a good mood; no Button to deal with, Margery seemed to like him, and the consensus was that Lilly liked him. And hopefully, in less than an hour, he should be pumping some senior pussy wearing a schoolgirl skirt, named Samantha. Oh yeah, and his best friend just set a world record the first time he ever attempted a squat.

And that rare feeling of relaxed content fell over Cord; life seemed pretty good. To which C cracked a crooked smile, hoping the high would last.

CHAPTER 152 – HE UNLOADED, WITH HER NOT KNOWING HER NAME

She didn't hear him pull his bike into the driveway; she usually did. So when the kitchen door suddenly jarred opened, it startled her; she jumped and gave a little yelp.

C smirked, as he clicked the door quietly shut.

But other than the involuntary yelp, she didn't acknowledge him; she didn't say a word, nor cast her eyes in his direction. She quickly recast her demeanor, and facing the stove, slowly stirred a pot of sauce. If there was such a thing as stirring sexy, Mae was doing it. Classical music played quietly in the background, *Haydn*, his favorite, as she well knew.

String Quartet, Opus 64, No 5 - Finale

He didn't comment on the selection, but rather focused on that other thing he was supposed to notice - the short black skirt, the black pumps with tapered heels, along with the black halter top, sans bra. And she wore those slutty hoop earrings; the ones a size too big – meant to look just a bit trashy. She faced away from him, but he knew her nipples were erect; they always were when she was juiced.

And she was.

And as he stared at her muscular back, while she slowly turned and cascaded the wooden spoon in the sauce, he knew the punishment was over. He had banked on her caving; he doubted she could've held out for another week….willpower, when it came to sex, just wasn't in Mae's deck.

He grinned at her weakness, and gave thanks for it, as his dick started to swell. This was going to quickly degrade into a down-and-dirty kitchen fuck. His cock got hard at the thought. Then he thought about banging Margery, and he went to rock.

And just like that, Catholic-girl Sam got tossed aside; and although he didn't know it at the time, C would never think of her again, jettisoned for his new best fantasy, his frail little ballerina….Margery. And he was going to fuck her, but good.

He slowly walked across the kitchen, in contradiction to the furious string work by Haydn in the background, pushed her hair to the side and gently kissed the nape of her neck, over and over, as he slowly ran his hands down her sides, light as a feather, down her hips, down her thighs, till he reached the hem on that pouty little skirt. His hands disappeared under the fabric, and headed north, a one-way to her panties.

Mae could never decide if she got more aroused when he tore them off, quasi-rape, or if he went to grab them, and realized there were none to grab.

But she wanted to be taken tonight, so the maroon lace panties were on, his favorite; the ones that let a little loose hair, stray strands, poke through the fabric here and there.

She knew they weren't going to be on for long.

He knew what she wanted; a split second after his hands found the fabric, without warning, he ripped them down to her ankles. She let out a gasp and her legs trembled a bit. She dropped the wooden spoon into the sauce and braced herself against the edge of the stove. She knew, she hoped she knew, that this was going to be a hard, rough fuck from behind, right where they stood. She liked to say *I'm gonna come*, when he did her like this. She would say it aloud, just above a whisper, over and over again, until she did. And it was rarely just once.

With his right hand, he spread her ass cheeks apart and ran his middle finger along the outside length of her lips, front to back, to see how wet she was.

Very.

Without warning, he took his middle finger and plunged it in, quickly making a large circle in her cunt, an exaggerated circle….deep, while he gently kissed the back of her neck. Up to now, he hadn't uttered a single word, since pushing through the kitchen door.

"Who's gonna come?"

He breathed into her ear.

"I'm gonna come."

And just as she finished the words, it took less than thirty seconds after the panties were down, she moaned loud for her first orgasm, and she purposely tried to hold out. But it was no use, it just felt too good, and a week had been too long to wait. She stretched the come for as long as she could; he loved when she did that – so she did it for him.

And her.

As she finished, she could hear him unbutton and unzip his pants behind her. God, she *needed* that cock.

And she got it. No warning, no tease, just a deep thrust into her cunt, right to his balls against the bottom of her ass. And he kept it in, his body tight against hers, and just partial-pumped her rough, with no daylight between his body and hers. He grabbed her hips hard, and kept her pinned between his groin and the top edge of the stove, grinding and pumping. She was repeating her motto over and over, forcing the whispered words out between his thrusts, till she came a second time.

When he knew she was done, when the moans subsided, he barked a simple question, a command more than a query.

"In your cunt or your mouth?"

"She *hated* that word, it made her feel trashy, but for that exact reason, getting fucked hard like this, it amped her. The answer came out in a throaty, forced breath, as he held her pinned against the stove."

"*Cunt.*"

Was all she said. And with that, he grabbed her hair in a cinch, spun her off the stove and roughly shoved her on the floor, doggie-style, and grabbed her hips hard, and pumped her fast. He always had to grab her hips and hold them tight, because Mae would invariably take two doggie-strokes and fold, down to her belly. For whatever reason, she couldn't, or wouldn't, stay upright, always trying to lay on her belly.

But he wanted this to be a dirty, dog-fuck, so he held her tight - so she couldn't fold, and counted the rapid strokes in his head as she was on all-fours, submissive, his for the taking, for as long and as hard as he wanted.

He got to eighty-five, thinking of fucking Margie on the flat bench in the gym, her legs up on his shoulders, her watching his cock go in and out of her snatch, which he imagined had more hair than it probably did. Mae kept looking back, watching him pump her rough; he loved when she did that.

He got to one-hundred-thirty and she started to moan loud, continuous; he thought of Margery moaning, and he was ready.

Mae started to come again….number three. And he almost asked Mae what her name was, so she could say it aloud, as she was getting pumped dirty on the kitchen floor, like she always did for him when he was ready to unload inside her:

Samantha

And he could say:

No, you're Margery, my new little gym bitch.

He almost did it; he almost asked her name....almost. But for some reason, he didn't.

And then he unloaded, with her not knowing her name.

CHAPTER 153 – HE CAREFULLY DIPPED HIS BIG TOE IN

"As usual, that was fantastic."

C chimed, as he sopped up the last of the sauce in the bowl with a ripped section of a long baguette from Sam's, from the new bakery he recently sourced.

"You make it spicy, I like that; are you sure it's not too spicy for you?"

She just smiled content and nodded no, staring at him, soaking him in.

He leaned back in the kitchen chair and stretched, crossing his legs and picking up his drink to tip it toward her.

"A baguette dipped in sauce, with an extra-dark kir royale, topped with a glass of port a little later on the porch, with a *DeMuth;* did I leave any *DeMuth's* here?"

Mae nodded yes.

"With a *DeMuth,* the best."

C closed his eyes in relaxed content.

"And?"

She prodded.

"And what?"

He asked, innocent.

"Is that it?"

C hesitated, and pondered.

"Yeah, I guess so; why?"

His face feigned innocence, confusion.

He knew she was blatantly fishing, so he teased her; but, as usual, since she was beyond gullible when it came to such matters, she didn't think he was kidding, and the insult soaked through."

"Are you kidding me?"

She snapped.

"What? What did I say?"

She stared at him in utter disbelief, which was quickly fermenting. So he ended the charade.

"Oh, you mean the good company, and the pussy? Yeah, that's pretty good too."

He smiled at her, and she finally realized the charade.

"You know, for someone who says they're so smart, I don't know why you believe me when it comes to stuff like that."

C said, matter-of-fact.

"Because you're a good liar, and I want to believe you, which makes me gullible, or a fool, I guess."

"But I was a good boy tonight, wasn't I? No more punishment?"

She grinned.

"Does it look like you got punished?"

He smiled sly.

She hesitated with the next line, not really wanting to hear the answer.

"Are you staying?"

He leaned across the table and, with a too-serious demeanor, looked deep in her eyes.

"Are you gonna get on your knees, between my legs, and blow me out on the deck while I smoke the *DeMuth* and stare at shithead's house next door?"

"Yes."

She said, a bit too quick.

"Swallow?"

She frowned, knowing he just wanted to hear her say the only answer she ever gave.

"Of course; as if I never do."

"And are you gonna let me wake you up at 2 am and drill you in the ass on your belly? Can you take it in the ass?"

"Yes, I took care of *that* problem."

"Man, if I shit once a week like you do, I would die. If I shit just once a day I'd be in trouble."

She cut him off and tried to change the subject; her constipation wasn't a topic of choice.

"Well, that issue is okay, for now, so the answer is yes, and let's stop talking about *that*."

"Anything else I want to do I can do….*anything*?"

She cocked her head and looked at him, knowing he knew the answer was always yes. She hated being so subservient, his little myrmidon, and his asking was simply his way to emphasize the point, to be in total control. But having him stay, which he did so infrequently, was worth the ingratiation.

So she played the game.

"Yes, anything you want. So do you want to go out on the porch and torment Joe? Or read the paper, or talk, or go to bed now, or whatever; I'll be your little bitch for tonight, just like you want - so you pick….whatever."

C thought a bit, and then he carefully dipped his big toe in.

CHAPTER 154 – THE FOOL IN HER BELIEVED HIM

Cord took a long drink of the kir royale and looked into Mae's eyes.

"How bout we go out of the patio and play a little game."

Mae leaned forward, anxious to hear. A new game meant more sex, and she was ready to go again; she was usually ready to go again.

"I met a girl today, a ballet dancer named Margery."

What happened to his myrmidon? Not more than five seconds after the sentence left his lips, the room was ice.

"What do you mean, you *met a girl named Margery?* What does that mean?"

He was taken aback at the vitriol. Mae had immediately turned vicious; it was a Lilly-like move.

"I don't know, I just met a girl; she owns a gym in Town I went to today; she's Lilly's boss."

Cord found himself stumbling over the words, like he was guilty of something he wasn't guilty of.

"Why were you there?"

Mae snapped at him, hard.

"What the fuck? What's the God-damn problem?"

He shot back, getting angry.

"Just answer the question; why were you there? And don't lie!"

"I was there because Earl and I went to Lilly's kick-boxing class. I *told you* I was going to her class to try and lose some weight, and Lilly told me the owner had some kind of gym with free weights, and I wanted to show Earl how to squat; I **told** you this *[C really didn't remember if he told her or not, but he said it convincingly - when in doubt, act convincing]*!

Trying to tell her about Earl's squatting phenomenon, to change the subject, briefly crossed his mind, but he quickly dismissed it; she was still livid, and the ruse wouldn't work.

"Why are you always following Lilly around? She doesn't want you!"

"That's not what I hear."

C was defensive, and that dagger slipped out.

"Really? If her boyfriend came back, she'd drop you in a fucking heartbeat....*history*. Everyone knows it, everyone! Except you, I guess; pathetic."

Mae's face was crimson.

"Whatever; anyway, that guy's long gone."

All of a sudden, C found himself backed into a corner, defending his *relationship* with Lilly; how did that happen? He followed himself, to move off that minefield.

"What are we arguing about, Lilly or the *new girl*?" *[he didn't want to evoke the name Margery....that somehow seemed evil]*

"Neither, forget it; I'm going to bed. Talk to you tomorrow, maybe."

She threw her fork down in disgust and got up in a huff, starting to angrily clear the table, slamming plates and glasses together.

"What the fuck is going on? I don't even know this girl, I just met her when I went to kick-boxing, and then she let me and Earl, and Buck, you know that kid Buck I told you about, she let the three of us use the gym to lift - that's it! End of fucking story."

"Then why'd *you* bring her up; you want to fuck her too?"

"No! It was just going to be a change from Sam, that's all."

"So you **did** want to fuck her! Jesus, are you kidding me, another one?!"

Christ, he was sinking deep, and fast.

"I didn't want to fuck her; I'm just getting tired of Sam is all. Fantasy, remember?"

"How about fucking just *me* for once! Is that so hard?"

Then he saw the wheels turning; Mae got a deeper red, and raised the decibel level.

"Wait a minute - did you fuck her in the kitchen tonight?! Did you?!"

"What kitchen? No! I fucked you! It's been two weeks and I fucked you, just you....in your kitchen!"

When lying, inflect decisive. But despite the try, that one didn't sound nearly as convincing; he better get off this subject in a hurry.

"Can we please drop this."

C asked, exasperated, seeing the prospect of future sex drying up fast.

"*You* brought it up again, and no, we can't. There are too many fucking girls already: Samantha, Lillian, Carol, that black girl - who the hell knows who she is - and anyone else I don't know about; any wives I should know about? We are **so** not adding another one, we're not! We're **not**!"

"Fine. Jesus, sorry I brought it up."

Mae just stared at him hard, and launched a new tirade. She was far from done.

"I'm not fucking kidding; no Margery, **ever!** I don't want you going to that gym anymore; I don't want you talking to her."

She almost finished the thought; she almost said what the proud part of her wanted to say: *or you're cut off, and were done.* She almost said it, but she chickened out, because the other part, the lonely part, knew he would probably leave, and never come back. Her only hold on C was sex, and it was only because he wasn't getting it elsewhere; she was pretty sure of that. And time was running out; if he did start fucking one or more of the others, she was done….she was sure of it. So she was stuck, and angry….and hurt. Why couldn't she just be good enough; the company, the common interest, the smarts, the cooking, the companionship? Why couldn't he see past her age? Why couldn't she just be twenty years younger, when *she* was surrounded by men who pampered her, pursued her; back then, *he* would be the one chasing, and she could ditch *him;* see how he enjoys the humiliation. Why couldn't…."

He broke in.

"What? Come on! I want to start lifting again and that is a kick-ass gym; she's got a fucking fiancé *[Cord couldn't believe he forgot that ace – that's the fucking answer - a fiancé! No worries for Mae; never mind that Margery having a fiancé just stoked the game fantasy even more for CJ!"*

"Yeah, right, that idiot is as much of a fiancé to her as I am to you."

He didn't touch that one.

"How do you know about Walt?"

C asked; yet another mistake.

"Oh, so the two of you discussed Walt? How lovely; I thought you just lifted? Now you know her life story? Did you fuck her? So help me, Cord, if you did!"

"No! I just met her I told you; she said the gym stuff was for him. I didn't bring it up, she did! Fuck!"

"She's never gonna marry that guy; the one good decision she'll probably ever make. He's a worthless bum."

"How do you know so much about this girl, and her fiancé? Did you fuck *him*?"

Oh the irony would be delicious, C thought. And that zinger seemed to derail her a bit; he could see she was formulating a response, calculating; her politician brain was churning. This was going to be a spin; a curveball was surely on its way. So Cord went on the offensive; there had to be a story behind all this.

"Well? You spread your legs for him too? Another boy-toy? That's it, isn't it? Maybe I should be offended."

She snorted.

"Nice try; don't deflect, I know the drill."

"That's exactly what *you* are doing, Ms. lobbyist."

Silence.

"I'm waiting; this should be good."

C snorted, suddenly feeling the driver's seat. Mae sighed, and settled into a dispassionate, professorial tone. She spoke slowly, deliberately.

"I never slept with that meat-head; please, don't insult me, more than you normally do, anyway. I lent her a bunch of money to start her gym, ballet classes and the like - I used to tan there, it was just a tanning place back then. Anyway, we were friends, kind of, for awhile; anyway, it went sour, and….it just went sour."

Mae frowned and looked down.

"I don't want to talk about her anymore….please."

C leaned in and put his finger under her chin, lifted it gently and looked into Mae's beautiful clear-blue eyes. And they were sad.

"Jesus, Mae, I'm not interested in the gym-girl, honest; I just wanted to lift with Buck and Earl is all. And I'm not fucking anybody but you, nobody, promise; let's just drop it, okay?"

"But you want to….fuck her, that is, don't you? Do you think she's pretty? Prettier than me? When I was that age? I guess you wouldn't know that."

Mae's voice trailed off. C didn't say a word, he just stared at her with hazel, puppy eyes. He could turn them on like a light; he was good at that. And it worked.

"Okay."

She forced a weak smile. But her mind festered, and she had to get one more in, to be sure.

"C, I'm serious, stay away from her, she's bad news. I don't want you pursuing her, or talking to her, or anything, you understand? I can take Lilly, and Carol, and all the rest, but not her. I'm not joking; this is important, stay away from her, or we're done. You know that's not easy for me to say, but it's *that* important to me. Please, at least this one, stay away, for me…*please*."

C never saw those eyes before, that anguish, looking back at him, never, and he had hurt her plenty of times. Not with Lillian, or Carol, or anyone; that face was real, and Margery was clearly a problem….a big problem.

"Okay, okay, no gym-girl…..promise."

And C flashed his signature uptick smile, with his arms gently wrapping around her hips, giving them a tiny squeeze, the kind that says *I get it, and were on the same page, we're okay*.

Mae smiled back, and the fool in her believed him.

CHAPTER 155 – JUST THINKING ABOUT THE BLOB

Thursday, July 13th; day eighty-five and all was still quiet; no unwelcome visitors to greet Cord.

"It's the coolest ever!"

Earl yelled.

"You never even *went*, Earl."

Lilly snapped.

"That's because you'll never go Lilly; you say you will, but then you never do. You never go anywhere! But C will go with me, right C?"

"Sure, I'm in."

"Yeah! See! We're going Lilly; C and me are going to the *Blobfest!* And you don't even have to come! How we getting there C? We can't ride our bikes, 'cause it's way too far, I think."

"We'll get a limo, go in style, stocked with booze."

"You're not getting my brother drunk again; stop getting my brother drunk!"

"Hey, what are you…."

C was going to say it, *his mother,* but he caught himself.

She spun around in her white Capris, one of thirteen colors she had, and planted her hands firmly on her hips, knowing what he was going to say; surprisingly, she didn't get mad, the typical result for most mom-related comments.

"Yes, as a matter of fact, I am."

"No you're not!"

Earl whispered to himself; head down.

"What?"

Lilly barked at Earl, hearing full well what he said.

"Nothing."

Earl murmured.

Then he turned and whispered to C, in defiance.

"I like getting drunk."

C grinned and whispered back.

"Me too."

They both smiled.

"So go 'head Earl, tell me again all about the *Blobfest*. I remember watching *The Blob* as a kid; the best part was when it rolled under the car and ate the mechanic, his legs wiggling and stuff – scared me shitless."

C recalled fond.

"Yeah, that was cool! Hey, remember when it climbed up the stick in the beginning, and stuck to the old man's arm, like a big slimy slug? He couldn't shake it off! That was pretty scary!"

"God, you two are nerds, you really are."

Lilly chimed in.

"Don't pay attention to her Earl, she's just jealous."

"Yeah, that must be it."

Lilly said sarcastically, as she stuck out her tongue. But it was a playful tongue.

C smiled; he was feeling good about things, about himself, about Lilly. He started to believe what he was hearing, that maybe she was starting to like him, maybe a little. Who would have ever guessed it.

Earl prattled on.

"It's the coolest ever, C. It starts tomorrow, and I don't know when we should go! They run out of the theater on Friday night, running away from the *Blob*, everybody screaming. We coulda run out too, even though it'd be scary, but Lilly never got the tickets, like she was *supposed* to. She always forgets to do things she doesn't want to do *[Earl shot her an annoyed glance]*."

"Careful Earl, or you're not getting any of what I was gonna make you tonight."

"Yeah, but Lilly, you *knew* I wanted to run out of the theater, 'scaping from the *Blob*; and you said you'd order three tickets, and you didn't."

"Sorry Earl, I forgot; you don't think I forgot on purpose, do you?"

Now both Earl and Lilly knew damn well she did, but Lilly would never admit it, and Earl wasn't going to call her out on it, and risk her not letting him go.

"No, you didn't forget on purpose."

He said, dejected.

"Good, I guess you can have some piccalilli then!"

"Piccalilli! I love piccalilli! Lilly makes the best piccalilli, just as good as my mom's; that's where she learned it!"

C shot a quick glance at Lilly, to see if she was agitated at the mom-comment; that was two in a row….not good. But for whatever reason, she let it slide. Earl was usually much more careful about such subjects, but he was simply too excited about the piccalilli, and let it slip.

"I know you do, that's why I'm making it."

Lilly smirked and turned back to the kitchen counter, and reminisced.

Growing up, Carol always made piccalilli for Earl and Lillian. It was one of Lilly's favorites as a kid, mainly because her name was in it, and she felt special, like it was named after her; that's what her mom always told her, anyway. It was one of the few mother memories she would tolerate, simply because she always thought of piccalilli being more about her than her mom. Earl liked it so much, even to today, because Lilly was always happy when she ate it; if Lilly was happy, Earl was happy.

"What's piccalilli?"

C asked the room.

"Cucumbers, onions and peppers, mixed with mayo, which I make a little bit spicy."

"Sounds good; I'm hungry, make some extra for me."

"No."

Was all Lilly said, in mock annoyance, which meant yes, she was already making extra for him.

Lilly was in a good mood, which although rare, was happening more frequently….lately.

But tonight, her mood was better than good; she was relaxed, almost too relaxed, too easy going. The incident at the gym with Margery three days ago was long past, and things had been good, better than good, since. It was as if Lilly unilaterally decided that she and Cord had turned some invisible corner; at least that's how it felt to Cord. And he wasn't complaining.

But today she was being especially nice, especially playful. And that scared C, because something was sure to screw it up before the night was over, he just knew it – it always played out that way. He just hoped it wasn't him that screwed up, but it usually was. Cord got a tinge of nervousness, worrying more than he should about playing neutral, being conservative, not popping the balloon. That was usually a sure sign, the first sign, that he would.

He took a deep breath to reset.

"Okay, so we don't have tickets for tomorrow, so what are we gonna do? Go tomorrow anyway, or Saturday? What do you want to do Earl?"

Earl furrowed his brow; this was important stuff, and he took this executive decision seriously. This was the 7th annual *Blobfest*, and he had missed each of the first six; he had some *serious* catching up to do. He thought some more, and decided to go for the ring.

"Can we do a sleepover?"

Before C could part his lips came the loud answer from the kitchen.

"We're not sleeping anywhere, Earl, forget it!"

"*We?* So now you're going to the *Blobfest?*"

C looked at her, with raised eyebrows.

She never even turned around.

"Just for Earl's sake; I don't trust you getting him all drunk *yet again* and stuff, getting him in trouble, and stuff."

"Yeah….and stuff."

C said, sarcastically.

"You're gonna come to the *Blobfest* Bibby? I knew it! You're a *Blobophile* too!"

"And apparently a nerd."

C said, with a big, fat smirk.

She spun around, cutting knife in hand, with a thin slice of cuke hanging on for dear life, pointing the blade at the two of them, raising it up and down as she spoke.

"I am *not* a nerd, and I'm *not* a *Blobo*-whatever; I'm just going to….protect….to be sure Earl is okay. I don't trust you getting him mixed up in….whatever; *you* are a bad influence *[Lilly pointed the knife ominous at C]*."

"I'm not a little kid, Lilly!"

"Right, you're a *Blobophile*….sorry, I forgot. Little kids aren't *Blob*-nuts, just adults, like you."

She cracked, pointing the knife directly at Earl.

"I *am* a *Blobophile*, and I'm proud to be one! I also like the smell of cow manure!"

Earl pointed right back at her.

C looked at him with a contorted face, wondering where that came from.

"Well I do!"

Earl shouted.

C just shook his head and chuckled to himself; Earl was definitely a keeper.

He turned to Lillian.

"Just what do you expect to happen at the *Blobfest* that I am gonna get your brother mixed up in? Exactly what *Blobo* high-jinx do I have in store for him?"

"I don't know mister, but knowing you, it has something to do with women and booze and trouble."

"Women, booze and trouble at the *Blobfest?*"

C contemplated, and then answered himself.

" I somehow doubt it; but we'll try our best, right Earl."

"Right!"

Earl shot his hands up over his head, fists clutched in defiance.

"And **that** is why I'm going with you, to stop you from corrupting my brother."

"Fine, but Earl and I aren't hanging around with you....*nerd.*"

And with that Earl and C huddled at the dining room table, talking in hushed voices, planning out the two-day stint, with an overnight stay in Phoenixville, Pennsylvania, the epicenter of the *Blob* world.

Lilly, still working on the piccalilli, smiled to herself as she hunched over the counter, listening to the two grown kids excitedly plan out the two-day extravaganza, filled with scream contests, tin-foil hat competitions, fire extinguisher parades, double-features of *The Blob* and *The Creature From The Black Lagoon*, The *Blob Ball*, where they could watch everyone in costume dance while they ate *Bloboli* pizza, and, of course, a VIP tour of movie sites – Doc Hallen's house, where the old man, doctor and nurse got sucked up by the ooze, Jerry's Market, the high school, and finally, most importantly, the Colonial Theater, where all the patrons ran out screaming while the *Blob* rolled over the ones too slow to escape.

Lilly felt butterflies in her stomach; was she really going to go? She had never really left Town, never, certainly not to a place as far away as Phoenixville. C said it was a two-hour car ride, all the way down by Philadelphia. She was excited and scared, more scared than anything. The blanket that was Belvidere was all she knew for the last forty-one years, and she wasn't sure she was ready to come out from underneath. Not just yet.

"When are we gonna leave C?"

Earl asked.

"Well, the running out of the theater starts at 7:30 pm tomorrow, and we don't wanna miss that, so we should leave at five, maybe four-thirty at the latest, just to give some extra time for traffic and getting lost. Then we can find the hotel, check in and get over to the Colonial. I can't imagine there are gonna be that many people."

"Yeah, it's gonna be all three of us….embarrassing."

Lilly yelled.

"Then don't go."

C shot back.

"Oh, I'm going; don't you worry about that mister. And don't think I'm sleeping in *your* room; don't get any ideas. You better get me my own room; you can sleep with your boyfriend, nerd-nick."

Lilly said, defiant.

"Indescribable! Indestructible! Nothing Can Stop It! The Blob!"

Earl shouted out the poster-line; he was so excited, he had to stand up when he yelled it.

"Good God."

Was all Lilly could say.

Earl sat back down and mouthed to C in a hushed, ominous tone; this was an important point, a key fact to remember for their trip.

"You know C, the *Blob, it creeps and leaps and glides and slides, across the floor, right through the door.* That's what it does, you know, that's what the song says; so just be careful tomorrow, okay? Stay close to me; I know all about this *Blob*, he's *very tricky.*"

And C smiled through it all. Earl was so happy, and maybe this was the weekend when something finally would happen with Lilly; how cool would that be?

C couldn't stop smiling, staring blankly at the wall.

"What are you smiling about? You look goofy."

Earl said, poking C in the shoulder. And C simply couldn't stop smiling.

"Just thinking about the *Blob.*"

CHAPTER 156 – LAUGHING, WITH GIGLI STUCK IN HIS TEETH

The boys each downed two heaping plates of piccalilli, sopped up with torn pieces of baguette from the Market, washed down with hearty gulps of *Vernors*, in clear glass bottles.

Haute cuisine.

They sucked down every last bit of it, the piccalilli, the bread, the *Vernors*....and they were both still hungry.

Lilly ate exactly two spoonfuls of piccalilli; she always had to have at least a bite or two, but was more interested in her staple....pasta. Lilly was a bird when she ate, but her downfall was pasta, always pasta. And until C redid the Market, her repertoire consisted of spaghetti, spaghetti, and more spaghetti; when she felt a little crazy, she would go for the linguine, or just maybe, angel hair. That was the extent of exotic: angel hair, and the extent of pasta selections at the old Sam's.

But now was a whole new ballgame; Cord's organic pasta section included shapes and sizes she couldn't even pronounce.

She would eat *buctani, vermicelli, roccheti* and *ancini di pepe,* and she liked them all.

But of course, her favorite, which was also Earl's favorite, was the *gigli*, the little cone-shaped flowers, with fluted edges, which meant *lilies*, according to Cord. She and Earl ate *gigli* at least once a week; she bought it in bulk. When it was just the two of them, Earl would always ask for the *gigli/spaghetti* combo, the whole Cord (since spaghetti were long cords) and Lilly mix. But when C was there, she *never* mixed the two; she didn't want Earl to do the *Cord-n-Lilly* jingle, which he invariably did every time he ate the two pastas together….Earl couldn't help himself, he thought it was too funny.

So while the boys ate piccalilli; she slowly ate the *gigli,* making more than she normally ate, and piling it all up on her plate. She had every intention of eating it all; she always did when she was hungry, but she never finished it….and Earl stood by for cleanup, like a hungry dog.

She had asked the two of them earlier if they wanted any, but they were so tied up in *Blob*-planning, they paid her no attention; big mistake. So now the boys were done, and were watching her slowly eat, forks in hand, upright, tines facing the ceiling.

"Are you done yet? Did you make any more pasta, Bibby? I like *gigli.*"

"Nope, made just enough for me."

Lilly said, casually stabbing the large pile of pasta on her plate and lazily eating it in front of the boys, the lioness crouched at the kill, the juveniles salivating in the periphery.

And so they sat and watched, and so she slowly ate. Almost imperceptive, Earl began to lean closer to Lilly's plate, moving like a spider.

"You get one inch closer Earl, and you are fucking stabbed; *last warning*!"

Lilly threatened. Earl recoiled in fear; no threat with a utensil by Lilly should be taken as idle. She smiled at him, and continued to eat….slowly. Earl tried to quietly push out his chair, to leave the table.

No luck.

"Where are you going? Sit down!"

She barked.

"But I was gonna get…."

"Sit down! It's rude to get up when someone is still eating; I didn't get up when you two were eating."

Lilly stuck her fork in for one last bite; her belly was full five minutes ago, but she was simply playing with them. She pierced a single cone, spun it around in the air, impaled on her fork, then slowly skinned it off the tine, chewing it slowly, staring at the both of them.

She took her napkin, dabbed her lips lightly and pushed away from the table.

"Be sure to do the dishes."

She said, as she headed for the couch, never looking back at what she knew what was about to happen; chaos.

Earl was quicker than Cord, he always was. He spun and staked a claim to what she left on her plate, beating C's fork to the punch. Cord stood up to try and muscle Earl away from Lilly's scraps, but Earl simply gave C a gentle stiff-arm to the chest, grabbing his shirt and holding him at bay, like putting your hand on a little kids forehead, while his fork started to reduce the pasta pile. C struggled like a fish on the line, and Earl couldn't concentrate with the fork, so he threw it down and stuck his face into the plate, eating like a pig at a trough, laughing and coughing down the pasta, all while C struggled against his arm, seeing the pile disappear into the big man's mouth, half of it falling out, back onto the plate, until he vacuumed it up on a second pass.

C was pulling away from his arm hard, trying an end around, getting mad.

"Share the fucking pasta Earl, let go!"

And just like that he did, and C went flying to the right, landing hard on the floor.

"That sounded like it hurt."

Lilly said deadpan, watching the inevitable spectacle from the computer desk; Earl was doubled over, laughing at his prone friend.

"Nice Earl, nice. Thanks."

Earl couldn't answer; he was too busy laughing.

"There's more pasta on the stove."

Lilly stated in an calm, indifferent tone, as she turned back to the computer screen.

"Want me to get you some pasta, C? There's more on the stove."

Earl said, holding out his hand to help up his friend, his smile a mile wide.

"You got pasta all stuck in your teeth!"

C said snidely, but he wasn't really mad; how could he be mad?

Cord grabbed Earl's mitt, and was yanked off the floor by his best friend, still laughing, with gigli stuck in his teeth.

CHAPTER 157 – JUST FOR A FLASH, IT CAME, THEN IT WAS GONE

"You wanna watch *Godzilla* tonight C? His real name is *Gojira*, in Japanese – *Godzilla* is just a made-up name. It's the first one; he's the *Incredible, Unstoppable Titan of Terror!* That's what it says, you know, on the DVD, bonus edition. But I don't think he's a titan of terror; I feel bad for him. They treat him bad C. I like *Godzilla*, a lot, but nobody else does; they just try and hurt him. They just never gave him a chance."

Earl dropped his head, sad.

"Didn't you just watch that last night Earl?"

"Yeah, so?"

"Did I ever tell you the story about *The Head*, Earl?"

"*The Head?* No, is it scary?"

"You bet, very."

"Oh boy, tell me! Does it smell like cabbage? Sometimes when I wake up, I smell cooked cabbage, and I figure, it must be my head, it must smell like cabbage; I don't know why; why is that C?"

"Maybe you farted in your sleep and it stunk so bad, it woke you up; ever think of that?"

C said, matter-of-fact. Earl gasped, never thinking of the fart angle. But then he dismissed it.

"Nah, my farts never smell like cooked cabbage, lots of other stuff, but not cabbage - no way; must be something else. Where does that cabbage smell come from? Is it from my head? It's a real mystery C, a *real* mystery. I bet Ken and Sandy could solve that one, couldn't they?

They're smart about cooked cabbage and *everything*; way smarter than me about important stuff like that!"

C shook his head and smiled in wonderment; the fact that cooked cabbage and Ken and Sandy somehow worked their way into this conversation was why he loved Earl. He refilled his glass to the brim with tawny port, and filled Earl's as well. They had moved from *Vernors* to port….a *smooth* transition.

"Are you enjoying the port, Earl?"

"I love port!"

Earl said, as he tried to slowly sip the wine with a dignified air, gently grasping the throat of the glass, his pinkie finger pointing skyward. But it was futile, down went port number seven, just short of a chug.

Cord topped off a third glass of tawny, and walked it over to Lilly, who was still deep mining for new porn sites to bookmark on the internet; she would spend hours trolling.

Both C and Earl knew when Lilly was deep in carnal research mode, you weren't supposed to go over and look at the screen, it was an unwritten Lilly rule; there were lots of those. So C walked toward the desk with the screen just out of ken and extended the glass of port toward her.

"This is number three, young lady; keep going and you might get sloppy drunk like your brother, and start talking about cooked cabbage. I'm having another *Stoli Elite* chaser."

C interrupted himself and yelled over to Earl, who was staring blankly at the far wall.

"Earl! Another *Stoli* shot?"

"I love *Stoli*!"

Earl quickly shouted back, like a recruit in basic training, still staring intently at a white spot on the white wall; *Godzilla* hummed in the background.

"Coming at ya!"

C said, and turned back to Lilly, smirking.

"Double-fisted drinking, you gotta love it."

"You're corrupting my little brother, you know that?"

"Someone has to; and he's not being corrupted, he's already there."

"Want to try some *Stoli?* Come on, but it will surely put you under the table, and you'll probably lose all that self-control you have; it *could* be dangerous."

"For who, you? Or me?"

C didn't answer, he just smirked at her.

"I'll just take the port for now; maybe I'll have a shot of the vodka in a bit....thanks."

And she just smiled at Cord.

C then broke the first unwritten rule; he leaned around the edge of the screen, and took a peak at the video on the screen. Lilly had the mute button on, but once she saw him looking at it, rather than yelling at him, she nonchalantly tapped the mute, and the audio, which was turned down to the lowest low setting, kicked in, and he could hear the blonde with tits a half-size too big moaning, as she was getting drilled on the hotel room bed.

"I can help you with some of that, you know."

1397

C said, pointing at the computer screen, while a muscular guy with a knit ski cap banged away, bottoming out, with her legs up on his shoulders."

She just smiled at Cord; no wisecrack, just a friendly smile.

Holy shit, he thought, that was pretty cool. Now if he could only get that *Stoli* in her, finally, he might be golden. He flashed back an up-tick smirk.

But if he ever did fuck Lilly, if it ever *really* did happen, he didn't want it to be a drunken fuck. He wanted her to be sober, and still want it. He figured that was a pretty stupid stand to take; if she ever opened the door, no matter what condition she was in, he would be foolish to let the opportunity pass – he never had a *no drunk* rule with anyone else.

But with her, for some reason, he didn't want it to happen that way. So he probably wouldn't ply her too much more tonight, even if she wanted more booze, just in case. She was already feeling happy, and at her weight, it didn't take much alcohol to put her under. So he vowed that this would be her last port, three and done, and he'd let the chips fall where they may.

Cord left Lilly's side and sat down hard on the couch by Earl, cracked his knuckles loudly and grabbed the remote, muting *Godzilla*, just as the first shot of the monster flashed on the screen, the first time you see him, right when he barely peaks over the mountain range, sneaky, like a cat, with big wide eyes. Everyone starts to scream and run; that was C's favorite shot in the movie.

Like Earl, Cord always felt bad for *Godzilla*.

"I don't know why they want to hurt him, C, they should just leave him alone! Just like they should have left Fred alone; maybe *Godzilla* likes sweet potatoes like

Fred! Maybe that would make him happy, and he'd stop stomping on all those little Japanese people."

Cord cracked a grin, thinking about the lizard sitting upright, like a squirrel, munching on an oversized golden tuber, the ruins of Tokyo at his feet. Maybe if they stopped shooting at him and just gave him a big potato, he'd be happy.

"Maybe Earl, maybe Emiko can feed *Godzilla* some potatoes; I wouldn't mind if she fed *me* some. She's a little hottie, isn't she Earl? Her running around in that tight little white top and dress; she probably has a nice looking bush, what do you think *[Cord poked Earl in the shoulder]?*"

Earl blushed and didn't say a word; he didn't want to think about Emiko's bush, or anything else about her. He just wanted to feed *Godzilla* some sweet potatoes.

C gawked at the thin Japanese starlet on the screen; man, did she have the perfect arms, and a great chin. And those Orientals always have full black bushes, always; and back in 1954? Guaranteed. Sweet.

Normally Lilly would have chimed in on C's baiting, making a snide remark or two, but she was silent, preoccupied, deep in the hunt for new porn, and wasn't paying attention to the *Godzilla*-talk.   What she was doing, in fact, was getting juiced; a potent combination of alcohol, C flirting with her, and the endless hardcore videos looping on her computer screen.

She discreetly rubbed her thighs together, creating a little friction in her crotch. God, she figured she could come right then and there; she could do it and neither one would be the wiser. But for some reason, she held out, for now, and closed her eyes.

She hadn't had sex, real sex, with a real cock, in three long *years*, ever since Button left. Lots of fingers and toys, lots of fantasies, but none of the real deal. She leaned back in her chair and tilted her head back, eyes still closed. Button's cock was the last one she let in, the only one that had been inside her, for years. God, she loved his cock; it just fit, perfect, like it was special-made, just for her pussy. And she wanted it, *bad* - right here, right now.

Even with what Button did to her, she still couldn't, still wouldn't, be with someone else; as foolish as it sounded, it would feel wrong, like cheating. And she had long ago convinced herself that Button was tricked by Carol; that CD, with all the horrible things he said about Lilly, and what he did with Carol, was all *her* fault. He must have been drunk, or tricked, or bewitched, or something, of that she was convinced. Button would *never* have said and done those things on his own, he loved her too much. It was all that bitch's doing.

And although Button didn't know it, Lilly forgave him, unconditionally, long ago. And she knew Button probably hadn't been faithful for the past three years, but she liked to believe he had been. And she would never ask, to ensure the answer conformed to her hope; that his last pussy was hers, and her pussy was the only one for him.

What she couldn't understand, though, was why he never called her once, not once, since he left. At times, just fleeting thoughts really, she thought - hell, he could be dead, and that's really why she never heard from him, and she'd never hear from him, *ever* again.

And her stomach would drop at the thought.

But she just knew he wasn't dead; she could never picture that day *ever* happening. He was too strong, too street-smart, too good-looking, too lucky. For sure, Lilly was convinced she would die before him; it ran in the family.

But in the end, she knew she would forgive him for the past three years, for all he did, and didn't do. And she really didn't want to know what he did, or who he did it with, she would just put the thought out of her mind and convince herself that she was the one he really wanted, and, in the end, she would be the one Button would always come home to.

Man, three years; she hadn't seen Button in three years! No real sex in three years!

She shook her head at the thought, as she rubbed her legs together, more friction on her already-stoked clit. She would have never believed it could happen. After the military jag, the longest stint she hadn't seen Button was six months, back in 1997; he never really explained why he went away that time, or where he went, and she didn't press – she was just glad he came back. He didn't call back then either, AWOL; which is kind of why she knew, this time, it was just again a matter of time. But three years? Why?

She still thought about him almost every day. She would miss him, and love him, and hate him, and miss him, in fits and starts, ricocheting around her brain; that pretty much summed the relationship. It was debilitating; it always had been.

But lately, for the first time ever, she found herself now and then going a day, sometimes two; rarely, but it happened, without thinking about Button. The days would just slip by. And that was a new sensation; it didn't feel good or bad, it just felt different. Maybe a bit guilty, but just a little.

But despite it all, she knew whenever he finally showed up, whenever he was standing in front of her, she wouldn't see anything else but him, couldn't imagine herself with anyone but him; in the end, she never could. The grip he had on her was iron. She never understood it; he certainly didn't deserve it. But when he cocked his head and flashed those little-boy blues, and gave her a smirk, she was all-but-done every time.

Stupid? For sure. Helpless to stop it? Without a doubt.

She opened her eyes and lazily looked over at the boys, the two of them, Earl enthralled while Cord spun yet another tall tale about his many travels; she never knew if some, or if any, of his yarns were really true, but it didn't matter to Earl....Cord was his world.

She smiled, remembering early on how she was threatened by C, afraid he was going to take her brother away from her. But C brought out the best in Earl, and she was sure Earl did the same for Cord.

And Earl still loved her, as much as ever. And he still needed her, but not quite as much. And to her surprise, she was mostly okay with that....mostly.

She sat up and looked intently at Cord. God, she remembered that first day, at Sam's, when she laid him out cold, him wearing Uncle Frank's smock. She chuckled to herself, not really understanding how she did that. Cord was tough, tougher than she usually gave him credit; she wondered how he would stand up to Button.

She thought of the two of them, the images flipping back and forth, back and forth, in her mind. That was a meeting she didn't want to see; that had bad written all over it. But in the end, she knew Button would get the best of Cord; Button always came out on top. If Button cared about something, he always won, and she didn't want to see anything bad happen to Cord.

And that's when she first had the thought, *the* thought, from left field.

Looking back, she would always remember this day, this time, when she was sitting at her computer desk. It was the first time she saw herself, *really* saw herself, in a relationship with another man, someone other than Button, even if Button was around for her to have.

It was fleeting, the image lasted less than a flash, but it happened; the thought processed in her mind….it *did* happen, and with a pull of the lever, the slot machine came up not as Button, but as Cord.

And this wasn't about sex. She fantasized about other guys all the time; hell, she fantasized about Cord that first night, as Earl reminded her in the Park the next day. God, that was embarrassing.

No, this was much different. This was about Cord, standing next to her, the two of them, together, as in *together*. This was about Button *not* being in the picture, when he *could* be.

She cocked her head and wrinkled her brow at the strange revelation; doubting herself, not knowing how that circuit somehow connected in her brain. That was a wire she didn't know existed. She's wasn't even sure that's what *she* really wanted to think, but her brain did, like it flipped that switch on its own.

Standing by her side, *with her,* it was Cord; for just for a flash, it came, and then it was gone.

CHAPTER 158 – SHE MOUTHED THE ONLY RIGHT ANSWER; *YES*

Earl was passed out on the couch, his face contorted and scrunched against a pillow, mouth partly agape. Even at three-hundred sixty-plus pounds, the two-punch of port and *Stoli Elite* finally put the big man down. He was out cold, no doubt dreaming of Carol.

The television was still on mute, *Godzilla* was long gone, nothing left but a skeleton, vaporized by the oxygen bomb in the ocean, yet again. Godzilla never got away, although Earl hoped every time, that this was the time, he somehow would. Earl always hoped for that day; he felt bad for *Godzilla,* because he loved him, like he loved Fred.

Cord had been leaning over Lilly for the past fifteen minutes, as she scrolled endlessly through her bookmarked web pages. She had never shown him, or anyone else, her favorites porn collection before; and as silly as it sounded, this was a *big* deal, and C knew it.

This had been Lillian's sex life for the past three years, and she was opening the cover.

As he stood behind her, C gripped the back of her chair for support, the thumb of his right hand rested squarely against her left shoulder blade. She was warm, and he liked the feeling of touching her, even as inconspicuously as this.

He wondered if she even knew he kept the contact on purpose, moving his hand now and again to create some movement, some friction, between them. There was no reason for his thumb to be there touching her, he could have easily moved his grip to a different spot on the chair top, and kept a respectable distance between his thumb and her top.

But he didn't.

She felt like a little kid, showing off a revered collection of some sort….coins, dolls, bugs….something important and secret, to a new best friend, one who, so far, didn't enjoy benefits. That's kind of how Cord felt, different; maybe it was the alcohol.

She saw C every day; he might as well have moved in, eating most meals with them, spending gads of time with Earl lounging around the apartment, raiding the fridge, getting her brother drunk again and again, endlessly talking about all the stupid stuff guys talk about, which invariably led to C weaving girls and sex into the conversation, with Earl trying to sidestep the subject.

To her surprise, she never tired of the dance.

And when the two of them went upstairs, for *guy time* away from her, usually after she annoyed them, on purpose or otherwise, she inevitably found a reason to wander upstairs and join them, and lounge around his apartment, raid the fridge, and generally mess up the neatness that marked his apartment, so he would straighten it, and she would muss it yet again.

She never tired of that game either.

And surprisingly, she found herself waking up in the morning in a good mood, looking forward to, anticipating, that moment when C would walk through the apartment door each morning, without a knock, looking for breakfast, that she would complain about making, but would always make. Always.

She liked that he never knocked.

When he walked through the door, it always made her smile, even though she rarely let him see it.

It was the small town nuts and bolts, mundane everyday life, that she cherished; it was safe, and predictable. And C brought it all back into focus.

As she sat and stared beyond the carnal acts on the screen, inches from her nose, her thoughts drifted to Earl, and Button; the blind hatred and hostility that infused them both.

Never once, in thirty-plus years, *never,* did she see the two of them speak nicely to each other. She knew Button wanted Earl to go away, forever, for good, to never come back. He wanted that from the first day the two of them met, as kids, when it was clear how much her mom loved Earl; how he was, and would always be, the most important man in her mom's life. It was clear, and she made no bones about it.

Button didn't want to share either of them with Earl; he wanted to be their mom's favorite son, and he wanted all of Lilly's love, in toto.

She didn't think Earl was really capable of hatred; but as close as he could come to that term, to ill will, he came to with Button, and she well knew why. Earl didn't care a lick if Button made fun of him, and Button really could never physically hurt Earl, on his own, not really. But it was the things Button did to Lilly, the things Lilly didn't admit, and weren't discussed, that were the real problem. And if her mom ever knew what he did to Lilly, she would have killed Button; she knew that for a fact; and if Earl was capable of it, he would too. If he knew, if he....

C's shifted his stance, purposely brushing his chest lightly against her shoulder and the side of her head, moving her hair just a bit.

And Lilly forgot about Button.

She wondered if he was doing it on purpose; knowing him, it was all part of a grand plan. But there was always this doubt as to his intentions; a mistake, or a planned mistake? She doubted anything like that was a mistake when it came to Cord.

She sat there, staring at the screen, hoping he would make some more mistakes; right here, right now, she was ready for more mistakes.

"Poor Earl, you always get him drunk!"

She pouted fake.

"Poor Earl, are you kidding? He's a happy pup, and he likes getting drunk, lots of catching up to do, a whole life's worth; leave him alone."

"Do you want to go up to your place? Nowhere to sit here, besides the table."

C couldn't believe it; she invited him up to *his* place?

"Yeah, sure, I'll grab the *Stoli*. There's still some left, but the port is drained; I may have another bottle upstairs."

"Yeah, you do, in the kitchen cabinet by the fridge."

He frowned at her, knowing she full well went through all his drawers and cabinets on a regular basis – his door was never locked - looking for hints to his past. Three months, and she was still rooting around, hoping to stumble upon a clue. Nothing in his apartment was sacred; nothing off limits, except, of course, the box. She respected the box, and didn't tinker with it, shake it or otherwise disturb it. It sat quietly on the top shelf in the closet, next to the three aluminum foil packs of money, patiently waiting for Jenny to arrive. It had all the time in the world.

Lilly grabbed her favorite comforter, rolled it in a messy half-ball, and led the charge upstairs to his place, C in tow. Walking behind her, seeing that tight little butt in those Capris, he couldn't believe this might really happen.

She pushed open the door and went right for the port.

"So, are you gonna keep coming to kick-boxing? You didn't last too long, you know."

"I know, I was there. I'm thinking of pilates."

Lilly shot him a look.

"Pilates? With Margery?"

Cord was so close to getting laid, and he was sabotaging himself; why did he always do that, play with fire?

"Yeah, maybe more my speed."

"You couldn't do pilates, trust me."

"And she's kinda cute; wouldn't mind seeing her in tight tights."

Lilly turned and looked at him again, raising her eyebrows, clearly annoyed. She extended her arm, ready to hand him the port bottle back.

"I'm kidding! Of course I'm gonna do kick boxing; I don't even know what pilates is."

"Is she better-looking than me?"

"No."

C said quickly, de facto. He couldn't have responded quicker if he tried.

"Good answer."

She smiled and retracted her arm, cradling the port and headed for the front room, and the couch.

"Is anyone in Town better-looking than me?"

She said, her back to him.

Cord hesitated, to feign weighing the question.

She turned, once again raising her eyebrows; they both knew who she was talking about.

Finally, C answered, in a sarcastic tone.

"No, Lillian, of course not, but you already know that, don't you?"

Smiling sexy, she mouthed the only right answer; *yes*.

CHAPTER 159 – A SWEET LITTLE SPOT IN THE BUSH

The bottom of the glass tilted high toward the ceiling, and the sixth glass of port ran smooth down Lilly's throat, chasing the burn from the last shot of *Stoli*. She held it aloft, waiting for the port clinging to the side of the glass to gather into a single drop. She kept it aloft, till the drip slowly coalesced and landed softly on her outstretched tongue.

She snickered a bit.

Oh boy, so much for the three port rule, C thought.

Sitting on the floor, she snuggled up next to him under the comforter, their backs against the couch, legs stuck out straight in front of them, four parallel lines, like two giggly teens. The comforter was cinched up tight to their necks, two bugs in a rug. She wiggled her toes and tilted her left foot to rest against his right; she watched it in fascination, like it wasn't hers, like she didn't control it, a loose cat playing under the blanket. Then her head fell lazily onto his shoulder. The warmth of his body and hers, trapped beneath the blanket, mixed in a comfortable cocktail.

She closed her eyes, a bit sleepy, and content.

"Tell me about *my* trip; I want my *own little blue fish*, named Lillian."

C cocked his head to look at her; she never opened her eyes, but she knew the stare.

"You're not supposed to know about little blue fish."

She picked up her head and lazily opened her eyes.

"I'm sorry C; Earl promised me not to tell. He was drunk about two weeks ago, your fault again, of course, and he slipped about the fish, about the coral and the lobsters. But that's all he told me; he didn't even tell me where it was, where you were going. When he realized what he said, he got upset and started crying, like he always does, and told me he was in *big* trouble; it was some big secret. He said it was *No. 2 of 10*, whatever that means."

C just looked at her, and didn't say a word.

"Well?"

She said, expecting an explanation.

"Well what?"

C said, turning his head and staring blankly at the cream-colored wall before them. The lights were down, only a lamp was on, away from them, so they mostly sat in the dark. The wall, at least now, was a lighter shade of gray.

"Well, what does it mean?"

C looked back at her and raised his eyebrows, not saying a word; she playfully harrumphed.

"You two are such girls."

C still didn't answer, but smirked.

"Well, then, what about my trip?"

"You wanna go on a trip? With me?"

"Are any of these trips real, or is it all just made-up?"

"Does it matter? You're drunk; you won't remember it in the morning anyway."

"Yes I will, promise; tell me about *my* trip, a *real* trip."

"Your trip, or our trip?"

"Our trip."

Lilly liked the sound of that – *our* trip.

"Okay, I'll tell you about *our* trip."

She laid her head gently back on his shoulder, half-turned toward him and wrapped her arms around his right bicep. C figured he could pretty much spend the rest of his life just like this. Girls came and went, and he usually didn't give a rat's ass about most of them, just about all of them, *all of them*, in fact, except Kristine. But now there was Lilly. Lilly's weren't supposed to happen.

"Well, the world's a big place; where do you want to go?"

"Anywhere! Anywhere but here!"

"Then why don't you just go? Why are you still here? Why haven't you ever left? You don't have a rope around your waist."

"Yes I do."

She said, in deflated defeat.

"Don't blame Earl; he's not stopping you."

"I never said it was Earl."

C didn't answer, and she said it a second time, just above a whisper, to herself, and to anyone else who might be listening.

"I never said it was Earl."

And Cord, without thinking, kissed Lillian, for the very first time. It was a gentle, dry kiss, barely a touch, on her forehead, right at the hairline. He exhaled slowly as he did it, and then breathed in the aroma of her hair; he didn't know the shampoo, but it smelled good.

She didn't pay it any heed, good or bad. She was just silent. He didn't know if that was a good sign, or not, but he figured good, so he did it again; this time, she tightened her grip on his arm.

But it wasn't a scared, or angry, grip, it was more the type you get when someone wants to get closer than they can really get to you, to crawl right inside you. It was *that* kind of grip, the best kind you can ever get.

C could hardly believe it; yeah, she was drunk, but, hopefully, when she woke up tomorrow morning, hopefully with him by her side, she would remember that arm squeeze, and be happy she did it....no take-backs.

"I've never left Town, not really; some school bus trips to other schools, down to Hackettstown, downtown Washington, Easton, but that doesn't count. Never left. I've been over every square inch of this shitty little Town, and I'm lost C....I'm lost. Do you know how many times I've said to myself: *just run away, don't even think about it, don't even pack a bag, just go, in the middle of the night, just go....somewhere else, anywhere else.* But I always figure out an excuse; I'm good at that. I'm too scared, so I don't go; I never do."

Lilly sighed.

"I'm scared, and lonely, and angry....and trapped."

She stared into the gray.

"I'm lost too, Lilly, just in a different way. I have no finish line; no place to stop, to catch a breath, to end, to call *home*. It's just the next place and then the next; I come, and go, and come and go; I don't control it, I can't stop it, and there's no end, *ever*, a carnival ride that never stops. Most times, I feel like a sinking ship, with no port to call home, so I circle endlessly, knocking more holes in the hull, hoping I finally just sink, but I never do, I never sink. I'm not allowed to just fucking sink, even though I want to, because sinking is the best option I have. That cycle has gone on for years, *years;* thousands of faces come and go, and I don't remember any of them, don't give a fuck about any of them, not in the end. And then, somehow, I end up here, in the middle of nowhere, and meet Earl, and you, and I suddenly care. That's not supposed to happen; that's not in the rulebook. My mom used to say *a three-minute egg is a three-minute egg, except when it's not.* I'm not sure why I just said that."

C's head was spinning, but not too much; most of what he was saying still made sense, he thought. Lilly looked up at him and smiled.

"What's your mom like, C?"

She said, squeezing his arm again.

"Guess what her name was?"

He said *was;* she must be dead.

"Is she dead?"

Cord smiled and gave a single nod of yes.

"Her name was Lillian; I *love* that name."

"Really? No way! You're not lying?"

Lilly quickly sat up, the blanket falling just past her shoulders, and looked deep into C's eyes, looking for the sarcasm, a hint that he was playing with her, and she saw none. She just saw a genuine smile looking back at her; she loved when he smiled that way. C had a good smile when he wanted to.

"I'm not lying; I would never lie about something as important as that. That was her name; my dad always called her Lillian, never anything else, just Lillian. Other people sometimes called her Lil. But she was never a Lilly, never heard that once. Just you, you're the only Lilly I know."

And that was the first piece of family Cord had given up to her, since the day he arrived in Town. And why his mom's name meant anything but coincidence didn't matter to Lilly one pinch; to her, it was gold, some sort of divine sign.

"Why didn't you ever tell me that?! Tell me more."

She said, hugging his arm harder, wanting to hear about his mom.

C put his arm around her shoulders, and she pulled in tight. Chicken walked into the room and curled on the corner of the comforter; in seconds her eyes were closed, fast asleep.

"I had another weird dream last night. I never dreamed you know, not for years, at least none that I remembered, till I showed up here. I was stuck in a picker bush, standing on some kind of sloped ground, like the edge of a lawn, next to the edge of the woods, I think. And the soil next to the picker bush was full of small mounds of loose dirt, like gopher mounds, but smaller, kind of like ant mounds, but bigger, all around my feet. And these big pill bugs, you know those things you find in the wet spots in the basement, with the armor-looking plates, gray, but they were big, the size of big roaches, even bigger, the size of a mouse, they were burrowing in and out of the soil all around my feet, and I kept trying to shift my feet, to not step on them, to not hurt them, while

I was unhooking and re-snagging myself on the picker bush thorns. I had to get through that bush for some reason, to get to what was on the other side, but I couldn't, I was just stuck there, endlessly unhooking and re-snagging myself, surrounded by pill bugs, who really paid no attention to me at all. What the fuck do you think that means? And why am I dreaming again?"

"Do you ever dream about your mom?"

Lilly said, barely above a whisper.

"Yeah, kinda. I had a strange dream about Polar bears and *Baby Magic*. I had that dream the night I told you about the puppet story, remember? God, that seems like a lifetime ago, that was the first weekend I was here, remember?"

It felt good to be able to reminisce with Lilly; they had finally accumulated enough history, that they could look back together, at shared times, even bad times, with fondness. And that was pretty cool.

Lilly half-shook her head yes as it rested on his shoulder. C couldn't see that she was smiling.

"That was the first dream I had in Belvidere, and the first dream I remembered having in years. I remember it just popped in my head, standing right over there in the hallway, right after you left, all wrapped in a blanket. Hey, that was this blanket *[C was surprised at the revelation]*! You looked like a big mashed potato *[Cord laughed, remembering that day with Marty]*. Why did you come up that night anyway?"

"You know why; that stupid puppet dream and Earl saying the puppet was coming in the front window freaked me out....stupid puppet."

C laughed, and kissed Lilly on the forehead for the third time, this one a bit longer.

And she let him.

"Anyway, it just popped into my head, just like that, out of nowhere. I don't know what the polar bears were all about, but the *Baby Magic* was definitely my mom. I remembered smelling *Baby Magic*, and that smell *was* my mom; she used to slather herself in that stuff every night before she went to bed, and when she kissed me on the forehead and tucked me into bed, it was always the last thing I remembered before falling asleep. *I loved that smell.* Lilly, it was so vivid, that dream; I swear it felt real."

"I had a dream about my mom."

Lilly said, somber.

"Really, when? Recent?"

"No, just once, right after she died. Well, a couple months later."

And Lilly didn't say anything more.

"You wanna tell me?"

C said, as he kissed her forehead for the fourth time, his lips barely touched her skin.

"I don't know, I might get upset. Earl knows, he's the only one, not even Button."

Why did she have to bring him up, C thought to himself. Was it good that he was going to hear something that Button didn't know – and this was the most important topic there was when it came to Lilly – or was it bad that she even had him on her mind, at an intimate time, really the first intimate time, between the two of them?

C didn't answer, and he didn't kiss her again. He just waited to see what Lilly would do, anything or nothing was okay with him. Her head was down, looking sullen at the blanket.

She spoke, barely above a whisper, in more of a plead, than a question.

"Do you think Earl really talks to my mom, for real? Or is it all just made up? I know he talks to you about it; I know it, so don't deny it. You don't believe him, do you?"

C kissed her forehead again, a long kiss; he could feel her trembling.

"Lilly, I don't believe in anything after death; I believe black is black and dead is dead - lights out, and nothing more.   Anything else is simply wishful thinking. I've believed that since I was a kid, and I believed that before I came to Belvidere. But now, I'm not so sure. What I'm saying is, that I *do* believe, I really do, that Earl talks to your mom, or someone, or something, inside his head. I don't know how, but he does; stuff he's said to me, stuff he knows about, he simply couldn't know that stuff. Lilly, I can't explain it any other way, I just can't.   It makes no sense."

Lilly was silent. So C asked her, just above a whisper.

"Do *you* think he talks to your mom?"

Lilly's upper lip started to quiver, and she began to softly cry.

"I hope so."

And for a minute or so, the two just sat beside one another, in silence, Lilly quietly crying to herself, cradled in C's arm.

Then she began, mid-sentence, as if she'd already started retelling the dream, to herself, for the thousandth time, in her head.

"…and I was running in the woods; it was sunny out, and I remember the sun speckled the ground all around me, between the leaves high up on the trees. I could feel the twigs and gravel and leaves crunch under my feet, and I was running fast, *so fast,* but I wasn't tired at all, not a lick, and there was no one around me, just me in the woods, alone, and I was running so fast, like I was floating on air….effortless. I was running with my head down, looking at my sneakers, looking at my shoelaces, and every now and then, I would look up and, and…."

Lilly started sobbing.

"….and suddenly I saw my mom was up ahead, *way* up ahead, on the path; I could hardly see her face, but I think she was smiling at me, I really think she was C, and she said: *just a little further, almost there sweetie, come on.* And I would run harder, I'd put my head down and run harder and faster, like my heart was gonna explode, and the harder I ran, the further she slipped away, further and further up the path. I yelled to her to: *Stop, don't go, wait for me!* But she wouldn't, she wouldn't C, she wouldn't wait; she kept going, getting farther and farther away. Why'd didn't she just wait C; why'd she go? Why'd she have to go away? Why?"

Lilly pleaded with C, wanting the answer she thought he might have; the answer she had been waiting her whole life to hear.

"I don't know sweetie, I don't; I wish I did."

Cord didn't realize he called her *sweetie* till it had already come out, and he cringed, afraid of her reaction. But she didn't seem to care.

"….then, all of a sudden, it was the middle of the winter, just like that, and I wasn't wearing winter clothes, but I wasn't cold, and there had just been a fantastic snowfall, the kind that's wet and heavy, you know, where it sticks to the branches and weighs them down, way down, like they're just about to snap. It was beautiful, the most beautiful snow I ever saw. And it must have just stopped snowing, just a moment before, because the scene was *perfect,* not ruined in any way, quiet….and perfect. And I'm running through the woods, along a path, which is kind of like a snow tunnel, because all the tree branches are bent down, and the path becomes like a long, arched tunnel. And way up ahead, there is someone running away from me, hunched over, shadowed in black against the white snow. I can't tell if it's my mom anymore, it might be a man; he runs like a man, but maybe it's my mom, so I chase along. And he, or she, I think it's a he, keeps stopping, and looking back at me; he has a long black trench coat on, but I can't see the face, and when I get a little closer, it runs ahead, along this switchback trail in the woods, like a line in the movie theater. I can see him, and I could probably catch him if I left the trail and cut through the woods, but, for some reason, I don't, or can't, leave the trail. Neither one of us talks, but I just run through the snow, and run….and run. Then he gets to a cave, kind of an ice cave, and ducks inside. I get there and the cave is bright, full of icicles, and snow; the ice looks blue. It's a long windy tunnel, like it's carved out of solid ice, with the tiny tips of rock sticking out here and there. It doesn't even look real. And he's way ahead, down the tunnel, so I follow him through, but he's always too far ahead to really see. The last thing I remember, I'm getting closer, and he ducks around a corner, then peers back around the corner to look back at me, and then disappears around the bend for good, and I never see him again. I run toward the corner, and I'm almost there, almost ready to see whatever is hiding around the corner, but I never quite make it. Then I woke up."

Lilly had stopped crying some time during the retell, her head down; her tone had become like one who is recounting the witness to a crime, trying to remember each detail, trying to figure out which ones really mattered, the ones that would solve the riddle.

"Lilly, is that's why you ran cross-country, in high school? To find your mom, in the woods."

Lilly just barely shook her head yes, face down.

"She was never there C; I ran and ran and ran, but she was never there. Every race I figured she'd finally be there; Earl talked to her, and she told me: *just a little further, come on.* So I ran as fast as I could, every time; but she was never there, C, she was never there. All I ever wanted was for her to be there, *just once*, just to talk to her again, just one word, even to just smile at her, and have her smile back, just one more time. I didn't care about anything else; but she was never there….so I gave up, forever."

Lilly had a hundred-pound weight wrapped around her neck; she couldn't pick her head up, even if she tried, so complete was the defeat in her voice.

C pushed down the comforter to expose Lilly's left hand; she had elegant, tiny hands, with thin fingers, smooth skin and pronounced, bony joints, enough to notice. But Cord loved the look of them.

Cord gently grabbed her hand, pulled it out from beneath the blanket and placed it atop the fabric, palm down. Then he carefully placed his atop hers, loosely interlacing their fingers as he slowly ran his hand back and forth.

It was the first time he held her hand, kind of.

"I like your hands; I've always liked your hands."

Lilly said to him, and C smiled.

"That's funny, so did…."

And he caught himself.

"So did who?"

"A girl I used to know."

Lillian looked at him.

"Not as pretty as you, though."

C quickly added; she smiled, and let it drop.

C leaned back, away from her, in an exaggerated manner, and studied Lilly's face, as a painter does a model: her straight blonde hair, chocolate eyebrows framing piercing, blue eyes, wild eyes, hiding behind the veneer. Lillian was beautiful in so many ways, no question, but her eyes, those eyes, were probably the very best part.

But the beauty couldn't hide the pain, and they were still a bit puffy and pink from her cry.

He looked down to her slight-upturned nose, her thin lips, with just the right amount of puff; pouty, yet belligerent. Extra-white teeth, straight and sparkling, with a beautiful smile, which she sported not nearly enough.

And a long, regal neck.

She loved the attention he was giving; she always did. One thing Lillian got more than enough of, but always thirsted for more, was attention.

"You know, everyone says I look just like my mom, like we could be sisters. We used to wear each other's clothes.   I wish you could've met her C, I think she would've liked you; I don't know why, but I think so."

"Do *you* like me?"

Shit!   That was too risky, too direct; the answer could screw the evening, and it came out too quick, before he really thought about it….*stupid* alcohol.

She smiled.

"We'll see, the night's not over yet."

And Lilly kissed C, lightly, on the tip of the nose, his first kiss….a tiny, tiny peck.

Lilly did her own painter's stare, and she was drawn to the three-inch scar, that she had seen a hundred times, on his right bicep.   She lightly ran her fingertip down the red and white, fading arched scar.

"You never told me what happened?"

"You never asked."

"Okay, what happened?"

"Lilly, I'm not ready to talk about that, please."

"Who's the black girl?"

He frowned and said nothing.

"What's in the box? Why does it say that? Why are you here? Why?"

Lilly's voice trailed off.

"Okay, okay."

He interrupted, and sighed.

"Lilly, I look at myself in the mirror, every morning, and all I see is damaged goods. It's like I've got a stain, on my skin, and no matter how hard I scrub, I can't get the stain out. And everyone sees it, eventually, and I can't hide it, and I can't shake it. So I just keep going away."

"I don't get it; what's that mean?"

"I was in Kansas City one time, and…."

"I don't want to hear about another stupid trip, or another stupid story! Answer my question, any of them, one of them…*just one!*"

C let out a long, steady exhale from his nose, looked at her, and resigned himself to answering a question.

"What I tell you now, where I was right before I was here, you can't tell anyone else, agreed? It's really important Lilly, *really important*, that you tell no one; understand?"

C stared at Lilly hard, and she nodded a single yes. And he believed her, he really did, so he continued.

"Back in April, right before I came here, some bad things, and sad things, happened, on a farm in a little no-name part of Kansas, in the middle of nowhere, between Wichita and Kansas City. Don't ask me how I ended up there; it's the same as how I end up everywhere. This place, there's not even a town, where this is, not really, just endless farms. After what happened there, but not because of *what* happened, but after, I got real drunk, worse than usual; that was after I opened the box, *the box [C pointed over at the hall closet with the box and aluminum foil packs].*

Lilly sat up, realizing just how important this story was going to be.

Every time, after I open the box, after a little while anyway, I always get drunk, I mean really ripped, that's the process; I don't ever change it, I can't. It's just the way it is; those are the rules, not my rules, just the rules. Always the same, every time, so far anyway.

And once I'm good and ripped, I take out a set of darts, which I keep in the box, with other stuff. Three darts, always three. They're in a little carrying case; they're up there, right now. Anyway, I flip it open and carefully take out three; there are four darts in the case, but I never take the fourth one out, I only keep it in case I lose one, one breaks, whatever. And I've never lost one, or broke one yet, so the fourth dart has never been used. Ever. And I've used the darts *many* times; too many times.

Anyway, in April, right before I came here, I take out the same three darts I always take out, close the case and put it back in the box. Nothing unusual in that.

I have a bunch of folded maps; I keep them in the box too. Don't remember where I got them all, along the way I guess....doesn't much matter. Anyway, I stick my hand in the box, blind, and pull out a map, any map, I've got the whole world covered in maps, every fucking inch, some are of Europe, some Africa, some Central America, some the United States, some are of parts of the United States, some are just individual states. I have about thirty maps, maybe more, bound with a big rubber band. I always shuffle them around before I pack them away, so I never know the order of the maps. Anyway, back in April, I stick my hand in, and pull out a random map from the bunch of them, and the map just happens to be Pennsylvania; don't know why I have a Pennsylvania map, just do....it's simply part of the bunch.

So I tape it to the wall of the bedroom I'm in, the best I can, 'cause I'm really jacked, and step back, no set distance, just whatever feels right; I'm drunk, so it doesn't really matter. Anyway, I throw the three darts, like I always do, and the first one that hits something on the map, a real place, not the middle of the ocean, or the map margin, or the ceiling, or the wall, I go to next. It's that simple. That's how I usually decide, or rather, that's how *it's* decided, where I go. Not always, there are some exceptions, like if I get in a jam, and some others, but usually that's the procedure. Again, not *my* procedure, just *the* procedure."

And C stopped. And Lilly looked at him. And he looked at her.

"So, finish the story."

"I did finish the story."

"No you *didn't*. Where did the darts land? What happened? Why are you here?"

"I don't really remember throwing the darts, Lilly, but that's not unusual."

C stopped, and Lillian just stared at him. C sighed, and continued.

"Okay, here's what I remember. I remember waking up, face down on the floor, in a puddle of drool, in the middle of the night, which was unusual; not the face-down part, I have that piece pretty down pat, but the middle-on-the-night part was different - I usually don't wake till the next morning. But this time, for some reason, I don't know why, I woke up, and I remember the time *[C shook his head at the memory]*. Trust me, I remember it; it was exactly 1:13 am, and that matters, that *really* matters, because that was the same exact time I got home that night I got stuck on the fence, when I was twelve."

"What fence?"

"I never told you that story? About the dam?"

"No, what story? Who'd you tell?"

C remembered it was Mae, when they were in bed after they fucked, so he didn't answer.

Instead, he slowly picked up his shirt; his belly was getting pretty flat, much flatter than the last time Lilly saw it, and he pointed to the four linear scars on his mid-section, the ones that traveled with him, his companion, every day, since 1975.

"I was twelve, and I got stuck trying to crawl over a real tall wrought iron fence, with real big spikes."

Lilly didn't respond, she just looked closer and lightly touched the closest circular scar, the same one Mae kissed. It was different than when she just touched his bicep earlier; it was the first time she touched him in a way that was, could be described as, sensual....and it was on purpose.

"I thought I was gonna die on that fence at twelve years old; in fact, part of me has never been sure that I didn't really die that night. That sounds crazy, stupid, right; I just told you black is black and dead is dead, right? And I've always believed that, right? And I have, I think. But, Lilly, I was skewered on that fence, pierced, all alone, at night, twelve years old, scared shitless, with no one around, no one anywhere nearby to help, and those sharp rusty spikes were dug into me *deep*, real deep. To this day, I don't know how I got off that fence; I was stuck like a pig, and sinking deeper, it just a matter of time till I pierced my heart, or something vital....*something*. And I remember, vividly, at twelve years old, not being afraid to die, or rather, being okay with it....I wasn't giving up, but I wasn't afraid, I just kind of accepted it. I don't know how else to describe it. Anyway, I must have just passed out, stuck up there, and surely my weight alone would have sunk those spikes right through me; *had to, right?* But later on, and I don't know how, there was no one around to help me, and no one knew I was there, I somehow woke up lying on the ground, all alone, next to the fence, with blood everywhere, but not as much blood as there should have been, with no explanation. And everything around me was eerie quiet, and the stars, I remember them being *so* bright, like they were fake. Like they weren't real, not like the stars you normally see. But maybe I was just in shock....I don't know.

So I walked home, alone, and I never looked at the holes, not close anyway; I was too scared to lift my shirt and really look at them.

When I got home, and crawled into bed, it was exactly 1:13 am; I remember like it was yesterday. The clock radio, that green glow from the clock, it dimly lit my bedroom, and the time, the 1:13, it *never* changed, at least I don't remember it ever changing, for way longer than a minute should last. It just seemed to stay 1:13 am....forever.

1:13 am.

And that's the night I first met the puppet, in a dream, the exact dream I told you and Earl about, with the crickets, and the flies; and it all seemed *so real* Lilly. And right after that day, after that happened, it was like my life bent a bit off-course. It was like running your hand up a smooth, straight branch, then coming to a kink, and veering off in a skew. I don't know how to describe it any better; my life, whatever my life was for the first twelve years, felt decidedly different prior to that day, and its always been *off* since, like that stain I can't get rid off."

She just stared at him, and for the first time, she felt the pang of what Earl had told her she felt all along. And she wanted to tell C right away, right then, right there. But somehow she couldn't; she couldn't get the words out, or figure how to say it. How to say that maybe, just maybe, she was falling in love; that maybe C was really, was finally, the right guy, for her.

She just stared at him, mouth about to speak, but not a word left her lips.

"You know Lilly, I don't know if that fence, hole-punching me open like it did, let him in, or let him out, but that fucking puppet has never left since. He's always there, offstage and to the left most of the time, but there nonetheless, hiding, and laughing, with the crickets and the flies, in my brain. And now and again he shows his face, just to remind me that he's watching, *always* watching, making sure the game stays played. I've never been able to shake 'em since."

"You're starting to scare me."

"I'm not trying to, I promise; I'm trying to explain why I'm here. I'm trying, for once, to honestly answer your question; Lilly, I really *don't* know why I'm here."

"What happened with the darts?"

C shook his head, left to right, as if he didn't really believe what he was about to say.

"I woke up on the floor, and looked over at the wall, and the digital clock, this one was white, it said 1:13 am. That had *never* happened before, seeing 1:13, after opening the box. And I've opened that box too many times, over too many years. Never once was it 1:13 am. So the hair on my arms rose, seeing those three scary numbers, just staring back at me, silent, like I was twelve all over again.

The lights were off, but the moon was bright enough to glow the room. I wiped the drool from my mouth and pushed myself off the floor, to look for the darts I threw, like I always did.

And that's when I realized one, the third one, the one I always threw last, was still gripped in my hand; I must have passed out and fell down holding it, before I even threw it. The first one, my favorite, was stuck in a ceiling tile. The second one was stuck in the lampshade by the bed, not even close to the map, and the third, as I said, was in my hand. That had never happened before; I never missed the map completely, and I never passed out with one in my hand, and as I said, I've played this game many, many times.

Too many times *[C shook his head in the negative as he spoke]*.

But as I stood there in the dark, still in a bit of a drunken fog, I noticed, on the far right side of the map, close to the very edge, what looked like a dart, sticking arrow-straight, driven deep in the wall, piercing the map....hard. Much deeper than it would ever normally be if you threw it, unless you threw it really hard, I guess, *really* hard. It was the *fourth* dart, the one I never use, the one that never comes out of the case, the one I had shut in the case and put back in the box; I *swore* I did, but I was drunk, so maybe I didn't. That fourth dart, the one I never toss, was sticking in the map, lit up by the moonlight. I'll never forget, it was a waxing moon, on it's way to full, and it was almost full that night, but not quite.

I stumbled over to the map, and had to put my arm on the wall to steady myself, and I stared at the fourth dart. It wasn't even in Pennsylvania, it was *in* the river, the Delaware River, closer to the eastern shore, kinda just off the shore. Lilly, it was sticking in the water, just downstream of the boat ramp; I didn't know it at the time, but it was, just south of where the Pequest comes into the Delaware, just south of the bridge, right where we always go, right where Al fishes. I looked and saw the town *Belvidere*, but it was in New Jersey, not Pennsylvania; so, I figured, that must be the place to go. And that's why I'm here, I think."

Lilly just stared at him; the hair on her arms was sticking straight and her fingers tingled.

"Did you throw that dart C?"

"I don't know, I must have."

"But you still had a dart in your hand; you couldn't have thrown it!"

"Maybe I threw it third."

But neither of them really believed that.

"Who threw that dart C? Who were you with?"

"*No one*, trust me *[C shook his head hard in the negative]*. Whenever I open the box, I'm always alone, always; that part of the game is always solo, always, has to be. That rule is never broken, *never*, it just can't be, it's not allowed, or there *will* be consequences. That much I know."

"What's in the box?"

"I told you what's in the box?"

"What *else* is in the box?!"

"Stuff that has nothing to do with why I'm here; I told you why I'm here."

"No, no you didn't, you told me *how* you got here, not why. Who threw it? Why'd that dart land in the river? Why there?"

"I don't know why, *do you*?"

Lilly eyes started to get red again.

"C, why does your box say that? Why? Why does it say *Open When You Are Ready? Why?!*"

Lilly was practically pleading with him. So C faced Lilly, practically nose to nose, and placed his hands firmly on her shoulders.

"Lilly, it's a coincidence, it is; I don't think what I wrote on the box has anything to do with Belvidere, or your mom. I don't think it has anything to do with….the note she gave to you."

And C braced for the aftermath.

But Lilly was beyond getting mad; she figured C knew about her mom's note anyway. Sam had a big mouth, and the two of them were too close, working together, for that bit to stay a secret. She knew Frank would never say anything, and Earl didn't know about the note, so it had to be Sam.

Little did she know Sam spilled about the note on the very first day they met.

"How do you know? How do you know it doesn't?"

C just looked at her; he was as lost as she was.

A single tear ran down Lilly's cheek, and her voice started to quiver.

"C, did my mom send you here? Do you talk to my mom?"

"Lilly, I don't talk to your mom; I wish I did, trust me. I don't talk to anyone, not like that. All I have is the puppet, the crickets and the flies, and I don't want them."

Then Cord sighed, and frowned.

"What's that face for? Why are you making that face?"

Her voice still quivering.

"Lilly, I don't know why I'm here, I really don't, and I can't explain the darts, and I thought the same thing about the box as you did, when I heard about your mom's note, and what it said, but I just think it's got to be some sort of weird coincidence. I've been using that same box for years, with that same saying written on it the whole time, not just this trip. But, but...."

"But what?"

"Some of the stuff Earl says to me, it makes me think, I don't know, that he knows a lot more about this stuff than you and I do."

"Like what?!"

A tingle of adrenaline shot up Lilly's arms again.

"This is crazy, it isn't real. I know you want it to be, me too, I really do; but it's not, Lilly....it's not."

"Like what?!"

"I don't know, a bunch of stuff. Stuff that seems a little odd stand-alone, but not really super crazy. But when you start adding them all up, it seems much more than a little odd....kind of."

"Tell me what the fuck you're talking about!"

Lilly pleaded.

"Okay, okay."

C looked at her like he was a kid, ready to confess, ready to get it off his chest.

"It was the very first weekend I was here; Earl and I were walking to the boat ramp, alone. I had just met Earl, *just met him,* I knew him for an hour, probably less; you remember that day *[Lilly nodded once, yes].* And I remember thinking that he and I had some sort of special connection, something like I never felt with anyone else, and the word that came to mind, right to mind, was that I thought Earl was a kindred spirit, to me, for me....kind of.   And I remember thinking that was pretty cool, having a kindred spirit, and how really special that was, and that not many people have that, *ever.* I certainly never did.

But I said that to myself, Lilly, in my own mind; I was just *thinking* about it. I never said it out loud, and I definitely didn't say it, or *anything* about it, to Earl. Ten minutes later, less even, I asked Earl why he talked to me, that first day in the Park, since I was told he *never* talks to strangers; and you know what he said? Did he ever tell you *[Lilly shook a no]*? I'm sure he didn't. He said *your mom* told him to, that she was sitting with us, right between us, on the bench, in the Park, *their bench,* and that she knew about me, that I had done some bad stuff in the past, but underneath I was a good person, and that I was Earl's friend, a *kindred* spirit...Earl said that to *me*! Then I asked Earl what the word *kindred* meant, and he just shrugged his shoulders; he didn't know....he had no idea what that word even meant, but he said it anyway. How do you say a word you don't even know? That same word I just thought about him? Coincidence? How do you even explain that? That's pretty fucking strange, don't you think?

And then he said that his mom, *your mom,* really believes in me; she told him she thinks I'm some sort of angel, a good angel, kinda. Me? Some sort of good angel? Are you kidding me? With all the stuff I've done? Bad, *really bad stuff* Lilly; stuff I can never tell you, ever. And yet I'm supposed to be some sort of angel sent here for him, and for you? It makes no sense....none."

Lilly just shook her head no; she wasn't really sure why she was doing that.

"Now Lilly, you can't get mad at Earl, and you can't tell him I said this; I shouldn't have even said anything to you at all, but this shit doesn't happen to me, and if anyone else said it happened to them, I'd call them a fucking kook and walk away….trust me."

Lilly just stared at C, mouth partly open, the hair on her arms still at attention. C just looked down and slowly shook his head, shaking the box of secrets, getting the last crumbs out, getting them all on the table.

"And Earl said, she said, your mom, that I wouldn't believe in her, at first, but I hopefully would, eventually, and I had something to tell Earl….*when I was ready*….that's exactly what Earl said, those were *his* words. And I don't even know what the fuck I'm supposed to tell him, or when I'm supposed to do it! When am I ready? I have no fucking clue! And I don't know where Earl came up with all this; I guess he could have just made up the angel thing, and the something-to-tell-him thing, but the *kindred spirit* thing, now that's a big fucking stretch, don't you think? How did he make up a word he doesn't even know, a word, and not a common word, by the way, that I just thought about not ten minutes before? Does he even *know* that word, for real?"

Lilly just shrugged her shoulders; she had no answers.

C looked exhausted, drained, finally setting down the bag of bricks he had been carrying for months. He looked up at her, confused, looking for answers from her, as much as she was from him.

"What do you think, about all that?"

Lilly was just staring blank at the wall, into the gray.

"Can we not talk about this anymore, for awhile….please?"

Lilly said, as she turned to him and hugged hard, burying her head in his chest.

"Sure, yeah….no problem. That's what I normally do, just stop thinking about it. It's the best solution, no solution at all."

And the two hugged tight, in silence. Then Lilly quietly whispered into his chest.

"Did she say anything about me?"

But before C could answer, she did.

"Forget it, please don't tell me, not tonight; I can't think about it anymore tonight, okay C?"

"Okay."

He whispered, as he gently kissed the top of her head, and slowly ran his hand up and down the top of her arm, rubbing her in comfort.

"You know, all I wanted when we got under this blanket was to have my own trip, and my own little blue fish, named Lillian. How the hell did we end up here, talking about all that stuff?"

"I don't know, but that was a pretty strange trip, wasn't it?"

C said, smiling at Lilly, which she weakly returned.

"But if you still want to go, I've got a couple places in mind. How about a little private island, in Belize, Central America, just you and me? You'd like that."

"Tell me."

Lilly said, as she closed her eyes, and dreamed of a place she'd never been, a place she couldn't even find on a map.

"This is a real special island; you can walk around the entire perimeter, the whole island, *all of it*, walking real slow to boot, with one foot dragging in the water, in a big lazy circle, in less than *six minutes*....that's it! I timed it, so I know. And that included a stop along the way to kick the generator, which sometimes works, and sometimes doesn't.

It's so tiny, there are only two huts, ours - which is Hut No. 4 - which makes no sense, and the one where the cook and the mechanic sleep, which doesn't even have a number. Just them and us, that's it, out in the middle of the ocean, the Gulf of Mexico, with some of the most beautifully-colored water in the world – I can't even describe the blue.

The only way to get to it, and to get off, is by their tiny boat, *real* tiny. It's a forty-five minute ride in the open ocean, so you can only leave if the surf isn't too rough, otherwise, you're stuck. But what a place to be stuck. Lilly, what a place! No phone service, no internet; only a beat-up radio that rarely worked. Your bags get thrown in a rusty wheel-barrow, and Alburn, he's the mechanic, wheels them to your hut, Hut No. 4.

A supply boat comes out once about once a week; it brings ice, diesel for the generator, food, takes away the trash....that's about it.

Lilly, you lay lazy in bed in the middle of the day, and it's nothing like you've ever seen. Your bedroom door is open, certainly no need for locks, the door is hung there simply to help keep out the wind and rain. And with it open, you look out to nothing but countless shades of blue water, clear to the horizon.   What a fucking bedroom!

And off to the left, lying real low, just above the water, a line on the horizon, you can see some hints of green. The first one *[C pointed across the room, slowly moving his finger left to right]*, that's *Tropp Caye,* then there's *Whiprey Caye*, the next one, that one doesn't even have a name, then *Little Lagun Caye* and then *Water Caye.* A series of tiny islands, nothing more than a bunch of tangled mangroves, really; nobody lives on 'em.

And I saved the best one for last.

If you lay on the bed, gaze to the left of center, and look out the door, across the deck with the hammock, about a quarter-mile away, a ten minute slow paddle by kayak, is the tiniest of the tiny islands....a baby really, just forming. Two small rocks, usually pelicans are sitting on them, and a single, solitary mangrove stem, which took hold in the shallow water and is desperately sending up shoots, trying to grow a tangle of roots and branches that will catch the shells and sand that someday may make a new caye, a new island, if it's lucky....if it survives.   Lilly, you're miles from any land, but the water by that little mangrove is only as deep as your ankles; it's sitting on this long, curved and narrow ridge of coral, maybe thirty feet wide at most, probably less, that runs for miles and miles through the Gulf of Mexico, hiding just below the surface of the water.

It's like your standing on water, walking on water, literally, in the middle of the ocean; you could walk for a full mile and a half, in the middle of nothing but blue, with the water no deeper than your knees, sometimes it barely covers the top of your feet.   It feels other-worldly; no other way to describe it.   But if you get stuck standing out there and a big storm rolls in, with big waves, you're pretty well fucked, pretty surely swept away....a goner. And storms out there can form and can sneak up on you real quick; way quicker than you can get back to safety. And that little island with Hut No. 4 is not so safe either, if the storm is big enough. It's a fickle place; beautiful and scary, both at the same time. Kind of like you.

[Lilly smiled at him – a good smile - and C smiled back. Then she simply closed her eyes and listened to Cord spin his tale]

But I swear you'll never experience anything quite like it; it's hypnotic being able to stand beside that little, single, struggling mangrove, and spin three-hundred sixty degrees and *all* you see is water, and the little island your hut is on, which is a pretty big God-damn island compared to the single stick of mangrove your standing next to. It certainly makes you feel vulnerable, and small. There's an awful big world out there Lilly, and we're pretty fucking small.

And I like that.

And if you tie your kayak to that single mangrove, and walk less than twenty yards to the left or right, the water gets four to six feet deep, and suddenly you're surrounded by coral outcrops full of huge, spiny lobsters hiding in the crevices; sometimes all you see are the tips of their antennae sticking out of a hole, under the coral. They swish them left and right, feeling around. And you'll see fish of every shape and color you can imagine: barracuda, spotted trunkfish – they look square – a *square fish*, for real, butterfly fish, orange and green parrot fish, huge angelfish, and you'll even see your blue ones....they're called blue tangs, by the way....pretty.

And if you peak just under the surface, you'll see massive schools of neon goby, darting back and forth, swimming like they're one big fish, till they scatter at the site of a bar jack, and just as quickly coalesce again when the danger passes. And conch, they're *everywhere*, living in huge shells; you have be careful not to step on them, there are so many, crawling slow along the bottom. And starfish, loads of starfish; they're crawling around too, looking for sea urchins to eat….and there are *plenty* of them to eat. And if you're lucky, you might find an octopus living in an old conch shell; I did the last time I was there….he was *so* tiny, just a baby! And sea cucumbers, they look kinda like a real cucumber, the shape, are everywhere; and if you touch 'em, they'll spit water at you!"

Lilly opened her eyes and smiled at him.

"Does that place *really* exist, C, promise?"

"You bet, real as rain. I wonder how big that little mangrove island is by now? God, it's been years since I've been there."

"How do you remember all this stuff, about everywhere you go?"

"I don't know, some stuff, I just do. I guess, for some reason, remembering is important to me."

"What's the name, of the island?"

"*Jeunesse Doree.*"

"What's that mean?"

"Gilded youth, in French. It's not really the name, but that's what I always call it. You certainly feel young, and carefree, and rich, and special, when you're there. The real name is boring, so we'll just call it *Jeunesse Doree,* okay? Just you and me."

"Deal. So what else? Tell me more; tell me about *our* island."

"I almost forgot to tell you about the best fish we'll see, if we're lucky. Wow, and this one's the absolute best! It's all black, with a bright yellow tail – it almost looks fake, and it has these little blue dots all along its back and sides – they're shiny, iridescent, like they're metallic! It's absolutely beautiful, the *most* beautiful amongst dozens of beautiful fish. It's called a yellowtail damselfish, but some people call it something else, they call it a *Lillian,* although no one knows that but you and me….our little secret."

"I got my own fish! A Lillian? Cool! Way better than Earl's little blue fish, for sure! What's its other name?"

"That's right, a Lillian Liddell, a *Lilly* for short, it's also known as, boring, a yellowtail damselfish. You'll never forget when you see the first one, for real, trust me."

Lilly was beaming, and C smiled.

"More, tell me more C! When can we go, for real?"

"Whenever you want; how's tomorrow morning, soon enough? You give the word, and were gone, first-class all the way....promise. Well, maybe getting you a passport would be nice, but, you get the picture."

She closed her eyes and waited for more.

"Okay, what else can I tell you. Well, right off the dock, less than thirty feet away, the turquoise water turns jet-black, because the coral reef drops off a cliff into the abyss. Don't know how deep it goes, but it's *way* deep….pretty spooky. And if you sit on the dock, and watch, every now and then you'll see a giant stingray float out of the ink, up to the shallow water right next to the dock, with wings six-plus feet across….so graceful. And as quickly as they glide by the dock piers, they slip back into the darkness, out of sight. They come and go all day long, and watching them glide by never gets old, never.

We'll eat our meals in our underwear, the staff laughing and telling jokes in Creole, smoking cigars and passing them around the table, drinking Belizean beer, and I don't even drink beer, but I drink it on that island….only on that island.

And at night, lying next to one another on a chaise, out on the deck which overhangs the water, just off the bedroom, we'll listen to the ocean lap against the piers below us, and raise our drinks, as we watch the moon cast a milky trail across the open water, right to us. That's until the clouds race across the night sky, shrouding the moon, then releasing it, over and over again….all night long.

That never gets old either; never.

And you know what? When you wake in the morning, and look on the floor, you'll probably see a crab sitting there; but it's not a real crab, it's a molt, right next to the bed. Some crab came into the room at night, and shed his shell while we slept, never the wiser, and slipped out again into the night. They do it all the time, in and out of the room, leaving a perfectly translucent crab shell, sitting on the floor, to greet you in the morning.

And you know what's for breakfast, *every* morning?"

Lilly just smiled and shook her head no; the answer didn't matter, it was going to be good no matter what C said.

"All sorts of fruit….local stuff that you've never had nor even heard of, even stranger than all the new fruits we have down at Sam's – like craboos, custard apples, coco plums and mamey, sea grapes and pitaya - dragon fruit. All good stuff. But despite all that, believe it or not, the best of the best every morning, is a big glass of watermelon juice served by Alburn. And every morning we'll tip our drinks to each other and smile, with the ocean breeze kissing our cheeks and the morning sky reflecting off the water, the waves hitting the sea wall below us. And you'll say: *Thank you C, the sex last*

*night was fantastic, like always; you really are the best!
Ever! Way better than Button!"*

Lilly elbowed him feisty.

"Nice try."

"And while we eat, we'll watch the crabs running sideways through the sun to find the next patch of dappled shade. And way out there, on this tiny island, in the middle of the Gulf, you'll see yellow butterflies, at least one or two, zagging like drunken sailors, flower to flower.

Later on, we'll pass the afternoon swinging in a hammock on the deck, watch the hermit crabs crawl by, leaving a tiny trail in the sand, and read a book together. *Tortilla Flat,* John Steinbeck, one of my favorites; I read that the last time I was there. We'll sweat and not even care about it, till we fall asleep, tired from doing absolutely nothing all day.

Then you'll wake, take an afternoon shower to wash off the hot and lazily paint your toes in the sun and write in your journal that this is just about the best day of your life. Till tomorrow, when you do it all over again, with a new best day.

Lilly, it's all those stupid little things that aren't so stupid, the crabs and butterflies and generators that don't work, that makes a trip an adventure, the little stuff that most people don't even notice. But I notice it; I notice it all."

"I wanna go! Do you think we can really go, just the two of us?"

"Of course! I told you we would, *whenever* you want."

"Have you brought anybody else there?"

C frowned; the one question he was hoping not to hear.

"Does it matter?"

"Yes."

"Then no, I haven't."

"Are you lying?"

"Maybe."

She raised her eyebrows.

"Who was he?"

She giggled at her own joke, the same one she always used on him; and he smiled in return. Then she asked the real question.

"Who was she?"

But before he could respond, she quickly answered herself.

"Forget it, I don't want to know."

The silence lasted less than ten seconds.

"Is she still around? Is she the black girl?"

"I thought you didn't want to know?"

"It's the black girl! *I knew it;* she's from Belize!"

"It's not the black girl."

"What about the first part?"

"What first part?"

"The first part of the question, who you went with; is she still around?"

"Right now no one's around, just me."

"By choice?"

"I guess. Circumstances....happen."

C bent over a bit and kissed her again, this time, lightly on the neck, working his way south. But at this rate, he would be kissing down around her crotch some time tomorrow afternoon; he had to pick up the pace a bit.

"I don't wanna go if I'd be sleeping in Hut No. 4, the same hut where you were with another girl, or girls, probably still the same mattress. And all those things you said, you did all that *already,* with someone else first. I want to be the first in something, not second, or third, or whatever....first."

"Okay, no Belize."

C said, matter-of-fact.

"But I miss it already. I wanna go back, and I've never even been there! Isn't that strange?"

Lilly said.

C kissed her neck again, and she actually stretched a bit away from him, to give him more room to get in; very cool.

"Forget Belize, we'll just have to go to my favorite all-time place....*best* place, bar none, out of anywhere in the *whole* world."

"But I already know all about Belvidere."

Lilly said deadpan, then laughed again at her own little joke, and C laughed at her laughing.

"You are so queer."

He said, which made her laugh harder.

"Of course Belvidere is *the* best place in the world, *ever,* but I'm talking about the best place in the world *outside* of Belvidere. And I've only been there alone….solo. So, do you want to go, with me, on a little conte?"

"A little what?"

"A little trip."

C said.

"Yeah, okay, as long as I'm the *first* girl to go, and you can't *ever* take any other girls there, *ever!* Promise?"

And with that, she slugged him, but light, in the arm. He feigned it hurt.

"Jesus, not sure why that was necessary, but yeah, promise. Okay then, we got a deal."

And C picked up the blanket and re-cinched it up around their necks, and took a deep breath.

"Okay, were gonna take a little trip, far, far away, just about as far as you can get from here. And they have cormorants there too, you know, just like Al. And they have a couple other animals too, ones you don't normally see roaming the streets in Belvidere.

"I'm thinking of a remote outpost, just a bit south and east of Belvidere, called *Makanyane,* nestled in the *Madikwe Game Reserve;* a sweet little spot in the bush."